BEYOND ALL
Thom

Copyright © 2025 Thom Tate
All rights reserved.

Disclaimer

This book is a work of fiction. Names, characters, places, and incidents either are the product of the author's imagination or are used fictitiously, and any resemblance to any actual person, living or dead, business establishments, events, or locals is entirely coincidental.

Without limiting the rights under copyright reserved above, no part of this publication may be reproduced, stored in, or introduced into a retrieval system, or transmitted in any form or by means (electronic, mechanical, photocopying, recording, or otherwise) without prior written permission of the author.

The scanning, uploading, and distribution of this book via the Internet or via any other means without the express written consent of the author or copyright owner is illegal and punishable by law. Please support y our independent authors and purchase only authorized electronic and printed editions. Do not participate in or encourage piracy of copyrighted materials. Your support is appreciated.

FOREWORD

I would like to express my heartfelt gratitude to my writing partner and editor, Henry Martin. Without his unwavering encouragement and relentless motivation to write, this latest saga in the Blake MacKay world would not have come to fruition.

I am also deeply thankful for my alpha readers, Holly McCarthy and Sherri Talbot. Their keen insights and discerning eyes have been invaluable; without their feedback, mistakes and plot holes may have slipped through, and this book would not be as strong as it is today.

1

Soviet submarine K-278 Komosomolets
3,700 feet deep The Arctic Ocean

March 8th 14:23 (13:23 UTC)

The metal groaned in protest under the relentless pressure, inching toward five thousand pounds per square inch. At such depth, it was a haunting reminder of the fragile balance between life and death. Trudging along deeper than any normal nuclear sub, the submarine surveyed the ocean floor an additional four thousand feet below. Special ground-penetrating radar and sonar constantly beamed and received signals from under the Arctic's silty bottom, revealing secrets tens of millions of years old.

Akram Saman, a man hand-selected by His Royal Highness, Prince Awadi Salib, read the data from the sophisticated instruments and double-checked his findings before leaving his station. He entered the bridge and approached the commanding officer. "Captain, I have the information I need. Please surface so I may communicate my findings with His Majesty."

An old, gruff man, scarred by the trials of war, turned and clenched the cigar he was smoking between his weathered, yellowed teeth. "Are we going to get our money?"

"Yes." Akram waved away the smoke as he coughed. The stench assaulted his senses. "You can get confirmation of the deposit before we dive."

He squinted, nodding in understanding, then turned. "Surface the boat. Up bubble, twenty degrees."

Once they finished communicating with the prince and the boat's crew confirmed their payment, they descended to one thousand feet.

Akram went to his berth and, from his locker, removed his prayer rug, Koran, and special box presented to him by the prince. After completing his prayers, he wiped the sweat from his brow and took a deep breath. Opening the box, he removed the compact, but powerful bomb.

Armed with double-stick tape, he fastened the explosive to the sub's titanium hull, stepped back to his rug, and sat on his knees. Now, he would complete the mission he was chosen for. Grasping the detonator, its cold metal sent a shiver through him, a stark reminder of the destruction it would unleash. He swallowed hard and closed his eyes.

"Allahu Akbar."

BAHRAIN POLYTECHNIC Research Center
Manama, Bahrain

April 23rd 14:07 (12:07 UTC)

The school sat on the shores of the Persian Gulf. Palm tree-lined walkways crisscrossed the property like veins running through the heart of an oasis. The gentle breeze from the sea whispered through the campus like a soothing lullaby, carrying the salty essence of tranquility and timeless wisdom.

Dr. Sagadish Agate was an accomplished innovator in deep-sea rover and submersible technology. He stood at his worktable, surrounded by the odors of saltwater and machinery, hyper-focused on his task. His white lab coat, almost touching the ground, enveloped his compact frame like a child wearing his father's oversized robe. The lights reflected off the bald spot on his head.

Dr. Madison Wyrick, his assistant, stood tall and commanding, her long, dishwater blonde hair pulled back in a ponytail and secured with an orange and white scrunchie. At the young age of twenty-seven, she was no slouch. When she was twenty, she earned her undergraduate and master's degrees in engineering from the University of Tennessee. She completed her PhD at MIT eighteen months later, specializing in underwater drilling. Her skill and knowledge were a major factor in helping to drill and access two major oil fields off Guyana for ExxonMobil a few years prior.

The expanse reverberated with the rhythmic cadence of footsteps. The scent of brine mingled with the faint hint of hydraulic oil. Crown Prince Awadi Salib strode purposefully into the main research lab. His presence commanded attention even before he uttered a word. His *Bisht*, a regal extended cloak in deep crimson hues, billowed behind him like a banner of authority, echoing his swift steps.

Behind the Crown Prince marched a contingent of Saudi Royal Guard Regiment soldiers, their disciplined formation contrasting with the chaotic jumble of scientific equipment cluttering the marine laboratory. Each soldier wore an immaculate uniform, tailored perfectly and gleaming under the harsh fluorescent lights. The royal blue fabric bore intricate golden embellishments that glinted with every movement, a mark showing their allegiance and unwavering loyalty to their leader.

The sound of polished boots against the tiled floor resonated through the room, punctuated by the occasional creak of leather belts, the rustle of crisp fabric leather, and the faint hint of gun oil lingering in their wake. As they advanced into the lab, shafts of sunlight filtered through small portholes, casting ethereal beams that danced across the soldiers' polished buttons and epaulets. The air hummed with suppressed energy as the Crown Prince's entourage navigated the maze of scientific wonders and experimental apparatuses, their collective aura exuding power and purpose amidst the mass of research paraphernalia.

Madison's heart raced as he advanced, his Elite Guard moving with a precision that echoed through the room like a relentless drumbeat. His piercing gaze swept over the surroundings, absorbing every minute detail of his approach to the individuals crucial to his grand scheme.

Madison stepped forward. "Mister—or Prince Awadi, we are—"

One of the Royal Guard approached, pointing an accusatory finger. "You will address him as—"

The Crown Prince raised his hand. "Enough! It is fine." He waved his attendant back. "You may address me as Your Highness, Your Majesty, Prince Salib, or in due time—" He leaned over, cradled her hand, and tenderly kissed her knuckles. "Just Salib." He smiled warmly, his eyes crinkling at the corners ever slightly. "Please. Continue Doctor Wyrick."

The blood flowed to her cheeks after not addressing the prince correctly. The pressure on her cheekbones was a constant reminder of her ignorance. "Apologies. I didn't mean to offend you."

She motioned with her hand. "But please, follow me, Your Highness."

As they advanced, the lab's core loomed larger before them. The ceiling stretched high above, a vast expanse of industrial metal soaring sixty feet into the air. Thick steel cables dangled above, supporting an enormous bright orange submarine that dominated the space. The vessel extended fifty feet long and towered thirty in height, casting an imposing presence in the room.

Next to the sub, a massive crane stood sentinel, its sturdy frame ready to lift and transport the submersible to the dock a hundred meters away. Ready to receive command, the colossal machine stood tall.

Its metallic arms prepared to lower it into the depths of the murky waters.

She gestured towards the colossal orange vessel. "We've repurposed one of Doctor Agate's existing models for this special project."

The Crown Prince extended his arm and pointed to the front of the sub. "And is this where the drilling apparatus will attach?"

"Yes, and if you'll please come this way, I'll show you."

As they walked, Madison continued. "We are sifting through different drilling tool options to determine the one giving the best results. We've narrowed it down to three; hydrothermal spallation, chemical plasma, which I have reservations about, and lasers. Your Majesty, I suggest the laser option is most suitable."

They stopped in front of a massive apparatus.

The prince tilted his head. "And why is the laser your tool of choice?"

"A lot of advancement has taken place in the past ten years. We use laser energy for thermal spallation, melting, or evaporation of rock. This specific system is MIRACL. It offers a penetration rate of ten to a hundred times faster than conventional drilling methods."

The prince contemplated her words. "And what does that translate to regarding speed?"

Her eyes went up in thought as she searched her memory for the information. "About four hundred and fifty feet per hour."

His eyes widened. "That is impressive, doctor."

She smiled. "It's never been used for drilling in this environment before, but it will offer us the most power while maintaining control of the submersible."

"And when do you expect to start drilling?"

Madison's eyes drifted away from the prince. Her finger traced an invisible pattern on the table. "Well, there is one more thing we need to work out, but I think I've found a solution."

"Go on." The voice echoed in her ears with a resounding authority and a hint of impatience.

She turned to face him. "As you can imagine, the laser will be creating an enormous amount of heat. We can't penetrate the oil reserve using a laser. We'd run the risk of igniting it."

He nodded his understanding. "Hmmm, yes. Good point. And your solution?"

"A hydro drill for the last one hundred feet or so. The water temperature at that depth is near zero Celsius and will help with the cooling. We can rig up a pump attached to the sub and use the seawater to make that last hundred feet."

Pursing his lips, the prince nodded once more. "Make it happen, doctor. I still didn't get an answer to my original question. When can we expect to drill?"

Madison's eyes shifted toward her colleagues for affirmation in her answer. "Oh—I'd say we're twenty—perhaps twenty-two weeks out?"

Dr. Agate nodded while he popped a dried date into his mouth. His words slurred as he chewed on the sweet fruit. "Yes, I would say it's a safe assumption."

One of the Royal Guards approached from behind the prince and whispered in his ear. The prince's eyes widened and soon narrowed as his irritation became apparent.

"Pardon me," he said through a forced smile. "I need to take this call."

He hurried to a far corner. Madison smiled at the members of the Royal Guard. They didn't return the kind gesture. The prince's voice rose in volume. She didn't need to speak Arabic to understand he was displeased.

As he strode back to the group, a scowl etched itself on the Crown Prince's face. Abruptly halting, he raised his hand and pointed to Dr. Agate.

"You have twelve weeks to complete this project."

His words hung heavy as the team braced themselves for the challenge ahead. As fast as he approached them, he turned and walked away, his guards following closely behind him.

Her expression twisted into a mask of panic as she whipped around to face her colleague. His stoic expression offered no comfort, making her feel alone and uncertain. "But Your Highness!" Madison pleaded. "There's no—"

As they exited the lab, he turned and called over his shoulder. "Twelve weeks, Doctor Wyrick. Do it!"

PRINCE SALIB EMERGED from the air-conditioned laboratory. As the automatic doors slid open, a wall of oppressive heat slammed into him like a physical force.

He paused, blinded by the harsh sunlight reflecting off the barren parking lot. Despite his dark sunglasses, the hot air and the brilliance of the sunlight outside contrasted sharply with the lab's cool interior.

Taking a deep breath, he steadied himself against the searing air scorching his throat. Though he was no stranger to Bahrain's punishing climate, the transition was still jarring after long hours spent in the controlled environment.

As he stepped free of the building's shelter, within seconds, beads of sweat broke out across his brow. The sweltering temperature, hovering near fifty degrees Celsius, sucked the moisture from his body.

He strode towards his vehicle, his Royal Guard flanking him on both sides. The shimmering asphalt offered no respite, radiating its absorbed heat upwards in invisible waves. His damp skin clung to his fine cotton robes within meters.

Reaching the shadow of his vehicle brought sweet relief. As he slid into the cooled leather seat and relished the blast of blessed air conditioning, Prince Awadi Salib thanked modern technology for sheltering him from Bahrain's brutal daylight furnace, if only briefly.

Sitting in the back of his custom Rolls Royce, Salib grasped a burner phone and called the man he'd picked to lead his teams. The voice on the other end answered. "Yes?"

"We have a slight problem."

"Go on."

"Canada Oil deployed an exploration ship to the North Pole several weeks ago."

"How do you know?"

Salib stared out the window. "That is something you do not need to concern yourself with. I am ahead of them every step of the way. Your team needs to be ready to execute on my command. If the ship finds what I am certain is there, we cannot allow them to announce it."

Salib waited patiently for an answer.

"I'll get started."

2

The DavCo Arctic Drill Deep Ocean drill exploration ship
Somewhere inside the Arctic Circle

May 6th 23:52 (23:52 UTC)

It has to be here! It just has to!

Richard Cathey slumped in his chair, fingers threading through his hair. His laboratory occupied the entire ship's midsection, tucked between cargo holds. The room enveloped him in a cocoon of stillness, shielding him from the tumultuous symphony of waves battering against the hull and winds wailing outside.

The room conveyed a sense of sterility with its pristine white walls and gleaming stainless-steel equipment. Harsh light from rows of fluorescent tubes cast a clinical glow over every surface, emphasizing the space's meticulous cleanliness.

An open layout facilitated a smooth transition between various workstations, creating a seamless flow throughout the room. On one side, the wet lab stood ready for sample handling, equipped with a bank of fume hoods and centrifuges to ensure the safe containment of any potentially hazardous materials.

In the distance, an array of servers and towering computer units emitted a constant low hum, processing vast amounts of data within the chilly environment.

On the right side, an impressive array of screens adorned the wall, showcasing advanced seismic monitoring devices and drill core mapping systems. High-tech instruments adorned the control room, displaying real time data with pinpoint accuracy. They revealed the ship's exact location and monitored every aspect of all drilling operations.

Meanwhile, nearby, they submerged the cores extracted from the seabed in solvents before subjecting them to detailed spectroscopic analysis to unveil their secrets.

The laboratory, resembling a spaceship stranded in an icy wasteland, exuded a sense of impermanence that contrasted with its advanced technology. As the ice surrounding it creaked and shifted, the structure seemed to sway with the undulating movements of the frozen sea. The dim light filtering through frosted windows cast eerie shadows on the metal surfaces, creating a stark interplay between light and dark within the frigid confines.

The ship lurched violently, throwing Richard off balance and snapping him out of his spiral of self-pity. The ear-splitting groan of the strained engines reverberated through his makeshift lab, rattling the surrounding walls. He sprinted towards the main deck, his heart pounding in sync with each thunderous clank from below. As he ascended the stairs, he leaped two steps at a time, the cold metal railing slick beneath his grip as he fought against the tilting floor to reach the source of the chaos.

Dale Simpson, an engineer for Canada Oil, was the first person he met.

"What's happening? Why have we stopped?"

Dale zipped up his heavy coat and slipped his hands back into his gloves. "The sonar. It's stuck on something. We'll have to get it loose before we can proceed. I'm headed aft to help."

For three relentless weeks, the exploration vessel cut through the ocean's dark depths, a symphony of sonar pings and ground-penetrating radar sweeps echoing in its steel hull. The endless daylight near the North Pole cast a surreal glow over the landscape as day and night merged into a continuous cycle while the crew toiled ceaselessly. The salty tang of the sea lingered in the air.

Back down below, Richard, brow furrowed in concentration, meticulously analyzed each blip on the sonar screen, his fingers dancing across the controls as he delved into the intricate patterns displayed.

Outside, the deep blue expanse stretched endlessly, occasionally disturbed by frothy whitecaps breaking against the hull. The rhythmic hum of the engines reverberated through the ship, vibrating beneath their feet like a steady heartbeat, keeping time with their mission.

As they ventured deeper into uncharted territory, anticipation hung in the air. Every creak and groan of the vessel seemed magnified in the silent underwater world. The crew sharpened their senses, paying attention to every subtle shift in pressure or temperature that could hint at what lay hidden beneath layers of sediment and rock.

Through it all, Richard's determination burned bright like a guiding beacon amidst the murky darkness. If his calculations held, if his instincts proved correct, they were on the brink of discovering not just any oil reservoir, but a colossal treasure trove buried beneath the ocean floor—a potentially fundamental change in the world's energy landscape.

———•———

WITH GREAT CAUTION, Dale made his way to the back of the vessel, radio in hand. He raised it to his lips. "Bridge, activate the aft controls at once. We're taking command from this end."

A crackling response came through. "Copy that. Controls engaged. The boat is all yours now."

He nodded and turned to Jimmy—a trusted co-pilot authorized to handle the ship's rear helm. With a quick gesture, he signaled for him to reverse, creating some slack.

Gesturing again, Dale directed two other men to assist him in dragging a heavy steel hawser onto the deck. They strained under the weight, sweat pouring down their brows despite the freezing temperature. Dale, breathless chuckled. "Who would believe we'd sweat like this in temperatures like these?"

The other crewmen laughed and nodded in agreement as they continued their arduous task. Despite the cold, they were determined to get enough play in the hawser to allow them to use the rear davit to raise it, maneuver it, and, with some luck, dislodge whatever obstacle was impeding their progress.

Minutes turned into what appeared to be an eternity as they wrestled with the stubborn cable. They wiped the sweat off their foreheads and scrutinized each other with exhaustion and satisfaction. At last, it was positioned on the deck exactly as they had planned.

Dale took a moment to catch his breath before addressing his crew again. "Excellent work, everyone. Now let's focus on operationalizing this rear davit so we can move forward."

A thunderous explosion rocked the air. Off the starboard side, an iceberg calved and broke into the water. The tidal wave, displaced by the ice, headed their way.

Dale's voice rose above the chaos as he tried to alert the people around. "All hands, brace yourselves! The ship is going to rock!"

Jimmy dashed back to the helm as the colossal surge struck. It propelled him into the controls, forcing the throttle forward, his body colliding with the deck. The engines roared to life, propelling the vessel ahead at full speed. The boat heaved, the violence causing all the men to be slammed to the steel deck at the same time, the steel hawser whizzed off the vessel and plunged back into the treacherous waters.

Wide-eyed and filled with dread, Dale rolled away from the cable zipping past him. His eyes locked onto Jimmy, trying to convey his urgent message. "The throttle!"

With an abrupt, violent jolt, the ship's acceleration flung him away from the helm.

Seth, one of the other deckhands, struggled to regain his footing and staggered towards the engine levers, driven by the instinct to take control.

Oblivious to his surroundings and without thinking, he stepped into an area where the hawser had looped upon itself.

In a fraction of a second, it constricted around his ankle, yanking him to the stern of the ship.

Seth's anguished cries echoed through the air as he clawed at the smooth steel plating. The horrifying spectacle left all the men frozen in sheer terror; their bodies paralyzed with shock.

Dale's trembling hand reached out towards Seth, his voice shaking with disbelief and horror. "Oh, my God! Watch out!"

The cable's relentless pull hurled the man's body against the back railing, causing it to groan under immense strain. With an unbearable force, the cable cut deep into his ankle, but continued its merciless trajectory, dragging him over the rail and into the frigid depths beneath. A chilling silence filled the air, broken only by the haunting sight of blood oozing over the deck.

The ship staggered to a halt, trembling from the catastrophic event. Moments later, it lurched forward again, its sonar now freed from the entanglement holding it captive.

TWO DAYS LATER

Deep within the ship's bowels, on a lower level hidden from prying eyes, Richard Cathey lingered in his lab. As he awaited the culmination of his research, the wait seemed endless. He had stationed himself below deck, surrounded by a maze of technology and screens displaying intricate data patterns.

For twenty-one grueling days, the vessel had navigated through icy waters south of the North Pole, precisely within the coordinates Richard had meticulously calculated as foolproof. His weary eyes stung with fatigue as they remained fixed on the streams of information flooding in from the ground-penetrating radar (GPR) and sonar readings. The sheer volume of raw data inundated his senses, each pixel, and line demanding his attention.

The glow of computer monitors cast an eerie light over his face, illuminating the shadows that danced across his features. Filling the air, the hum of machinery was a constant backdrop to his solitary vigil. Every detail on the screens held a promise—a puzzle waiting to be solved—but until the processors completed their task, it was all a jumble of incomprehensible symbols and lines.

Confined to luminous monitors and dancing streams of information, Richard's reality was limited to his secluded hideaway.

The weight of anticipation hung heavy in the air as he yearned for those elusive moments when everything would click into place, revealing secrets buried beneath layers of silt and rock.

He pinched the bridge of his nose. One eye closed while the other glanced at the screen. *Processing... 86.8%*

"Jeez, hurry the hell up!" Removing his hand, he reached for a bottle of eye drops. He tilted his head back and relished the cool comfort of the droplets in his eyes.

"Ahhh, what a difference it makes!" He peered around the room to ensure he wasn't seen talking to himself. After some moments, he stood from his workstation chair, arched his back to stretch, and peeked again at the computer.

Processing... 87%

Oh shit, how much longer? He grabbed his favorite mug and sauntered over to the coffee station.

The hot liquid cascaded into the container, emitting a soft gurgle that enveloped him in a cocoon of warmth and comfort. With a contented sigh, he shut his eyes, allowing the rich aroma to swirl around him. Suddenly, the pungent scent jolted him back to reality, his eyes snapping open in alertness.

Grasping the vessel, its heat seeping into his chilled fingers, he turned towards the source of the intermittent banging and scratching against the icy hull. As he walked over to the port side of the room, a mesmerizing sight greeted him, illuminated by the ethereal glow of the midnight sun.

At the level of his gaze, he witnessed an enthralling sight. Massive ice blocks drifted peacefully on rippling waters, performing a captivating ballet as intricate snowflakes pirouetted around them in a graceful waltz. This picturesque view stirred recollections of bygone Christmas celebrations with his soon-to-be former spouse, their last festive season together colored with a mix of poignant reminiscence.

His heart weighed heavily with shame, a bitter companion to the looming sadness that engulfed him. Joining Canada Oil as the head exploration scientist had extracted its price. Throughout their three-year marriage, he had only been present at home for a mere eleven months.

It's not the way to treat your wife and start a family. His younger sister, Evelyn, who worked for the Canadian Security Intelligence, told him jobs like theirs offered no room for relationships.

He could picture it like it was yesterday. Christmas, Dad was still alive, and they were all at their cottage in the mountains near Banff. She pulled him aside after he announced the engagement.

"Rich." Her striking green eyes, wide with concern, stared into his. "What in the hell are you doing?"

He giggled, unable to believe she was serious while wearing the oversized, idiotic Christmas sweater.

Her eyes narrowed while she scrunched her lips. "What are you laughing at?"

"I don't know what's stupider; all the flashing lights on your dumb jumper or the expression on the elf's face as he's staring at Santa's fat ass."

She cracked a grin and handed him a loving pat on his chest. "Dammit. I'm serious."

He rolled his eyes and took a sip of his wine. "Yeah—Whatever."

"Richard! Listen to me."

His eyes met hers. "Ok, Sis. Go ahead."

"Your job." Her eyes danced back and forth as she searched for her words. "It does not work well with marriage. I mean, you're gone what, eight—nine months out of the year?"

"Yes, but."

"No buts. Bubby, please—trust me on this." Her eyes locked with his in a heartwarming plea as she placed her palm on his chest. "You'd be doing her and yourself a favor by not going through with this."

Richard let loose a sigh as Evelyn turned her attention back to their father.

She was right.

Chiming digital harps flashed him back to the present. The program was done.

The mug hit the lab table with a crash, spilling its contents as he dashed into the 3D rendering room to view the results. A few strokes on the keyboard and a mouse click doused the lights. He was ready for the show.

The center of the room illuminated by a fuzzy three-dimensional blob.

"What the—crap! The glasses."

Richard grabbed a pair from the shelf just inside the room, slipped them on, and they focused on a sharp, 3D image of what was below the surface of the ocean floor.

"Oh—my—God!"

3

The DavCo Arctic Drill
March 7th 00:36 (00:36 UTC)

After a few unanswered knocks, Richard's excitement got the best of him. He tore open his colleague Mike's cabin door. "I found it!"

He flipped on the light and his friend's black rear end stared at him, and a woman's leg protruded out from underneath him.

Oh, crap.

"Hey! What the hell, dude? Turn it off!"

"Sorry, you have to come—"

"I was about to till your stupid ass barged in here. Close the damn door! Give the lady some privacy."

The blood rushed to his cheeks. "Right! I apologize." He stepped into the corridor and closed the door, embarrassed at interrupting Mike's recreational activity. The two men were about the same age, under forty, but Mike had never married. Probably the wiser of the two.

A young woman, Darla from the galley crew, tumbled out the door wrapped in a sheet and clasping her clothes near her chest. Her shoes hung by her fingers from the opposite hand. She wore a frown and scanned him as if he were an alien. "Way to go." She grumbled as she passed him in the hallway. "Asshole."

His focus met the floor as he waved. "Sorry." Mike strode into the passage wearing sweatpants and a "Funkin Gonuts" T-shirt. "What the hell, dude? This had best be something spectacular."

His smile widened. "Oh, it's better. Come on!"

Back in the 3D room, Mike put on his VR glasses as Richard started the virtual reality presentation.

"Do you see it?"

His eyes focused on his colleague in anticipation, eager to study his reaction.

Mike's jaw dropped. "Well, I'll be damned."

He waited for him to take it all in.

"Is this real? You're certain?"

Richard's eyes sparkled. "Yep."

"You're sure? I mean, guaranteed one hundred percent?"

He folded his arms. "Yes, I am. You're looking at the single largest oil reserve in the world."

"How immense are we talking?"

He shifted his weight to his other foot and rubbed his chin as he eyed the image floating in the middle of the room. "Mmmm, at a guess—I'd say as much as triple or perhaps four times larger than Venezuela."

He whistled and removed his VR goggles. Glancing about the empty room, his voice quieted. "You know this is an issue, don't you?"

Richard switched off the presentation and shook his head. "No. Why would this be a problem?"

"What is our precise location?"

"Why does our—"

"Come on! Follow me." Mike pivoted and dashed out of the room. Richard tagged close behind.

Under normal conditions, an entire complement would have exceeded one hundred and fifty members. This voyage, however, focused only on seismic exploration rather than drilling, which required less than a fifth of a full crew.

Positioned on the bridge, the First Mate stood at the helm, guiding the ship through treacherous waters. Enormous ice flows loomed ahead, forcing them to navigate with extreme skill to avoid collision.

The icy landscape surrounded them in a breathtaking show of shimmering whites and blues beneath the Arctic night sky.

Engines hummed as they cut through the frigid ocean, creating a constant background noise reverberating throughout the vessel. The air carried a sharp chill seeping through layers of clothing, causing the most seasoned sailors to shiver involuntarily. The scent of saltwater and diesel fuel reminded them of their isolation in the vast expanse of the open sea.

Amidst this frozen world, where time appeared suspended in perpetual sunlight, the crew relied on their senses to maneuver safely. The sound of cracking ice echoed in the distance, signaling potential hazards ahead. Each crew member scanned the horizon, searching for any signs of movement or danger lurking in the shadows cast by towering ice formations.

As midnight approached and the sun still sat relatively high in the sky, it was not uncommon to see a fellow crew member, sporting sunglasses—a surreal sight against the backdrop of an Arctic sky. Whenever this happened, the song *I Wear My Sunglasses at Night*, a Cory Hart number, got stuck in his head.

In this harsh and unforgiving environment, where nature reigned supreme, every decision could mean the difference between survival and disaster.

Mike spoke to the navigator, Henri. "Can you show us our location on the chart?"

"*Certainement*. This way." Henri's French-Canadian accent was thicker than most people Richard had worked with. Growing up in Vancouver, the furthest away from Quebec, he had never cared to learn to speak the language. After the First Mate pointed out their coordinates, he nodded and waited for Henri to leave.

Mike clasped Richard's shoulder. "Yep, as I suspected. We're in an exclusive economic zone. This is a problem."

He furrowed his brow. "What does our location in an EEZ have to do with it?"

Mike put his hands on his hips and started to respond when the one of the crew interrupted.

"There's a helicopter inbound. Are you expecting anyone?"

Both men's eyes met as they simultaneously answered. "A chopper?"

The chopping of the blades filled the inside of the ship's bridge as the Seahawk with Danish markings approached. The radio squawked with a message in broken English. "DavCo Arctic Drill. This is OY-HKR. Permission to land. We have news and a piece of equipment to deliver from the Canada Oil office out of Copenhagen."

Henri raised the mic to his mouth and responded. "Hello, OY-HKR. You are cleared to land."

Above the bridge of the drilling ship, a helipad stood as a marvel of design. Surrounded by cranes and the towering derrick dominating the vessel's space, it was an inconspicuous spot, hidden from view. The only indication of its existence came from a monitor near the helm, displaying a grainy image captured by a camera amidst swirling snow churned by the rotor blades.

As Mike droned on about territorial disputes between nations, his focus shifted from the conversation to movement beyond the ship's expansive windscreen. His attention honed in on three figures clad in black battle fatigues suspended from ropes outside. Clutching assault rifles, they swayed in the icy wind, their presence sending a chill down his spine.

The scene outside unfolded like a tense ballet against a backdrop of steel-gray clouds and turbulent seas. The men's movements were sharp and deliberate, their breath visible in puffs of frosty air. Metal on metal as they secured themselves to the hull, its clattering reverberated faintly through the howling wind.

Richard's pulse quickened as he observed their calculated approach, each detail etching itself into his mind with vivid clarity. The subtle creaking of ropes under tension added an eerie soundtrack to the unfolding drama, heightening the sense of imminent peril lurking beyond the safety of the ship's walls.

"What the—"

Shards of glass exploded like crystal rain as a hail of bullets pierced the reinforced windows of the bridge.

The metallic tang of blood and the acrid scent of gunfire enhanced the horror as crimson splattered across the once pristine control panels, painting a macabre masterpiece of chaos.

In the blink of an eye, before he could register the hazard,

Mike crumpled to the floor, his life abruptly ended with only half his skull remaining intact, a gruesome sight searing into his memory.

The harsh reality crashed down on him like a tidal wave as he glanced at his feet, where brain matter now decorated his shoes in a grotesque mosaic.

The squelch underfoot sounded louder than any gunshot, imprinting a visceral reminder of the brutality unfolding in front of him.

"Oh, my God!"

He bolted through the heavy metal door to the first flight of steps he could find. Automatic weapons echoed throughout the ship. He couldn't tell which direction it was coming from.

Three levels down, and he still wasn't below deck. His chest hurt from sprinting, and his heartbeat thumped in his ears. Panic was setting in.

He slowed to catch his breath, scouring the area for a secure hiding place. These guys wanted something so much it was enough to kill for. But what?

Two more bursts, three rounds each. A scream followed by another long burst.

The findings. That had to be what they were after! But how could they know? There's no possible way!

He was hit with sudden insight.

The laboratory! Holy shit!

After five more levels, he reached the lab deck. Longer periods elapsed between the screams and blasts of staccato fire.

Richard froze at the main deck level door. He grasped the lever, closed his eyes, and inhaled, the frigid air burning his lungs.

His heartbeat still filled his ears. A wave of nausea crept in as a flash of Mike's split skull entered his mind.

He shook it away and opened the door to listen for anyone else on the deck. Three doors along was the entrance to his laboratory. The corridor was clear. He bolted for it but slid to a stop.

Oh no. The door.

Too late. The self-closing door slammed with an echoing boom. He froze. A voice yelled. "Down a level!" Thundering steps racing down metal stairs.

He dashed into his lab and to his computer. He searched for his external backup drive at his workstation. Lifting papers and opening drawers, he mumbled under his breath. "Come on! Where the hell did I put you?"

The door banged closed again. The assailants were inside the facility.

Oh, my God!

Voices rattled on and a female screamed.

He opened a drawer.

At last!

He fumbled with the drive.

Fucking come on!

Once inserted, he started copying the essential data from the network drive. A woman's voice pierced the air as she begged for her life. It was Darla, the woman whose evening he ruined earlier, with Mike.

A single shot rang out. The thud of what could only be her body hitting the steel floor penetrated the walls of his lab. Footsteps came closer. The door to the room next to the main laboratory door creaked open.

Sweat dripped from Richard's brow. *Come on, come on!*

The computer emitted a sharp, metallic chime. He ripped the drive from its slot. As he turned to leave, the door swung open, revealing two imposing figures brandishing raised weapons, casting menacing shadows in the narrow corridor.

Reacting instinctively, he pivoted and sprinted towards an adjacent back exit. Adrenaline surged through him as he burst into a cluttered supply room, his heart pounding in his ears.

With a tug, he pulled on a nearby shelving unit. It teetered precariously before crashing to the ground with an ear-splitting clatter of metal and plastic trays scattering across the floor.

"Stop!" in a foreign accent, penetrated his ears. The bullets ricocheted off the metal equipment and glass shattered. He crossed the room to a door on the other side, leading to another corridor. An arrow on the wall pointed to the ship's galley.

Eyes wide, his panic was in full swing. He dashed into the galley and searched the room for a hiding space. He stashed the drive where he hoped it would be safe and ran out the door on the other side as the two men entered. More bullets flew in his direction.

Up the stairs, skipping every other one, the first thing entering his mind was to get a message to his sister, Evelyn, but how? He reached the main deck. The lifeboats were forward, on the upper bow deck.

Only one more to go.

Shouts echoed from the deck above, urging him into action. Without hesitation, he bolted up the stairwell, the frigid air biting at his skin. Snatching a fire extinguisher from its mount, he wielded it like a weapon, relentlessly pounding the door handle until it warped and wedged the door shut from the outside.

Raising his gaze, he locked eyes with a menacing figure on the other side of the glass—a cold-blooded killer with half his ear missing. The man spat foreign curses and unleashed a barrage of bullets through the window. Heart racing, Richard emptied the extinguisher's contents at the window, then dashed away, adrenaline fueling his escape.

Leaning perilously over the starboard railing, he scanned the ship's length, spotting the vivid orange hue of a lifeboat tethered near the bow. With no other option but to ascend two levels via the outer railing, he steeled himself against his fear of heights.

As he tentatively placed a foot on the icy steel railing, a searing cold pierced his hands as they clung desperately above. Ignoring the chaotic sounds reverberating around him—metal doors clanging shut and hurried footsteps resonating through the ship—he pushed past his trembling limbs, clambering towards safety sixty feet above the glacial waters. The numbing chill gnawed at his palms and fingers with each careful grip on the icy metal.

The vessel heaved violently, threatening to hurl Richard into the icy depths of the ocean. He squeezed his eyes closed, drawing in a lungful of the salty sea air. After what felt like an eternity compressed into two agonizing minutes, he clambered inside the relative security of the lifeboat.

Hands trembling, he rummaged through a box stashed in one corner. His hand met something solid and rectangular—a satellite phone.

A lifeline capable of transmitting voice calls across vast distances, sending electronic missives and brief messages even from this barren spot in the middle of nowhere.

Abruptly, another burst of gunfire echoed off the water's surface, each shot a thunderous clap propelling icy tendrils of dread snaking down his spine. He fumbled in his pocket for his phone. It's cool glass screen slippery with sweat. Evelyn's number was there among his contacts—an anchor amidst the storm.

His fingers were numb from cold and terror, making it hard to coax them into tapping her number on the tiny keypad. But at last, they obeyed him, and he hit call. The signal bounced off satellites in the skies above him before hurtling back to Earth and towards Evelyn.

Her phone rang once... twice... three times, and then her voicemail clicked on.

The sound was as jarring as a gunshot in this silent seascape. Panic surged within him like a wave cresting over its peak, and Richard ended the call before he could betray himself with his voice.

The footfalls were getting nearer now—ominous thumps against wooden planks appearing to echo around him like a dreadful heartbeat. And those voices. They were growing louder too—harsh whispers carried over by the wind chilling him to his core.

God dammit! You're so stupid!

I'll send her a text.

The door to the lifeboat mooring station opened. He typed as fast as he could, but what to say for his final words to his sister?

"Check the other lifeboat." The sound penetrated his mind as the door flung open. The hair on the back of his neck stood on end.

"Got him!"

The man's satisfying, third-world smile greeted him as he raised his weapon.

A tear rolled down Richard's face as he pressed send.

4

Kotelney Island
East Siberian Sea

June 15th

04:00 AM (21:00 June 14th, UTC)

Nestled between the Laptev and East Siberian Seas, Kotelney Island emerged as a majestic gem among the fifty largest islands globally. Originally untouched, it witnessed human presence in the early 1930s when the Soviet Union established a naval station on its rugged terrain. Despite remaining uninhabited post-Cold War tensions and whispers of undersea oil reserves breathed new life into its once deserted shores.

The island's vast expanse unfolded with an awe-inspiring grandeur. The landscape, a tapestry of untamed beauty, stretched endlessly before the eyes. Rolling tundra carpeted the earth, only interrupted by defiant rocky formations jutting out like ancient sentinels guarding their realm. Crystal clear lakes glistened like scattered jewels under the Arctic sun, casting mesmerizing reflections dancing with ethereal grace.

In this wilderness, where silence reigns supreme, nature thrives resiliently. Arctic foxes darted through the undergrowth, their fur blending seamlessly with the snow-kissed ground. Majestic reindeer traversed the rugged terrain with regal elegance, their hooves echoing against the historic rocks. Above, migratory birds painted intricate patterns across the vast sky, their melodic calls harmonizing with the whisper of wind weaving through valleys.

The frigid waters surrounding Kotelney Island teemed with life unseen elsewhere.

Seals lazed on ice floes, basking in the sun. Their sleek forms glistened like polished silver under the Arctic light.

Santiago Dias detested the biting cold with a passion running deep in his bones, urging them to hasten their departure from the icy wasteland.

Despite the month being July, the air still carried a frosty sting at a mild minus three degrees Celsius.

Their high-tech American cold weather gear, designed for such harsh environments, faltered after enduring five grueling hours on the desolate tundra, allowing the icy tendrils of the frozen landscape to creep insidiously beneath his protective layers.

A voice pierced through the frigid silence from behind Santiago. "How much farther do we have to go?" Lupe Moreno, Santi's steadfast companion and former comrade from their days serving together in the National Army of Colombia and later in the AFEUR's Urban Counter-Terrorism Special Forces, posed the question.

Having realized it was more lucrative and less dangerous to engage in conflicts abroad instead of the treacherous Colombian drug cartels, they had founded *El Talon Negro*, known as The Black Talon—a mercenary group forged through years of shared battles and bloodshed. Their recent exploits had taken them to Yemen, where they had engaged in skirmishes under contract with the Saudi military for nine arduous months.

Seven weeks prior, a proposition unlike any other had arrived from Nazir Farhi, a mercenary whose tactics were known to be excessively brutal, even among others with the same occupation. He offered a job backed by someone of great wealth, but didn't mention who. The five-million-dollar deposit into his account was all it took to agree.

Santi's finger pierced the icy air, guiding their path. Without a word, his friend's breath formed misty clouds in the bitter cold. A pang of longing for Yemen crossed his face, hidden behind protective gear, as he motioned for the group of ten men to move ahead into the barren, snow-covered landscape.

After a strenuous trek over jagged terrain, Santi sank to the ground. He reached into his coat pocket and retrieved binoculars, scanning the distance from his prone position on the rocky incline. "Five hundred meters out. The generators lie eastward, within close reach. Intel suggests a constantly manned radio room adjacent to them. Two barracks stand nearby. Our mission is to ensure they send an emergency distress signal upon attack. Once confirmed, cut off power and eliminate any survivors."

Lupe knelt beside him, seeking details. "How many are inside?"

"Roughly a dozen to eighteen at most. Their lack of arms is evident except for a lone rifle meant for bear deterrence."

Checking his watch by rolling back his sleeve, he verified the time. "It's four in the morning now—daylight has crept in an hour ago and will only intensify." With a swift motion, he revealed a concealed U.S. Flag beneath a Velcro cover on his attire.

The desolate landscape echoed with serenity as they prepared to execute their covert operation under the relentless gaze of the rising sun, casting elongated shadows across the frozen wasteland like ominous premonitions of impending action.

His gloved fingers grazed the cool metal of his whisper mic, activating it with a soft click, barely disturbing the icy stillness around them. "Let's move."

The ten operatives marched to where they had concealed Russia's latest winter vehicles, the TTM-1901 "Berkut," sturdy machines designed for harsh Arctic conditions.

These snowmobiles were like stealthy shadows against the snow, their sleek frames ready to carry out their mission.

Each vehicle had a compact cabin meant for two agents and enough space in the rear for three soldiers or essential gear weighing up to six hundred pounds.

Their stolen transport was a blend of camouflage and efficiency—if spotted from afar, they would be mistaken for routine military movements, evading unnecessary attention.

As they approached the barracks, Santi veered towards the closest building. Lupe disembarked near another barrack while Santi continued to the farthest one.

Santiago and four comrades waited poised outside their target, awaiting confirmation from their teammates stationed at strategic points.

A crackling voice broke through their muted communication devices. "Ready for your signal." In this isolated outpost where security was lax, doors were unlocked as an invitation to those who dared challenge its vulnerability. Santi's directive was swift and concise.

"Go."

Entering the barracks with silent footsteps barely disturbing the slumbering peace within, Santi found himself amidst rows of bunk beds shrouded in darkness.

Five forms lay under blankets like dormant shadows on half-filled cots. As he approached, one of the sleepers stirred and mumbled incomprehensibly in Russian, adding to the tension-charged environment permeating the room.

Probably something to do with the door. You die first.

Aiming his M16, he fired three silenced shots at the man, the suppressed cracks almost inaudible in the tense atmosphere. Perfectly synchronized and silent, the other four operatives moved towards their designated targets, with speed and efficiency neutralizing them without a sound.

Startled by the sudden commotion, a figure in the farthest bed bolted upright and made a desperate dash towards the rear of the barracks, only to be met with a relentless onslaught.

Bullets from all directions tore through him, turning his frantic movements into a macabre dance of death. His lifeless body tumbled to the ground in a grotesque display, crimson streams of blood intertwining as they painted a chilling tableau on the floor.

Reacting swiftly, he signaled his partner with a subtle gesture before Santi smashed open the door to the radio room.

Inside, a young man stood frozen in shock, his eyes wide with fear as he hesitated with his hand hovering over the microphone, uncertainty etched on his face.

He swiveled around. The eyes of the timid Russian shifted to the American flag on his sleeve.

He smiled, firing off a burst of three into the frightened man's right shoulder, and closed the door behind him as he departed.

Outside, he rendezvoused with Santiago and the others.

"All taken care of?"

"Not yet." He motioned to another member of his team, who retrieved a compact device from his gear and activated it.

They waited in tense silence.

After what felt like an eternity, a distress signal crackled through the airwaves. The young operative sent out a desperate plea for help, pinpointing their assailants as U.S. Soldiers.

Santi spun around, excitement gleaming as he pumped his fist in victory. "Okay, one more thing."

The vehicles glided out of the camp, halting at a safe distance of about a hundred meters away. Lupe emerged from his all-terrain vehicle, reaching in the rear to retrieve an American LAW rocket.

The missile soared towards its target, leaving a trail of smoke behind it before impacting with a deafening explosion. The blast lit up the early morning sky in a dazzling display of destruction.

The sound of splintering wood reverberated through the rugged terrain, mingling with the acrid scent of burned debris filling the air.

Against the backdrop of the glow painting the desolate landscape, the billowing black smoke etched into their memories.

THISTLE OIL PLATFORM
Norwegian Sea
June 16th, 23:50 (22:50 UTC)

The commanding steel towers and cranes on the platform contrasted with the dank surroundings of the Norwegian Sea. Beyond was a vast watery void, expanding north to the Arctic Circle. It rose from the water, like a city floating in the air, and in some sense, it was. Standing forty stories tall with a crew of 189, it was a self-sufficient metropolis.

Outfitted with stealth technology, eight Zodiacs, each carrying six men, slowed to a crawl as they came within two hundred meters of the metal beast.

The cool, ice-kissed wind blew through Nazir Farhi's hair as he fiddled with his earpiece and pressed his throat mic. "Lower your speed. No wake from here out."

Though the sun was still shining, most personnel would be asleep, or winding down, and most windows had thick blocker shades drawn to keep out the midnight glare.

The gentle wrapping of waves was the only interference over the steady hum of the electric motors propelling them through the cold waters of the Norwegian Sea.

"Boats one and two, navigate to the nearest platform anchor. Three and four, southeast corner, five and six, northeast. Everyone else, take the northwest."

After mooring the boat and steadying himself on the makeshift dock, Nazir tilted his wrist. *00:05*. He repeated the words in his mind, *Toropit'sya. Poshli, Toropit'sya. Poshli*, and pressed the throat mic again.

"All teams—on my mark—Go!"

Nazir and the forty-seven mercenaries commenced their incursion. They were clad in black hooded tactical gear and fitted with the latest Russian weaponry.

They chambered rounds into their silenced AK-12 assault rifles and began the silent ascent to the rig's four central platforms.

The hired gun sent thirty of his squad to the accommodation area on the top deck. He divided the rest among the other decks to sweep the tool and generator rooms, well bay, cellar level, and all other areas.

He took the two remaining guys, Vicente, a Chilean, and Gojko, a Serbian, with him to the operations center. It was adjacent to the helideck on the other side of the rig from the flare boom. They ran in silence in the direction of the platform, slowing as they approached the control room door.

"Remember, we leave one alive and do not say a single word."

Movement inside the window of the room caught Nazir's attention. Seconds later, one of the engineers came out. The three crouched behind pallets of empty barrels as their target strode past their cover and onto the helipad; the only designated smoking area.

Vicente aimed with his rifle. "I have him in my sights."

"Not yet. Wait for my signal."

Nazir waited for the target to move out of sight from the office. Once the coast was clear, he signaled Vincente by tapping his thigh. Without a moment's hesitation, the mercenary squeezed the trigger.

Blood erupted in a macabre display as bone fragments and gray matter scattered into the air upon impact with their target's skull.

The engineer staggered, his cigarette tumbling from slackened lips as life ebbed away in a crimson tide.

His body crumpled to its knees with grim finality, before gravity claimed its due. In a heart-wrenching descent, he plummeted forty stories into the embrace of the sea below—a silent witness to the ruthless efficiency of their mission.

Advancing, rifles engaged and prepared, the three hustled to the door. Nazir checked for an acknowledgment of 'ready,' two deliberate nods from his men.

He pushed on the door, their weapons sweeping the room, locking onto their targets. Three quick rounds to the chest of the nearest target on the right.

Farther back, a woman stood, wide-eyed, holding a steaming cup of coffee and biting into half a doughnut. The ceramic vessel shattered against a console as her body slumped to the deck with two slugs through the head.

An engineer in his late twenties froze in front of an electric panel, his mouth agape. Nazir broke the silence in his best Russian accent.

"Hey."

Not daring to meet his eyes, the terrified man stared into the bank of switches and lights.

"Hey!"

Bullets tore through the instrument panel and three brass casings settled on the flooring near the guy's feet.

He pressed the tip of his rifle under the young man's chin and raised it, forcing eye contact. His voice was clear and slow as he spoke in his practiced dialect, "Radio—control—panel. Where is it?"

A quaking hand pointed five yards across the room. "There."

He tilted his head towards his men, and they opened fire, destroying everything. Shell casings clinked on the floor and a few sparks crackled and hissed, igniting the wires deep inside.

Grabbing a fire extinguisher, he emptied the chemical contents into the electrical casing.

"Wha... what do you want from me?"

The cold killer ignored the question and regurgitated one of the three words he learned in Russian into his mic. "*Chisto?*"

"Yes, all clear," chimed into his earpiece.

He activated his mic and moved his finger in a circle in the air. "*Toropit'sya. Poshli. Toropit'sya. Poshli.*"

All the men exited and headed for the elevator when Nazir stopped. "You go on. I'll be there in a moment."

Unveiling his head from the concealing hood, he welcomed the crisp embrace of the Nordic breeze, mingling with hints of raw crude and distant sea salt. The wisps of smoke teased his nostrils, coaxing him to inhale deeply, filling his lungs before he released a controlled exhale, a visible cloud dissipating into the air.

His gaze swept across the panorama in front of him, absorbing the stillness of the office beyond. Satisfied by the absence of movement within, he indulged in one final drag of his cigarette. He flicked the butt over the side and watched it as it arced over the edge. Satisfied, he re-joined his comrades assembled at the foot of the platform.

Descending to the waiting Zodiac boat, with a subtle nod, he acknowledged one of his team members responsible for external communications. Using silent gestures, he conveyed instructions indicating they should communicate with the Saudi Prince. "Inform Salib we have successfully executed phase three out of four."

5

CSIS Atlantic Headquarters Halifax, NS
June 17th 12:16 (16:16 UTC)

Evelyn stood in her office cubicle. Her elbow rested on the top of the partition while her head leaned against her cell phone. She watched the birds fly by the ground to ceiling plate-glass windows. "Yes, Mom, I will—no, I still haven't found a man." She rolled her eyes and smiled at her partner, Josh Hardy. "No, I haven't. I told you already—yes. Yes. I will, Mom. Mom… Mom! I gotta go—love you, too." She mashed the end button.

Josh smirked, his body lightly shaking as he suppressed a laugh.

She smiled. "And just what the hell are you laughing at, eh?"

He shook his head. "Oh, nothing. There's nothing like your mom busting your ass for not being married and giving her grandkids. Am I right?"

Evelyn paused before answering with a schoolgirl grin. "Partially, but there's more."

The wheels on her chair rattled as she pulled it back and sat. She effortlessly logged onto her computer and attacked the keyboard.

Her concentrated look gave her away. The smile on his face dissipated. "Hey, in the six years we've been partners, I know when you bite your lip like that, something's wrong." He strolled over and put his hand on her shoulder.

"Is something wrong?"

Her fingers danced across the keyboard until a marine tracking website flashed onto the screen. She remained silent while she navigated the page and clicked on different links.

"Hey!" Josh snapped his fingers twice.

She flinched and blinked at Josh. "I'm sorry. What?"

"I asked if everything was okay. You're acting strange. What did your mom say?"

Her chair squeaked as she turned around, glancing back out the tall windows behind her partner. "She asked me if I'd heard from Richard recently."

"Your brother?"

Her stare wandered toward the beige commercial carpet. "Yeah."

"Okay, is it odd you haven't? When was the last time you did?"

She raised her eyes, inspected the tiny holes in the ceiling tiles, and caught the flash of a fluorescent tube. "It's not so much I haven't heard from him. It's my mom. Ever since dad died, Richard has tried to call her a few times a week. I know he's been on an expedition in the middle of nowhere, but even then, he still manages to talk to her at least once a week."

Josh pulled an apple out of his lunch bag, inspected it, and shined the red skin on his blue polo shirt. "And when was the last time you heard from him?" He bit a large chunk and munched while she spoke.

"Ya know… I'm not sure." She reached for her phone and scrolled through her text messages. "The last thing I got from him was a text from a phone number I don't recognize. I remember thinking how weird the message was."

His brow furrowed while he took another bite and spoke with a mouth full of fruit. "Weird, eh?"

She searched for the text, then tossed her phone to him. He dropped his apple, and it rolled on the floor. "Shit."

"Sorry."

"No worries." He took a moment to read the text on her phone.

This is Richard. It's in the oven. The Dane's.

His nose wrinkled at the odd message. "It's in the oven? What the heck does that mean?"

Evelyn shrugged. "Or the Danes?" She spun around and refocused on her computer while Josh set her phone down on the desk.

He reached for his apple and blew off any errant hair or speck of dust. Satisfied it was safe, he took another bite and laughed before he spoke. "Maybe some Danish guy got his wife pregnant."

"I'm so glad you can crack yourself up. However, as unfortunate as it is, that wouldn't surprise me."

He chuckled as he went back and plopped into his chair. "So, what are you looking for?"

"As you know, he works in oil exploration and is gone for weeks, sometimes months. I'm looking to see if I can find his ship's last known location. This website tracks every commercial vessel worldwide and tells you where they are. Do me a favor and read me the date and time he sent the text."

Still chewing his food, he sounded off the timestamp. "Ten forty-seven PM on May the seventh. That's more than a month ago."

Her eyes scanned the screen for any detail or bit of information. "Okay, hmmm. And that's our time. He's at least four hours ahead of us. That would be May eighth his time. Interesting. There is some significance to that. Come here. I want to show you something and get your opinion."

Letting loose a slight groan, he pried himself from his chair and stepped over to her. She felt him over her shoulder and pointed to the screen. "Look here. This is the ship's last known location. It was moving but at a crawl. Almost like it was drifting." She pointed to the screen. "But check out the last timestamp from their location."

He squinted as he leaned forward. "Two in the morning. Same day."

She turned in her chair and Josh backed away. "Don't you think it's odd? Did the ship turn off its transponder?"

After another bite and a few chews, he shrugged. "Odd? I'm not sure I understand what you're getting at."

She sighed. "He sent a cryptic text just before two, and about ten minutes later, the transponder goes off. If the ship had been in trouble, he would have said so. We're sinking, we've lost power or pirates have boarded us."

"Ha! Pirates."

"You know what I mean."

He swallowed. "Have you tried to call that number?"

"No, but that's a great idea." Evelyn reached for her desk phone. By the time he chewed his apple to the core, she had dialed and listened for a moment. Her expression was vacant, she gently placed the phone receiver back onto its cradle.

"Nothing."

"Nothing? You had the phone to your ear too long for it to be nothing, eh?"

"It was a recording saying the phone was either off or not in service." An overwhelming sense of foreboding washed over her, akin to a sinister shadow descending upon her. The intuitive twist in her gut appeared when she knew something was amiss. "I'm calling his office."

Evelyn searched for the corporate headquarters for Canada Oil and dialed the number listed on the main webpage. After negotiating the multi-levels of their automated phone system, she finally spoke to someone. Even after identifying herself as a Canadian Intelligence officer, it took another three transfers before she reached the right department, and they connected her with the CEO.

"James Gallagher," a deep voice announced.

"Yes, sir. My name is Special Agent Evelyn Cathey with CSIS, and I am investigating the whereabouts of one of your drilling ships, the DavCo Arctic Drill. Can you tell me the last time anyone on board checked in with someone at your company?" She tapped her fingers on her desk and listened to the response.

"May I put you on hold, Special Agent Cathey?"

"Yes, I can hold, but it shouldn't be a difficult question. You are the one in charge, are you not, Mr. Gallagher?"

"I'll be with you in a moment." His voice took on an acidic tone. Evelyn heard background music.

She placed her hand over the mic on the handset. Josh tossed his apple core into the trash. Her eyes met his. "Bout damn time you finished that thing."

Josh smiled. "What's he saying?"

"Nothing, but I sense he knows something, and maybe..." She raised her index finger and listened intently.

"I'm here. Yes, Mr. Gallagher. I understand." She gave her partner a wide-eyed look as she listened. She reached for a pen and started writing. "I see... Okay... Yes." She turned her wrist to glance at her watch. "Tomorrow morning. Ten AM. Yes, sir. We'll meet you then."

She put the phone on the cradle and tried to make sense of everything she was told.

Josh rested his elbow on the top of her partition. "What did he say?"

She tapped the pen lightly against her mouth for a moment. "Hope you've got a go-bag in your locker because you and I are about to take a trip."

"Where to?"

"Canada Oil's corporate headquarters."

"What about your brother's ship?"

Evelyn closed her eyes and sighed.

"It's missing."

6

Somewhere in the Venezuelan jungle SE of Caracas.
June 18th 08:12 (12:12 UTC)

Seasoned clandestine agent, Blake MacKay, stepped off the boarding stairs from the Gulfstream G700. He raised his hand to shield his eyes from the unwavering early morning light. A sleek black SUV sat waiting, its system blasting cool air, yet even the short thirty-meter trek from the company jet to the vehicle left him drenched in sweat, his shirt sticking uncomfortably to his back.

Closing the passenger door, he looked to the driver and saw a familiar face. Marty Goldmann, a man who had gone through training with him at "the farm". They'd only worked on the same assignment once before. This was the second, but they always stayed in touch with each other and compared notes when they caught themselves in sticky situations.

"Welcome to the jungle."

Blake chuckled. "Have you got fun and games?"

They both laughed. Marty held out a hand, and Blake grasped it. "How ya doing, Blake?"

"Meh. I was doing okay until I heard about the shit show you got going on in this—paradise."

The Yukon started to roll. The bumps in the primitive road evident as his body bounced with the vehicle.

Marty's brow scrunched. "Shit show? What? You know we have things in complete control."

"Yeah, yeah, yeah. Like you did with that little wannabe terrorist in—Liberia, was it?"

He pointed a finger at Blake while attempting to suppress a laugh. "Hey now! I knew you'd go there. Let me say in my defense. I had no idea he was actually going to fuck that goat."

Blake burst out laughing. "And you blew his balls off!"

Both erupted into laughter. Marty had to stop the SUV. "And he had his pants around his ankles. And goat guts and his nuts were splattered all over...over his face."

"Ahhh, good times."

"Yeah."

They continued to chuckle. Blake wiped a tear from his eye. "All right. Now it's business. I understand you have someone here requiring my services to make him blab a little?"

Marty rested his elbows on the steering wheel as he drove toward the bunker. The road from the airfield, carved out of the jungle by the cartels for their drug smuggling operations, was less than stellar. Even with the air-con blowing, Blake felt the oppressive humidity wrapping around him like a weighted shroud, clinging to his skin. Every bump in the dirt road added to his discomfort.

"Well, you've read about the election they had here, right? Mister dictator asshole Valdez, lost to Montero, but he has no intention of relinquishing his seat. At least not without a fight. We're pretty sure there will be an attempt on Montero's life and—no scratch that, we *know* there is. The chatter is so loud it's like they're not even trying to hide it. Problem is, we don't know the how, who, when, where of it all. Bottom line—we have to protect the democracy they tried so hard to build and it is hanging on by a thread."

The Yukon rolled to a stop and Blake cleared his throat. "And this person you have. You suspect he knows something?"

Marty shifted the SUV to park. "That's what you're here to find out. Come on. I'll show you around before we have a chat with our guest."

They entered the concrete bunker. The outside was still crumbling and dilapidated. Vines climbed the walls. Their roots penetrated the cracks in the mortar, but the inside had undergone retrofitting with modern amenities. Electricity, computers, secure networks, and most importantly, air conditioning. It smelled of plastic-coated wire, floor adhesive, and fresh paint. Marty motioned toward his office. "In here."

Upon entering, Blake noticed the picture of a young woman on his desk. "Did you get married, or do you have a sister?"

Marty's brow furrowed. "Huh?" His eyes shifted to the simple wooden framed photograph. "Oh." He smiled. "If only." He grasped the frame while admiring the brunette staring back at him. "We met a few years back. Started to date. But—you know how it is with our jobs."

Blake nodded. "Don't I ever."

"She understood and was pretty cool with it, but after several times of me not calling her for weeks on end and not being able to tell her where I was or what I was doing... we decided it wasn't going to work and should stick to being friends."

"With benefits?"

"Oh yeah. For sure. Well—at least for a little while. Last time we talked, she said she was going to be getting engaged. I haven't talked to her since." He sighed. "But I can dream, can't I?"

Blake's thoughts drifted away as he thought of Adriana, his lost love. Not knowing if she was even alive, it was eating at him and tearing his soul apart. He shook away the thought. "Yeah."

Marty tossed the frame into the trash. "So, what about you? Mr. poster boy." He chuckled. "I remember we'd frequent some dorky bar while we were at the farm." He snapped his fingers twice. "What was it called?"

Blake shook his head and smirked. "Chugger's."

"Yeah, Chugger's. What a stupid name. I don't think I've ever seen a dude get so many drinks bought for him. You had the ladies *begging* for your attention. You and your chiseled features. I hate you. I bet you've got side chicks all *over* the place, right?"

"Meh, not my thing. Besides, like you said, in our line of work, not having a relationship is collateral damage. I can wait until I'm out of the field. It's too distracting and I'm not interested in one-night stands."

Marty shook his head. "Yah, I don't understand you. If I had your looks and chicks were fawning all over me—man, I'd be loving life."

Adriana's smile filled his mind's eye, and his heart ached. "Yeah, I said that's not me. So, drop it."

An awkward silence filled the air.

Blake's last long mission took a toll on him physically and emotionally. People he trusted betrayed him and a woman he fell hopelessly in love with, he lost. Add on top of it all, a new boss he historically didn't get along with. The extended leave of absence he took to decompress wasn't enough.

Marty cleared his throat. "Hey, how are you getting on since the change in leadership?"

"You mean Veronica? I don't want to talk about it. Let's say she and I keep it professional and leave it there."

His buddy nodded. "Okay. I hear ya, bud. All right. Hey, I'm sorry about—"

Blake raised his palm. "Forget about it. Let's go meet our guest and work out a way we can get some answers."

THE THICK, SUFFOCATING humidity clung to the jungle like a damp blanket, smothering every living thing in its clammy embrace. Deep inside the ancient bunker, with a continuous hum, the whirring fans fought relentlessly against the oppressive air, their blades slicing through the dense atmosphere. But their valiant efforts could not drown out the grunts and screams echoing from within the shadows of the bunker's depths, where fists collided with flesh. The stench of sweat and fear lingered, mingling with the metallic tang of iron and the musty scent of decaying earth.

They entered the room. The steel door groaning in protest as it creaked open on rusted hinges. Blake flicked on the light. Sitting in the middle of the gray concrete room with his hands tied behind his back and his legs bound to the chair, was their prisoner. His head drooped onto his chest. Blake grasped the suspect's chin and raised it to inspect the damage inflicted from hours of enhanced interrogation. The man's swollen eyes opened. Dried blood cracked around the edges of his mouth.

"When was the last time he was fed?"

"Um, yesterday I believe."

"No wonder you're not getting anything. You're making him comfortable."

Marty's eyes went wide. "Comfortable?" He pointed at the man tied in the chair. "You call that comfortable? He's pissed his pants and is probably sitting in his own shit."

A quick glance at his watch and Blake shot back. "He's eaten within the past twelve hours and he was asleep when we walked in here. That's comfortable, and it stops now." He started to look around the room.

"What are you looking for?"

"An outlet."

Marty pointed toward the door. "Over there."

"Okay. Good. How far to town where I can get some speakers and an amplifier?"

"Thirty minutes."

"All right. Let's go. We're going shopping."

THREE HOURS LATER, they were back in the cell with multiple stacks of acoustic equipment. No less than six contractor lights on stands stood, each filling the room with a blinding light of four to six thousand lumens each. Four additional fast moving strobe lights would add to the misery. To top it off, Blake connected his phone via Bluetooth and chose the band *Cannibal Corpse* and their album, fittingly titled *Torture,* and cranked it to 130 decibels.

Marty scrunched his nose as he cupped his hands over his ears. Blake smiled wide and motioned for them to leave. After closing the door behind them, Marty turned to him.

"Oh, my God! What in the hell?"

Nodding in agreement, he smiled. "Yeah, we'll check on him tomorrow and see if he's more cooperative."

The wrenching sounds of their prisoner's screams faded as they walked away.

7

Isola di Montecristo
   Tyrrhenian Sea

June 19th 11:07 (10:07 UTC)

A repeating gentle crash of waves against the breakers calmed the tensest nerves and the canvas canopy kept the temperature at a comfortable twenty-one degrees Celsius. The inlet on the tiny island was picture-perfect, but barren, with several coral rock formations rising out of the sea.

The impressive mega yacht, *zayt muntasaf allay*, translated, *Midnight Oil*, lay moored a few hundred meters offshore. Awadi Salib poured his guest a glass of wine and then served himself. No less than seven staff stood by ready to serve them; but only if he signaled them.

"I'm pleased you accepted my invitation to get away from your project for a brief getaway."

Madison smiled. "How could I turn down a prince? Besides, I've never flown in a private jet before."

He handed her the glass. The dark liquid inside glowed a deep red as it captured the rays of the midday sun.

"I hope you enjoy this. It's from the Marchesi di Barolo winery in northern Italy." Raising the glass, he brought it to his nose, closed his eyes, and inhaled. He swirled the dark red liquid. "You should oxygenate it to bring out the bouquet." Repeating the gesture with eyes shut, savoring the wine's esters and tannins. "You try it. You'll notice a distinct difference between the nose and bouquet."

Dr. Sagadish Agate had enlisted Madison Wyrick's help. She came from Knoxville, Tennessee, and was now developing an underwater drilling system to be used by a deep-water submersible. They investigated hydrothermal spallation, chemical plasma, and lasers. Based on the limitations of the craft, they decided lasers would give them the best results.

She had a classic southern drawl. "Pardon my ignorance, but isn't drinking alcohol forbidden by Islam?"

He smirked. "The benefits of living as a prince." Taking another sip, he outstretched his arm. "And being so far from Saudi Arabia and their overbearing regime."

Her brow furrowed. "But he's your father? Are you saying he's oppressive?"

"Old ways from an older generation." His gaze focused on her cleavage. "Do not think I refrain from indulging in other sinful pleasantries."

Her lips tightened into a thin line as she adjusted her position while tugging her cover-up over her bathing suit.

He placed the glass on the crisp white linen-covered table. "But I don't want to discuss such things. Tell me your progress with the sub and its drilling capabilities."

He frowned. "You and Dr. Agate were to have a working prototype three weeks ago and I have yet to see anything. You're being paid more than enough money, and I expect results. What is keeping you from making the deadline?"

She reached for her glass and took a healthy swig of her wine, forcing a giggle to lighten the mood. "Speaking of which, where is my lab partner? Wasn't he supposed to join us?"

"He is en route as we speak. The delay, doctor."

She brushed her long dishwater blonde hair to the side and tucked it behind her ear. Salib's temper and impatience were legendary among his staff, and she did not aspire to be on the receiving end of his hostility.

"I, uh, I mean, we did some testing last month and discovered there was potential for a dangerous malfunction without some kind of blowout prevention system. I'm also concerned about the proximity of the laser to the hull."

The rhythmic chopping sound of an approaching helicopter abruptly interrupted their dialogue's growing uneasiness.

The prince shuffled in his chair, indicating his waning patience. "Forget about the chopper! The delay, doctor. Continue."

"We've designed a preventer and had to have the parts sourced for manufacturing and..."

A faint scream grew to a shriek, and she was startled by a thump when a body slammed into the coral rocks. She cried out. The hair on her nape stood on end as the mangled corpse rolled off the reef into the ocean. It was her colleague. He had been hog-tied.

She stared wide-eyed, frozen by the sight of her former associate as his corpse bobbed in the sea. The waves knocked it against the steep slope. Salib remained calm as he spoke to her. "Delays can cause accidents, Doctor Wyrick. I hope for your sake you remain accident-free."

He snapped his fingers and rose. His staff rushed in to set everything right as he stepped toward her with his hand outstretched. "Come! I've had the chef prepare a wonderful *kabsa* for us on board. We have further things to discuss now you're in charge of the project."

She raised her chin. Her stomach was in knots and a tingling numbness filled her being. What mess had she gotten herself into? Forcing a smile, she took his hand and stood. "Certainly."

The 24-ft Chris-Craft was minuscule as it docked next to the 358-ft mega yacht. A crew member helped her out of the boat. The ride back was unnerving. She forced herself to think about anything else. Like a skipping record, the image of her colleague's lifeless body striking the rocks kept replaying in her mind.

The prince stepped onto the craft and walked over to her. His voice was amplified to speak over the helicopter rotors, now landing on the yacht's helipad. "We will eat in thirty minutes, aft on level three. We will discuss the project further. Do not be late." He leaned in and kissed her once on each cheek. She contrived another smile. "Of course. I'll freshen up and meet you there."

SALIB EXITED THE 3RD level's saloon and out to the aft deck. Nazir Farhi was standing at the bar pouring himself a whisky.

His Majesty stopped. "Help yourself."

Nazir turned to him and smiled. "I did." He raised his glass and took a gulp.

The prince returned an unamused smirk and gestured to the white, rounded couch. "Sit." His guest sat comfortably with his left ankle propped on his opposite knee. He relaxed and stretched his right arm across the back of the sofa. With his left, he took another sip of his drink. The sun reflected off his Ray-Ban Aviators.

Salib rummaged through several figs in a silver bowl before making a selection. Once satisfied with his choice, he leaned back. "I'm impressed with what you and your team have accomplished already. There are rumblings in the intelligence community, and each side is blaming the other."

His hired man nodded and tipped his glass.

Next, the Canadians will turn their attention to attacking American interests. What are your plans?"

He uncrossed his legs. "The largest oil field in the U.S. is in Prudhoe Bay, Alaska, about three hundred miles west of the Canadian border. Employees work two weeks with a minimum shift of twelve hours a day, every day. Some longer. We'll be hitting them at the end of their stint. They have shoreline drilling stations, and these will be an easy target."

"And you have everything you need? Canadian uniforms and other identifying measures?"

"Yes."

"When?"

"Four days."

"No. Too long."

Nazir straightened and removed his glasses. "What? But I—."

"Move—it—up. You have thirty-six hours. That is all!"

Three of the Prince's well-dressed bodyguards stepped closer, arms inside their jackets ready to draw their weapons.

Nazir's eyes moved from man to man, considering his options, and nodded. He placed his drink on the coffee table. "Very well then. Thirty-six hours."

As a former member of the Syrian Special Mission Forces since its inception in 2014 and the 15th Special Forces Division for ten years prior, he was used to acting with speed and making changes on the fly, but to have to make this drastic change for an assignment halfway around the world with such a short timetable left him agitated.

The prince popped the last bite of his fig into his mouth. "The helo is waiting. You'd better get going."

He stood, put on his glasses, and tugged on his sports coat. "I'll let you know when it's done," he said as he turned and marched to the helipad.

Salib leaned forward to snatch another fig. "I'd expect nothing less."

MADISON STROLLED OUT of the saloon's quadruple-wide glass doors as strange guests headed to the port side stairwell and up to the helicopter. The mangled half ear on the man's head made her pause.

Was he the one who bound my colleague and hurled him to his death?

Queasy, she stopped, placing her hand across her belly. Her host called out, "Are you ill?"

"I'm a little nauseous. I'm... I probably don't have my sea legs yet."

Snapping his fingers, two crew members went to her aid and helped her over to the couch.

As the crew seated her, he clapped his hands. "Champagne!"

She needed to forget the event from earlier and please the prince, but there was no doubt her situation was dire.

A crewman set down a silver champagne bucket on a stand next to the prince. A plain brown bottle made of old glass sat buried in sun-sparkled crystal ice. Another crewman placed two glasses on the coffee table.

He removed the bottle and began to pour. "In two-thousand and ten, some divers were in the Baltic Sea. They located a nineteenth-century shipwreck, discovered a chest buried in the mud, and brought it to the surface."

He tilted the bottle to show her. "When they opened it, they found this champagne inside. By sheer luck, there were twelve bottles, perfectly preserved. Their perfectly horizontal orientation and ideal depth saved them from destruction." He handed her the glass. Madison brought it to her nose as he showed her on the beach before the unfortunate mishap.

He chuckled. Louder than she would have preferred. "You don't have to do it with champagne. The effervescence masks the delicate bouquet."

The blood rushed to her cheeks as she took a sip. Her eyes widened and her lips curled upward without hesitation. "This is superb. When did you say the ship sank?"

"Nobody knows for certain, but it is at least two hundred years old."

"Oh, my. I bet it was expensive." She enjoyed another gulp.

"I got a steal. I purchased the case. Eleven bottles for only one hundred and fifty-six thousand dollars."

She swallowed abruptly, preventing herself from spurting the golden liquid in her shock. "That's a steal? I dunno, but in my experience, a case includes twelve bottles. Someone screwed you."

"No!" The abruptness of his response startled her. "Nobody screwed me over."

She tensed at the forcefulness of his reply. His shoulders relaxed as he sighed and gazed at her. "They had opened one of the bottles to test its potation. I, of course, understood there were only eleven."

She contrived another smile. "Ah, I understand. Well, it's fantastic."

The head chef stepped out into the sun. She was thankful he had broken an awkward situation. "Your Highness, your meal is prepared. Please." He gestured them into the saloon and toward the less formal dining area amidships on the yacht.

The informal dining area occupied three-quarters of the ship's beam. A dark mahogany table sat upon a gold-inlaid marble floor. Above was a multi-layered ceiling with mirrors, and wood trim with backlighting. At the center was a massive crystal chandelier. The plates were trimmed in gold leaf and the royal family crest was hand-painted on the surface of each plate.

The servers brought their meal of traditional Saudi cuisine—*harees*, a dish made with coarse wheat and meat. *Shawarma* is another meat dish, marinated, split, roasted, and served with *amba*, a pickled mango sauce. *Kabsa*; is a dish of lamb, rice, and spices. In addition, there were numerous flatbreads, dates, hummus, other jams, and jellies.

She continued her idle chatter, making their repast as enjoyable as possible to ensure her welfare now and in the future. The chef entered, carrying a plate with dome-shaped pastries on it.

"Ah, wonderful." He rubbed his hands together in anticipation. "Now, these are *Ma'amoul*, an ancient cookie, and they're filled with various fruits and nuts. I hope you like walnuts and pistachios."

"I do, but how can you tell which is which?"

He pointed to the air. "An excellent question. Unlike American chocolates, where you must bite into each item to discover what they are, these are all somewhat different."

He reached and selected one. "Take this one, for example." He rubbed his finger across the top. "This one is rounded, so this has walnut."

He placed it back on the plate and gestured to another. "This one, the top is elongated and oval. Pistachio."

He moved to the next and picked it up. "And this one. It has a flat top, and it is my favorite. It contains a sweet date."

He sank his teeth into the confection and smiled as he chewed the doughy treat.

She couldn't help but enjoy his company during their meal together. He was intimidating, but also charismatic. His confidence was often mistaken for arrogance, hubris, and smugness. She bit into her *ma'amoul* and took a sip of her dessert wine. As she enjoyed her dessert, she listened to him carry on and on about the different foods. She gulped more of her sweet drink. His words gradually became a distant murmur, and the illumination surrounding her dimmed. Suddenly, complete darkness engulfed her.

8

Canada Oil Corporate Headquarters
Toronto, Ontario

June 19th 09:50 AM (15:50 UTC)

Evelyn and Josh approached the steel and glass circular desk in the middle of the massive lobby at Canada Oil headquarters. A MUZAK version of Depeche Mode's *World in My Eyes* played over the foyer's speakers. She checked in with the guards as her partner stared up at the almost seventy-foot atrium, highlighted by an all-glass and chrome bank of elevators on the lobby's west side.

"Here!" She slapped the RFID card on Josh's chest to get his attention. His eyes switched to the lanyard holding it.

"What's this, eh?"

"Just follow me."

They both put the cards around their necks and headed for the lifts.

A shiny barrier surrounded the elevators. As they got closer, a friendly voice came out of nowhere. "*Elevator five, please.*"

Josh quipped, "Gotta just love technology, don't ya, eh?"

She smiled. "Now you know why we're issued RFID-blocking wallets. Damn scanners can steal your information in a heartbeat. Not ideal for people in our line of work."

He nodded as he placed his phone in his pocket. "Yeah, the sad thing is—most people have no clue."

By the time they reached their designated spot, the lift had arrived, doors open. They stepped inside and were taken to their destination, the executive level on the 77th floor.

The elevator opened into the CEO's reception area. A slim brunette greeted them and directed them to sit on a black leather sectional. She offered them coffee while making idle chat about the usual banal things.

"I hope you had a pleasant trip here."

Evelyn nodded. "Yes, we did. Didn't we, partner?"

He glanced from the *Car & Driver* publication he was perusing. "Hmm? Oh, yeah, excellent flight." He leaned toward her and flashed a page in the magazine. "Have you seen the new Corvette?"

The receptionist came from behind her desk and gestured them forward. "He will see you now." She ushered them into the office of James Gallagher, CEO of Canada Oil.

The executive was distinguished, dressed in a navy-blue pinstriped suit, snow-white shirt, and purple tie.

He was mostly bald, but what little hair he had left was colored too dark for his age. He rose from his glass and steel desk before approaching the agents, offering his hand in greeting. He was taller than she had imagined. After exchanging pleasantries, he directed them into a conference room where six other people were sitting: the Senior Vice President, The Chairman of the Board, and four corporate attorneys.

She scanned the room. "I didn't realize this would be so formal, Mr. Gallagher. I just had a few questions regarding the missing ship."

Gallager's down-turned lips indicated his displeasure. "When we deal with multi-million-dollar equipment, the company's employees, and Canadian Intelligence, we want to ensure we cover our bases, Agent Cathey. I'm sure you can appreciate how sensitive this matter is."

She nodded, glanced toward her partner, and the pair sat in the plush black leather desk chairs.

One of the suits at the end of the table initiated the meeting. "It is a pleasure having you both here today. It was somewhat shocking to have heard about your call with Mr. Gallagher, but since you requested this interview, why don't you start? We're here to cooperate."

She paused to gather her thoughts. *Fucking corporate lawyers—always covering their asses.*

"Mr. Gallagher, the other day on the phone, you mentioned my brother's ship, the DavCo Arctic Drill, was missing. What were they doing and where were they?" She sensed their hesitance as one of the corporate lawyers interrupted. "Unfortunately, such information is privileged, and I'm afraid we can't divulge it at this time."

Josh started to speak when she raised her hand to stop him. "I can appreciate your position. But, for your information, I'm not here officially. The agency is not initiating a formal inquiry into your company or the missing ship. They don't know anything about it. Be aware I can change this if you piss me off."

She pointed an accusatory finger at the attorney, who had spoken. "And statements like—like the shit she just said—pisses me off." She paused to allow her words to sink in.

"Especially when it comes to preventing me from locating my brother. I can, and will, make it official, and rest assured, it will be painful and rather expensive for you. Now, I'm not here to cause you problems, so I highly recommend you tell me what I want to know."

She turned to Gallagher before she continued. "All I care about is finding my brother. We can do this the easy way, and I can help you, or we can do this the hard way. Your choice."

She scanned the group for an eternity when, at last, the CEO stood. His attention drifted to the attorneys at the end of the table, and he dipped his chin. "I trust you can keep this confidential for now?"

"If you're trying to insult me, it's working." Pointing to her partner and herself. "We're both members of Canadian Intelligence. What sort of question is that?"

He nodded and cleared his throat. "Of course. What I meant was—until we make a public statement. Which, at this point, can't be avoided." He glanced toward the group of attorneys at the end of the table. The lead attorney nodded.

"Yes, we'll be making a public statement shortly after this meeting."

The CEO grasped the back of his chair. "Your brother, Agent Cathey, had the idea a massive oil reserve lay at the bottom of the Arctic seabed. For months, he tried to convince our board all he needed was some specific equipment and a ship, and he could find it."

She leaned in and rested on her elbows. "And?"

"We believe he did." He walked over to a glass panel and hit a switch. It illuminated a map of the North Pole.

A spot glowed pinkish red. "This area is known as an exclusive economic zone, or EEZ. It's a boundary under extreme scrutiny for who owns the mineral rights, if any are found."

Josh raised his hand. "Who is scrutinizing it?"

Gallagher chuckled. "Who isn't? But if you want to know specifically; us, the Russians, the Americans, the Danes, and a few others, perhaps. Everybody wants a piece of the action."

Upon hearing the Danes, Josh locked eyes with Evelyn. A subtle head shake backed him down. "How does this tie in with my brother and the missing ship?"

The CEO took a deep breath and exhaled. "Miss Cathey—apologies—Agent Cathey, our business is a bit unique. It's not uncommon for pirates to capture our ships, ask for a ransom, and then be on their way."

She shook her head in disbelief. "You're kidding me. And you just pay it?"

Nodding, he sighed. "Yes. It's more economical to pay it than to lose a billion-dollar ship and pay out hundreds of millions to the families of those killed. It's more common than you think." He walked slowly toward the attorneys at the end of the table and rested his hands on the back of an empty chair. "Sometimes it can be weeks before we hear from them and that's what we were assuming here, but it's been too long. And, if your brother was right; and I have every reason to believe he was, there are a lot of other nasty people prepared to go to extreme measures to get the information he found."

A gleam of hope appeared in her eyes. "So, he *did* discover something?"

He shook his head. "Purely speculation on my part. I don't know. But—your brother is a smart man. So much so that he convinced us to dispatch him on this expedition. If anyone could uncover something, it would be Richard."

Josh flipped open a notepad and readied his pen. "And where was the ship when you heard from it?"

The CEO turned to his pool of lawyers when a younger woman with a dark brown bob, somewhere in her late twenties, answered. "We'll send the exact coordinates to the email address you left with us. You'll have it within the hour."

Evelyn stood, approached the CEO, and offered her hand. "Thank you for this information. I trust you will inform me if you locate the missing ship?"

He accepted her hand and grasped it while he spoke. "We will."

With a sneer, her eyes scanned the row of attorneys pointing back and forth between Josh and herself. "And for future reference, it's *Special*—Agents."

She called over her shoulder as she left the room. "I'll be expecting an email within the hour."

THEY CONVENED IN THE coffee shop across the street from the Canada Oil building. She sat with her elbows on the table, grasping and enjoying the warmth of the mug; her eyes shifting in deep thought.

The plate scooting along the table knocked her from her momentary trance. Josh had purchased a couple of chocolate croissants. She placed her mug on the surface and focused on him. "Those look good."

He pulled back the chair. "One is for you. Do you plan to tell me your thoughts when he mentioned the Danes? Do you think it's what your brother spoke about on his odd voicemail?"

She picked up one of the croissants and bit into the flaky pastry. The warmth made the chocolate soft and gooey. She took a few seconds to savor the flavor. While still chewing, "I know, as soon as I heard—that..." Bits of flaky pastry fell onto the table.

Josh's brow furrowed. "Ev?" She was staring past him and focused on the television on the wall. It was broadcasting a BBC Worldwide news station.

She leaped from her chair, darted to the TV, and increased the volume.

"*...sources say the attack was unprovoked. Authorities are still trying to figure out a motive and on the diplomatic side, both ambassadors are meeting with heads of state of Denmark and Russia. We caught up to the lone survivor earlier, and this is what he said.*"

The picture switched to a young man with a microphone tilted his way. The banner at the bottom read *Anders Siversten – Lone survivor in Oil Platform Attack*.

"They just came out of nowhere. Russian soldiers everywhere. They killed everyone."

Reporter off camera: "And why do you think they left you alive?"

"I don't know. I don't know." There was an awkward moment of silence. The scene returned to the BBC News desk. *"And that was Bridgette Stone reporting from Bergen, Norway. Next up on the news hour..."* She turned the volume down and stepped over to the table and let loose a deep sigh.

"I'm going to Norway."

9

Awadi Salib Property
   North of Trongisvágur
Faroe Islands

June 20th 08:00 (07:00 UTC)

Madison's eyes fluttered open. She yawned, freezing in place a second before her eyes went wide and she spring-loaded upright in bed.

Her surroundings were comforting. Devoid of color, modern light-hued furniture rested on a floor with the tone of weathered driftwood. The goose-down filled duvet matched the fifteen-foot-high curtains across the room. She ripped back the covers, surprised to discover she was dressed in tasteful satin pajamas.

"Where in the hell am I?"

She hesitated before placing her bare feet on the floor. Anticipating a jolt from the cold white tiles, a broad smile creased her face when she discovered they were heated.

She walked hurriedly to the curtains and yanked them open. A rocky landscape extended for only a short while before descending to meet the sea. The water reached out to the horizon.

A knock at the door disrupted her thoughts. She moved a few steps closer to the sound originating on the other side before replying.

"Yes?"

An older-sounding woman, called out, with an accent she couldn't place. "Dr. Wyrick? Are you awake? May I come in, dear?" Before she could answer, an elderly lady entered carrying a tray. Upon it was a Turkish coffee pot, a cup alongside a pitcher of cream, and a small jar of sugar cubes.

"Good morning, dear. My name is Arna, and I'll look after your needs while you are here. Here is some fresh coffee for—"

"I'm sorry." Madison extended her arms from her side and shook her head. "Where is here? How'd I get—here?" She tugged on her pajama shirt.

"And—and who fucking dressed me?" Her ire rose to near boiling. "What the fuck is going on?"

Arna spoke while she placed the tray on the small table. "I'm so sorry, please—please calm yourself. I thought you were aware. This is the research station owned by Prince Salib. You are working for him on a special project, are you not?"

"Wha—yes. Yes, I am." Shaking her head once more. "But not here. This isn't where my lab is—or was? I don't recognize the landscape. Where are we?" Returning to the window, she stretched her neck to look as far as she could to her left and then right.

"Are we on some kind of island?"

"Yes."

She continued to peer through the glass and waited for the woman to finish, but she was met with silence. Turning back, she noticed her caregiver pouring a cup of coffee. Growing impatient, she shrugged. "Well?"

"Well what, dear?"

"Seriously? Where in the fuck are we? Precisely. If I were to open a map and ask you to point to where we are, what would you say and where would you point? I wanna know specifically where the fuck we are. Do you think you can do that?"

"Yes, yes. I'm so sorry, dear. We are on a private island south of Trongisvágur." The woman smiled and handed her the mug. Her smile quickly dissipated when Madison didn't reply, and only stood—a blank look on her face.

"Oh, apologies. In the Faroe Islands."

She accepted the cup with an unwavering gaze, savored the aroma, and then took a sip. The bitterness seized her tongue like a bear trap, yet she swallowed, closed her eyes, and drew a deep breath.

Her exhalation was a growling whisper, forcing her to keep her composure. "And where the fuck is that?"

The old lady frowned and gave a disappointing stare. Madison felt like she was back in the 4th grade, misspelled an easy word, and was about to feel her teacher's wrath.

Arna gave a stern reply. "We'll, if you insist on specificity—we're southeast of my home, Iceland, by about five hundred and forty-five kilometers. Scotland is four hundred kilometers south and Norway is to the east about six hundred. Do you still need a map?"

Madison sensed the shift in her demeanor and, as the only person she'd seen and one who started out being kind, she decided to change her tone. She returned a warm grin. "Thank you. And this coffee is something else."

"You're welcome." She turned to leave, then stopped.

"A more substantial meal awaits you in the dining room. It's out and to the left. The Crown Prince wants to meet with you in his study after you are done. But do not take too long. I understand you're in enough trouble as it is."

Anxiety reared its ugly head when she heard those words. What did she mean by trouble?

The tingle on the nape of her neck erased any further thoughts of eating. Arna exited and started to close the door when it reopened. "Oh, I put on your sleepwear. Your clothes are in the closet. They've been washed and pressed."

Madison dressed and hurried out. Strolling past where breakfast was placed, plates of various pastries and rolls were laid out. A large bowl of fruit was the centerpiece of the table. Two silver warming trays wafted the scent of spices and citrus her way.

That smells good. I wonder what's under those lids.

Ignoring the grumbling of her stomach, she sought someone to whom she could get directions to the prince's location.

A formidable pair of imposing doors guarded the entrance to the study. Heavy, dark wooden beasts, battle scared with deep grooves and black iron hinges with a Thors Hammer knocker in the center of each. They reminded her of something in a Viking fortress. She reached out when it suddenly opened. Its hinges moaning under the tremendous burden the door's weight carried. It was one of the Royal Guard.

"Come in, Dr. Wyrick." Salib was wearing a more traditional Western suit; dark blue, a pink shirt, and no tie. He rose and moved around the massive wooden desk with various Nordic designs carved throughout.

"I imagine you have questions. I'll provide answers."

She stood with her fists clenched and worked to control her breathing. Her former partner had been chucked out of a helicopter and she had been drugged. But she was in the company of a Crown Prince from a country where women had no rights. To make things worse, she was surrounded by his Royal Guard.

She had to maintain her self-control. The only sense of unease she experienced stemmed from the distressing realization of being involuntarily drugged, with no recollection of what had happened or if anyone had taken advantage of her.

"Please. Come forward. I promise not to bite." There was a long table with cushioned chairs. She assumed it was used for dining or formal meetings. Most likely the latter. He motioned for her to come and sit in the chair at the head of the table. "Did you get breakfast?"

She hesitated and replied in a tone above a whisper. "No."

"Excuse me?"

She cleared her throat. "No."

The familiar snap of his fingers instructed his guards to leave the room. She walked cautiously toward him and grasped the back of the chair. "Where am I?"

He sat adjacent to her and once again indicated for her to take a seat. "Please."

Defiant, she stuck to her guns. "Answer the question first."

A sudden slap with his palm on the wooden slab startled her. "You sit, goddamn it, or I'll have you dismembered and thrown into the sea!"

Her eyes widened as she inhaled and held her breath. She crossed the line and was now terrified. The numbness seemed to resonate from her gut out and to her feet.

"Now, woman!"

She pulled back the chair and did as commanded. Her hands clasped in her lap.

He stood and wagged his finger in her face. "I am tired of your insolence! I have told you before that I am giving you some leeway, but you have now tipped the scales and pissed me off, doctor. If I command you to sit, you fucking sit! If I tell you what to wear, what to eat, when to sleep, you do it!"

He leaned close to her ear. The stench of alcohol permeated her nostrils. She focused on a knot in the wood. "And if I want to fuck you like a whore, I will fuck you like the whore you are."

Tremors wracked her body as a torrent of thoughts flooded her mind. Acting on impulse, she lifted her head and locked eyes with him. "And did you? Fuck me like a whore?" The disdain in her voice flowed from her lips like a venomous river.

He straightened. His lips down-turned and snubbed his nose. "Hmph! No. I would want you awake."

She sat motionless.

He exhaled a heavy sigh and sat opposite her. "Now, as I mentioned, I am here to answer your questions. Proceed."

She searched the back of her mind for the queries that escaped during his tirade.

"What is this place?"

His voice adopted a monotone quality, absent the warmth and amiability it once exuded, as his responses became terse and devoid of embellishment.

"It is another laboratory, on an island closer to our drilling destination."

"Am I a prisoner here?" she asked, immediately wishing she could take it back, fearing it would acknowledge an answer she didn't want to accept.

"There is a village on the adjacent island. You are free to come and go as you please."

She felt a small amount of numbness fade with the answer.

"Why here?"

As he started to speak, the ancient doors parted and three men brought in the food she had passed by outside his study, including the buffet warmers. As they were arranging them on the table, he replied. "I have reason to believe—a very strong one, there is a huge—no—a gargantuan oil field laying beneath the ocean floor and stretches well into the North Pole. If we are the first to drill it and cap it, I can and will claim it."

"But isn't that in—oh, what do they call them, an—EE zone, uh, exclusive economic zone?"

He gently tugged a grape from a bowl and ate it. He rubbed his fingertips together while he chewed. "Fuck the e e z."

Her stomach growled, and the prince must have heard it as he took on a new demeanor. His lips curled, and he chuckled. "Please. Eat. I will continue to answer your questions."

She stood and grabbed a plate. She filled it with rolls and some fruit, and removed the lid to one of the warming trays. As the steam gently ascended, it carried a tantalizing medley of scents—the odor of freshly caught fish and the zesty essence of lemon. As she lifted a fillet from the tray, she inquired, "How long was I out?"

"Close to twenty hours."

She paused. *No wonder I'm so damn hungry.* She continued filling her plate until a repulsive thought occurred to her and she stopped.

As if reaching into her mind and plucking her thoughts, the man holding her capture released some of the pressure bearing down on her shoulders.

"Nobody touched you or violated you, if that is your concern. But—" He reached for another grape. Before popping it into his mouth, a sinister smile creased his lips. "It is only because I didn't allow it. Otherwise, they would have had their way with you." He motioned with his arm to some men standing around the room.

She felt the guards' eyes on her, but she ignored them.

"Why the theatrics?"

"So you'll always know who is in control."

She forced a smile and nodded her complacency. *You can take your control and shove it up your ass.*

"Why was I out for so long?"

He picked another grape and popped it into his mouth.

"That, I am afraid, was an unfortunate miscalculation. Inexcusable. You were given too much."

She let out a nervous giggle. "What happened to him? I hope you threw him off the boat." When the prince didn't reply, she turned to see a stern and serious look on his face. She wisely decided not to press him.

She sat and started to eat when one more thing occurred to her. "You cut our timeline from twenty-four to twelve weeks. Why?" She took a bite of her fish and relished the taste. She scooped another in while she was still chewing.

"As you can imagine, young lady. Throughout the world, I have contacts, informants, spies, if you will, in different oil organizations. I received word a couple of months ago that a Canadian oil company was sending out an exploration vessel to the North Pole. Through my connections, I was able to—let's say, make arrangements as to its status in real time. When I was informed they were getting close to the location where my team of scientists believed there was a deposit. I needed to guarantee we are the first to drill and cap."

She washed down her food with a swig of orange juice. "And what if they beat you to it?" Salib placed his elbows on the table and clasped his hands. He leaned in and his stare cut through her.

"Rest assured, good doctor. That's not going to happen." His confident aura permeated the room as he rose and pushed in his chair. He nodded. "This is why you are here. We need to beat them to it." He extended his arm. "Come with me and I'll show you your new lab. I also have an incentive I'd like to discuss with you."

She grabbed a croissant and followed him to the laboratory.

10

Prudhoe Bay, Alaska
June 20th 07:00 (15:00 UTC)

The Gulfstream 650ER touched down in Deadhorse, Alaska, also known as Prudhoe Bay. It was a dank and dreary place. White, slush-stained double-wide mobile homes dominated the landscape and comprised over half of the structures. The remainder consisted of single-wide trailers, pole barns, and buildings fashioned from colossal corrugated pipes, called Quonsets.

Nazir peered out his window. It was flat. Not a tree or mountain anywhere. Flatbed trailers, white SUVs, and pickup trucks littered the parking lots. Everything was filthy from the season's extended snow, mixed with salt and sand. Not what he was expecting, and a huge contrast to the corporate jet's luxurious leather, marble, and wood interior. He rolled his eyes and unbuckled his belt.

"This place looks like a real shit hole. Let's get this job done and get the hell out of here."

The jet was marked with the tail number of an aircraft registered to Canada Oil. Three prominent petroleum corporations controlled most of the North Shore Oil Fields, none of them affiliated with the Canadian Oil Company. However, it was not uncommon for engineers with precise knowledge, or a particular skill set to be contracted for specific projects.

It was nearing the end of a three-week shift, so air traffic coming in at this time wouldn't be seen as unusual. The co-pilot opened the cockpit door while the plane taxied to a hangar.

"Looks like we're getting a welcome."

Nazir nudged his way through his men to the front and glared out the windscreen with narrowed eyes. His co-pilot pointed out to the right. "Over there. He just pulled up."

A dark green pickup with *Prudhoe Airport Security* partially visible through the caked-on, dried slush, sat waiting with its filthy dark yellow light flashing on the roof.

"Shit. We don't need this distraction. I'll take care of him."

The aircraft entered the hangar and parked. As the drone of the engines subsided, the door swung open, and the stairs unfolded. Nazir was the first to exit. As he was descending, the man from the truck approached. He wore a navy-blue jumpsuit with a badge projecting his authority. Adorned on his right collar, just above his nametag, was a card equipped with a magnetic strip. There was no sidearm he could see. His dark-rimmed glasses hung ever so crooked on his face, giving him a disheveled charm.

He approached with a clumsy gait step, resembling that of an old oaf. "Wow, that's a beauty ya got there, eh?"

Nazir focused on the nametag pinned crooked across the man's chest. "Yeah, thanks... Colton."

Three or four other men started to deplane, and he noted the rent-a-cop shifting to get a better view of the plane.

Nazir cleared his throat. "Is there something I can help you with, buddy?"

"Ah, you can call me Colt. Uh, you folks are with Canada Oil, eh?"

"We are. Are you familiar with the company?"

"Oh, fer sure, eh? I'm from Canada too. Alberta. Panoka, it's a wee bit south of Edmonton, but nobody knows where the place is, so I say Alberta or Edmonton."

"You don't say." He raised his arm and glanced at his exposed watch.

Colton met Nazir's glance. "Hey, the supply plane came in yesterday and I've got a bunch of Timbits and Timmies back at the station, if you guys want some." He twisted and motioned with his thumb.

Nazir's eyes narrowed. "Timmies?" He saw a concerning brow rise on the little guard's face. His speech became less welcoming.

"Yeah.... Timmies. You lot aren't from Canada, are you?" He leaned to his left. "And that isn't engineering gear, is it?"

He spun around. Two of his men were carrying rifle cases.

Shit!

They placed them on the floor. He could hear the slow scuffling run as Colt rushed to his vehicle. Nazir withdrew his pistol and took careful aim. Two quick, silenced rounds exited the chamber and struck the guard in the back of the head. His corpse hit the tarmac, his right leg twitching as his life force drained. The rest of the team stopped when they heard the spent brass from Nazir's gun clinking on the ground.

Nazir snapped his fingers. "Get the body. Put it in the truck bed and cover it." He walked over to the dead man, knelt, and plucked the security card from his collar. "This might come in handy."

WITH THE HELP OF COLTON'S badge, they gained access to an exit on the opposite side of the airport, far away from any prying eyes. Several Chevy Suburban SUVs, a van, and a pickup all leaving in a line would be a memorable event. Heading south on the Dalton Highway, they soon found themselves surrounded by absolute desolation. Not a single building, tree, or bush in sight—just a lifeless canvas, painted in somber, muted hues of brown.

The unmistakable clanking of mud and gravel reverberated through the air, bouncing off the fender wells like a percussive crescendo. A voice from the rear filled Nazir's ears.

"This sucks. I can hardly hear myself think. What are the secondary roads like if they call this a highway?"

"We're almost there. Try not to hurt yourself thinking." After a few more miles, they exited the road. In less than a minute, the top of a Quonset hut came into view.

Inside, the building was raw and smelled of smoke and gun oil. Fluorescent lights hung from the metal ceiling by chains. One tube in the distance flickered in an unbalanced pattern. The oil stains on the concrete floor indicated where vehicles used to park, replaced by oversized tables crafted from two-by-fours and particle board. Upon them were maps, beer cans, a bottle of Evan Williams bourbon, and a hoard of weapons and ammunition.

Nazir greeted Marcus Stanley, who arranged for the vehicles and assembled most of this team. He and three other men were former Canadian Special Operations Regiment (CSOR) members.

From 1994 to 2010 they provided tactical or strategic effects to the Operations Forces Command (CANSOFCOM) and the Canadian Armed Forces (CAF).

After widespread public outrage, the government responded by implementing policies many saw as an attack on their freedoms and right to bear arms. This led some people to get involved with a right-wing extremist group called the Three Percenters.

While the group was officially dissolved at one point, there were still suspicions that it remained active behind the scenes.

Marcus and his other men, Jackson, Wayne, and Tim, had been doing contract mercenary work ever since. The rest of the team consisted of two soldiers for hire from South Africa, two from New Zealand, and one from Croatia. Nazir set his Heckler and Koch 9mm carbine on the table. "Okay. It's eight-thirty in the morning. You said you had an easy target. What is it?"

Marcus had his back to him. "I do." He turned, gripping a stainless Yeti tumbler full of coffee in one hand and something rolled tight in the other. His muscles bulged as if trying to escape the moss green T-shirt displaying *Infidel* across the front. A tattoo in Latin, *Molon Labe* covered most of his outer forearm. After setting his beverage on top of a tool chest, he unrolled a map and pointed to a location.

"Here. Endicott Island."

Nazir eyed where he was pointing and then back to Marcus. "And?"

"Well, hold on. I only want to say this once. Everyone, come here!" He waited until the men gathered around the home-built table. He tapped twice at the place circled.

"This is Endicott Island. It is a man-made island and sits four klicks offshore. A causeway accesses them all. It's less than thirty klicks from here."

Nazir shifted his weight. "I assume this is our target. What is it?"

He chuckled. "What is it? It's only the first continuously producing oil field in the Arctic."

"And what is your plan?"

"Boss, this is going to be easy. In and out. There is a crew who has been there for three weeks. Tomorrow afternoon, they swap crews."

Drew stood chewing on a toothpick. "How many?"

"Twenty-five. Perhaps thirty."

He leaned in. "You don't know? You don't fucking know?"

A scowl formed on Marcus' face. He straightened and shifted his eyes to the man. "No! Does it matter?"

He tossed the sliver of wood to the ground. "Hell yeah, it matters!" Both men raised their voices and began shouting over each other when a loud whistle interrupted them.

"Shut the hell up!"

Jackson stepped toward the table. "Listen to what Marcus is telling you. It doesn't matter. We have the firepower, we're trained, we have the element of surprise. And—we have a plan. Hear him out. I think you'll like what he says."

The two alpha males ended their staring competition. Marcus pointed to the beginning of the causeway. "This road delivers everything to the island. Pipes of fresh water, electricity, communications. There is no cell service, but they have sat phones and satellite Internet as a backup to the main line, but when we cut the power lines—."

The New Zealander rolled his eyes. "But they'll still have the satty" Making a phone gesture to his face with his thumb and little finger.

"Yeah, but I doubt they'll be using it."

Nazir kept studying the map. "What do you mean?"

An evil grin creased Jackson's face. "A toxin—in the water. If it doesn't kill them, it will make them very weak. It's a slow killer, but it will get most of them."

Drew shook his head. "No—no. That's not gonna work. This was supposed to be in and out, you said. Now we have to go and inject this poison and do what, wait around for a few hours and hope they get thirsty? No. What a stupid fucking idea." Jackson stepped over to him. His six-foot-five towering over the shorter Kiwi. He leaned in. "Are you through or do you want to bitch some more before I finish?" Drew backed off and Jackson turned back to face Nazir.

"We did it this morning at oh-three hundred. We tapped into the line and installed a slow-release system. So, by the time everyone was getting up, brushing their teeth, taking showers, making their coffee..." Jackson paused and let everything sink in. Out of his peripheral, he saw someone nod. He turned to see it was Drew. "No ingestion is necessary; the effectiveness is through skin contact. While it may act slower, it still gets the job done. There will be perhaps a handful of men we didn't get, but—" Jackson raised his weapon and smiled. "We'll just shoot them."

Laughter filled the air.

Nazir pointed to Marcus. "This is a good plan. Everyone, gather up the weapons, and load them in the vehicles." He glanced at his watch. "We'll leave here in twenty-five minutes." They loaded the additional gear into the vehicles and drove to Endicott Island. Nazir and Marcus took the lead in Colton's truck. A wry smile creased his face as Nazir put the vehicle in gear. "This will be one the Americans will never forget."

11

Prudhoe Bay, Alaska
June 20th 09:12 (17:12 UTC)

Colton's body splashed in the otherwise calm waters as it was dumped from the beginning of the four-kilometers-long causeway. Nazir was driving the dead man's airport security truck. Marcus was riding shotgun. The other eight men were spread among the two trailing Suburbans.

Team one was the three Canadians and Luca, the Croatian. The second team included the remaining four. Nazir separated Drew from his fellow countrymen to avoid any inside conflicts. Markers indicated the distance in tenths of a kilometer.

At the half-klick sign, Marcus pointed. "See that marker?"

Nazir nodded. "What about it?"

Marcus flashed a satellite phone. "This bridge is wired with charges, from here to the next one. A call from this will detonate it. I can wait until we're in the air and long gone before I blow it."

"What if someone gets out before?"

A wry smile creased his face as he turned towards Nazir. "They won't." He returned his attention out the side window. Peering over the bay, he watched as the never-ending horizon sped by. "Besides—does it matter?"

The bridge carried them on and over the greenish-gray expanse of Prudhoe Bay. After a few minutes, a structure appeared with a flimsy gate stretching across the road. A lone man came out of the guardhouse with his hand raised. Marcus adjusted his buttocks in his seat and reached into his jacket. "Slow down and stop. It's okay. I was expecting this." He withdrew a silenced Sig Sauer, and yanked back the slide to reassure himself there was a round chambered. "I'll do the talking."

The truck came to a gentle stop, and Nazir opened the window. The guard eyed them suspiciously and turned toward the other approaching vehicles.

"I'm not sure of your business here, but nobody can come in or out. We have a virus or something going around. You'll have to leave. You can turn around—" The metallic clank of the pistol's slide moving and ejecting the shell interchanged with the simultaneous explosion of bone and brains. The guard's body was violently thrown to the ground. Nazir's eyes widened.

"What in the hell were you using?"

Marcus chuckled. "These are my little secret. One hundred and thirty-five grain, rapidly expanding. They're called the Overwatch."

"Where did you get those?"

"Maker bullets. An old buddy of mine north of Atlanta started a projectile company as a hobby. It turned out to be pretty damn successful."

"Well, they certainly do the job."

The island's structures consisted of five buildings related to petroleum production. All the structures lined up in a row, with the living quarters at a right angle to the two farthest buildings. It connected to the second building via an enclosed, raised walkway.

Nazir activated his throat mic. "Alpha team, go."

Jackson responded. "Alpha. Acknowledged,"

"Delta Team, go."

Drew replied. "Delta. Acknowledged."

Alpha team drove north to the living quarters, while Delta went to the four production buildings and started with the furthest south. Nazir and Marcus went to the second structure connecting with the residence hall to eliminate anyone trying to escape via the raised walkway.

With caution, Jackson and the rest of the Alpha team entered the main entrance of the dormitory. Everyone wore beige military fatigues with the Canadian Special Operations Regiment patches displayed on their shoulders. They carried a combination of silenced C8A3 Carbine and H&K 9mm MP5s.

The lobby was small, but welcoming. A common area to the immediate right shared a cozy sitting space with a green couch and a few armchairs of varying shades of brown. An older plasma television stood upon a worn buffet. To the left were two vending machines and a coffee machine. Further in and to the right was a bar-height surface. To its rear was a front-desk-style manager's workstation.

Jackson peeked over the counter, waved his arm in a gesture to Tim, and then pointed to the floor. Tim nodded and proceeded through the double doors. Seconds later, he appeared behind the counter. He removed his glove, knelt, and checked for a pulse.

"He's dead. From the feel of him; body warmth, no rigor around the eyes yet—sixty minutes. Maybe less."

"Alright." Jackson pressed his throat mic. "Magneto, copy?"

"Magneto here, go ahead."

"Looks like the stuff we put in the water is working. We've got a guy, tits up, in the lobby. Tapeworm says he's been dead for about an hour."

"Okay, clear the main floor. We'll start at the top and will meet you in the middle."

"Right, Jackyl out."

———◆———

DELTA STARTED THEIR sweep in the building closest to the causeway. It was a loading and receiving bay divided into several areas: a dedicated spot for waste and recyclables, a shop for vehicle repairs and maintenance, and one for unloading supplies. One spot was occupied with a box truck, its lights on and engine running.

Raising their weapons, they approached the vehicle with caution. When they closed within twenty meters, the driver's door opened. Drew raised his hand and the team stopped.

A figure approached and they were half blinded by the headlights shining in their direction. Drew tightened the grip on his rifle.

"That's far enough."

A twenty-something kid with long unkempt hair, wearing a Green Bay Packers beanie raised both arms. "Whoa. Hey man, I mean you no harm. I'm just trying to figure out what the hell's going on around here. It's like it was a viral terrorist attack or something. Do you guys know? Is that why you're here?"

He removed a cigarette from his pocket, placed it in his mouth, and patted his pockets. "Shit, man, I left my Bic in the truck. Any you guys...?"

Drew sighed and outstretched his arm with his lighter ignited. The young man leaned in, lit his smoke, and took a draw. "Thanks, dude." He exhaled his plume of smoke. "Hey those are some wicked-looking guns you got there, eh?"

Drew rolled his eyes. "What are you doing here?"

"Oh, well, I was supposed to be making a delivery, but." His brow furrowed as he inspected Drew and the other three men. His eyes narrowed. "Hey, why are you wearing Canadian military uniforms?"

In perfect unison, Arno and Johan opened fire. Bullets tore through his body. Blood and chunks of flesh littered the concrete surface. Drew squeezed his button. "Magneto, copy?"

"This is Magneto. Go ahead."

"This is JD. One down in the first garage. He was some delivery driver and not one you had accounted for. I'm letting you know if you're keeping count."

"Copy. Out." *You prick.*

He smirked, knowing he pissed off the man on the other end of his conversation, then motioned the team to move on. As they entered the next structure, they came upon a glass-enclosed room belonging to the refined petroleum testing unit. Tables lined in rows displayed various-sized beakers containing oil in differing stages of refinement. Two men and three women, all wearing white lab coats and masks, approached the glass entrance. A middle-aged woman stepped forward and knocked on the glass. "Don't come in here. We think there's been a viral attack. We're not sure. Is that why you're here? Are you here to assist us?"

Drew shifted his attention to Anthony while he answered. A wicked smile spread across his face. "Yes. Yes, we're here to help. But first, I need you all to spread out and face us." The four chemists did as they were told. "Okay, good. Now, turn and face the other wall." As they turned around, he nodded, and all four opened fire.

Bullets ripped through the panes of glass. The noise was deafening as it collapsed like a wall of water to the floor. Black oil, petroleum, and blood splattered the white walls and ceiling, creating a scene Jackson Pollock would admire. Arno entered and tapped a corpse closest to him with his foot. A low moan came from one of the chemists. He shot him in the head, then stepped over the body. "Like fish in a barrel, guys." Back in the dorm, Alpha methodically went through all the rooms, one by one. A majority of those they found had already expired from ingestion or topical exposure to the poison.

They made their way to the mess hall. More than sixteen casualties were sprawled on the ground or hunched over a table. Jackson activated his throat mi. "Magneto, copy?"

"This is Magneto. Go ahead."

"Looks like that shit was more potent than we thought. We've counted about twenty bodies in the living quarters and there's gotta be at least fifteen more in the dining area."

"Copy, Jackyl." Marcus released the button and turned to Nazir. "I wonder if my intel was off, and the other crew is already here. If so, the numbers here will be higher."

He pressed his transmit button. "Jackyl, copy?"

"Go ahead."

"Proceed with caution. There may be as many as sixty or seventy here."

"Roger. Magneto out."

The team dispersed throughout the dining room, checking the bodies for survivors. Luca found one still breathing and slit his throat. A rattling came from behind a swing door. Jackson snapped his fingers twice and motioned for Wayne and Tim, closest to the door, to investigate.

When the pair approached, someone barreled out. The door knocked both men to the ground. The worker ran at full speed to the exit of the hall. Luca was too far away and risked shooting his partner if he opened fire.

"Shit!" Jackson raised his weapon and fired. As the bullets whizzed by, it seemed as if they were relentlessly chasing the running man, showering the wall with a hail of gunfire, narrowly evading their mark by a mere breath. With adrenaline pumping, the sprinting man burst out into the passage.

"Fuck!" Jackson took off after him. He exited the room and went down the corridor. It was empty. A door at the end clicked close. He activated his mic. "We've got a runner! Magneto, he's headed your way."

Marcus and Nazir were outside the entrance to the walkway in the adjacent building.

Marcus re-checked his weapon to ensure it was loaded, a habit he found hard to break. "He'll be on here in a few seconds. We'll let him get halfway across."

The opposite door flew open, followed by the sound of pounding feet.

The two mercenaries grasped the handles of the double doors. As the footsteps grew closer, Nazir nodded. They both pulled and stepped into the passageway. The man running stopped. His sneakers squeaked as they screamed for a grip on the vinyl tile. His eyes were wide in fear, and the glistening beads of sweat on his brow shimmered, reflecting the radiant glow of the overhead lights. He stumbled as he changed direction to run back.

"Oh, God. No!"

Bullets ripped through his flesh, exiting out of his chest. One demolished his kneecap. Another shattered his femur, while a third took out half of his jaw and nose. His body hit the floor with a thump. Smoke wafted from the barrels of their rifles. Marcus pressed his mic. "Target eliminated."

The teams continued their sweep and discovered only three more bodies, all deceased. He called out to the team, "Everyone convene back at the vehicles. Be certain you are seen on the cameras."

THE SOUND OF AN ENGINE starting resonated off the aluminum structures in the parking lot as the men stowed their weapons.

Johan was a few feet away smoking and cocked his head. "Do you all hear—?"

Marcus raised his hand. "Shhh!"

Silence filled the air.

"Goddammit!" He ran toward the water. "That's a boat! Luca. Take the truck, kill him."

"You got it."

Luca was the bunch's resident sniper. Hired by a private company, he had honed his skills helping to protect container ships as they sailed off the East African coast.

On multiple occasions, he had to fire on Somali pirates to deter them before they got in range to use their AK-47s.

As he drove to the other side of the island, the wake of the patrol boat pointed to the target as it motored toward the mainland. At this point, it was about 350 meters out but getting further as each second ticked. He hurried out of the truck, reached in back for his Barrett 50 caliber sniper rifle, and rested it on the truck's hood.

The wind meter he pulled from his vest gave him a reading on its speed, air temperature, humidity, barometric pressure, and density. They were all the things to be considered when making a long-distance shot.

He raised his weapon and brought the scope to his eye, finding his target. Now at close to 1000 meters away, he lowered it, raced to make quick adjustments and once again sighted his quarry. It was traveling at about thirty knots. Thankfully, it was moving away in a straight line. He observed the boat rising and falling with the rhythm of the waves, patiently waiting for the perfect moment when his aim aligned with the crest of each wave. He held his breath and thought to himself; bob—bob—bob—on the fourth one, he squeezed the trigger. Less than two seconds later, he witnessed the inside of the boat's windshield painted with blood.

AIRPORT SECURITY SUPERVISOR Brian Paulding entered the office and approached one of the women near the radio. "Have you seen Colton anywhere? His shift ended hours ago. He didn't bring the vehicle back and nobody's set eyes on him."

"I dunno. Did you try the radio?"

He rolled his eyes. "For Christ's sake. Yes. Check his truck's GPS."

"Well, I had to ask, eh." She spun around in her chair and her fingers danced on her keyboard for a few seconds. Her brow furrowed. "That's odd."

"What?"

She turned the monitor toward him. "GPS shows he—well, at least his truck—is on Endicott Island."

"Why the hell is he out there? I'm calling Rob. He's working the gate out there this week."

After several rings and no answer, he pressed the end button and tried another number. As he placed the phone to his ear, he nodded to Carol. "Can you have them call the main switchboard out there?"

"I'll get the number."

There were no responses after multiple attempts to contact various people, so he went to the coffee station and poured himself a cup. "Something is wrong. Together, we should have reached at least one of these people. I'm going out there. Let me know if he comes back. And keep trying to reach them."

Upon exiting the airport, two black Suburbans shot past him.

"Holy Shit!" He swerved out of their way, the back end of his truck fishtailing across the gravel road. He glanced in his rearview mirror. *Goddamn oil executives!*

Twenty-five minutes later, he started on the causeway to the refinery when the bridge in front of him exploded into a mushroom cloud of fire, flying concrete and dust.

12

Somewhere in the Venezuelan jungle SE of Caracas.
June 20th 15:30 (19:30 UTC)

Agony shot through his hand as the sting pierced between his knuckles. Blake lifted his hand to examine the damage, finding blood and a dislodged tooth. He was grateful it hadn't been embedded in his skin, which could have led to infection.

He stood in front of his prisoner, glaring and shaking his fist. "Shit! Look what you did."

The man, still zip-tied to a chair, spat blood on the floor and groaned with pleasure from the pain he caused his captor.

He pointed to the defiant captive and spoke to his colleague.

"Hey, Marty. He thinks this is funny. I bet he'd like a closer peek to see what he did to my hand."

The guy mumbled past the cigar hanging from between his teeth. "Probably so." He struck a match and lit the tobacco. The smoke wafted around his dark crewcut. He puffed a few times, ignited it, and drew it away from his mouth. "You should show him."

Blake nodded, reared back, and slammed his fist into the captive's eye. The force of the impact sent the chair flying to the ground. The man's head took a healthy bounce as it hit the dank concrete floor.

"Oops! Sorry 'bout that."

He motioned to Marty. "Get him up." The metal door to the room groaned open, flaking beige paint as ragged as the prisoner. Its once proud surface was now a mosaic of rust and decay. Trevor Tyson stepped in. Sweat glistened off his forehead and a circle of moisture stained through the light blue dress shirt under his armpits.

Blake chucked his chin at his associate. "Still hot outside?"

"What gave it away?" His jaw was clenched as he held back his frustration with his boss. He had the stressful task of reporting to Emilio

Briggs, the Chief of Station in Venezuela, and after a conversation with him, his mood was rarely happy. After a moment, Trevor motioned for the door. MacKay grabbed his backpack as they exited the windowless room into the hallway. The door slammed shut and echoed throughout the old concrete bunker. Trevor grasped the back of his neck and rubbed it as if massaging away stress. "Anything?"

"No! Not a damn thing. I don't understand it. Two days of bright flashing light and blaring death metal. I've never seen anything like it. This piece of shit is locked up tight. He could be a loyal asshole or completely terrified. Either way, we still have no idea if, when, or who plans to attack Montero."

"But you think he knows something?"

Blake nodded. "I do."

Trevor wiped his forehead with his sleeve. "Montero was just recognized at the UN as the true president. He's supposed to be flying back here three days from now. He's giving a public speech in Caracas two days later. It could be our window."

"Yeah, I know." His eyebrows rose in thought while Trevor rubbed his chin.

"Oh, by the way, Briggs asked me to say your boss is looking for you. She said to, quote, answer your goddamn cell phone. It's what you have it for. End quote."

Blake exhaled forcefully and rolled his eyes.

Trevor cocked his head. "Are the stories about her being a bitch and difficult to work with true?"

He chuckled as he removed the cap from his water bottle. "I'm going to go ahead and plead the fifth."

"Well, she wants you to call her ASAP. She said something about pulling you out for something else. She said to tell you there is a—" He made air quotes. "'situation developing' and you need to know about it."

He and his relatively new boss, Veronica Slocum, had never gotten along. They didn't think along the same lines. However, since he saved her life before taking over the position, she tended to look the other way and let Blake be himself. Not to say they didn't have terse conversations from time to time, but for the most part, they were cordial towards each other.

"Yeah, ok." His eyes shifted down toward his backpack. "You said it would be three days before he flies back here, right?"

"Yep. Why?"

Raising a finger, he cogitated. "It might be enough time." He dug through his gear. "Found it." Pinching a bag with the tips of his fingers, he smirked.

Trevor shrugged. "I give up. What is it?"

"I only use this for extreme situations when I can't get someone to crack. And—I think it's time. It's a unique soap. They have to package it in this rubber lined bag to ensure it doesn't get wet and leak through the packaging." He opened the bag and retrieved a wrapped bar.

His colleague shook his head. "I still don't get it. Looks like regular soap."

"This shit has been infused with concentrated oil from poison ivy. It's about two hundred times more potent. Let our friend in there take a shower. By tomorrow, he'll be tearing his skin off and begging to tell us anything we want to know for a cortisone shot."

Trevor roared with laughter while Blake handed him the bar. "Clever."

"Okay, you attend to it, and I'll go make the call."

MACKAY, NOW A SEASONED field agent, strode the short distance from the interrogation room back to the central office, an old weighing station and prep area used before to smuggle cocaine out of Venezuela. The mass corruption in the country over the past eighteen years created a drug superhighway. A promise to combat this was one large part of what got the new president, Valencia Montero elected. The former cartel airstrip made it a perfect location for the CIA to conduct their in-country business.

The building appeared old and derelict from the outside. The inside had been retrofitted with the most modern comforts and best technology the CIA had garnered from DARPA, the Defense Advanced Research Projects Agency. Having assumed the identity of Blakes 'Q,' also known as Alice, Kyle Moran established an Area Security Operations Command Center.

It was a combination of secure channels used by the Navy's Multiple Threat Alert Center referred to as MTAC and satellites deployed by the National Reconnaissance Office, or the NRO. It was a hidden channel within a protected network. Blake placed the call and the seventy-two-inch monitor in front of him awakened.

Veronica's image filled the screen, her red hair contrasting with the dark blue blouse, her skin blended in with the boring beige walls in the background.

"I understand you needed to talk to me?"

The scowl on her face prepared him for the onslaught he was about to receive. "Perhaps if you'd answer your fucking phone, you'd know what I'm calling about. Why didn't you answer?" He took a deep breath to slow his rising heart rate and reminded himself to respond calmly. "I don't have my mobile with me when interrogating. It's standard opera—"

"Correct! I know. How's it progressing? Please tell me you're not torturing him. Wait, I don't want to know."

His lips parted, unveiling a dazzling, pearly white smile, lighting his entire face. "Boss, you'd be pleased to know he's enjoying a hot shower right now."

"Shower? You don't mean at a forty-five-degree angle with a towel over his face?"

His laugh helped him lower his anger and her temperament. "I can if you prefer."

She was quick to interject. "No, no. It doesn't sound like you. Being... pleasant."

"Do you want me to send you a pic?"

"Save it for Christmas. Please advise me if you've gotten any answers."

"I suspect he'll be telling us everything we need to know by tomorrow afternoon, if not sooner."

She cleared her throat. "Well, let me know ASAP. I've got the DCI breathing down my neck and President Pennington is demanding a report from him, and you know how she can be when she gets commanding."

"Yes, Ma'am, I do."

Another high-definition screen adjacent to the one displaying Veronica came to life and showed a "Google Earth" like world map, but much more detailed. The globe tilted down and zoomed in to the northern pole.

"I don't want to tell you *I told you so* when extracting information from people. You don't have to mistreat them physically."

Those final few words reminded him of just one of the reasons why they didn't get along. Veronica's anti-torture stance could have cost millions of lives in the past. One particular mission came to mind.

After blasting death metal for thirty-six hours at 130 decibels, with no sleep or food, an Al Qaeda militant having pertinent information kept his silence. At last, when the strike was imminent, Blake got the nod from his old boss. He shut off the cameras, forced everyone to leave, and entered the room with a knife. Ten minutes later, he exited the room. With the intelligence he obtained, they stopped a dirty bomb attack in three U.S. cities. It saved over nine million lives. Torture worked and he would only use it when there was no alternative. Veronica had no former military experience. She'd never been in the field and didn't get it.

He turned around out of her sight to retrieve a remote for the other screen and worded *Bullshit* to himself.

He refocused and diverted the conversation. "What am I looking for? There's a lot of ice and barren sea in this image."

"Blake, over the past seventy-two hours, multiple parties have attacked a couple of different oil exploration outfits." The globe rotated east and focused on Kotelney Island.

She continued. "Sometime after four a.m. local time on June sixteenth, a group of men attacked an oil camp run by the Russian gas and exploration company, Roseneft. It's state-owned. Everyone was killed but not before a mayday was sent out about the attack."

The globe zoomed in and focused on the old Soviet Naval base, now a camp. Wisps of smoke wafted up from the buildings. Blood-stained snow and crumpled bodies dotted the outside of several barracks. A trail of bloodstains led away from the building and ended in a mangled pile of flesh. Three bear cubs appeared to be feeding while their mother kept a watchful eye on the surrounding terrain.

"When were these taken?"

"About thirty-two hours ago."

"And the mayday? Did it give us any clues? Do we know who did this?"

Veronica cleared her throat and took a deep breath. "It's the reason I'm calling. The message said they wore military uniforms and were all identified as American soldiers."

"You're a higher pay grade than me. Unless there's something you're not telling me, I call bullshit."

"Same here. I've checked and there were no U.S. operations, including off-the-book ones in the area. Period. Not even close."

The globe on the screen moved westward, capturing his attention as she continued her briefing. "The second attack happened about two hours later on an oil platform in the Norwegian Sea. One hundred and eighty-eight people perished."

"Let me guess. They sent out a mayday."

"Yes. But they left a witness—it appears to be on purpose."

His eyes widened. "I knew it. There may be a pattern here."

His boss nodded as her eyes shifted to read from her notes. "The survivor is an engineer, in his late twenties, single. He lives in Ladegarden, Norway. He claims they were Russian."

"How does he know?"

"He only spotted two other people, and only one guy spoke. He communicated over the radio. The man said it sounded Russian, but he wasn't sure. Security footage showed men clad in Russian gear carrying Soviet weapons."

"So, where am I going?"

"Norwegian Intelligence is working with Kripos, their National Criminal Investigation Service. Review the video of the assault and inspect the forensic evidence. Go talk to the witness." She took a quick peek at her notes. "Anders Siversten. Check out what he knows. Hell, go to the damn platform if you have to. Just do what you do, Blake. You'll have to rely on your colleagues to finish with your prisoner there."

"Have they picked up any chatter on this yet?"

"Quiet so far, however, there is one more thing I need to mention. We believe it's related."

The screen switched to an image of the DavCo Arctic Drill.

"This ship was on a lease to Canada Oil and was on a standard exploration mission. About a month ago, they lost all contact with it. Someone turned off its transponder, and they have no idea where it is." The monitor returned to the globe. "Its last known coordinates were almost six hundred miles due north of Greenland, which puts them right on top of the world. But with almost five and a half million square miles, there's no way to search for it."

His eyes shifted from screen to screen. Taking a deep breath, he drummed his fingers on his chin. "Yeah, too coincidental. It's related."

He heard Veronica's phone rang. "Do you need to take the call?"

"Yes. Hold on."

She muted her microphone, but her eyes grew large and darted back and forth between him and the surrounding equipment. She disappeared off the screen and reappeared. This time in the background at her laptop; her focus intent. She placed the phone face down on the table and approached the camera on the wall. Her lacquered crimson nails glinted in the light as she rubbed her chin.

She unmuted the microphone and took a deep breath. "There's been another attack."

13

The White House
June 20th 16:00 (21:00 UTC)

Veronica thumbed through her notes while she sat in the war room with the Joint Chiefs and other high-ranking staff members. POTUS called the briefing to discuss the series of recent attacks, which had left the world on edge and several nations on the brink of conflict.

Ceiling spotlights lit the oval table in the contrarily darkened space. High-definition televisions filled the wall behind her. Each one displayed a satellite image of where the incidents occurred. The most concerning was Russia and how they would respond to a supposed attack by a U.S. special operations group.

The door opened and President Pennington walked in. She was a no-nonsense woman who got things done.

She chose her team with care and, with that, complete autonomy to do what they needed to accomplish their tasks, but if they made mistakes, she had no compunction about removing them and replacing them with someone more competent.

Veronica recalled how she acquired her position and shook away negative thoughts.

The president slapped a manila folder onto the table but remained on her feet. The overhead lights highlighted her graying brown hair, usually cascading down her shoulders, which she had swept up into a bun.

"Gentleman!" She glanced toward Veronica and the Secretary of Defense, Sonja Southwell, and gave them a nod. "Ladies. Can somebody please tell me what in the holy hell happened? Why do I have the Russian ambassador, the Prime Minister of Denmark, and the PM of Canada all ringing my hotline, talking about attacks on each other?" She scanned those present around the conference table. "Anyone? General?"

Like a wolf circling its prey before an attack, each step reminded them of who was in charge. Her hands caressed the back of every chair as she passed. She stopped across from the gentleman responsible for the Coast Guard.

"Commandant Halsey. What in the hell is going on? Somebody attacked us off the coast—of Alaska! You know—the coast. Isn't that your department?" She slammed her palm on the shellacked wood surface. "And by the fucking Canadian's no less. Canada! Seriously?"

The recipient of her ass chewing, swallowed hard. "With all due respect, Madam President, the attack was initiated on land, not by sea. We patrol the area, but mainly stick to the western side, towards Russia. We've never considered our northern neighbor a threat."

The president responded to his reply with an icy gaze, leaving no doubt about her disapproval.

Veronica cleared her throat to break the awkward silence. "Madam President. We don't believe these were the operations of individual countries." Pennington shifted her focus to her.

"Well, no shit! I know, for Christ's sake. Do you know how I know, Ms. Slocum?" She raised her arm and faced her palm toward Veronica. "Don't answer. I'll tell you. No one had informed me of any activities involving U.S. military personnel in Russia. And another way. Do you want to know another way?"

She strode to the wall of screens and pointed to a smoldering refinery in Alaska. "Because Canada isn't that fucking stupid!"

She turned and marched back to her seat. Before sitting, she removed her blue blazer and put it on the back of her chair.

"And we're not dumb enough to think they would attack us. That's how!"

She pulled her chair back, sat, and rolled the sleeves of her white blouse to her elbows. "But someone does. Somebody thinks we're all damn idiots."

She took a sip of water and placed the glass gently on the surface, rotating it as she collected her thoughts.

The light reflected off her bright red nails as she focused on the condensation trails.

"Now, Ms. Slocum, it appears you have some information, so please enlighten me with something I don't know."

Veronica stood and grabbed a stack of classified folders with red and white markings decorating the edges. She distributed them to all the Joint Chiefs, beginning with the Commander-in-chief.

As she started speaking, POTUS opened her folder.

"This is what we've confirmed so far. There have been three verified attacks, on locations revolving around oil pumping, exploration, or refining. And each attack has been between differing nations. The U.S. and Russia, Russia hitting Denmark, and today, what appears to be Canada, striking us. If we look, there are four countries—"

Chief of Naval Operations, Admiral Geoffrey Cutforth, blurted out, "There is going to be more."

Her hazel eyes narrowed, and she crossed her arms as she responded to his interruption. "And what makes you so confident?"

"To close the loop. To pit them all against one another."

She pointed at him with the folder. "Right! And who will it be between?" He placed his thumb and forefinger on his chin and rubbed it. "The Danes didn't respond, and the Canadians haven't been struck."

The President leaned in. "So, you're saying there will be another one?" She then turned to Veronica. "Director, is the intelligence you've gathered leading you to believe this?"

"No."

The president's eyes widened. "No? Why not?"

Veronica unfolded her arms. "Because we think it's already happened." She opened her folder. "Everyone, please flip to the last page in your packet." Various papers rustled. "This vessel is the DavCo Arctic Drill. It is an exploration vessel owned by Canada Oil. It's gone missing somewhere in the Arctic."

Pennington kept focus on the image of the ship. "How long ago did it disappear?"

"About a month, Madam President."

"Do you have any intel indicating an attack took place? If so, what is the nature of it? And by the Dane's, no less?"

"I'm afraid none. It's only a hunch, but it fits the narrative of everything else that's occurred." POTUS turned to Cutforth. "James, do we have any ships in or near the Arctic right now?"

He shook his head. "No. Well—we may have some near the south coast of Greenland, but nothing so far north."

"And submarines?"

He frowned and stroked his chin. "There's a definite possibility."

Pennington let out a sigh, clearly conveying her displeasure with his response. "I'm not looking for oxymorons. I demand either a yes or no. Now, which is it?"

He shifted in his seat and cleared his throat. "You need to understand, the fleet is fluid. Ships and subs are always on the move. The last time I knew for sure, it was yes, but that was twelve hours ago. I'll make a call, and you will know as soon as I do."

"Fine." She redirected her attention to her Director of Intelligence. "What else do we know?"

Taking her cue, Veronica walked over to the monitors on the wall and pointed to the naval base on Kotelney Island.

"In the instance of the ambush on the Russian substation, someone got a message out they were being attacked by soldiers decked out in BDUs with U.S. markings." She took a few steps back to reveal the Norwegian oil platform.

"In the case of the rig at sea, they left a survivor and there is camera footage of men wearing Russian military fatigues." Veronica shifted to face the other monitor.

"As far as Endicott Island, it has been too recent and we still have intel coming in, but from what we know, there are also recordings and one possible witness. We presume once we review those tapes, it will show the assailants clothed in Canadian combat uniforms."

Sonja, the Secretary of Defense, tapped her pen on the table. "I think it's clear to everyone that a solitary faction is orchestrating all of this. There has to be a reason for these attacks. Why are they doing it? And if we can figure out why, we can discover who."

"The opposite also holds, as well." General Richard D. Thayer, Chief of Staff of the Army added, "If we find out who, we'll reveal why."

Pennington glanced at all those in the room. "I think we can all agree the United States isn't involved, and it falls upon me to persuade the other nations of this fact too. Some group is attempting to pit us all against each other."

She continued jotting a note. "Cutforth. Get with your counterpart at Canadian Intelligence." She stared toward the ceiling and searched the back of her mind. "Remind me, what's his name again?"

"Admiral Juneau, Madam President."

She wrote it on her pad. "Right! Find out the last known location of this vessel. Offer our assistance in finding it. Employ the sub already deployed and get a ship or two to the last known coordinates. Screw it. Get whatever you or they need."

"Yes, Madam President!"

"I'm off to Geneva in a couple of days to strive to un-fuck this mess. If there are any updates I can use to try and calm everyone's nerves, I must have them ASAP. Understood?"

There was a collective confirmation from around the table.

She pointed her pen at Admiral Cutforth. "Oh, and make it abundantly clear to the public and press we're helping Canada to find this ship. This will reinforce our stance that we were not the victims of their aggression, thereby enhancing our image on the international stage."

"All right. Everyone get to work." She stood and turned to Veronica. "Director, I trust we have an asset going to interrogate this lone survivor?"

"Yes, Madam President. He is en route as we speak."

The president spun and handed the classified file to the handler. "Someone good, I hope."

Veronica grasped her folder with both hands across her chest and rolled back on her heels. She grinned. "It's uh—MacKay."

The president nodded and smiled. "Good. He'll get us some answers. You have my direct line. Use it."

As she started heading to the door, she paused and turned to face Veronica.

"Director Slocum, I'd like you by my side when we speak to these people in Switzerland. I know they'll be asking for any updates on who may be behind this, and I'd like to give them the latest instant updates. Do you think you're up for it?"

The tingle of anxiety up the back of her neck gave her pause.

"Director?"

The president's voice snapped her back to the moment.

"Oh, sorry Madam President. Yes. Absolutely. If needed, I'm more than willing to share our most recent information and updates."

POTUS chuckled. "Well, you'll be called on for just that. Have your ducks in a row, Ms. Slocum."

14

Awadi Salib Property
   North of Trongisvágur

June 21st 18:00 (17:00 UTC)

The Prince and Nazir, followed by two of the Royal Guard, sauntered into His Majesty's grand office. They had finished a meal of roast lamb with vegetables and rice. The scent of spices lingered in the air but faded as they strolled across the room.

Salib walked over to pour a drink. His extensive collection of potent potables was next to his Norse-themed wooden desk, and he motioned for his guest to sit in one of the facing chairs as he made his selection.

The bar exuded exquisite elegance, mirroring the charm of his desk. Both spaces captivated onlookers with a Nordic ambiance. Crafted predominantly from a lustrous, dark, opulent wood, Viking-inspired designs carved into the ancient timber unfolded gracefully. Round wooden shields adorned the front, displaying intricate Scandinavian symbols in remarkably crafted detail.

"What you executed in Alaska on such short notice was impressive. I have to admit, moving the timeline distressed me. You did well."

Nazir sunk into the oversized brown leather chair and crossed his legs. "Thank you, Your Royal Highness."

With a mischievous grin, his Majesty shifted his gaze towards the stone wall, which showcased an enchanting display of shelves adorned with a striking assortment of bottles. Each shelf showcased a precise arrangement housing an impressive collection of the world's most exceptional spirits.

With a firm grip, he reached for a decanter brimming with amber-hued liquor, its depths shimmering enticingly. Submerged within the vessel's base, an exquisite crystal eagle stood proudly, as if frozen in time, evoking the grace of a majestic statue. He removed the matching eagle stopper and chuckled before speaking.

"Please—Prince, or, to be honest—when we are in seclusion from others, call me Salib." He raised his glass.

"But *only* in private."

The drink's aroma filled his nostrils, and he took a slow, deliberate sip, closing his eyes as he savored the taste.

"Remarkable!"

Reaching for another glass, he poured an equal share, walked over, and handed it to his guest. The prince's grip remained as his guest's fingers grasped it. His eyes met Nazir's.

"Double Eagle Very Rare, twenty-year-old American bourbon. I think you will enjoy it."

Nazir accepted the drink. "Thank you. I appreciate it."

The prince remained on his feet but leaned his buttocks on the edge of his desk. "Now, tell me about Alaska. Did you leave behind any survivors?"

Before answering, he sipped his bourbon and waited for the heat of the 101-proof spirit to escape his throat.

"No. Most of the crew were dead before we got there. The advance squad had contaminated the water source with a substance effective on contact and when consumed."

"Hmmm, interesting—and quite ingenious. Your idea?"

"Yes." He enjoyed another taste.

One eyebrow arched, demanding a more satisfactory response. Salib folded his arms across his chest as his trust started to waver.

He straightened and moved away from the desk and walked beside his man. "But, tell me. You managed to get on camera, correct? You made sure to display the Canadian markings on your uniforms?"

He nodded. "Of course, Your Majesty. I mean—Salib. Multiple times. We were certain to be seen. Those were your orders."

He continued to circle to the rear of the chair. Nazir uncrossed his legs and took another sip of his drink. The prince sensed his tension. "Did the cameras capture your ear?"

The mercenary started to turn. His brows pinched together as he raised his hand to his chin. "What?"

One guard raced to his side and grabbed his right arm. Another pinned his left onto the chair.

"Your ear!" Salib plucked a pair of pliers from his pocket and clamped them on Nazir's right ear. "Did they *see* your fucking ear?"

In a cacophony of pain, the mercenary's anguished screams pierced the air. The cocktail glass shattered when it impacted with the ground. Reacting with swift precision, another sentry rushed into the front of the seat and grasped the screaming man's thrashing legs, immobilizing him.

"Ahhhhh! What are you talking about? Please! Stop!"

Salib yanked hard while squeezing on the plier's grip. Blood oozed out and spattered at each thrash. "You—need—to, be... Stop fighting!"

The former soldier screamed. Salib whipped out a knife with his left hand. With a quick flick of his wrist, the saw-like blade flipped into its locked position. He sliced the back of his prisoner's ear.

"Oh, God! Stop! What are you doing? Stop!" Nazir fought and wiggled in his seat. The three sentinels gripped tighter. Escape was impossible.

"Hold him, dammit!" The prince sawed back and forth on the last part of the dangling ear. The serrated edge chewed through mangled cartilage. Blood poured out. Satisfied with his handiwork, he threw the ear into the screaming man's lap. The guards released him. Panting from the adrenaline rush, he stepped to face the punished man. He wiped his bloodied hands over Nazir's pants. "I said you need to be more careful!"

He frowned as he surveyed the blood-ravaged chair and floor. "You've made an awful fucking mess!"

Bent over and rocking back and forth in a feeble attempt not to go into shock, Nazir pressed his hand to his head and wrenched. "God! Why in the hell did you do that?"

The prince glanced at one of his guards. "Get him a towel. He's ruining my chair." He meandered over to the wet bar to wash and dry his bloodied hands. After straightening his hair in a mirror on the wall, he turned and grabbed a newspaper off his desk. On the front page was an article in the London Times. He held it out to the still whimpering man.

"Look at this!"

Nazir remained bent over and rocking. Salib slapped him across the side of the head. "Look at it, goddamn it!"

He straightened himself and leaned in to read.

Interpol Investigates Lead in Deadly Attack on Norwegian Oil Platform

Interpol is speaking to the lone survivor of the violent invasion, which occurred one week ago at the Thistle Oil Platform in the North Atlantic. Anders Siversten of Ladegarden, Norway, was the only person lucky to be alive. Siversten said only one man spoke and despite it being Russian, the underlying accent and his physical description, lead Interpol to believe this to be the work of either a terrorist group or independent contractors and not the Russian army.

"After he left the control room, he went out and removed his hood to smoke a cigarette. I'll never forget him." – Anders Siversten

On the 23rd, Interpol is bringing in a world-renowned crime sketch artist, Dr. Risa Lindman, to speak to Siversten and sketch a likeness of this mystery man. Detective Agent Jack Kingman says, "Once we get a decent sketch, we can run it through our extensive facial recognition database. I feel confident we'll know who he is within a week."

Nazir leaned back and lowered his chin. A guard threw him a towel. He folded it and pressed it to the side of his head.

Salib slapped the newspaper back on his desk.

"You fucking idiot! I should kill you now!"

He walked back and poured another drink. After chugging the whiskey, he helped himself to another and gestured with the hand holding the glass toward the bleeding man. "But you know what? I'm not going to do that. Lucky for you, you're still useful to me." Swigging his bourbon, he poured another before walking back toward his one-eared mercenary.

Still pressing the cloth to his head, he raised his chin as his employer approached. He removed the makeshift bandage, found a dry spot, and reapplied it. "What do you want me to do?"

"Smart question." He leaned forward, pulled back the towel, and inspected the wound he'd caused. "Hmm, nasty. But you'll be ok, I believe. Once we complete our task here, I will send you to medical."

Resting once more against his desk, he folded his arms. "Here are the orders I expect you to fulfill. You will go to Ladegarden, find this man, and kill him before he talks to the sketch artist. I have also received credible intel; the Americans will be watching him. They may want to speak to him. Keep an eye out for them and, if necessary, eliminate any threat they pose." He continued to grin.

Wanting to stay compliant, Nazir nodded and glanced back at Salib. His superior's smile faded and his eyes narrowed. "And if you fail me this time, I will pull out your eyeballs and feed them to you. Do you understand?"

He stood; his eyes met those of Salib.

"Yes, Your Majesty."

"Okay, now go. I have things to do." The prince dug his phone out of his pocket. Dr. Wyrick answered at the other end. "I hope you are well and adjusting to your new lab. I am coming to visit you. There is something we need to discuss."

TWENTY MINUTES LATER, Salib entered the lab with a high level of expectation. To make his claim on the most expansive oil reserve in the world, he gave them the impossible task of making the submersible operational with a shortened deadline of twelve weeks.

Spotting Madison near the submersible, he made his way across the expanse of the high-tech lab. Eyeing the sub as he walked, it hung from chains made of thick steel, exposing its underbelly where the drilling apparatus would attach. Four other technicians ran around, doing various tasks. She was holding a tablet and directing someone toward the front of the submarine, where another technician was working on the drill attachment.

He paused to appreciate what she had done for him so far with his quest for world oil domination. Her signature Tennessee-Orange scrunchie held her blond ponytail. She placed the iPad on the table, with her dark-rimmed glasses, when she glanced toward him.

Stepping over to her, he cleared his throat. "I understand you're making good progress, doctor. Is this the laser you spoke of the last time we met?"

After wiping her brow with her wrist, she let out a sigh. "It is."

He gave her a brief nod while gesturing a smile. "Good. So, it would seem you are ahead of schedule. I am overjoyed."

Her brow furrowed. "Well, I wouldn't exactly say that."

He stood tall, arms crossed, and chest puffed out. "What else needs to be done? You've attached the drill, and the sub is operational, so you should be close to being finished."

"Your Highness. We've still not tested it. We have several tests we must complete. After each test, adjustments need to be made, and errors corrected. This will take several weeks. Then, we still have to work out the blowout preventer."

Salib frowned, raised his hands, and voiced his displeasure. "No! Too long. You can finish this before the deadline."

She stood her ground and shook her head. "I'm sorry, You're Highness. This isn't some elementary thing. We're talking about operating at twelve thousand feet or more. At that depth, the force will be more than two tons of pressure, per square inch. This is a delicate operation. Do you want this to reach the bottom and implode? We'd have to start all over, delaying us months, if not a year. Not to mention killing everyone on board."

She reached for her tablet while the information sank in.

"We're on track to finish at the—near impossible deadline you set. Let us do our job."

The prince paused, then strode to a steel countertop, strewn with assorted parts and wires. He picked up a coupling and examined it closely. Returning to where it originally sat, he took a deep breath and exhaled.

"Dr. Wyrick. You have a brother. Do you not?"

She massaged the back of her neck and took a deep breath. "Yes, but—."

Salib raised his index finger. "My understanding is he has—" Rubbing his beard, his eyes, trained on the chains affixed to the industrial-sized crane overhead. "How do I put this?" He turned his attention to her. "Medical issues?"

Her arms dropped to her side, and she frowned. "What does any of this have to do with my brother?"

"I understand life is—difficult for him at the moment and will only get harder." Salib strolled toward her from behind the table. "But I have also confirmed there are new procedures available to be performed; followed by a year's long rehabilitation and therapy, but in the end, he would recover and go on to live a normal life, free from pain and his current—handicap."

He searched her expressionless face for an answer to what or how she was feeling.

She glanced away, then back. "How do you know this?"

He grinned. "Do not worry about how I came about this information. I have many sources. Also, I know this would be an unbearable expense—one his insurance company refuses to pay, and unsurmountable for you and your family."

Stepping closer to her, he leaned in and whispered in her ear. "I can help."

He sauntered over to the table and turned back toward her. Her eyes narrowed, and she cocked her head.

"How?"

Shifting his focus to the team scrambling around the sub, then back to her. He motioned with his head. She nodded her understanding and approached her co-workers. "Hey, guys. Take a ten-minute break."

After everyone had disappeared from view, Salib, again, invaded her personal space. "I'll move straight to the point. I have access to some of the best doctors in the world. Get this sub operational, and the moment we cap the well, I will deposit twenty-five million dollars into a Swiss bank account for you."

He studied her reaction. She stood agape. Her green eyes were wide. "I—I."

Once again, he rubbed at his beard as he grinned. "You do not need to say anything. Get it done, doctor."

Madison's gaze focused on the floor. Her body remained still as her eyes moved back and forth in deep thought. Raising her head, she outstretched her arm for her tablet and remained hyper-focused as her fingers danced across the screen. Replacing the tablet to its resting place, she kicked a step ladder, forcing it to slide across the floor to the subs entrance.

Salib's eyes narrowed and his head tilted from side to side as he let her complete whatever calculations she had running through her head. Climbing up the ladder, her slim body disappeared into the steel orange tomb.

A few moments later, she reemerged. "Your Highness, do we have a ship that can transport this sub out to sea so we can test its capabilities?"

"What are you thinking, doctor?"

She gracefully climbed out and descended from the ladder, her excitement evident as she rubbed her palms together. "If you can get a ship here in the next few days, with some extra hours and a sprinkle of luck, I am confident I can have this project ready for testing in approximately four days. However..." She paused, momentarily diverting her attention back to the table, where she swiftly retrieved her tablet and skimmed through her meticulously organized notes. "If all the tests go smoothly, without any hiccups, we will be ahead of schedule and poised to commence drilling by the deadline. But that's *if*, Your Highness. I can't make any promises."

The corner of his mouth curled into a half smile. "I will have the vessel here in four days. I suggest you get busy."

As he turned to leave, she shouted over his shoulder. "I'll need more help."

"You're in charge, doctor. Double your team. Whatever it takes."

15

CIA Gulfstream Jet
      Somewhere above France 42,000 feet
June 22nd 07:30 (06:30 UTC)

Blake leaned against the bulkhead with his eyes closed, enjoying some music. The jet engines offered a subtle vibration, lulling him into a doze. Alice slid into the seat across from him and placed a container on the table. The light thump piqued his curiosity, and he opened his eyes.

"Oh, hi. Sorry, I didn't wake you, did I?"

Blake rubbed his eyes and removed one of his earbuds. "What?"

Alice smiled. "Never mind. Whatcha listening to?"

"Music."

His co-worker pursed his lips and frowned. "Well, I figured as much. Don't you listen to—kind of unusual or alternative stuff?"

He grinned while he pulled out the case for his earbuds, placing each one in its charging slot and closing the lid. "I suppose you could say so. It depends on where you are when you ask the question. *Lord of the Lost* is popular in northern, central and western Europe. They are less known in the U.S., but their music is spot on."

Shrugging off the information, Alice kept his attention on the muted silver box. "Meh. perhaps I'll give 'em a try sometime."

Blake took a deep breath and straightened himself. He stretched, slapped the table with both hands, and focused on the container before him. "Okay! A box. What's in it, Alice?" His brow furrowed. "By the way, have I ever asked you about your nickname? I don't think I have."

"No."

"Well, tell you what." He stood. The top of his head, millimeters away from brushing with the ceiling of the six-foot three-inch cabin. "You explain to me how you got a girl's name while I get myself a coffee because I need to wake up a bit. Then you can show me what neat little gadget you've brought me."

He chuckled. "Okay. Fair enough. Well, I'm a born and bred Hoosier. In Indiana, basketball is king. And not only at the collegiate level. It's all of them."

"From pre-school up. Everyone learns how to play. I love being a spectator. But watching college ball is my favorite. March Madness is the best."

Standing in the galley as he made his coffee, he listened with interest. "Okay. Go on. I'm sure you're aware you are freakishly tall. No way you didn't participate."

"No, that's the crazy thing. I'm not athletic at all. I've always been a nerd, interested in gadgets and technology. Part of me *wanted* to have fun and my mother enrolled me in the youth program at the Y when I was nine. By the time I was in sixth grade, I was over six foot four. But at only a hundred and seventeen pounds, it was a challenge to control my body. I was so skinny."

Nodding in agreement, Blake blew the steam wafting from the top of his mug. "Well, your muscles hadn't had time to develop yet."

His colleague chuckled. "Yeah, my mother said I reminded her of a baby giraffe trying to stand for the first time."

He closed a cabinet door in the galley and laughed along. "I can picture that."

"Yes, but anyway—I couldn't dribble worth a shit. Hell, I couldn't make a free throw to save my life."

He walked back, slid behind the table, and sipped his brew. "Okay, so what's with the cute moniker?"

"It was our high school team name, the Alice's. Long story there as well. I'll tell you sometime, but they were always a fantastic basketball team."

"I assume you had friends who played for them?"

The youthful scientist placed his palms on the container, his fingers beginning to toy with its edges. "Yeah, not so much. I had graduated by sixteen and was already attending MIT."

Alice grinned. "But I was still monitoring them on live streams and such. And of course, my new classmates thought it was funny, or unusual for me to be following a high school team. And soon they found out their name, the Alice's, and somewhere, I don't know how long ago it was, but somebody called me Alice, and—" He shrugged and curled his lips. "It stuck."

With a heavy sigh, he turned to gaze through the window, where a handful of clouds raced past in a flurry.

Blake smiled. "Well, there ya go. Now I know." He clapped his hands. "All right. So, show me what you've got."

"Okay. Sorry." Alice spun the silver case around and toggled the latches. He raised the lid and withdrew a pair of digital binoculars. "So, looking at these, they appear to be a normal set you can get on Amazon."

He rotated them in his hand. "Seven X optical, two x digital zoom." He flipped them over and pointed. "Take a photograph with this button, and here, on this side, a sixty-four-gig micro-SD card slot."

Blake accepted them and gave them a once over. "And this pair is special, because?" He sat them on the table and enjoyed another taste of his coffee.

"Oh, right. Let me see your phone." He slid over his device. Alice opened his laptop and connected the mobile. "I am putting an application on here to connect to the binoculars. If you snap a shot of someone, you can access our face recognition database and find out who they are."

"Fantastic." He snatched them and inspected them again. "Well, those are indeed cool." At that moment, his laptop made the familiar ring of an internal video call. Alice took the queue, grabbing his computer and cell phone. He mouthed, *I'll be in the back of the plane* and gave Blake a pat on the shoulder.

He nodded his understanding and answered the call. "Good morning, Veronica."

Her pale complexion reflected off the glow of her monitor. The camera failed to pick up much else in the dark background. "Yeah, that's debatable. I wanted to talk to you before I went to bed. What's your ETA?"

He glanced at the clock in the corner of his monitor. "I think we've got about two and a half more hours until we land."

"Okay. I'm sending you his address, but we may have to make this more clandestine than we thought. They announced he would be talking to a world-renowned sketch artist to make a rendering of one assailant. Here she is."

A picture of Dr. Risa Lindman appeared on his screen.

He rolled his eyes. "Oh, shit. That's a problem."

She nodded. "Right. If the public knows, they know, and they might make a move to kill him. And truth be told, I'd be surprised if they didn't."

His eyes narrowed, and he cocked his head. "Hmmm, not necessarily."

She pinched the bridge of her nose, closed her eyes, and sighed. "What are you thinking? Why wouldn't they?"

"Well, up to now, this Anders guy hasn't publicly described this bloke. If they, the ones who made the attack—if they don't think it's important enough—they might do nothing."

Veronica shook her head. Her red curls flowed with the movement. "I'm not following you. What do you mean?"

"Okay, let's say Anders gives a brilliant description of the individual in question. Which, honestly, is doubtful because it's been over a week. But for argument's sake, let's say he does, and Doctor Lindman makes this phenomenal rendering. That's already working against us because it's a drawing, not a photo."

He sighed. "You've got maybe a three to five percent chance, at best, it will find the right person. And that's *if* they're in the database. Knowing the technology could bring back a thousand suggestions for us to comb through, how much of a waste of time will that be?"

Veronica nodded. "I'm with you. Go on."

"However, what if this guy had a unique set of features, something so obvious the chances of him being detected is near almost certain? Then they would have something to worry about, wouldn't they? It would give them a reason to take him out."

Her eyes shifted in thought. "What kind of feature or aspects are you talking about?"

"Uh, I dunno. Perhaps a dragon tattooed on his face, or half of his nose is missing. Something like that. The fact they would risk exposure tells us this guy would be identified easily and could—or more than likely, would tie him back to somebody powerful."

"All right, Blake. I follow you. All excellent points and thoughts. Get with him as soon as you can."

"Will do. And when is he supposed to meet with her?"

"The twenty-third is all I know. I'll get with the COS in Oslo and get you a location and exact time."

He took another sip of his drink. "That's unnecessary." He smiled. "I'll ask him when I see him."

With closed eyes, her head shook. "Of course. I'm tired."

Alice approached and handed him his phone. Veronica nodded. "Okay, we'll monitor all channels and let you know if we get any chatter."

"Sounds good. I'll have them push the throttle and get us there a little sooner. Go to bed."

He shut the laptop. After he asked the pilots to double-time it, he went to the back of the plane to shower and prepare for his meeting with Anders Siversten.

BERGEN, NORWAY

June 22nd 14:22 (12:22 UTC)

Blake relaxed in his blue Volvo station wagon on Øvre Blekeveien, which translated to Upper Bleke Road. He was south and on the opposite side of the road from Anders Siversten's home.

The house was at Blake's one o'clock. It sat at an elevation about three hundred feet above the harbor. It was a light yellow with a red clay tile roof, matching the surrounding dwellings.

The adjacent lot to his right had no structures, other than a pool, or non-working fountain, so he had an unobstructed view of the front and side of the house.

To his north, looking well beyond the building, was a fjord from the North Sea, and mountains surrounded him, all dotted with homes and buildings. The air was a comfortable sixteen degrees Celsius. He kept the windows open, allowing the refreshing sea breeze to roll through the car.

The CIA doesn't have an official Chief of Station, or COS, operating inside Norway. However, because of the recent threats of Islamic Terrorism, the CIA and the Norwegian Intelligence Service resurrected a bastardized version of a post-World War II stay-behind service, allowing American intelligence and MI6 to operate legally within Norway's borders.

Blake and his team were piggybacking off that agreement in case they had to reveal their presence. As of now, this was to remain a covert mission.

Veronica had put Anders' house under surveillance after his interview on the BBC news. They'd been looking for anomalies to indicate he was being watched by another group or subjected to any threat. Blake's job was to speak to him and gather any intel to expose a lead for him to follow.

So far, there had been no communication between our intelligence and the witness, so he needed to get a message to him to arrange a face-to-face meeting. In this instance, because of multiple unknowns, he insisted on going "old school" rather than risk possible electronic interception of his instructions.

Blake gazed out over the fjord and admired the scenery. He glanced at the clock on the dash.

"Shit!" He grabbed his radio.

"What's the delay?"

The radio squawked back. "The gray BMW parked out front?"

"Yeah. What about it?"

"This is the first time we've seen it since we started surveillance. They reviewed the video, and it got here about an hour ago."

He peered in his rearview mirror and identified the front of a yellow van stop and park around a corner. "What's your twenty?"

Dave chuckled. "Fantastic instincts, but don't worry. It's me in the van. I'm waiting for the green light from you to proceed."

"Roger. Do we know anything about the BMW? Occupants? How many? Where they were headed?"

The radio was silent for a minute. He was losing his patience when Dave finally answered him. "Sorry for the delay. I got info on the beemer. It's a single female occupant. She knocked on his door and has been in there ever since."

He massaged his temples with his middle finger and thumb. "Okay. Let's give it a little more time." Blake grabbed the binoculars Alice had given him, zoomed in on the license plate, and captured a picture. He forwarded them to Dave. "In the meantime, have them run these plates. See what materializes. Should she fail to emerge within the next quarter of an hour, we'll need to reconsider our game plan."

"Roger."

Blake planned to have a package delivered. Dave, the man behind him in the van, was delivering a verbal message, along with written instructions and a square sign displaying the logo for Norway's national football team. Once Anders got the orders, he was to flush them in the toilet and put the board in the window facing south. This signaled his agreement to meet him at the designated location at 15:00.

After about ten more minutes, he radioed Dave. "Anything on those plates?"

"Negative."

"Oh! Wait! The front door opened." He peered through the binoculars. An attractive brunette standing about five feet, eight inches exited the home. He zoomed in. She reached for the handrail and slowly stepped onto the six-step flight of stairs. She wore a tight red skirt, hemmed a few inches above the knee, and a tight, thin, knitted long-sleeve sweater that accentuated her breasts.

"Okay, hold on. I'll try to snap a picture of her face so we can run it through the database." Blake maximized the zoom on her face. Her long wavey hair partially hid her features.

"Dammit!"

"What's wrong?"

"It's her long hair. The damn wind is obstructing—oh wait."

As soon as she reached the bottom of the stairs, she turned and said something to Anders. She brushed her hair behind her right ear and then turned to return to her car. "Gotcha!" He captured a picture and started searching the facial recognition database.

Blake's radio squawked. "We got an answer back on those plates. It's a rental. We're waiting to tap into the rental company's database to find out who rented it."

Blake was focused on his phone. He grabbed the radio to answer. "You may not have to worry about that. I'm running her through facial rec—" His phone dinged. "Hey, I got an answer."

He focused on the screen as an image appeared. His eyes narrowed as his brow scrunched in disbelief.

"Canadian Intelligence. What the hell?"

16

Bergen, Norway
June 23rd 12:34 (10:34 UTC)

Blake sat at his laptop, studying the layout of Bergen and the surrounding area. He made mental notes of where the main roads were, and what areas typically had congestion if there were tunnels, bridges, et cetera. The best routes to use for an escape, and which roads to avoid at all costs. He was finishing his lunch when his phone rang. He turned it to see the screen. Veronica was calling.

"Good afternoon. I hope you've got some information about the woman I saw coming out of Anders' house."

"Well, I reran those pictures you sent to see if I got the same hit and then cross-referenced our internal database where they matched. You were right. Her name is Evelyn Cathey, and she works for Canadian Intelligence. We generally have a co-op with them and as far as we know, they have no operation in progress over there."

Blake took a sip of his Coke to wash down the last bit of the sandwich he'd been chewing while his boss spoke. "Okay, I'm sure with your extensive contacts list, there's someone you can call. I'd like to know what the hell she's doing here. Maybe she knows something we don't."

"Easier said than done. As I said, we have a co-op, but that runs both ways. To the best of my knowledge, we've yet to disclose any information about our activities over there. Acknowledging our awareness of her would inevitably unleash a flood of inquiries from them."

He sighed. "Understood."

"Maybe you can go old school and if you see her again, you could just ask her."

"Hmph. I'll keep that in mind."

Veronica chuckled. "I'm sure you will. Now. On to our asset, Mr. Anders Siversten. We did get a few hits on some suspected mercenaries coming into Norway this morning."

"Wonderful. I'm assuming they came on a private jet?"

"Well, of course. What better way to bring in contraband, like automatic weapons and whatever else they need to complete their deeds?"

He recognized her attempt to be sarcastic and laughed it off. "Right. The only way to travel. Anyone we know?"

"Nobody of significance."

"Any chance they *didn't* pay off customs and we have something to get the locals to arrest 'em for?"

"I'm afraid not, and so far, there is no chatter on any open contracts. None had any outstanding Interpol warrants, so there was nothing we could detain them for."

He shook his head. "Figures. Okay, if anything changes, let me know."

"Of course. You'll be the first person I contact. Let me know how the interview with this witness goes."

"Will do."

He disconnected the call.

TWO HOURS LATER, BLAKE glanced at his watch as he stood on the roof of a high-rise office building. He was supposed to meet Anders across the street near the cruise terminal's front doors.

He peered toward the terminal through his binoculars. The view of the road was clear both ways from this vantage point. The trees slightly obstructed his line of sight up the hill, allowing him only a glimpse of Anders' house's red roofline.

He raised his radio. "Dave, do you have a visual? Over."

"Affirmative. I'm viewing the house now. No sign of the asset, yet. Over."

"Copy. He drives a shitty, red Toyota Yaris. I told him to take his car and not any public transportation. Let me know as soon as he leaves. Over."

"Roger. Out."

To enhance the scope of surveillance, Blake introduced extra layers of security.

He stationed Dave outside the witness's residence, making him responsible for watching Anders' activities.

In addition, he stationed two other agents in opposite directions, strategically placed to account for the possible routes their witness might take to reach the meeting location.

He glanced at the time again and pressed the button on his mic. "Christy. Jerome. Copy?"

"This is Christy. I'm in position. Over."

"This is Jerome. Same here. Over."

"Copy. Thanks. The asset should leave any minute. Once we get confirmation on his direction, I'll let you know. Whoever ends up being the follower, tell me when he passes. If he doesn't come in your direction and you're not following him, proceed to your next station. Copy?"

Before he could get confirmation from the other agents, his radio squawked. It was Dave. "Control. A gray mini pulled in behind me. A fighting-age male has exited the vehicle and is approaching my side of the van. Over."

"Copy. Describe him. Any sign of nervousness?"

Dave glanced in his side-view mirror while he readied his silenced Glock 19. "Negative. White male, blonde hair. Early to mid-thirties. He seems to be holding a package with both hands."

"UNDERSTOOD. I KNOW I don't need to tell you to be cautious." Blake switched from the radio to his phone and dialed Alice.

"This is Alice."

"Hey, I need you to get that drone in the air ASAP with eyes on Dave. Do it now."

"Uh, yeah, but the battery might not last too—"

"Fuck the battery. You've got a hot swap on standby, don't you?"

"Yes."

"So be prepared to use it. Now get it in the fucking air. Now!"

DAVE ROLLED HIS WINDOW down.

The man held out the package. *"Kan du hjelpe meg er du snill?"*

Dave grinned, shaking his head. "No idea what you're saying, dude. Do you speak English, *oder sprechen sie Deutsche?*"

The man flashed a white set of teeth as he smiled. "Ah, English. Good. Sorry. Can you take this for me? It's going to Warsaw."

Dave's brow furrowed. "What? No. I only do deliveries."

"Please. I need to mail this to my mother."

Dave shook his head. "No. I don't have—I can't weigh it. I don't have any way to take payment." He started to close the window, then stopped. "There is an office near the cruise port. Have a nice day."

The window closed. Dave glanced toward the blue sky as he heard the familiar buzz of a drone's tiny propellers splitting the air.

The man lifted the package. "Please!"

Two bullets exited the box, shattering the window, and piercing into the veteran agent's torso.

BLAKE'S PHONE RANG. The caller's ID showed Alice.

"Yeah. Do you have eyes on him?"

The panic in the young man's voice was evident from its shaking. "Holy shit! The blonde guy shot him! I think he had a gun in the box he was holding, or something, but he shot him and took off in the gray car."

"Shit! Okay, follow him. Which direction did he go?"

"Uh, towards the white sedan."

"Okay. Stay with him. I'll call her."

SIXTY YARDS FROM ANDERS' home, Agent Christy Bellamy sat in a white Peugeot. A gray mini approached her, its tires screeching as they struggled for traction on the hairpin turn.

Her radio squawked. It was Blake. "Gray mini. We've been compromised. After them!"

"On it!" She shifted to first gear and floored the accelerator.

She closed in on the mini, the engine revved to full throttle. As the compact she was chasing made another hairpin turn back in the other direction, its rear end slid out, but the driver regained control. She made a classic handbrake turn, tires squealing and leaving a black patch on the road. Two more tire-screeching handbrake turns and the smell of burning rubber, mixed with the stench of hot brake pads, seeped into the vehicle.

They exited the bottom of the hill without stopping and headed north. Brakes screeched from behind her as other road users attempted to avoid a collision. She stomped on the gas pedal and followed the mini through three red lights. They drove like maniacs, accelerating, braking, dodging cars and motorcycles as they went. A box truck slammed into the back of a white Saab. The vehicle smashed into the SUV in front and spun off the road, rolling over, finally impacting a power-line pole. A transformer burst into flames as sparks rained onto the pavement.

Alice relayed the chase to Blake as it unfolded

"Shit!" Blake mashed his radio button. "Jerome. We're compromised. Go get the asset and transport him to the terminal. Now!"

Jerome put his car in gear and headed up the hill. Blake called Alice. "How's the battery life on the drone?"

"It's at eighty percent."

Blake typed feverishly into his phone. "I'm sending you the coordinates to Anders' house. I need eyes on him. Unbelievable. This mission has turned to shit. Call me back when you have him. Red Yaris."

Two motorcycles moving caught Jerome's attention in his mirror as he sped toward Anders' home.

He slammed on his brakes after a glance forward. A black Range Rover was backing out of a driveway, impeding his progress. He glanced in his mirror. The bikes were no longer behind him.

He exhaled a relieved sigh, then mashed on the horn. "Come on! Let's go!"

Movement on his left. It was one of the bikers. He turned to his right and saw the barrel of an automatic weapon. Throwing the car into reverse, he stomped the pedal to the floor.

A hail of bullets tore through windows and the bodywork of the car, shredding holes and shattering glass. The steel-jacketed messengers of death were followed by a stream of crimson spurting from his body as they sliced through vital organs.

His twitching corpse slumped over the wheel as the car continued rolling, coming to a halt as it crashed into a tree. The door flew open and the horn blaring, the cadaver hung out of the car, held only by the seat belt, dripping a puddle of red horror onto the green grass.

Desperately, Blake pressed the button of his mic. "Jerome, come in, for fuck's sake, where are you? Answer me."

He called Alice. "Where's the drone? I need it asap!" A car's horn was steadily blaring off in the distance.

Alice's voice was broadcast through the phone. "I'm at the cruise terminal and am sending it back up the hill. You should hear it any moment."

The horn stopped. Blake heard the faint buzzing of the drone and shielded his eyes from the sun to see the tiny black spec heading towards its destination to intercept Anders.

———•———

CHRISTY SWERVED TO avoid a group of pedestrians about to cross the street. As she passed, angry voices pierced her ears.

The mini turned a sharp right and returned toward the top, to the cobbled and narrow road. Buildings of different hues towered on both sides, resembling the walls of a vibrant canyon.

A hard left, then another right.

Her gaze darted in all directions.

She remained hyper-focused as she swerved again, avoiding cars and vans parked on either side of the cramped street. She followed the tiny two-seater as it made a sharp left, careening into the side of a small blue Nissan before continuing.

The road ended, and her mark screeched to a halt between two cars.

"Ah, Ha! I've got you now mother fucker!"

A van halted behind her, the sliding door facing her. She turned around as the door opened and a man stepped out.

The lone gunman raised his automatic rifle.

Her pupils dilated.

"Shit!"

She ducked as her rear window shattered by the onslaught of flying lead. Pulling out her pistol, she peered over the steering wheel.

The driver of the mini also climbed out and raised a weapon.

She shot four times through her front windscreen as bullets ripped through the back of her sedan.

Slamming the shifter into reverse, she stomped on the gas.

She collided with the van, slightly behind the passenger door, knocking it halfway across the narrow road.

The shooter stumbled into the vehicle's open door. He lost his grip on his MP-5 and it slid across the pavement.

Maneuvering it back into first, she accelerated.

BLAKE'S ANXIETY EASED as the whirring of drone blades made its way towards Ander's home.

He hadn't heard anything from any of his co-workers and assumed the worst.

Realizing his death grip on his phone, he loosened his fingers and pressed the speed dial for Alice.

"Alice. I'm looking for a red Toyota Yaris or a light blue BMW Jerome drove. He was headed to the house but had gone silent. Do you see the BMW or the Yaris? Do you know what those look like?"

"Sorry Blake, I'm not much of an enthusiast."

"Can you send the drone's camera view to my phone?"

"Yeah, I think so. Hang on a sec."

"Fuck, come on. Do it, now!"

He concentrated on his phone's screen and waited for the connection. Buildings' rooftops appeared. As the drone gained altitude and climbed the mountainside, Anders' home came into view.

He checked the time. It was 14:53.

"Scan around back. He parks there."

A few moments later, his voice rose. "Someone is coming out of his house. Get closer."

The camera zoomed in.

"It's him. He's about to get into his car. Zoom out and give me a three-sixty when he's gone. I need to confirm if he's being followed."

BULLETS CONTINUED TO pepper the Peugeot. One of them found its prey and ripped through her bicep. She drove on, ignoring the excruciating pain.

Taking a sharp right, she began climbing the hill. A glance in her rearview mirror revealed the van colliding with a small vehicle.

The car careened in a wild spin, yet her relentless pursuers closed in without faltering.

She tried to make a sharp left using the handbrake, but the searing pain in her arm made it impossible.

Her turn took a wide arc, resulting in a collision with three trash cans placed near the curb. Undeterred, she maneuvered her vehicle over the sidewalk, resolutely forging ahead in her determined escape.

Bullets shattered her door mirror as she approached a hairpin turn on the left.

She slammed on the brakes and spun the wheel hard. The tires screamed in protest, but she navigated the difficult curve, seething in pain. Revving the Peugeot's tiny engine, she raced along a residential street.

Her pursuers closed in.

She slapped her hand on the top of the steering wheel.

"Come on, you piece of shit!"

The pursuing van continued to draw ever closer.

It was only a few feet away from her bumper.

She stomped on the brakes. The van tried to stop but rear-ended her. Christy's body jerked forward from the impact. Navigating the shifter like a seasoned race car driver, she floored the gas pedal and achieved some distance.

A main road intersection near the bay came into view.

Another hail of bullets ripped through the exterior sheet metal.

There was a warm sensation on her side. She felt around her waist. As she inspected her hand, it was covered in deep crimson gore.

The approaching traffic light ahead was red. She clutched the wheel with both hands, fighting against the slickness of the blood covering her grip.

A tandem bus T-boned the side of her sedan at high speed as she drove through the intersection. The collision pushed her into an adjacent petrol station and ripped a fuel pump from its base. The badly damaged vehicle landed on the toppled pump.

Christy raised her head. Blood was gushing from her side and a gash in her forehead.

The acrid smell of sweat, gunpowder, and fuel vapor filled her nostrils.

She heard screams and warnings. The ensuing explosion sent a black and orange fireball thirty feet into the air and engulfed her.

THE DRONE'S CAMERA completed its three-hundred-and-sixty-degree scan. Blake didn't notice anything unusual, other than a black plume of smoke from about a mile away. The BMW was nowhere in sight.

"Okay Alice, let's focus on Anders. You must keep him in view but change your vector often. We need to make sure he's not being followed."

The drone followed Anders. Blake heard sirens in the distance.

"Alice, he's approaching a sharp turn. Get higher and then skip to the next area of the road. Ensure the drone is positioned so we have a clear view of his car as he approaches. The area seems tight, and I haven't spotted any vehicles around."

"Will do."

The drone gained altitude and flew to a more favorable position. It spun the camera to face the red Toyota as it negotiated the sharp curve. As it came around the corner, Blake noticed something.

"Where in the hell did that motorcycle come from? Did you see it earlier?"

"I don't know. It must have been in an alley we missed."

Blake rubbed the back of his neck. The tension was making it tight. "Spin the camera one-eighty."

Completing its graceful pirouette, the camera captured every angle. Blake witnessed a gray van with no markings pull out ahead of Anders.

"Hey, get down in front of that van and see if you can zoom in on the driver or passenger and run—"

"I know exactly what you're looking for."

He navigated the drone down close enough to capture images of the occupants in the front seat. As soon as he snapped the photos and input them into the facial recognition software, the results immediately popped up. In under thirty seconds, it came back with a match.

"Hey, I got a hit. Both of them are bounty hunters and contract killers."

"That was fast."

"I think they were at the front of the line. They were the pair that Veronica said were recognized coming into the country."

"Son of a bitch! They're trapping him." Blake ran to the door to exit the roof. "Keep talking to me Alice and give me turn-by-turn feedback."

"What are you going to do?"

"I'm going to stop them."

17

Bergen, Norway
June 23rd 14:36 (12:36 UTC)

Blake rushed to his Volvo station wagon and started the engine. Without hesitation, he accelerated away, tires screeching against the pavement in his race to intercept his valuable asset.

As he ventured forward, to his left, the majestic peaks of the mountains emerged on the distant horizon, stretching across the Sea of Bergen. The wheel was clammy in his hands as anxiety crept in. The intel this Anders guy had was too important to lose. Alice monitored the area from above, relying on the drone's high vantage point for observation.

"Alice, any change? I'm talking about the van and the one following him on a bike. Where are they?"

"Uh, as far as I can tell, it's still just the two. They're coming along the street on the ledge above you. Sand—vik—sv..."

He gunned the accelerator, the Volvo hurtling on the winding coastal road known as the 577. The deep blue waters of the Byfjorden inlet stretched out to his left, while steep hillsides rose on the other side, winding residential streets and homes clinging to the slopes overlooking the fjord below.

What seemed like an arm's length to his right were the sheer rock walls leftover from when they carved the roads out. Sanviksveien Street was atop the ridge, thirty feet above him.

Blake chuckled at the young technicians' struggle to pronounce the street's name.

"Sanviksveien."

"Yeah, what *you* said. They are above you."

"Hey, shit. Blake. Another motorcycle just joined them. He's clad in all black like the other."

"Okay. Thanks." *Dammit. I've got to get this guy now!*

He flashed his lights and overtook a slower-moving SUV. "Well, he must take a left to get down here. How far are they until he can make the turn?" He started to overtake another vehicle but dodged back behind it when a tour bus came his way.

Son of a bitch!

When it passed, he gunned the motor and buzzed by the next motorist. A horn blared.

"Hey, Alice! What's going on? You've gotta guide me, dude. I'm driving blind. Come on. Keep feeding me details."

"Okay. Uh... yeah, they just turned. It's a ramp and it will intersect with the street you're on."

"How much further?"

"Huh?"

"How fucking far, Alice?"

Jesus, this kid's got to get it together.

"Okay. Sorry. The road curves to your left. It's around the corner you're approaching now. About a hundred yards beyond."

With a surge of adrenaline, he slammed on the accelerator. As he reached the next intersection, he executed a handbrake turn, maneuvering the wagon to the right. The tires screeched, their protest cutting through the air. Inside, the pungent odor of burned rubber drifted into the interior.

Cresting the hill, Anders and the two mercenaries on motorcycles bore down on him. Blake's eyes widened in dismay, teeth sinking into his lower lip as he frantically searched for a target. The roar of the engines filled the air, drowning out all other sounds, while the acrid scent of burning rubber mingled with the sharp tang of alarm gripping him.

Do I ram the van, the car? Take out the bikers? Fuck!

He jerked the wheel to the left and then back enough to clip the rear bumper of the lead vehicle. All of them stopped.

Blake jumped out of his car and took four quick steps to the van's window. "Hey, I sure am sorry. I don't know what I was thinking." He withdrew his Glock and fired two shots into the head of the driver.

The passenger disappeared into the back as a third man tried to hide. He trained his sights on the most exposed biker and emptied three rounds into his chest and one into his helmet. The other motorcyclist escaped, using the opposite side of the van for cover.

He opened Anders' door. The young blond man was white-knuckled, gripping the steering wheel, paralyzed in fear.

"I'm Blake MacKay. The guy you're on your way to meet. Come with me now. Your life is in danger."

Back in the car, he threw it into drive, headed to the next intersection, and turned left, toward the top of the hill. The road was just wide enough for two cars. Houses lined each side of the narrow street. At the end, he turned left and drove to the main highway.

"Are you okay?"

Anders' eyes widened in fear, darting around as if searching for unseen threats. His chest heaved with rapid breaths, the adrenaline still coursing through his veins from the harrowing ordeal. A sheen of cold sweat glistened on his forehead.

"Who? Who were they?" His words quivered with raw emotion, barely above a whisper. There was desperation in his tone, a silent plea for reassurance in the face of unknown horrors. "What were they going to do to me?"

"You don't want to know."

Alice's voice came through Blake's earbuds. "Hey, you're about to have company. The van turned around and so did the biker. They're going to turn left and be at your rear."

He glanced into his mirror and saw the mystery rider. The van soon followed.

Oh shit, I've got to lose these guys. I can't let them get to this dude or they're going to kill him.

He twisted to face his frightened passenger. "Buckle up."

Accelerating, he whizzed by several cars and came to the intersection for the 577 and was once again next to the Bergen Sea on his left. He sped along the two-lane street.

A black pickup with a trailer pulled out in front of him.

He pressed down on the brakes while wailing on the horn. Turning the wheel hard left, then right, he passed them. The move allowed him to gain some distance and then, glancing in his mirror, both antagonists were in pursuit.

Concentrating on the road, he could sense the terror flowing through the man he was trying to protect. "Spill it, what do you know? What happened on the oil rig? Who's after you?"

His peripheral vision caught a subtle shake of the man's head. His passenger's voice continued to quiver with fear as he spoke. "I don't know. I saw one person remove his hood. He had a fucked-up ear. I'm to meet with some expert sketch artists to describe him. That's all I know."

"What do you mean by his ear?" He accelerated and overtook three cars. A semi-truck was facing them head-on and closing in fast. His passenger grasped the dash and held his breath.

I've got this.

The wagon slid back into the right lane. The Doppler effect of the truck's blaring horn as it passed filled the car's interior. His passenger's eyes were closed tighter than a clamshell on a stormy sea.

"Hey! My question. His ear?"

Anders opened his eyes. "I can't remember precisely. It was all mangled. It looked like someone put it in a meat grinder and didn't bandage it to heal."

"When are you supposed to meet her?"

Alice broke in. "They're on you."

Hot lead blasted out the Volvo's back window.

"Hold on and get down."

The man on the motorbike came alongside the passenger's rear door. Blake veered right. The motorcycle backed off. Shots shattered the back right glass.

"Fuck! Stay down!"

Alice chimed in. "Hey, you're approaching a tunnel in about a quarter mile."

The van closed in and hit the back left quarter panel, causing the rear end to shake. The bike slowed and got behind the other men in pursuit. Then it slung around and was on their immediate left. Bullets peppered the back door. He swerved left. The motorcycle reciprocated.

As he gazed ahead, his eyes fixed on the looming mouth of the tunnel, mere feet away. The towering shadows cast by the encircling mountains enveloped them, obscuring the sunlight and intensifying the overwhelming sense of impending doom. The pursuing vehicle hit the rear again. His passenger cried out.

"Oh, my God! Help me!"

"Shut up! He won't help you. What do you think I'm doing?"

Before the entrance into the mountain, the road split into four lanes, separated by a concrete divider. They entered. Their pursuers pulled alongside him. Blake glanced at the speedometer. It read 145 mph. "What kind of engine does that fucking piece of shit have in it?" He swerved left and clipped its front fender. Sparks flew. Its driver braked. The faster motorbike sped past them.

That's not good. What's he up to?

The rock walls closed in around them. Like the cold embrace of a vengeful specter. He navigated to the left lane. The motorcycle loomed ahead. Its rider turned back and unloaded a fury of lead stitching a line in the hood, with a final round penetrating the center of the windscreen.

"I need you to brace yourself!"

"What? What are you doing?"

Anders' body tightened. Every muscle flexed, preparing for the unknown. Blake slammed on his brakes. The pursuing men smashed into the rear of the station wagon. From his mirror, He could see their bodies jolting forward with the force of the collision. Standing strong, the Volvo's sturdy frame absorbed the blow, shielding its occupants from the full extent of the crash.

He laughed. "Take that, assholes." With a firm grip on the steering wheel, the seasoned agent's foot floored the accelerator, desperately seeking an elusive escape. An anxious prayer slipped from his lips as he glanced in the rearview mirror.

There, a billowing cloud of steam and cascading radiator fluid betrayed the damaged state of the mercenaries' vehicle. Limping forward like a wounded predator, the van's headlights gradually dwindled in size, a fading beacon as it relentlessly pursued them towards the tunnel's exit.

As they emerged into the sunlight, flying lead shattered the passenger window. A lone bullet hit its mark and tore through Anders' right thigh. His body stiffened. He pressed his hands against the headliner as he inhaled and held his breath. Both eyes were wide open in shock.

"Argh shit! My leg!"

Blake crossed two lanes to an exit, drove to the bottom of the slip road, and turned left. He steered under the main street and then onto the ramp to head in the opposite direction. Leaning over Anders, he opened the glove box and grabbed a handful of napkins. "Here. Apply pressure to the wound." He grabbed the wad of paper and pressed it on the asset's wound.

His eyes clamped shut, and he gritted his teeth. With his right hand clenched into a fist, in rapid succession, he pounded the door panel.

"Ahhh! Holy shit! Damn, it hurts!"

"Yeah, I know it does, but you've got to stop the bleeding. Now do what I say."

He scanned the mirror. There was no sign of the other gunman.

"So, when are you supposed to meet this sketch artist?"

"Tomorrow. Noon. At the Hotel Oleana."

Driving back through the mountain, as they exited, he saw a lone headlight of a motorbike approaching fast.

"Son of a bitch."

Increasing his speed, he dodged cars, trucks, and panel vans as he returned to Bergen. The sea appeared on his right. Bullets penetrated the seats behind them. What little glass remained intact, shattered, and flew within the confines of the estate saloon.

"I truly want to kill this guy."

Anders chuckled. "Yeah. Me too."

Automatic weapons fire continued to pepper the back of the wagon. Alarms sounded and lights flashed on the dash, indicating a sudden loss of air pressure in both back tires. He pressed further on the accelerator.

The bike matched their speed on their right. Blake grabbed his Glock.

"Duck."

He fired over his passenger. The pursuing assassin braked and then maneuvered to their left side. Gunshots once again assaulted their ears. The pair of them felt the front tires explode as the vehicle dropped a few inches and more warning chimes sounded. In moments, the sharp, rhythmic whapping sound of shredded rubber relentlessly slapping against the pavement filled the air. The cacophony echoed throughout, intensifying the sense of urgency enveloping them. As the chase progressed, showers of sparks erupted from the exposed wheels, a display of friction between metal and road.

Blake's fist pounded the dash of the car. "God dammit!"

Anders' hands clutched the dashboard, his eyes widening in alarm. "Look out!"

The Volvo slammed into the side of a panel van, and came to an abrupt halt, as it entered the 577. Both airbags deployed. Acting on instinct, Blake snatched his knife and deflated the bag. As he attempted to get out, two arms reached inside, grabbed him, and pulled him from the vehicle.

A punch to the gut made him hunch over. He flew backward and darkness surrounded him as a knee connected to his forehead.

As he lay prone on the hot asphalt, his eyes shot open. Shaking his head vigorously, he was determined to brush off the disorienting effects of the powerful blow. As he attempted to rise, muscle memory and reflexes took over.

Blocking a potential life-ending kick to his skull with his arms, he then reached out and yanked the aggressor's planted leg, sending his assailant to the ground. Still wearing a helmet, his body slammed onto the pavement. The assassin used a 'kipping up' move to spring to his feet in a rapid move and immediately went into attack mode.

Blake raised his arms to defend against the kicks. Rolling backward, he righted himself and stood. The attacker pulled a nunchaku from his jacket and swung it relentlessly, connecting with Blake's arms and shoulders as he tried to block the onslaught. Still punch drunk from the crash, and the devastating knee to the head, he was seeing double-vision.

As he shook his head to try to right his sight, a vicious blow landed squarely on his face, sending a jolt of pain coursing through his body. The all too familiar taste of copper and blood filled his mouth, a bitter reminder of the violence inflicted upon him. His eyesight was fuzzy, and he felt vertigo.

Oh shit, I cannot pass out.

The aggressor, clad all in black, twisted and delivered a roundhouse to his head. He face-planted on the ground and struggled to right himself. An empty click, then the well-known sound of an empty magazine hitting the pavement urged him to rise. He turned as his attacker inserted a fresh mag and loaded a bullet with his name on it into the chamber. Darkness was closing in. The weapon before him raised.

A yellow blur of a DHL van whooshed by him, impacting the black-clad would be killer, swiftly erasing him from existence. Crumpled sheet metal and bystanders' screams filled his ears as the weight of the delivery truck smashed into his assailant. Strong hands wrapped around him, assisting him to rise amidst the chaos.

Struggling to his feet, his body ached with every movement. Pedestrians hurried over to assist him, their concerned faces a blur as he tried to focus. His arms throbbed from the relentless blows of the nunchaku, bruises blossoming like dark flowers on his skin. Every breath sent a sharp pang through his ribs, a reminder of the vicious assault he had endured moments before.

As he stood shakily, the taste of blood lingered in his mouth, metallic and bitter. The world swayed around him, dizziness threatening to pull him back down. With each step forward, the pavement seemed to tilt beneath him, an unsteady ground for his reeling senses.

The distant sound of sirens pierced through the haze in his mind, growing louder with the passing seconds. The echo of footsteps and concerned murmurs surrounded him as he tried to piece together what had just transpired. Every movement sent sparks of pain shooting through his battered body, a symphony of agony that drowned out all other sensations.

With trembling hands brushing against the support offered by the pedestrians, He took a shaky breath. The aftermath of the brutal beating was etched into every fiber of his being. He sat on the side of the pavement. He tried to get everything in perspective again.

Alice's voice came over his earbuds. "Blake! You there?"

Sirens filled the air.

"Yeah. I'm here."

"Are you okay?"

"Uh. No. But I'll survive."

"I've got help coming. EMTs should be there in a few minutes. I was mistaken about Dave getting killed. He was wearing a vest. He was only stunned. I was able to direct him to where you were, and I suppose he plowed the asshole over."

"Yes, I guess he did. Thanks."

Dave exited the truck and approached him. "I thought you were toast."

Blake smirked. "I could say the same about you. Alice was sure you'd been killed."

Patting his chest, he smiled. "Yeah, I never go into the field without my body armor."

Blake nodded. "Smart man. Now help me get our buddy outta here so we can take him somewhere safe until his meeting tomorrow."

"No problem."

———◉———

TWO DISHEVELED MEN disembarked from the van in the tunnel. One put his phone to his ear.

"We didn't kill him. I don't know if he escaped, but I'd err on the side of caution."

Nazir exhaled. "Imbeciles! Go ahead and execute Plan B."

———◉———

HOTEL NORGE
Bergen, Norway

June 23rd 23:02 (21:02 UTC)

Blake examined the needlework on his face in the bathroom mirror. The medical technicians meticulously stitched up the gash on his cheek on the side of the road. Afterward, they handed him a bottle of pills, promising it would dull the ache that would linger for days. As he stared at himself, feeling the throbbing in his face, he winced. They weren't kidding.

Submerged in the ice bath, to keep the swelling to a minimum, he shivered, as the freezing water enveloped him, sending a cold shock through his body. The scent of minty menthol from the bath salts filled the air, mingling with the sharp aroma of bourbon that he sipped from a crystal glass. As the icy chill numbed his skin, he emerged from the icy water, feeling almost weightless and refreshed. After patting himself dry with a plush towel, he wrapped himself in a soft, white robe, hugging him like a warm embrace.

Using the last swig of bourbon in his glass, he popped a couple of capsules of naproxen and exited the bathroom. Pouring another, his phone rang. It was Veronica.

He took a deep breath to prepare himself before answering. Swiping the green dot to answer, he put the phone to his ear and spoke first.

"I'm sure you know."

"You're damn right I know."

Damn you, Alice.

"I understand the day wasn't a total fucking debacle. You at least kept the witness alive."

Taking a deep breath to push down his rising ire, he chose not to reply.

"Which is more than you can say for Jacob and Christy. What the fuck happened, MacKay?"

He clenched his jaw. That comment cut deep and was unnecessary, and he searched his mind for the right thing to say. He didn't choose wisely.

"That's on you."

She barked back with a ferocity he hadn't heard in a while. "Excuse me? I gave you that intel and—"

Blake felt the pressure increase in his temples. His anger rose to a level rivaling that of an erupting volcano. "And *you* did nothing with it! *You* knew they were in the country! *You* control the teams! *You* have contacts with the Norwegian police and intelligence! It's *your* job to get someone to follow those assholes and let us know about it! You didn't! We were taken completely by surprise and now two agents are dead! Two more unnamed stars for your fucking lobby wall!"

An uneasy silence filled the room, no sound other than his panting as he tried to catch his breath. The anticipation of the fury of a redheaded woman scorned about to rip through the earpiece unsettled him. But it never came.

He chugged his bourbon and poured another shot.

"POTUS has a meeting on the morning of the 25th in Geneva and she's asked me to come with her so I can relay any intel you've found. We'll be there talking to members of the UN Security Council, the PM of the

Netherlands, and Canada, and the Russian Ambassadors to the affected countries. Let me know when we have a positive ID on this mangled ear man."

He let out a sigh. "All right."

"Have a good night, Mr. MacKay."

As he dwelled upon the events that had transpired, the frigid numbness that the ice bath had bestowed upon him melted away, giving way to an inferno of fury that surged through his veins. The smoldering embers of his ire ignited, propelling his anger to a scorching, fevered crescendo. With a clenched fist, he tightened his grip on the rocks glass, the weight of his rage palpable in his trembling hand.

He gulped back the remaining liquor. Its ninety-proof burned his throat and intensified the inferno that raged inside him. In a swift violent motion, he hurled the glass across the room. It collided with the wall, shattered into a myriad of minuscule fragments, and scattered across the room.

18

Ladegarden, Norway
June 24th 11:28 (09:28 UTC)

Evelyn sat on the bed in her hotel room, resting against the fluffed pillows. As she waited for Josh, who had momentarily stepped away, she activated the phone's speaker function. Her patience waning, she stood from the bed and strolled toward the window, peeling back the curtains, she glanced outside. The sky stretched above in a serene shade of blue, adorned with fluffy white clouds. Not a single rain cloud threatened to dampen the day. Nestled gracefully by the port, her hotel, the Clarion Havnekontoret, offered a picturesque view of the harbor, where ships of all sizes commanded the scene—their majestic presence and the bustling of people added to the vibrant atmosphere. The flags on the tops of other buildings waved to the gentle breeze as it caressed the air. Her phone displayed a comfortable 14 degrees Celsius. Perfect for a light jacket.

Her partner returned to the phone. "Okay, sorry 'bout that. Stupid dog kept scratching to be let in."

She released the curtains and turned back to face the television. "No worries. I thought you put in a doggy door. Does she not know how to use it?"

"Oh, she does, but it's in the basement and would require her to go off the deck, down the hill, and into the house. Besides, it's raining. She is a self-proclaimed little princess and doesn't like to get her paws wet. So..."

Evelyn heard slurping as Josh took a sip of his coffee. After he swallowed, he cleared his throat. "So, what have you found out so far? Did you talk to the survivor we saw on the news?"

"Anders? Yes, I spoke to him yesterday."

"Did he have anything revealing to tell you?"

She removed herself from the picturesque scenery, went to the desk, and read from a scratchpad. Inscribed was the address for the Hotel Oleana, with

12:00 circled at the top. "He's meeting a sketch artist in about thirty minutes. It's about a five-minute walk, so I'll head over there and determine if I can discover the identity of the mystery man she'll be drawing. The investigator from Interpol will be there, and if I flash my credentials, hopefully, he'll fill me in."

"But—you're not there in any official capacity."

"Right. *I* know, and *you* know. But it doesn't mean *he* needs to. That's why I called. If he asks, I am going to give him your number. You get to be my boss and confirm I'm here on official business. I don't think he'll ask, but it's best to be safe. Okay?"

"Ha! Fine. But you'll owe me, eh?"

She smiled. "Of course. I'm sure you'll find a way for me to pay you back, too."

"Like maybe dog sit, eh?"

A chuckle escaped her breath. "Sure, why not? Hey, I gotta run, but I'll call you later and let you know if I find anything interesting."

NAZIR AND HIS TWO REMAINING men sat in a rented Mercedes twelve kilometers away. Across the street was a construction site where they were pouring the foundation for a new parking garage. Concrete trucks buzzed by, delivering an endless supply necessary for their work. The incessant symphony of beeping emitted by the truck's warning as they maneuvered in reverse filled the air.

From the driver's seat vantage point, Nazir locked eyes on them both in his mirror. He handed the man directly behind him a folded piece of paper over his shoulder.

"I need that sketch artist dead. All you need to know is in your hand. Do *not* fuck this up like you did the last one or you won't get paid."

The man directly behind him cleared his throat. "If you're worried about that witness, why not take him out?"

Nazir's eyes shifted in the rearview mirror to the man who spoke. "That's been arranged. No loose ends in the event something goes wrong. Now go do your job and don't screw it up."

Both men turned to each other and nodded. The furthest one from Nazir removed his pistol and chambered a round. "We won't"

"Good. Remember, I'll be watching. Now get the hell out of my car."

THE HOTEL, SITUATED in a picturesque area, faced a rectangular city park. It was open, with a thick carpet of grass reminiscent of fairways from some of the finest golf courses in Norway. Walkways cris-crossed the area with berms of flowers, colorful bushes, and foliage scattered about. People were walking their dogs, jogging or resting on the various wooden benches, reading, or enjoying the cool summer air. Lining the brick-laid road were lines of tall downy birch with an occasional Norway spruce.

The entrance to the hotel was modest and unpretentious. A wide brick staircase led up three steps to a charming patio adorned with a few tables and chairs on the left, likely serving as overflow for the quaint sidewalk café next door.

The glass front door, framed in black aluminum, featured three elegant windowpanes. Above the entrance, flags from all the Nordic nations fluttered proudly, adding a touch of regional pride to the inviting facade.

Still reeling from the injuries he sustained the previous day, Blake hobbled into the lobby of the boutique Hotel Oleana. He found himself immersed in a vibrant kaleidoscope of hues. The room burst with an explosion of color, courtesy of a pastel velvet rainbow stretching before him. To his right was a wall adorned with a light violet velvet, illuminated by the twinkle of sparkly lights. The scene exuded an aura of sophistication and whimsy. Neatly arranged black tables stood decorated with chairs covered in a tapestry of purple, teal, silver, and green suede, inviting guests to indulge in comfort and style.

Oh man, did the Lucky Charms leprechaun throw up in here?

Dave stood in front of a doorway about ten meters away. As he approached, another gentleman exited the conference room to the right.

Blake outstretched his hand to his friend. "Good afternoon. How's your side feeling?"

Laughing as he spoke; he placed his palm on his side. "Ahh, yeah. The bruises are expanding as I speak, but it beats the alternative. Speaking of which, *how* are you doing? You look like hell."

Blake rubbed his face, the bruising setting in. "Uh, yeah, it looks worse than it is. I was able to block most of his blows with my arm."

"Oh yeah? What's that look like?"

Blake pushed up his sleeve to reveal dark black, purple, and yellow bruising all up his arm.

His colleague gritted his teeth while scrunching his nose. "Yikes. Well, you'll heal."

Dave extended his hand toward the guy in the dark suit. "Blake, this is Jack Kingman, from Interpol. He's the one who arranged for the sketch artist to come and draw what our buddy, Anders, saw and hopefully, we can get a match. Jack, this is special agent, Blake MacKay, from the CIA."

They shook hands.

"Ah, yes, Mr. MacKay. I've spoken with your superior, Director Slocum. She has nothing but praise for you."

Blake smiled. *Yeah, sure she does. Whatever.*

"I thought I felt my ears burning. It's a pleasure to meet you, Detective Agent. Is Anders here?"

"Yes. He's inside speaking to the Dutch diplomats. It seems they sent an army of them, including an adviser who works under the PM. He told me what happened yesterday. Is that how you got your cuts and bruises?"

Blake nodded his confirmation, stepped to the doorway, and peeked in. The young man he saved was engaged in conversation with several people in dark suits.

The Detective Agent cleared his throat. "We're waiting on Dr. Lindman. She should be here any moment. We'll have a few minutes while she sets things up, so if you have any questions, you can ask him."

The glare from the sun on the lobby door as it opened, grabbed Blake's attention. A young lady entered and strolled in his direction, turned to her left, and headed to the concierge desk.

He nudged his colleague. "Hey, the woman there. Isn't she the one we saw coming out of Anders' house the other day?"

Dave turned to see. "I dunno. Sorry dude, I missed her."

"I think it was. I'm going to find out."

Kingman's phone rang as Blake searched for the Canadian Intelligence officer. There was a voice at his rear. "Agent MacKay, Dr. Lindman's car is one minute out. It's a big black American SUV. Can you meet her at the curb and bring her in?"

Are you kidding me? Horrible timing.

"All right. I'll go out and wait for her."

He scanned the lobby for the woman he saw enter but he didn't see her. As he walked away and exited the front doors, he glanced at the couples leisurely seated at the charming café tables. A pang of envy washed over him. They reveled in the midday bliss, savoring delectable lunches and refreshing cocktails. His mind wandered, pondering how many were on a well-deserved holiday, relishing moments of respite from their children's joyful chaos. Perhaps young couples were embarking on the exciting journey of blossoming romance.

Stepping out past the trees that lined the road, he cast his gaze in both directions, searching for the SUV while taking in the picturesque scene unfolding before him. The street was adorned with elegant white bricks, meticulously arranged in a captivating scallop pattern. A serene grassy knoll lay past the bricks, followed by another brick street welcoming traffic in the opposite direction. Beyond the curb, souvenir shops, clothiers, and cafés greeted travelers and locals with their welcoming embrace.

Refocusing his task, he looked again left and then to the right. A black Lincoln Navigator approached the crossroad, heading toward the hotel.

That's got to be her.

A sense of serenity enveloped him, soothing his frayed nerves, and he felt the burdensome weight of anxiety dissipate into thin air as he released a deep, cathartic sigh. Looking toward the intersection of precisely placed bricks, he rubbed the back of his neck. A feeling of uneasiness caused him to scan the area again.

Nothing. I'm imagining things.

A dark cloud crossed the sun, and a shudder ran down his back.

EVELYN'S PHONE RANG. It was the corporate number for Canada Oil. She stepped outside the hotel to the peaceful courtyard to hear better.

"Hello?"

"Yes, this is the Canada Oil office of James Gallagher for special agent Evelyn Cathey."

"Yes. This is her."

"Hold please."

The line clicked.

"Ms. Cathey. This is James Gallagher from Canada Oil. How are you?"

"Fine, thank you. I'm—I'm kind of surprised to hear from you. I can only assume you have some new information since you're calling. What's going on?"

"Yes, I do. I am pleased to tell you that I've been informed the Arctic Drill ship's transponder has turned on and we can track it."

Her brow raised, accompanied by a broad smile. "What? Are you serious?"

"Yes. It happened early this morning."

Evelyn abandoned all thoughts of Anders and the identification of the unknown man. As if on auto-pilot, her feet moved as she retraced her steps to her hotel at a hurried pace.

"Well, this is great news. Have you talked to them? How is my brother? What happened?"

"I'm afraid there is still some mystery surrounding the details. So far, nobody has answered the radio, and the vessel is drifting. It's not under power. But we know the location."

Evelyn's thoughts raced as to the possibilities of what transpired. Was Richard alive? Was this now a ghost ship? Were there any survivors? Where is it?

"Mr. Gallagher, were you going to send a team out there to investigate? If so, I'd like to go with them."

"Uh, well, frankly, we don't own that ship. We only leased it. It's owned and operated by DavCo Drilling. They had a majority of employees on the vessel. Only your brother and a handful of others worked for Canada Oil. It's my understanding that they're in charge of any investigation. You might be best to contact them."

Evelyn stopped at a corner to get her bearings and continued walking when the light indicated it was safe to cross the street. "I see. Do you know where they're out of?"

"Aberdeen, Scotland. It's on the east coast, north of Edinburgh."

"Mr. Gallagher, please send me the last known coordinates, the direction of the drift, and estimated coordinates for the next five days. I'll contact DavCo to see if I can get a ride out to the ship. You have my email address, eh?"

"Yes, I do. I'll send it right over. It'll take a few hours before I can get you a projected course. I hope that's ok."

"It is. Thank you."

Evelyn ended the call, her mind spinning with possibilities about her brother. Meanwhile, only a few hundred feet away, another crisis was unfolding.

THE BIRDS IN THE TREE to his right drew Blake's attention. A mother had just delivered nourishment into the eager beaks of her chirping offspring, their tiny bodies pulsating with newfound life.

Suddenly, the horrific crunch of steel upon steel and the screeching of rubber and smashing of glass drowned out all other sounds. As he returned his focus to the intersection, the blur of a concrete truck slamming into the SUV permeated his view.

Holy shit!

The collision unleashed a devastating and violent force. The sheer inertia of the heavy truck tore the SUV apart as if it were nothing more than a tin can. Upon impact, the fuel tank erupted, sending a searing fireball soaring into the sky—a sight both horrifying and grotesque.

He took off at a full sprint toward the accident when his instincts flashed him back to reality.

This was a professional hit. She's dead. They're going after Anders next.

Blake stiffened his legs and stopped. The chaos and frenzy were tangible. He returned to the hotel, running as fast as his legs could move. Onlookers from the café had leaped to their feet from their relaxing meals. Some ran toward the devastation to render aid. Screams filled the air. As he approached the front entrance, the initial sound of the explosion filled his ears. Instinctually, he knew what was happening before the glass blew out the establishment's front windows. The force of the concussion wave struck him with pitiless intensity, abruptly sending him crashing to the ground. During the chaos, he could sense the scorching heat of the flames, their fiery tendrils reaching out like the sinister claws of a dragon as it expelled its hellish breath, stretching through the hotel's entrance and shattering its once pristine facade.

In the chaotic aftermath, the blaring car alarms and piercing screams of the injured and bystanders managed to break through the veil of temporary deafness and ringing in his ears. With a determined effort, Blake rolled over, propping himself on his left elbow, taking in the devastating scene before him.

A thick plume of black smoke ascended into the sky, resembling a haunting tower of death. It was a grim reminder of the lives lost - his colleague, Dave. The innocent bystanders, and Anders, the person he had sworn to protect. Their absence weighed on his heart, amplifying the gravity of the situation.

The acrid stench of explosives and burning materials filled his nostrils, triggering a flood of memories he had desperately tried to bury. It was a scent that evoked a mixture of anguish, regret, and painful recollections, threatening to consume him amid this harrowing experience.

Amidst the disorder and devastation, he grappled with the enormity of the tragedy, as the sights, sounds, and smells merged into a memorable symphony of sorrow and despair.

OPPOSITE THE GRASSY knoll, concealed behind tinted glass in the confines of his car, Nazir smiled with greedy satisfaction at the macabre spectacle delivered by his hand. Satisfied with his completed work and hearing the approaching sirens, he shifted the Mercedes into drive and slowly left the area.

19

Geneva, Switzerland
June 25th 09:00 (08:00 UTC)

The President and Veronica found themselves ensconced within the plush confines of "The Beast," the Presidential limousine, gliding along Route de Ferney. The scent of fresh leather upholstery and the faint hint of polished mahogany from the limo's elegant interior created a comforting yet sober atmosphere.

A phalanx of Secret Service agents, stern-faced and vigilant, formed a protective cocoon around them in their black SUVs. Their journey from Geneva Airport to the meeting location was fleeting, set to conclude in under five minutes.

Rebecca let out a soft sigh, her breath fogging a patch on the thick bulletproof glass before it disappeared into nothingness. She turned her gaze from the outside world to Veronica, her eyes reflecting an odd mix of regret and resignation. "I always find it disheartening our drive to the UN Building is so brief. This is such an enchanting city. They rob us of its beauty by not allowing us to explore more."

She gestured towards the window where sunlight was streaming through the tinted glass, casting dancing shadows across their tailored suits. The warmth seeping in was gentle on this radiant day.

"Look at the view out there." Her voice held a tinge of melancholy. "The sun painting everything gold outside while we're confined within this metal beast." The hum of tires against asphalt resonated throughout the car's cabin as they moved along. "And soon enough, we'll find ourselves trapped inside another structure - surrounded by people I'd rather not engage with—all to stave off World War Three."

Veronica smiled. "You have a way with words, Madam President."

"Ha!" She slapped her hand on her knee. "That's a bullshit compliment if I ever heard one." She paused and judged Veronica's response. "I trust you slept okay on Airforce One last night?"

"Oh yes. I've got to be honest with you. If I were president, I'd want to serve two terms just for the plane. The shower is exquisite. I appreciate you allowing me to use it."

Rebecca leaned toward her. "I'm going to tell you a little secret."

Veronica moved as close as her seat belt would allow.

Her boss smiled. "I agree with you."

THE VIBRANT COLORS of tulips, roses, and other blooming flowers had caught Jasmine's attention. Broad beds of blossoming plants and decorative bushes lined the road leading to the Palais des Nations—originally built for the League of Nations in the 1930s.

Although the official building of the UN is in New York, this structure has served hundreds of meetings, galas, and celebrations over the years. It offers stunning views of Lake Geneva and the majestic mountain scape only the Alps can offer.

Birds chirped, their joyful melodic songs echoing as they perched in the lush green trees. The temperature, a pleasant seventeen degrees Celsius, created an ideal atmosphere. With a gentle breeze caressing her, she was at ease in her tailored suit coat, which not only exuded sophistication but also discreetly concealed the formidable firepower it held within.

Jasmine Gibson was in charge of the advance team for the Secret Service. Their primary purpose was to conduct thorough assessments and preparations before the POTUS arrived at specific locations. This included understanding the location's potential threats and risks, detecting escape routes, assessing critical entry points, and identifying any weaknesses in local security. Since her first term, she was on President Pennington's advance team and became elevated to the Advance Agent upon re-election.

John Postlethwaite, who joined the detail three weeks earlier, approached her. "Hey, when is The Melungeon expected to arrive? It's only five minutes from the airport and she landed hours ago."

"The meetings aren't supposed to start until oh-nine-thirty and not everyone else has arrived." He glanced at his watch. "She doesn't stick around for anyone, does she?"

Jasmine stole his attention with her green eyes. "The Melungeon waits for no one. They wait for her."

He chuckled. "I understand. Shows who is in charge."

She glanced at the horizon and furrowed her brow. "Exactly."

He adjusted the wire for his earpiece. "Hey, what the fuck is a Melungeon anyway, and how'd she get such a codename?"

She walked past her colleague toward the barriers on the approaching road, brushing his shoulder with hers as she passed. "They're people rooted deep in Appalachia's history. Most keep to themselves and live back in the hallows between the mountains." She chuckled. "Of course, up there, they call 'em hollers. But, anyway, they're a mix of immigrants from Northern and Central Europe and Sub-Saharan Africa."

He poked at a small rock in the road with his foot. "Hmph, that's interesting."

She nodded in agreement. "Yeah, it is. In the mid-eighteen hundreds, they befriended and bred with the local Indians. The majority of them were Cherokee."

She strolled further along the road, reaching the barricades, and turned back. "Do you hear anything?"

John shrugged. "No. POTUS came from that part of Virginia, didn't she?"

"Indeed, she did."

"Who thought to call her Melungeon? I mean, it's a kind of fucked-up name. They sound like a bunch of inbred hillbillies."

Her eyes narrowed and her jaw clenched. "She did, and she picked it to honor me."

His nose scrunched as he scratched the back of his head. "You? How so?"

"Because I'm Melungeon, you stupid fuck."

His face turned scarlet as he stared at his shoes.

The radio on her shoulder squawked.

"Jasmine. I'm—I'm so—"

"Shut up!" She pressed the button on her microphone. "Go ahead."

She and John both listened to the transmission. Their eyes shifted as they took in the information being relayed.

She snapped her fingers at her partner, whose face was still red with embarrassment. "Contact the Swiss Guard. Get them to reinforce the barricades while I call POTUS."

She released a deep sigh. "God, I hate these assholes."

AS THE CARAVAN NAVIGATED the picturesque Route des Morillons, lined with lush trees and vibrant shrubs, 'The Beast' came to an unexpected halt. Veronica's eyes widened in astonishment as she glanced out of the window, only to be met with a startling sight.

A disheveled, yet determined woman stood before them, her naked form displaying the words "STOP BIG OIL" in vivid red across her broad, bare chest.

Within seconds, four Secret Service agents sprang into action and pried her away from the side of the car, restraining her in handcuffs.

The glass divider separating the driver from the passengers slid open. POTUS cocked her head. "I'm guessing you're going to tell me this is part of what caused this slowdown."

Julian Spencer's face occupied the divided area. "I'm afraid a group of protestors have blocked the road."

She wrinkled her nose. "Can't they move them?"

"Negative. Some of them have glued themselves to the pavement."

She shook her head in exasperation, her palm meeting the smooth leather seat with a resounding slap. "Oh, for fuck's sake!" Pennington glanced to her right where the agents were lifting the protesting woman to her feet, once again displaying her opposing viewpoint across her saggy breasts. "This is those stop oil assholes, isn't it?"

"By the looks of it. I believe so."

"Okay, well, fuck them. Imbeciles like this will not disrupt my day with their—their foolishness. Turn around."

"Ma'am?"

"You heard me. Prep the choppers. We'll fly."

"Yes, Ma'am." He turned to shut the divider.

"Julian. You tell the pilot to fly all three birds low and slow over these idiots. Open the throttle, too. I want to piss 'em off and give them a whiff of my aviation exhaust fumes."

He grinned. "Ten-four, Ma'am."

THREE IDENTICAL HELICOPTERS made their way to the UN Building after she gave the order to annoy the activists. After arriving at the destination and being given an "all clear", two decoys flew back to the airport while the one carrying the President, and her envoy went to the helipad. Marine One had slowed and hovered as the landing gear deployed.

President Pennington settled into an opulent, overstuffed white leather chair across from Veronica. To the President's right, on the bench seat, was her trusted Chief of Staff, Logan Cash. With a subtle pucker of her lips, the President's narrowed gaze drifted towards the window, capturing a fleeting glimpse of the world outside before refocusing on Veronica. She glanced at her watch. The constant hum of the chopper's blades permeated the cabin, creating an audible backdrop to their conversation.

"Well, today isn't starting too well. It's already a crappy day because of the circumstances of why we're here. I hope it doesn't get any worse."

Veronica's phone buzzed, and with a glance at the caller ID, she held up a hand. "Excuse me, I need to answer this."

She disconnected the call as the President was finishing a discussion with Logan. Biting her upper lip while she twisted her necklace with her finger, she contemplated a way to break the news.

Sensing something was amiss, Rebecca leaned in. "Director? What is it?"

"Remember when you said you hoped the day didn't get worse?"

"Oh, for God's sake." She reclined in her chair, closed her eyes, and let out an exasperated sigh. "What is it?"

"MacKay called. The agent I—"

"Yes, yes, I know who he is. What's happened?"

"In a nutshell, our only lead is dead."

Straightening in her seat, her eyes grew wide. "Details! I need to understand what's happening, so I don't go into this meeting blind."

From behind her, one of the crew members of the HMX-1 Nighthawks prepared to open the door.

The President twisted around. "Hold on Calvin. Not yet." Turning back to Veronica, she nodded. "Go on."

After a deep breath, her eyes clamped tight before continuing. "Blake was at the location in Bergen, Norway, where the witness to the attack on the Danish oil rig was to describe to the sketch artist so they could run it through the Interpol database."

"Right. Dr. Lindman, if I remember from the brief."

"Yes, Ma'am. Anyhow, he left the hotel to greet her and when she was a block away, a concrete truck t-boned her SUV. Nobody in the vehicle survived."

Pennington gasped. "Oh, my God."

Veronica nodded. "I know. It gets worse. As Blake turned to go back into the hotel, an explosive device detonated and killed everyone on the main floor of the building. Anders, the detective from Interpol, and one of our own, all perished."

The president's brow scrunched. "And this happened when?"

"Uh—yesterday."

"Director, why are you finding out about this now?"

Still in shock from the news, Veronica's face was pale. "MacKay. He was concussed from the explosion. He wanted his mind to clear and gather some intel before calling."

"I see."

Peering from the helicopter window again, she was met with a scene pulsating with excitement. Swiss officials stood in perfect alignment—their faces filled with anticipation of her arrival. The international flags behind them danced in unison with the soft breeze, a silent homage to her imminent presence.

"Madam President?"

She turned to face Veronica. The blank stare on her face said it all. Out of respect for her boss, she allowed her a moment to allow it all to sink in.

A sergeant from the Marine Helicopter Squadron approached her from behind.

"Madam President, they're waiting for you."

"Oh. Yes. Thank you." She stood. "Miss Slocum, how's MacKay? Physically and mentally?"

"Other than his raging headache, he doesn't let me know those things. But he said he is awaiting your orders."

"Have him remain where he is for now. We may gather some intel from this meeting today, and I want him in the region if something arises. I assume Interpol is going to screen through the destruction and determine if they can get a signature on this explosive device?"

"SOP Ma'am."

"Excellent. Well. Put on a cheerful face and let's go see if we can't diffuse this situation before it becomes a global catastrophe. It can't get any worse, right? Oh, shit, I hope I didn't jinx us."

TWENTY MINUTES LATER than the scheduled time, the leader of the free world entered the conference room reserved for smaller parties, followed by her Chief of Staff, Logan Cash, and her Director of Clandestine Affairs. Secretary of State, Terrance Thayer was on assignment in Japan.

The room's walls boasted exquisite murals masterfully crafted by the renowned artist Karl Hügin. Complementing the surrounding scenes, intricate woodwork added a touch of timeless elegance to the room. The scent of tobacco intertwined with the rich aroma of cognac, evoking a sense of history and the weight of important decisions made decades ago. The well-worn leather chairs, witnesses to countless discussions and negotiations, carried a unique aura, whispering tales of diplomacy and camaraderie.

"Apologies for being late. Please know it wasn't intentional." She extended her hand to the first person she came to. "Lara, so good to see you again. I wish it were under better circumstances. I trust your excellent police force is handling our protesting friends out there?"

The graying, middle-aged woman, sporting a red pantsuit and waist-length jacket, accepted her hand and returned her smile. "Good morning, Madam President. Yes, they're clearing the streets as we speak. They're an annoying bunch of clowns. If only they'd understand their actions pit people against them rather than making them willing to listen."

The President smiled. "I'll call them fools and leave it there."

The U.S. leader and her staff made the rounds and dispersed with formal pleasantries before taking their seats around the table. Logan sat to the President's right, and the opposite was Veronica. Next to Logan was Switzerland's Minister of Foreign Affairs, Lara Krieger, followed by the Russian Ambassador to Denmark, Alexi Kozlov, and Minister of General Affairs of Norway, Heidi Lund. To Veronica's left sat the Danish Prime Minister, Harold Rasmussen, and then the Canadian PM, Merrick Toussaint. Plush leather chairs against the wall accommodated the other staff members.

After the Swiss representative brought the meeting to order, she motioned for President Pennington to speak and handed her the gavel.

"Thank you all for being here. I understand the gravity of this situation speaks for itself." She nodded to her COS, who stood from his chair and began distributing folders marked 'Classified,' in bold, red letters. "Instead of pointing accusatory fingers and laying blame, we can optionally spend our time addressing what appears as an act of war. However, I have faith in our collective intelligence and believe we can all substantiate our innocence in each instance. Am I mistaken in such a belief?"

A rumbling of confirmations came from around the table, along with nods of agreement.

Alexi addressed Denmark's PM. "Prime Minister Rasmussen. On behalf of the Russian Federation, you have our condolences on such a tragic loss of life. Rest assured; our agencies are investigating this to their fullest potential to discover who is guilty of this heinous act. You have our full support."

Merrick Toussaint shifted his eyes from the classified folder to the group at the table. "Agreed. We, too, are looking into this. I think we can all concur that none of us is responsible. But the burning question is who and why are they doing this?"

President Pennington nodded. "Well, let's study this and find a common denominator."

The Danish Prime Minister raised his hand. "We can all agree it has something to do with the world oil market. Who would benefit the most from having us in conflict with each other?"

Toussaint chimed in. "You don't think it's OPEC, do you?"

"Ladies and gentlemen, esteemed ministers." The President's gaze swept across the room, capturing the undivided attention of every individual present. "Please understand, my words do not mean to offend anyone here or the countries they represent. However, it is a fact that with oil production, other than the OPEC nations, few can rival the prowess of the United States and our esteemed Russian allies."

She chuckled. "To be blunt, you're not a threat to them. There is no reason they would initiate the start of World War Three. It has to be something deeper."

The gentle hum of a vibrating phone resonated through the air, catching the attention of those sitting at the table. In her periphery, Veronica observed one of the seated staff members behind her rise and approach the grand double doors. As they swung open, a distinguished woman from the Swiss military entered and handed a folder to the staff member, who nodded to the Norwegian Minister.

Heidi Lund pressed both hands on the table to push her chair back. "Pardon me. It seems I have an urgent matter I need to attend to."

The rest spoke among themselves while they allowed her a few minutes to address the issue when the President turned to her intelligence officer.

"I'm going to call on you in a moment to give an update. Do you have any more information on what Mr. MacKay told you this morning?"

She started to answer when a sudden movement from behind the president caught her attention. It was the minister from Norway. She held a manilla folder outstretched over her head, with a scowl across her face.

Shouting above all in the room, she hurried back to the group. "Prime Minister Toussaint!"

Veronica's gut twisted into knots. "Oh God, now what?"

The Canadian PM swiveled in his chair toward the commotion, his expression wide with surprise as she approached him with fire in her eyes.

"What?"

The folder landed on the slick wood surface with a slap. "Explain this! If you did not have anything to do with the bombing in my country yesterday, then why am I receiving intel to the contrary?"

"Don't be absurd." He turned his focus to the folder before him and opened it. Sitting on top of the stack of documents and evidence was a ten-by-twelve color photo of a woman standing outside the hotel minutes ahead of the explosion. It appeared she was talking on her phone.

"I—I don't understand. Who is this person and what does she have to do with us?"

She leaned in and pressed her finger to the photo. "Her name is Evelyn Cathey. A senior agent for your Canadian Intelligence. She exited the hotel and left moments before the explosion killed the one and only witness to the attack on the Thistle oil platform. And don't tell me it was a coincidence."

"Ms. Lund, did it occur to you? Is it possible she was there aiding in the investigation? Perhaps she stepped outside to take the call?"

"Nice try. The director of NIS has already contacted your agency, and they employ no one assigned to investigate this over here. They didn't know this woman was out of the country. It seems you have a rogue agent or someone who has infiltrated your intelligence operation for this coup between our nations."

The Canadian Prime Minister's face turned red. With a clenched fist, he pounded the table and stood. "Enough!" He wagged his finger in her face. "How dare you accuse Canada of being involved with something like this. We also experienced an attack. By your friends to the south, no less. Perhaps you both are in cahoots with each other so you can enjoy all the oil in the North Sea to yourselves."

PM Rasmussen shouted, "What? Don't be ridiculous. We would ne—"

"On the contrary, Mister Rasmussen, assailants in Danish military fatigues boarded—"

The insulted leader shot to his feet. "They weren't *our* men!"

"Excuse me, I am talking! Men wearing clothes with identifying markings from *your* country infiltrated our ship and killed everyone on board!"

The President glared at all who were arguing. "Ladies and gentlemen. Please."

The Danish PM shot back. "What about your soldiers attacking the U.S. plant?"

Toussaint's eyes narrowed as he shook his head. "Oh, complete rubbish. You know damn well it wasn't us."

The gavel banged on the table four times. "Gentlemen!"

Rasmussen spread his arms while puffing out his chest. "So, the soldiers in Canadian uniforms aren't yours, but the ones in my country's uniforms are ours? Pardon me Merrick, but fuck you!"

"Gentlemen!" She forcefully rapped three more times on the unyielding surface, each strike resonating with increasing intensity. The resounding clash of wood reverberated throughout the chamber, its echoes bouncing off the walls.

"Fuck me?" His eyes were wide with rage.

Minister Lund chimed in. "You leave me no choice. I'm afraid I'm issuing a bolo on her for her arrest, and questioning."

"What? You're insane! Get out of my way, you stupid hag!" With his left arm, Merrick pushed the Norwegian Minister out of his way and pointed to his Danish aggressor. "And fuck you, you son of a bitch!"

The President pressed a button on her necklace, signaling her detail to help.

She slammed the gavel on the table no less than ten times. "GENTLEMAN!"

U.S. Secret Service, Canadian PMPD, the Norwegian Statsministerns Kontor, and the other nation's protective details entered the room. They rushed to the two men, about to engage in fisticuffs, and restrained both while President Pennington tried to calm them.

"Shut up!" When the voices subsided, she continued. "Enough of this. This is exactly what whoever is doing this is hoping for. Now stop it. Let's all be civil and work through this."

The Canadian Prime Minister, still breathing heavily, shifted his eyes to the U.S. leader and nodded. The Danish leader tugged at his jacket and returned to his seat.

"Mr. Toussaint. I suggest you contact your head of intelligence and find out why this woman was over here and inform us all as soon as possible."

He poured himself a glass of water and chugged it. "Yes, Madam President. I'll work on it and have the information for you moments after I do." He waved one of his staff toward him. A young woman in her late twenties with dark hair pulled back in a ponytail approached. He leaned toward her and spoke loud enough so they all could hear. "Get the director on the phone. I want to speak to him immediately."

"Yes, sir."

As she trotted off, President Pennington stood. "We've had an emotional meeting so far. I believe we're all in need of a distraction. Let's take a thirty-minute break. It should be ample time to obtain the answers we seek."

As everyone disbursed, she leaned into her director by her side. "Call MacKay and let him know what's going on. He must find her before the Norwegian police do."

Veronica nodded. "I'm on it."

MINISTER LUND STEPPED out of the hall and into a small conference room, where the stench of cigar smoke hit her like a brick wall. Her breath was still heavy from her earlier engagement with the Canadian Prime Minister, and each inhalation felt as if she were licking an ashtray. She fought to suppress the rising urge to vomit, struggling to regain her composure in the oppressive atmosphere.

She entered her contact for Norway's Ministry of Justice, which was in charge of the PST or Police Security Service. They're the group responsible for domestic intelligence and security. Unlike regular police, they operated directly under orders from the MOJ. After several deep breaths, her nerves had calmed, and she called Bendik Ovesen, the man in charge.

"We have a problem."

"What's the issue?"

"The bombing yesterday. We have a suspect. A rogue Canadian Intelligence officer was seen leaving right before the explosion. CSIS doesn't know anyone investigating the attack on the oil platform."

The man on the other end of the call shifted in his seat. The sound of creaking wood and worn leather came through the phone. "Do you think she's covering something up?"

Digging through her pants pocket, she retrieved a tube containing some aspirin. Placing the phone between her face and shoulder, she pried open the lid, shook out two pills, and popped them into her mouth. "I don't know." She took a sealed bottled water from the center of the table, opened it, and washed down the medicine. "It could be revenge over the first attack on some ship the Canadians had leased for some oil exploration they were on."

"So, what do you want me to do, take her out?"

Taking another sip of water, her eyes danced around the room. A picture of the Matterhorn loomed over the buffet perched against the opposite wall. "No. But I wouldn't be opposed if you wounded her. It might give her some incentive to cooperate and answer our questions."

He cleared his throat. "You sure? She could be our scapegoat."

Glancing at her watch, she felt the weight of such a decision press down on her, like a mountain resting on her chest, stifling her breath and clouding her judgment. "Yeah, I'm sure. I want to punish her. Go get her."

20

175 Miles NNE of the Faroe Islands, North Atlantic
June 25th 08:30 (07:30 UTC)

Both of the Atlas diesel engines slowed to a near stop. The 220-foot vessel was custom-built for oceanographic research.

The mode of transportation was a stark departure from the luxurious mega yacht he typically frequented. Prince Salib spared no expense, investing a further ten million dollars, to enhance its seaworthiness and incorporate lavish amenities uncommon on similar ships.

Besides the ship's opulent royal stateroom and saloon, the most impressive feature was the two-thousand square feet of clear deck and the Nautilus 5,000lb crane and 13,000lb aft-mounted A-frame over a 14ft wide sloped stern ramp.

The bridge bobbed delicately, as if in sync with the rhythmic ebb and flow of the North Atlantic waves. The horizon rose and fell in perfect synchronicity with the vessel. Captain Sparkman let his binoculars hang from their lanyard around his neck and turned to his boss.

"We've reached the coordinates you gave us, Your Highness."

He nodded. "Excellent. And how deep is it here?"

"Twenty-five-hundred and fifty meters."

Salib pressed his fingertips together and formed a triangle. "Hmmm, how unfortunate. I had hoped for something closer to the depth we'll face at the drill site."

"I'm sorry, Your Highness. We'd have to travel more than another thousand miles due north before we can reach waters as deep as that."

"Yes, I understand."

The sound of tearing paper from a printer behind them filled their ears. One of the crew handed the captain the information. His eyes danced across the sheet as he nodded.

"Excellent news. The sky is promising, hinting at favorable conditions ahead. It's too deep to anchor, so the alternative is to keep the engines on and man the helm. Do you know how long we will be here?"

Salib placed his hand on the captain's shoulders and squeezed. "As long as it takes, Captain. Success is the leading factor. We will not let the length of the visit dictate to us when we are to be finished."

He turned and stepped outside, greeted by the refreshing sea air. The sun's bright rays reflected off the water, causing him to squint. He reached for his sunglasses and put them on, shielding his eyes from the dazzling glare. Before him was a steep set of stairs. As he descended to the main deck, he spotted Dr. Khalid Fadel.

"Sabah al-khair, Doctor."

The man spun around. He was in his mid-fifties with finger-length black hair parted on the side with an unnatural, dyed tone. His pencil-thin mustache rested above minuscule lips. His green dress shirt accentuated his olive-toned skin.

"Ah, Your Highness." He extended his arm. "Yes, good morning to you. Thank you for choosing me for this operation. I am curious though, what are we looking for in this area? As far as I know, no sunken ships or other treasures are nearby." He leaned in and smiled. "Or is there a surprise to tell me about, huh?"

They shook hands. "No. I'm afraid it isn't anything quite so exciting. You are here to pilot an HOV and test a drilling apparatus attached to the front."

His brow furrowed. "Hmm, well, you've aroused my curiosity."

"Yes. I'm sure I have. Come." He outstretched his arm. "Let me introduce you to Doctor Wyrick. The brilliant engineer who put this together."

"But of course. It would be a pleasure to meet him."

A smile creased Salib's face.

MADISON CONCENTRATED on the laptop's screen and brushed a wayward hair from her face for the third time. She placed her pen in her mouth and redid her ponytail in her signature orange scrunchie. Chains rattled as they flowed through the pulley systems on the crane in preparation for launching the submersible.

"Satish, can you double-check the coupler near the hull to ensure it's tight? I'd hate to lose the laser on the test run."

"Yes, Ma'am. It would make the mission suck if we did."

A laugh escaped her breath at his response. A familiar voice filled her ears from behind.

"Doctor Wyrick. It's pleasing to have your presence on this fine day."

When she turned, she glimpsed her boss accompanied by a shorter gentleman wearing khakis and a green shirt approaching. Forming a salute to shield the rising sun, she forced a cheerful grin. "Good morning, Your Majesty." She glanced at the man to her right and wondered why he was frowning. "Who's your friend?"

"Ah, yes. This is Dr. Khalid Fadel from the Oceanographic Institute in Saudi Arabia. He will be piloting the sub for our tests."

She offered a greeting. "It's a pleasure to make your acquaintance."

He hesitated and turned his focus to the man in charge. "A woman?"

She withdrew the offer. The smile faded from her lips. "Is there a problem?"

His expression was void of all emotion. His eyes were full of contempt. "I was not expecting this." He refocused his attention on his host. "I am surprised you employed a female for such an important endeavor, Your Highness. Was there nobody more qualified for this you could have hired?"

Her ire reached its boiling point. Her left hand still shielding the sun's light, she quipped back. "Excuse me?"

He stiffened as his nose scrunched. "No offense, but you are a woman. I can understand—"

Her right hand rolled into a fist. "I said, excuse me."

The prince moved closer to her to form a divider between the pair. "Doctors! *kafā!* Enough!" He stepped back and tilted his head toward the grumbling scientist. "I can assure you she is more than qualified." A sly grin formed on his lips. "Perhaps she has more credentials than you, Khalid. I caution you to take care in choosing your words and don't make hasty decisions, only because of her gender. I would hate for other opportunities for you to slip away because of a simple misunderstanding."

Madison felt the man's anger rising, evidenced by his olive complexion turning a deep red. She stayed muted, taking in the prince's concept of justice and growing to admire it as he defended her.

"Now, Doctor Wyrick. As you can see, we have stopped and are at the coordinates you requested. I am curious. The depth of the sea. It is nowhere near where we will be when we begin to drill. Is it not important at this time?"

"Excellent question, Your Highness, and the answer is no. Our main reason for being here is to test the performance of the drilling apparatus on the type of rock we'll be breaking through. The ocean floor here most closely resembles the geologic formation at our final target. I want to observe how the submarine's hull reacts to the intense heat created by the laser."

Dr. Fadel blinked and cleared his throat. "The near-freezing water temperature will make sure the hull is fine."

She smiled and nodded. "I concur with your opinion, doctor, but this laser boils the water almost at once, so cross your fingers and hope the deep currents keep the cold water washing over it."

Salib removed his sunglasses and rubbed his eye. "How deep are you going to drill before you have the information you need?"

"I don't have a precise number, Your Highness, but it should be less than a thousand feet. Perhaps five or six hundred will be enough."

He replaced his Ray-Bans on his face. "Okay, so when do we start this mission?"

"Ten AM." She locked eyes with her new friend. "Doctor Fadel?" She pointed to a young Indian woman standing by the sub. "The person over there is Zaanjar. She has a PhD from MIT. I trust that's acceptable to you. She built the laser and knows every detail about it. And that young *woman* is going to teach you how to use it. I would suggest listening intently."

He nodded and walked over to where she was making final adjustments to the drill. When he was out of earshot, Madison turned to the prince. "Thank you."

He waved his hand in dismissal. "Not necessary. Some in our culture don't have the respect for women they deserve. I'll allow you to get back to work."

She started to walk away, but stopped. "I was going to get some breakfast first. Would—you like to join me?"

"Thank you, but no. I have tasks I need to address. I'll see you back here at ten o'clock."

AFTER EATING, MADISON went to the transom to take one last walk around the submersible and run through the sequence to power up the drill. Satisfied all items on her checklist were in perfect working order, she walked to the command room. It was here where she would monitor the descent and the mission. In the room, sitting on a metal table, was Sam, a Croatian scientist specializing in underwater acoustics. His legs swung freely as he sat chatting with Zaanjar.

"Hi Sam, how are you getting on with readying the hydrophonic mics?"

He gave the "OK," sign with his fingers. "They are a go. I can listen to everything the sub does and should be able to detect when the rock starts disintegrating."

Although she nodded, she appeared anxious. "That's fine, but I'm concerned about the hull. Will you hear any buckling, or hear the hull giving way?"

"Oh, a hundred percent. Sounds like those resonate through the water like a thunderclap. But—the submersible is rated for depths well beyond where we'll be. Why the concern?"

"I only want to verify we'll operate and be as safe as possible. We take technology for granted sometimes, and it eases my mind to ensure everything goes smoothly."

The door opened and Dr. Fadel walked in. "I'll be entering the submersible in a moment. I trust you know what you're doing?"

Madison's eyes narrowed, a subtle arch forming in her brow as she tilted her head to the side in response. "Of course."

"Excellent. I wouldn't want you to make any mistakes. I will be in charge of the descent. Expect me to go about ninety-eight feet per minute. It should take me an hour to reach the sea floor. Do everything I say. There is no room for error."

Madison turned to face him. "Doctor, we'll also be monitoring every aspect of this dive. If I detect any potential problem, you'll be the first to know. You *must* pay attention to me if we run into any issues."

He chuckled. "I've been doing this for more years than you've been alive. I'll pay attention to my voice of reason rather than listening to some woman."

He closed the door before she could respond. Her mouth stood agape as she turned to her colleagues. "Do you believe this arrogant jerk?"

Sam's lips scrunched as he nodded. "Yep, he *is* an asshole." He hopped off the table. "I'll be at my station and tell you if I hear funny noises."

She opened the door for him. "Does that include anything Dr. Dick says?"

They all laughed, and Madison felt a bit of anxiety slip away.

THEY WERE FIFTY-FIVE minutes into the descent and there had been little radio communication between them except for the required intervals every three atmospheres, or one hundred feet.

"Atlas, this is Nautilus one. I have a visual on the bottom."

Madison leaned into her microphone. "Excellent news, doctor. The coordinates for your drilling—"

"I have them. Turning eighteen degrees and heading that way. ETA is 5 minutes."

She monitored the hull pressure as her thoughts wandered.

I hope this isn't the guy working the sub when we get to the real drill site. I'm not sure if I can handle his attitude.

Should I say something to the prince? No? Perhaps? I dunno. This guy's an asshole. I'll be able to do so much with those twenty-five million dollars. And I will get it. Nothing will stop me from finishing this project.

Hey! I'll get a suite at Neyland Stadium. I can't wait until football season. Stupid Alabama. God, I hope we beat them this year now that Saban is gone. Where are my checkered overalls?

The voice crackling over the speaker interrupted her musing. "Drilling commencing."

"What? There are procedural steps you need to—"

"I've completed those. Now, at what depth are we going for this test?"

She flipped through a chart. "I've decided we're going to at least six hundred feet. A small percentage of what we believe the well will be."

"Affirmative."

Madison toggled a switch on her panel to connect to the other room. "Sam, he started drilling. Keep your ears peeled for anything unusual."

"Copy. I am receiving a lot of noise from the rock breaking, but no problem. I can filter most of it out."

The next 45 minutes were uneventful. A red light with an intermittent chime stole her complete attention. The hull temperature had risen far above normal operating conditions.

She flipped the switch on her panel back to speak to the man operating the sub. "Doctor Fadel? Can you check your hull temp reading, please?"

"In a minute. I'm getting close to our desired depth."

"No doctor. Now. Do you have any warning bells sounding?"

The ensuing ten seconds were an eternity.

"It's fine. I can't hear anything with the sound of this damn drill and these headphones on.

Two more minutes. I'm almost there. Five hundred and fifty feet."

Another alarm went off. Something was wrong with the hull integrity. Madison suspected the heat from the laser drill.

She pressed the call-out button to make an announcement the entire ship would hear. "Prince Salib, please come to the sub-control room at once."

Back to her headset, she pleaded. "Mister Fadel! I need you to stop!"

The door to the control room burst open.

"What is it? What is happening?"

Madison removed her headphones. "This person you have operating the sub. He's jeopardizing this mission and the submersible."

His eyes went wide. "What? How?"

"He's not listening to me. I need him to stop drilling."

Placing both palms on the console, he leaned in and inspected the gauges and screens. "What's going on?"

She pointed to the hull temp warning. "The immediate heat the drill emanates and the instantaneous cooling from the cold water has created stress points. Too much back and forth. It's like bending an aluminum can over and over until, in the end, it tears in half. The hull is weakening, and it will be catastrophic if he doesn't stop drilling."

The prince snapped his fingers. "Your headset. Now!"

She handed them to him. "Doctor! Stop drilling immediately!"

"Dammit, woman! Hold on! Ha Ha. Five ninety! Five ninety-five and a half. Almost there. Ninety-nine."

"Imbecile! This is Prince Salib, and I order you to stop this instant. Do you understand?"

He removed his headset and flipped a switch so they both could hear.

They waited for him to proclaim victory. But it never came.

"Doctor?"

Nothing but static greeted them from the other end.

"Doctor!"

Sam burst into the control room, his eyes brimming with worry and regret. The soft glow from the portal behind him reflected in his rimless glasses. He stood there, hesitant, as if seeking permission to speak.

Anxiety swirled around her, tightening its grip on her conscious mind. She sensed the truth already but needed to hear it from Sam's lips. Her voice trembled with anticipation.

"Sam! What did you hear?"

His gaze shifted to the floor, and his voice was almost inaudible as he mumbled under his breath. "We had an event."

Confusion filled her voice as she repeated. "A what? An event?"

His eyes met hers, then to the prince, revealing the weight of his words. "Yes. An event."

Impatience mingled with anger, and she couldn't contain her frustration for another moment. "What the fuck does—"

Cutting her off, Sam uttered the word that sent a shiver down everyone's spine. "An implosion."

Shock washed over her, her eyes staring in disbelief and reflecting the devastation within her soul. Despite having a gut feeling before he entered the room, hearing it spoken aloud solidified her greatest fear.

"An implosion?"

Sam nodded; his voice was heavy with sorrow. "An implosion. Yes. The sub. It's... It's gone."

21

175 Miles NNE of the Faroe Islands, North Atlantic
June 25th 10:51 (09:51 UTC)

All three stood in stunned silence as the prince closed his eyes, his emotions overwhelming him. His fists clenched so tight; his knuckles paled. After a moment, he released his grip and turned to face Sam. "Leave us."

Sam's brows furrowed as he sighed a breath of relief. After a glance and nod to his co-worker, he spun around as if escaping a major ass chewing. He slammed the door as he left. Her anxiety rose with each fading step.

She inhaled as if to speak. Only to be stopped by a raised index finger inches from her face.

"Silence! Do not say a word to me."

With a calculated stride, he clasped his hands behind his back and advanced menacingly towards her. His chin dipped, casting a shadow over his narrowed eyes, glinting with an unsettling intensity. Frozen in place, Madison stood statuesque as her fear gripped her like invisible shackles.

He circled her. From her rear, the weight of his gaze bore into her, searing through her skin and leaving an indelible mark on her senses. She could feel the blood pumping through her veins. Her pressure elevated from the stress.

He turned back to face her—his jaw rigidly set. As he cleared his throat, an atmosphere of anticipation hung in the silence, as if awaiting the unleashing of a formidable scolding. The intensity of his stare and the ferocity of his presence felt like a dragon's fire, destroying everything in its path, scorching the surrounding air.

Locking eyes with her, she braced herself for the expected eruption of emotion. Instead, his words flowed forth with serene tranquility, reminiscent of a gentle ebb and flow of a wave upon the tranquil waters of a Tennessee lake.

"What happened?"

Madison's anxiety lifted, cascading away like a delicate veil caught in a refreshing breeze.

"You were here. I told him to stop drilling."

His eyes closed as he shook his head. "No!" He took two steps back and placed his hand on his chin. She could sense his ire mounting. "I mean. What the hell occurred?" His volume and intensity were rising. "What the fuck happened? How and why did the sub—the one *you* built? The one *you* were in charge of. How could you let this happen? Why did it implode?"

He started to pace as she searched her mind for an answer that wouldn't make him want to kill her. "I won't know for sure unless we can get some of the debris."

He continued to pace, now rubbing the back of his neck.

Madison knew the problem. "I suspect it was the laser."

The prince stopped in his tracks and turned to her. "The laser? Clarify."

Panic set in. Her voice trembled. "I—I don't know. I think it—"

He closed the gap between them in under a second. His anger was in full view, his volume elevating with every syllable. "Unacceptable doctor! You know what it is. Tell me."

She flinched as each word stabbed at her. "It was too close. The laser."

He pursed his lips as he stared her down. "To what? The seafloor? The hull? Explain."

"Yes, the hull. It should have been mounted further away. The heat from the drill and the cold water over and over created a weak spot on the side of the submersible. After so much, it couldn't take it and failed, causing the implosion."

He sneered at her. "You should have known." His finger raised and directed toward her face. "That was *your* responsibility. This, now—" He opened his arms. "Colossal disaster is your responsibility."

Her eyes went wide. "My fault?"

"Yes!"

She pointed to herself. "Oh, no you don't! You're not going to stick this on me! You heard me telling him to stop!"

His brow scrunched. "That's not what I'm referring to, and you know it. I'm talking about the design." He stood and clapped his hand back into his other palm. Each strike emphasized every word. "The fucking schematics, doctor."

The pressure behind her eyes continued to rise. Her cheeks felt flush. She could not hold back any longer. Slapping the cold steel table, she screamed. "Aughhhh! You rushed me! I told you and explained we needed time to ensure we got this right. But nooooo, you had to have this damn sub done now! *You're* to blame, and now you're fucked!"

His eyes widened, then narrowed as his jaw clenched.

Madison immediately knew she had gone too far.

Oh-Oh.

He hurried towards her; his movements fueled by a surge of adrenaline. Without warning, the back of his hand sliced through the air, striking her cheek with a brutal force, sending her sprawling. The impact was so powerful it lifted her off her feet, leaving her stunned and disoriented.

As she lay on the steel deck plate, massaging her throbbing face, he loomed above her, a menacing figure. His arm remained coiled, poised to deliver another punishing blow, his intent clear and unyielding.

"You do not talk to me in such a manner! I've killed men for less."

She resisted the urge to wipe the spit off her face. His presence continued to hang over her.

"I suggest you obtain a way to get us back on schedule, doctor, or you'll suffer the same fate as the late Doctor Fadel."

The prince stormed out of the room, leaving Madison to her thoughts and failure.

Once she rose off the floor, she gathered her composure and returned to her quarters, slumping disconsolately on the bed. After a few minutes of self-pity, her mind turned to her brother. Feeling emotionally drained, the boat's gentle rocking lulled her into a light sleep.

She was four years old when her mother brought her younger sibling home from the hospital. He came into the world with an unusual affliction that caused his legs to develop in reverse, each foot positioned askew. One foot was noticeably more skewed than the other.

Growing up had been an arduous journey, marked not only by the relentless taunting of other children and the daily hurdles of life but also by the repeated let-downs of emerging technology, holding the promise of correcting his legs and granting him a semblance of normalcy.

These assurances, however, only left behind a trail of shattered dreams, as they failed to materialize into anything tangible, and life went on.

Then, two years ago, a friend who graduated from MIT contacted her. He had been working with other scientists at a bio-engineering company, striving to develop innovative technologies in artificial hips, knees, shoulders, and ankles. He felt Madison's brother was an excellent candidate for some of their new implants. Unfortunately, because it was experimental, insurance would not pay the outlay. They worked to get grants and even set up a go-fund-me page. To date, they have raised over one million dollars, but it was only around a third of the actual expense. The biotech firm agreed to pitch in another million, but they were still shy over seven figures to cover the procedure. And then, after the surgery, was the grueling physical therapy. They expected the recovery would be two years and another six to eight hundred thousand bucks.

The twenty-five million Salib offered her would more than take care of everything. It was easy money. All she had to do was drill a damn hole.

As she awoke, a renewed sense of determination coursed through her veins, pushing her forward. However, the harsh reality of not having a sub to handle the task weighed heavily on her shoulders, causing them to sag with the burden of uncertainty. How would she conquer this challenge and find a way to get it done?

She shuffled to the tiny basin in her room and splashed water on her face. Grabbing a towel, she strode over to the porthole and stared out over the rolling waves of the North Sea. She watched the ebb and flow as she blotted her cheeks when a memory slammed into her head.

She tossed the towel onto the bed and grabbed her cell phone. After a few minutes of searching, she found what she was looking for. Double-checking the date on her phone confirmed she was correct.

Am I crazy for thinking this? I couldn't get away with it. Or could I, with the right help?

She flashed back to the image of her former colleague plummeting from a helicopter. Then she thought of the man with the mangled ear. He and the Prince shaking hands. Her brother's smile.

"Screw it. I'm doing this."

She exited the room, and with tenacity in her step, searched the vessel for Salib.

He was talking to the captain on the bridge when she flung the door open. Both men spun around to face her, and each wore a frown from the day's events.

Salib sighed. "What do you want, Miss Wyrick? Unless you have a remedy for the clusterfuck you created, I do not wish to speak with you."

She stepped forward and raised her chin to meet his dark eyes. "Well, I've got to talk to you. And you're going to listen. I have a solution to our problem."

He snickered. "Our problem?" He turned to leave when she reached out to snatch his arm.

Coming to a halt, his gaze shifted to her hand, firmly gripping him. Then, his eyes darted to the captain and the other man steering the ship. A chuckle escaped his lips as he forcefully freed himself from her grasp. "I must admit, doctor, you possess an extraordinary amount of audacity to pull off something like that."

Raising both hands, her palms facing him, she closed her eyes. "I'm sorry, Your Highness, but yes, our problem. You want me to drill a hole, and I require a sub to do it."

"And?"

"I know where to get you one. It can do the job."

She stood waiting for a response. None came.

"Like, in a day or two. It's close, but I require your assistance."

He shifted his weight to his other foot. His eyes narrowed as he studied her. "How?"

Madison stood in thought. Her eyes shifted from the floor back to his. "How—what, Your Highness?"

He shook his head. "Oh, for." His lips scrunched as he played with a ring on his finger. "How do you need my help?"

"I think we should talk privately."

He scanned the bridge at the look on the two men's faces who appeared to have inserted themselves into the conversation. Years ago, he learned not to trust anyone and to keep business private whenever possible. Nodding in agreement, he gestured for her to follow.

They entered his lavish quarters. He held out an arm and gestured to the overstuffed sofa as he continued toward the bar. "Have a seat. Can I get you something to drink?"

"No. Thank you."

She saw the disapproving look on the prince's face.

"Suit yourself."

"Actually. I rescind that. I would like one. Gin and tonic, please."

"Well, okay." As he prepared her drink, he glanced between her and the bar. "I detect some redness on your right cheek. I do hope it isn't tender. You must forgive me." He shrugged. "It was the heat of the moment." Stepping over, he handed her the glass. "There were a lot of emotions to process." He sat, sipped his drink, and crossed his legs. "Now, tell me about this sub you claim to have miraculously found."

Taking a deep breath, she started to speak, but the words wouldn't come. Clearing her throat, she smiled. "Excuse me." In a single gulp, she drained her cocktail.

The prince smirked.

Wiping her mouth with her sleeve, she followed with another deep breath. "Okay. This is going to sound crazy, but I've been thinking."

She paused for some witty comeback, but the man remained focused on her.

"We need another submersible. I read the Deep Wave Institute is doing deep diving on an ancient Viking shipwreck off the coast of Norway."

The lack of interest on the man's face caused a shiver to run down her back.

"We can get their sub."

He took a sip, uncrossed his legs, and leaned toward her, resting his elbows on his knees. "How, doctor? Are we going to ask them if we can borrow it? Rent it?" He straightened and chuckled to himself.

Her face lost all emotion. "No, Prince. We're going to steal it."

His attention focused on her. Setting his drink on the table, he rose and extended his hand towards her empty glass. "Well, doctor, I'm taken aback by your audacious thoughts. What leads you to believe I possess the ability or resources to assist you? Besides, what you're speaking of is highly illegal."

As he walked to the bar to refill her drink, Madison felt confidence wash through her. "I'm not stupid, Your Highness. The man with the mangled ear. I know he threw Doctor Agate from the helicopter."

She watched his expression. The smirk on his face when she mentioned the killing of her colleague made her stomach turn, but it solidified her suspicion he'd go along with the plan.

"I also know he's done other—tasks for you. Things I don't want to know about, but I suspect they're a lot more illegal than this. You can get him and his team to help me."

He handed her the fresh icy libation. "And let's say I do have these—resources. What about the drill?"

"We have another."

"Won't it cause the same problem?"

"No. We'll build a longer brace for it. It will be further from the hull."

He sat, leaned back, and intertwined his fingers over his belly. "And what's caused this renewed sense of determination?"

"My brother."

He chuckled. "Right. Or is it the money?"

She tipped her glass to him. "Keen observation." Taking a sip, she leaned back into the soft brown leather chair and crossed her legs. "Ok. Full transparency. Both."

"Let's say I agree to this. How long to get the submersible ready?"

"Three weeks. And that's *with* testing it. Don't rush me."

"Fair enough."

His eyes searched the room as he thought. He took a deep breath and raised his glass. "You concentrate on the new bracket and the laser. I'll work on getting the sub. Do we have a deal?"

They leaned forward and clanked glasses. Madison nodded while taking a sip.

"Deal."

22

Air Force One
Geneva, Switzerland
June 25th 13:13 (12:13 UTC)

Veronica had already taken her seat and was catching up on the unread emails on her mobile phone. The screen's blue-white glow cast a soft light on her features. The low hum of Air Force One's air conditioning provided a soothing backdrop as she scrolled through the influx of messages, her brow furrowing slightly with each new bit of information.

Across the cabin, President Pennington removed her crisp, black sports jacket, the fabric rustling as she shrugged it off her shoulders. With a casual flick of her wrist, she tossed the garment onto the nearest plush charcoal leather couch. The coat landed with a dull thud, the supple material sliding across the smooth surface before resting on the plane's deep-piled, slate-gray carpeting. Shaking her head in a dismissive gesture, the President waved off the carelessly discarded jacket, allowing it to remain where it had fallen.

"Well, talk about a shit show," Pennington declared, her voice tinged with frustration as she ran a hand through her hair. The aroma of premium roasted coffee from the galley mingled with the faint scent of the President's citrus-infused perfume. "We come here trying to stop World War Three and almost inadvertently start it." She let out a heavy sigh, her shoulders sagging momentarily before she straightened her posture. "Good God, can this day get any worse?"

A genuine laugh escaped the Director as she held the phone to her ear.

"You've jinxed us once already. Don't do it again."

The President responded with a soft chuckle, lighting up her eyes and a subtle nod conveying agreement. Veronica, raised a slender finger as she rose from her seat the moment her call linked through.

"Yes, Janice Tomlin, please. Tell her it's Director Slocum."

The President's sharp gaze narrowed, and a single eyebrow arched in curiosity, as she lifted her chin. Veronica's hand, adorned with shimmering nail polish that caught the cabin lights like scattered diamonds, moved to mute the conversation on the phone. Leaning in closer to the President, her voice dropped to a hushed whisper, almost inaudible above the hum of the aircraft engines.

"She's from the Directorate of Operations," Veronica began, her words tinged with a hint of reverence before pausing for effect. With a deliberate gesture, she raised her index finger in a momentary pause, hanging like an unspoken question.

"Yes, Janice. It's a pleasure to speak again as well. It's been, what, less than twelve hours? Is that a record?" Veronica laughed, the warm timbre filling the lavishly appointed cabin of Air Force One. POTUS leaned back in her plush leather seat. The soft upholstery creaked beneath her as she listened and gazed out the window at the tarmac as the ground crew scuttled to prepare the plane for take off.

"Listen, I'll be brief 'cause I'm in a hurry." Her tone shifted to one of urgency, her brow furrowing as she spoke. The rumble of the powerful engines provided a steady backdrop to her voice, underscoring the sense of motion and purpose permeating the presidential aircraft.

"We've got a person of interest and need to know the hotel and room she is in and for how long." POTUS's fingers drummed against the polished wood of the table before her.

"The name is Evelyn Cathey. With an 'ey' at the end." She paused, her gaze focused and intense as she consulted the notes before her, the rustling of the pages punctuating her words.

"She works for the Canadian Security Intelligence Service (CSIS)." She cast a glance around, her gaze darting across the confines of the cabin, as though to confirm the secrecy of their dialogue.

"No. We don't believe she is traveling under an alias." She shifted in her seat, the plush upholstery providing a comforting embrace. "Last known location was Ladegarden, Norway."

Veronica's sharp nod sent a cascade of her sleek, ruby hair tumbling over her shoulders as the officer echoed the details. "Exactly right. And about my time constraints—"

POTUS gestured with a commanding sweep of her hand, requesting the mobile. Veronica nodded and handed her the phone.

"Janice? President Pennington here. This is crucial. We need this information as a matter of urgency. Crystal clear? Excellent. Get in touch once you pinpoint the exact place."

She handed back the cell phone. "I assume she is the individual who handles searching for all of your P.O.I.'s?"

"Affirmative."

The president's eyes flickered with relief as she absorbed the confirmation. A soft exhale escaped her lips, carrying a hint of tension. "Fantastic. Let's hope she uncovers something as soon as possible."

With a decisive clap of her hands, her fingers created a sharp sound in the confined space of the plane. "Well, I don't know about you, but my stomach is protesting. Those dainty finger foods, tapas, hors d'oeuvres—whatever fancy name they gave those measly offerings—didn't cut it for me." Her words held a note of playful exasperation.

Veronica turned to gaze at the ceiling above her seat, her lips pursing in contemplation. After a moment, she met the stare of her companion. "You know what? I think I'm famished too." A faint smile played on her features.

A glint entered Pennington's eyes as she made up her mind. "All right. Let's remedy this hunger situation. I'll ring for them to prepare us a proper meal." Her voice carried authority as she planned their next steps.

"While we wait for our food and the anticipated call from your contact." She leaned forward in her seat. "Let's delve into some of the other details we picked up during the chaotic meeting." She gestured towards Logan with a nod, indicating she required his presence.

"I want to ensure we've covered all bases. Let's go over Logan's notes together. We must make certain nothing slips through the cracks."

BERGEN, NORWAY

June 25th 16:50 (14:50 UTC)

Evelyn sat at the desk her guest room provided and read through the calculated coordinates her brother's ship might be at over the next few days.

It was adrift in the frigid North Atlantic and was caught in a mix of competing currents. The vessel drifted in a circle over one hundred miles in diameter near the North Pole. Sitting straight in her chair, she rubbed her eyes.

The constant staring at the monitor was getting to her and a dull ache was setting in.

"Ugh, enough of this."

She rose from her seat and strolled into the bathroom to retrieve some pain relievers. Shaking two ibuprofens into her hand, she popped them in her mouth and chased them down with a swig from her bottle of Fiji water when her mobile rang. Hustling back to her phone to glance at the screen, it was the call she'd been waiting for.

"Special Agent Cathey speaking."

A man with a thick Scottish accent introduced himself.

"Miss Cath— Ah'm sorry aboot that, lass. Special Agent Cathey, it's Kenny MacIntosh here fae DavCo Drilling, returnin' yer call."

"Yes, I appreciate you getting back to me. I'll get to the point. My brother was part of the crew on your ship, the Arctic Drill. Being I'm with Canadian Intelligence and it was one of our companies leasing the vessel when it disappeared, you can understand I have a personal connection to investigate and determine what took place."

"Aye, and ah'm truly sorry fer yer brother. A right unfortunate turn o' events, it is."

A wave of fear and a chill went down her back. "So, are you saying you know what happened? Was everyone on board killed?"

Dread slithered along her spine as she awaited his response. A whirlwind of thoughts consumed her mind, from the daunting task of breaking the news to her mother to the haunting image of a funeral for her beloved Richard.

"Aye, nae ma'am. I'm no' sayin a word. We dinnae ken a bloody thing. That's why we're sendin' a squad oot there as soon as we can."

She smiled, closed her eyes, and shook her head, trying to make light of what the man with the thick accent on the other end of the phone was saying.

"I'm sorry. Did you say you were sending a team out to the vessel?"

"Aye."

Evelyn strolled to the window and pulled back the curtains. The sunlight streamed through the glass, enveloping her in a gentle warmth, like a comforting embrace. She gazed out toward the horizon, where the vast expanse of the Arctic waters met the sky.

"I need to be on your ship, Mr. MacIntosh. Can you make it happen?"

"I dinnae ken, lass. Whaur d'ye be located?"

"Bergen, Norway."

Silence filled the air for what appeared to be an eternity. "Mr. MacIntosh?"

"Hang on, lass. I'm lookin' intae it."

After another long pause, the line came back to life.

"Apologies fer the delay, Special Agent. We're more than willin' tae cooperate wi' ye. Our ship'll be passin' by there in about seventy-twa oors, 'bout a hundred and fifty kilometers offshore. We can send the chopper tae retrieve ye, but ye'll need tae cover the fuel costs."

"Not a problem. I'm more than happy to."

"Awright. Gies yur mobile, and oor pilot will gie ye a call a couple o' hours afore pickup tae let ye ken the location. He'll need tae find somewhere tae land."

Evelyn pumped her fist. *Yes.*

"Mr. MacIntosh, the number you called me on is my mobile. Thank you for your cooperation."

"Naebody's problem. Oh, and Special Agent, ye'd best pack somethin' warm. It'll be bitter cold whaur ye're headin'."

"Oh, yes. That's correct. Fantastic idea. I'll go get some things now."

Evelyn's heart quickened and anticipation painted her features with hope and apprehension, her eyes alight with a newfound purpose.

With every breath, Evelyn felt closer to unraveling the mystery shrouding her brother and the fate of all those aboard the vessel, propelling her towards an unknown future fraught with both peril and possibility.

She grabbed her purse and left to shop for warm clothes for her upcoming trip.

IN FRONT OF THE CLARION Hotel was a circular driveway of intricate brick pavers. Nestled within this circle was a small, green oasis featuring an assortment of bushes and peculiar trees. Their thick branches had been pruned to bare stubs, giving way to new growth. Dozens of vibrant sprouts emerged, transforming the grove into what resembled an otherworldly display of alien foliage.

Blake had parked himself on one of the park benches and pretended to read the daily paper as he waited. A skill he'd learned, practiced, and implemented many times.

He stole a sporadic glance at his phone to remind him of Evelyn's appearance.

To his left was the harbor, where an occasional cruise ship would glide by, transporting its payload of tourists to fresh adventures, as they explored the stunning fjords and attractions the country had to offer.

He studied the facade of the building. It was underwhelming for a hotel. Sitting five stories high, the front entrance was a small wooden double door painted red. A stark contrast to the light, brownish brick covering the frontage. Framing the entrance was an ornate column structure, with an intricate carving, situated at the top with the inscription Nordemfjeldske Dampskipsselskap positioned in the middle.

What the hell does that mean?

The translator on his phone displayed, "The Northern Fjord Steamship Company".

Hmph. Interesting.

As he focused back on the door, it opened and the woman he was looking for stepped out and proceeded to the street. He stood and placed the paper in the nearest bin. As he approached the sidewalk, he saw her disappear around the next corner.

He made his way into the hotel and strode towards the staircase. Each flight of stairs climbed brought him closer to his destination on the fourth floor. Earlier, Veronica had provided him with Evelyn's hotel and room number in a call that had compelled urgency. Luckily, the Clarion boasted an advanced keyless electronic guest access system, a security measure that proved no match for his hacking skills.

He raised his phone to the reader and effortlessly gained entry into the room. As he crossed the threshold, a breathtaking view of the bustling harbor unfolded before him through the window. Across from him, a panorama of hotels, shops, and restaurants lined up in neat rows.

To his right was a grand king-sized bed, exuding comfort and luxury. On his left, a sturdy bureau and desk awaited his scrutiny. His eyes fell upon Evelyn's laptop, open on the desk beside a manila folder overflowing with papers and photographs. Intrigued, he delved into its contents with a sense of anticipation.

Among the assortment of documents lay a striking photograph capturing an immense ship unlike any other – 'DavCo Arctic Drill' boldly emblazoned along its dark blue hull. The vessel sported an imposing polar bear's head at its prow, accentuated by bright white lettering spelling out 'ICE'. Yellow cranes dotted its sides while a tall davit loomed at its center. An octagonal heliport perched above the bow added to its formidable appearance.

Drawing out his phone from his back pocket, he captured images of the vessel before continuing to sift through the folder's contents. Among them were numerous pictures featuring Anders, the unfortunate witness to the oil rig attack, whose demise had set off this chain of events just days prior in a tragic explosion that rocked their world.

Upon further investigation, he found newspaper clippings and internal CSIS memos on the attacks in Russia, the oil rig, and the U.S. on oil-based targets. To the laptop's left was a sticky note with the name Kenny MacIntosh, CEO DavCo Drilling, and a phone number.

That might be a number worth calling.

He snapped a picture of it and attached it to a text to Alice with the message; *Get me all the intelligence on this guy you can.*

He meticulously scanned the remaining documents, snapping photos of any intriguing details, and then proceeded to the bathroom. Inside, he sifted through her toiletries and medications until his eyes landed on a bottle labeled Xanax.

You're in the wrong business if you need to take this.

A sudden sound echoed in his ears, causing his stomach to twist into tight knots. Emerging from the bathroom, the door creaked open slowly. Evelyn glided in, her eyes narrowed and focused. The cold metal of the pistol gleamed menacingly under the dim light—its barrel aimed unwaveringly at his temple.

23

Bergen, Norway
June 25th 17:38 (15:38 UTC)

Blake's eyes went wide with surprise. He raised both his hands.

"Hey, hey! Woah. Can you not point that thing at my face?"

Everlyn crouched, holding the gun in both hands and keeping it out of range of his arms and feet.

"Who the fuck are you?" She glanced along both sides of the hallway to make sure nobody could see her and turned her focus to the intruder.

"Back. In the room." She gestured with the pistol, making sure it was always aligned with his body. "Further. To the window."

Her grip on the gun never wavered. She kept a calculated distance, just beyond the reach of his arms and legs. Her eyes dissected his every move, analyzing his stance and assessing the limited choices laid out before him. The smell of gun oil lingered in the air, a reminder of the danger he faced. With each step he took towards the opposite end of the room, the weight of helplessness settled deeper within him, knowing there was no viable way to disarm her.

When his back was against a wall, he could go no further. "All right. You're as far as you can go. Now, who are you? What are you doing in my room? Who sent you? Did you go through my things?"

He rolled his eyes. "Jesus, lady. Let me answer your first question before you ask me ten more."

She nodded. "Fair enough. Out with it."

He took a deep breath. "Maintenance. I got a report of a clogged toilet."

Between puckering her lips and trying to suppress a smile, she tilted her head to the side. "Bullshit, and I'm Betty Crocker. Where's your ID? Why aren't you in uniform?"

As Blake teetered on the tightrope between weaving a fresh lie or unveiling the harsh truth, a sudden crimson dot danced ominously on

Evelyn's chest. With her gun still aimed at him, he risked everything and lunged forward in one swift motion. One arm ensnared her gun arm as they both crashed to the floor.

"Get down!"

They lay sprawled out on the cold floor, his muscular frame shielding her petite form from any imminent danger. He disregarded the relentless pummeling against his kidneys as she pounded her fist against him.

"Help! Somebody help me! Get off of me!" Her panicked cries echoed through the room, bouncing off its high ceilings.

His voice was a low growl that reverberated through their entwined bodies. "Shut up!"

Fueled by adrenaline and fear, she squirmed and thrashed beneath him, legs kicking wildly in an attempt to knee him where it would hurt most. "You son of a bitch! When I buck you off of—"

"Someone took a shot at you." His interruption came as blunt as a sledgehammer.

She froze mid-struggle, her brow furrowing in confusion. "What?"

"Somebody tried to shoot you."

He motioned with his chin to the bullet hole in the window and the subsequent one in the opposite wall.

Evelyn stared in disbelief. Her brow creased and her nose wrinkled. "But—but, why?"

He removed the pistol from her hand, rose to his knees, and backed off of her. "Stay low." He crawled to the curtains and pulled them shut to block the view of whoever was shooting. "When you were facing me, a laser sight pointed at your chest. So—I tackled you."

She sat upright and leaned against the bed. "How do you know they weren't aiming for your head? Cause you sure as hell aren't maintenance. I don't know who you are, and I want to kill you."

His eyes narrowed and his lips pursed. "Funny."

Crawling to her, he helped her to her feet, out of the window's line of sight in case the shooter decided to take some blind shots. "We need to leave now. If someone took a shot at you from across the harbor, they have men in the building. Grab your laptop and anything else vital and let's go. Now!"

He reached for her arm, and she jerked it away. "Hold on, asshole. You still haven't told me who you are."

"My name is Blake MacKay, and I'm with the CIA. We need to go."

Her head swiveled in a quick jerky motion as if searching for something. She retrieved her laptop and all the documents and stuffed them into her bag.

He returned her pistol to her, and we waved her on. "Come on."

Cracking the room's entrance, wide enough to peer out, he inspected the hallway. "Okay. It's clear. We'll take the fire escape."

As the stairwell door opened, and he entered, the echoing of footsteps ascending caused him to pause. He peered through the gap between the stairs. Armed men, clad in black, were racing upward.

Closing it, he sought a way to jam it. "Not good. They're coming." Yanking an extinguisher from its mount, he pulled the pin. "When I say run, take off for the other stairwell. Understand?"

"Yes." She raised her pistol.

He turned around to her. "No! Nothing lethal. I know why they're after you. We'll get it straightened out. I need you to trust me for now."

She nodded and lowered her weapon. The entrance opened. He hoisted the extinguisher and slammed it into the face of the first man. Falling back into his partner, the other man's eyes went wide in shock. Blake squeezed the handle and let loose the chemicals inside toward both men. He threw the metal cylinder at the two pursuers and kicked the door closed.

"Go, go, go!"

Both ran the length of the hall. The wall sconces whizzed by their peripherals as their speed increased. Dashing past the elevator and to the next exit, Evelyn opened the door and was eye-to-eye with another man dressed in black, his partner on the steps behind him. Instincts took over. Grabbing his extended arm, she pulled him to her, lifted her right leg, and kicked him twice in the chest and once on the side of the head. Still grasping his sleeve, she placed her foot against his torso, pressed hard, and released him. The shocked man's momentum sent him into the other, the pair tumbling to the landing below and stopping with a thump and some groans.

She headed to the opposite side and ascended the stairs toward the roof.

"Keep going! Head to the top." He glanced back. Two men were struggling to their feet.

She reached for the maintenance access and pushed.

"It's locked."

He motioned for her to come to him. "Back here. Behind me." After she was out of the way, he aimed his pistol. The bullet struck its mark and made a hole where the lock once was. Barreling up the steps, he leaned in with his shoulder and forced the door open to the hotel's rooftop.

The sun still loomed over them in the early evening Nordic sky. Heat radiated off the black pitch, invisible waves beating at their skin. He scanned the area. To his right was the harbor and the road in front of it. It was too high and too great a distance to jump. The flat roof over their shoulder connected the building to another hotel. "Over there. Go."

They rushed over to the next structure. The thud of the stairwell door slamming open behind them sent an adrenaline rush.

"They're closing in. Gotta move faster and find a way to the street."

Bullets whizzed past them, narrowly missing their mark. One round struck the rooftop ventilation system, causing the fan to rattle, before resuming its task of sucking air out of the interior.

Evelyn rounded the corner of a maintenance shed on the connecting building's roof and readied herself. As Blake came in after her, he was breathing heavily. Recognizing the signs; her jaw clenched, and all her senses were on heightened alert. She was preparing for a fight.

"Are you sure about this?"

She nodded. "Yes! Why are they after me? Who are they?" Before he could respond, two men flanked the agents, effectively boxing them in. Blake delivered a punch to the man dressed in black, sending him crashing to the ground. He seized the opportunity and pounced on the fallen assailant and unleashed four elbow strikes to his forehead, rendering him unconscious.

Evelyn seized the other man's wrist, extending his arm and twisting his palm upward. She ducked in, positioning her shoulder beneath his elbow, and yanked toward her feet. The sound of his arm snapping was loud and unmistakable, followed by a howl of agony piercing the air. Without missing a beat, she twisted toward him and delivered an elbow strike to her assailant's temple, sending him crumpling to the scorching roof in a heap.

Blake could hardly suppress a smile after what he had witnessed. "Wow. Nice."

Her eyes met his, and she smiled her approval. They sprinted to the opposite side and gazed five stories below at the cobbled pavement.

One story beneath them was a ledge about two feet in width. A balcony rail indicated a door to a room out of sight, hidden from the roof's edge. Without hesitation, she climbed over the edge and extended her hands. "Here. Hold me until I tell you to let go."

He squeezed her hands tight and lowered her as far as she could go. On her signal, he released her. She landed, but as she tried to grasp onto the side of the building, she lost her balance. As she started to plummet to her death, she lurched to her left. Desperate, her left hand reached out for the safety of the balcony's rail spindles. Her fingers were outstretched as if trying to grasp the thin air itself. With a final, desperate lunge, she caught the spindle. Blake could sense the fear in her eyes as she grasped the solid metal beneath her fingers.

As she hung, he looked back for the approaching threat. Her struggling groans filled his ears. Returning his attention to her, a wave of relief poured over him as he saw her swing her legs over the railing. He watched as she disappeared under the roofline and waited for her signal.

To his rear, three more would be-killers, weapons drawn, were running his way. He called out. "Hey, we've got company. I'm coming." He reached out, grasped the roof's edge, and flipped each leg over. Right before releasing, they all rushed toward him.

He dropped to the ledge while she positioned herself by the glass door. When he opened it, they pushed the curtains aside and entered. A woman pushing a vacuum cleaner and listening to music from her earbuds had her back to them. The two rushed past her. She gasped in surprise as they zipped by and exited the room.

Once in the hallway, he scanned for an elevator. A couple were already waiting. They were dressed for a night out. The older gentleman wore a dark blue pinstriped suit, while the woman, a few years his junior, wore a silver and black off-the-shoulder dress paired with a blue wrap. Her hands, adorned with multiple diamond rings and polished nails, grasped a sequined clutch, catching the light.

"Come on. Let's slow ourselves and act—normal."

"Ha. Easy for you to say. Your hair's not a hot mess. I look like I finished a tennis match."

He smiled at the couple. "Dinner?"

She nodded, and her lips parted to reveal gleaming white teeth. The man stepped forward, reached, and pressed the already illuminated button. "And then the Opera."

"Nice."

The doors opened, and they all entered. The ride was brief, lasting only a few seconds without any stops, yet it was long enough for them to savor the intoxicating blend of cedar and spice from his cologne mingling with the delicate floral notes of cherry blossoms from hers. As they reached the main floor, Blake stepped aside to let them exit first, blocking the view of anyone who might be searching for them.

The lobby was empty, except for the concierge behind her desk to the left and two clerks stationed at the front counter to their right. In the center, two black leather couches rested on a white and gray patterned rug, while four swivel chairs completed the inviting common area.

He grabbed her hand and pulled her as they ran toward the side exit. Outside, he went to his right and peeked around the corner. No less than eight police officers were standing next to their cars, adjacent to his.

"Well, that sucks. They're all parked and hanging out next to my car. Do you still have the BMW?"

Scrunching her nose and dipping her chin, she stared back at him. "What the fu—how'd you know I had a BMW?"

He shrugged. "Seriously? You have to ask?"

She shook her head. "Unbelievable. Yeah, it's over here."

As they rounded the corner, the echoes of police radio chatter bounced off the surrounding buildings. A few scooters zipped past, their tiny engines humming like restless bees darting through the urban landscape.

Blake glanced to his left as they crossed the street toward her car. "Keep your head down. Maybe look at the things in the window of the building over there. Give me your keys."

"Hey, I can drive. I've been through special agent driving training too, Mr. CIA man. You worry about navigating me through these streets to get us the heck outta here."

They reached the car, and as she opened the door and started to step in, the last thing they wanted to hear filled their ears.

"Dere to. Stopp! Politi!"

Both captured the wide-eyed stare of the other.

Blake opened his door. "Get in. Start the car." Looking across the street, two officers dressed in black military fatigues, like the men in the stairwell, came toward them.

"Sorry, only English."

He climbed into the inviting leather seat and fastened his belt. "Go! Go!"

As she reversed, the officers were racing back to their vehicles consisting of sedans and motorcycles.

He turned to her, eyes narrowed, and his voice was urgent. "We have to lose them fast. We can't afford to have half the police force chasing us, and we cannot cause any accidents or injuries. If we can get away, I can clear this up with a single phone call. But if we end up hurting anyone, especially civilians, then it becomes a whole different ballgame."

Evelyn's knuckles whitened as she gripped the steering wheel. "If you can clear this up, then why not do it now? Why are we running?"

Blake's jaw tightened. "First off, it's because they shot at us, unprovoked. They might have a shoot-to-kill order out. I'm not willing to stop and find out the hard way." He pointed ahead. "Turn right at the end of the block. Then keep making lefts and rights. We need to keep them guessing—if they don't have a visual, they can't radio ahead."

The tires squealed as Evelyn executed the sharp turn. An old stone wall was nothing more than a blur on their left.

"I'm trying to call my handler now, but the call isn't going through."

She shifted into second gear, panic edging into her voice. "I hope you're right. Keep trying to make that call."

The wail of sirens grew louder, closing in. He pointed. "Go right, then the next left."

He grabbed the dashboard as Evelyn rocketed down the narrow lane. "You're doing great. Keep doing this until I get a connection and can get this all cleared up."

The car hurtled down the dark, winding streets, the sirens hot on their trail—and the inescapable realization if his call to Veronica didn't connect soon, someone would get injured or killed and they would be in even more trouble.

Evelyn's eyes widened as she caught sight of the CCTV camera mounted on the street corner. She moved the gearshift to third. "I don't think it's going to matter if we lose them or not."

He placed his phone to his ear. "Oh yeah? Why is that?"

"Cameras. They're tracking us."

24

Bergen, Norway
June 25th 18:11 (16:11 UTC)

The road ahead bent sharply, looping back in the direction they'd come. Approaching the next intersection, Evelyn's foot hovered over the brake pedal.

"Don't you dare slow down," Blake growled, his knuckles turning white as he gripped the door handle. "We need to keep moving, no matter what."

Ignoring the hesitation in Evelyn's expression, he pointed ahead. "There, take that left turn. We'll lose them in the side streets."

"Look! There's traffic. I can't go that way, It's—"

"What do you mean? Who cares about them? It's a rental."

"This is a one-way street. You said not to cause any accidents."

He ran his hand through his thick black hair. "Oh, for fuck's sake. I knew I should have driven."

The road took them back to an intersection they would have been at had they not turned earlier. As they approached, a policeman on a motorcycle met them.

"Shit!" She floored it and passed a small truck, blocking her path.

"Oh, my God!" Blake slapped his hand on the dash. "No. Not this way! We're back, right in front of your damn hotel, and there's no outlet!"

"You told me to go this way!"

"No! I wanted you to go left! Shit!"

They whizzed past the collection of police he saw earlier mustering near his vehicle. All of them ran to their cars and engaged in the pursuit.

He raised his hands. "Wonderful! So much for the fast escape and low engagement."

"Where to? There's no access to the main street from here."

"Oh, you don't say." He outstretched his arm. "Left. Go over the curb."

He grabbed the handle on the headliner next to the window, while they bounced over the paved sidewalk. She went left. The calm harbor waters were on their right, and the evening light sparkled off the gentle waves like pinpricks of light through holes in a dark canvas.

A charming walkway, bustling with locals and visitors alike, was separated from the harbor by the road. People strolled, jogged, or biked along the pathway, enjoying the vibrant atmosphere. The area had scattered benches, with many individuals occupying them and savoring the pleasant weather, watching the world go by, or finishing refreshing drinks purchased from one of the cafes across the street.

A slow-moving box truck blocked their escape. "Dammit!" She laid on the horn and attempted to pass. A motorcyclist was in the lane. She jerked the wheel back as the tiny horn blared past her. Sirens from the pursuing police reverberated inside the tiny cabin of the car.

She attempted again, but this time it was a city bus. She went right, bumping over the concrete median and into the pedestrian path.

Blake twisted around to look out the rear window. He braced himself with his hand on the dash. "Careful. Don't hit anyone."

Her stare was intent with heavy concentration. "Shut up. I know what I'm doing."

"Sure you do."

Through the rear glass, motorcycle police weaved through pedestrians as they dodged out of the way. The cars remained on the roadway. Blue lights flashed as their sirens blared a symphony of out-of-tune instruments.

He suppressed a laugh as several folks dove into the water to avoid being hit, but one gentleman's exaggerated fall was too comical.

"Ha, ha, ha."

"What's so funny?"

He faced forward. "Nothing. I have an idea."

She continued driving on the walkway, honking her horn as a warning and weaving in and out of people. A green building, the public restroom, was approaching. She spotted an opening in the traffic and ran over the curb with another thump. An intersection approached.

He dug out his phone. "Take your next left."

"You sure?"

"Yes! And don't wait for traffic. Hit 'em if you have to."

"You said no accidents."

"Ugh. Just go!"

The tires screamed in protest once more as she made a left turn in front of an approaching car.

"Oh, shit!" She weaved expertly around it. Blake put the phone to his ear as they heard a hard thump. He looked behind to witness the motorbike officer flip over the vehicle's hood they had almost collided with.

She glanced into her mirror. "What happened?"

"Don't worry about it. He'll be fine. You concentrate on driving."

They came to the end of the road. He pointed. "Go left."

"I can't! It's one-way!"

He motioned twice with his arm. "We're only going one way. Go, will you? They'll avoid you."

The call connected. "Veronica!"

They continued to bob and weave as she tried to negotiate the unfamiliar terrain.

"Blake, where are you? Were you able to find Miss Cathey?"

"You could say that. She's involved in a police chase through Bergen. Right now."

"What? Why? You need to go after her."

"Well, that's why I'm calling. I'm in the car with her."

"What?"

"Listen. I think someone took the bolo they had on her too seriously. Somebody tried to kill her and now they're chasing us. She had nothing to do with the bombing. I need you or anyone with enough iron fist to tell them to turn off the pursuit."

Evelyn turned to him. "What? Do they think I had something to do with blowing that place up? Are they freaking insane?"

He held his palm to her. "Shh. Quiet!"

She applied the parking brake and made a hard right. The smell of burning rubber and hot brakes permeated their senses as they slid around the corner. Sirens continued to blare. "Why would they believe I was involved?"

"Would you just drive? I'm taking care of it."

"Blake, I'm on the plane with POTUS. We're returning to D.C. from our meetings in Geneva. Let me drop a bug in her ear. I'm more than sure she'll call whomever you need her to. Who do you suggest she call first?"

"I dunno. The Prime Minister? The Chief of Police? Anyone who can call off their dogs before someone gets hurt."

She made a sharp left. Another car joined in the chase. It screeched in directly behind her, its siren screaming.

"Okay. I can hear the sirens. I'll get on it."

He ended the call and turned to her. "Hopefully, you'll see them back off in a minute. Go right, then your next left."

Inertia took charge of the sedan as it protested, its tires fighting against physics. The tail end whipped around and sideswiped a trash can. The chasing cruiser did the same thing, as did the car after as it slammed into the lead car's rear fender. She gained some distance. It reversed, and both continued after them.

"I have another idea." He dialed Alice.

"Hey! It's Blake. Track where I'm at and kill all the CCTV cameras within a five-square-mile area. Just buy me some time."

She burst through a stoplight. Looking to her left, a line of buses started through the intersection. Their creeping movement provided a temporary moving wall to allow them to gain some more distance.

His tech was typing on his keyboard. "I'm almost in... almost; and—"

As he waited for an answer, he motioned with his head. "Turn right"

Alice broke in. "All righty got it! You're good to go."

"Thanks!" He tucked his phone in his pocket. "Okay, he took care of the cameras. Glad we don't have any cops behind us."

A police car turned the corner immediately after they passed the intersection. It's lights and sirens protesting.

He let out a long sigh. "Oh, for Christ's sake."

She floored it. He rolled his eyes. A car pulled onto the roadway. She jerked the wheel to the left, then back, and checked her mirror. The authorities were still on their tail. He glanced at his watch.

Come on Veronica!

Three more cruisers came into view in her mirror. The road widened. Blake scanned the road ahead for some way of escape. Blue lights on several cars blocked their path in all directions.

Evelyn's head bobbed left and right as she scanned the concrete landscape. "What's going on? They have all the side streets blocked."

He searched around, out the rear window. "I don't know, but I've got a bad feeling."

She pointed. "Look. Ahead. It's open." She downshifted and mashed the accelerator. As they barreled forward, He looked all around at the surrounding blocked intersections. She turned the wheel and headed for freedom.

"Wait! No! Don't go that way. It's a trap!"

"Too late."

"No!" His stomach jumped to his throat, anticipating disaster.

She turned down the boulevard. City buses entered the roadway from alleys on both sides, blocking their path. Following were no less than a dozen police cars that trailed each bus. She slammed on the brakes. They came to a stop. Dozens of armed officers had weapons drawn and pointed in their direction.

He let out another deep sigh, allowing his tense muscles to relax as he sank into the plush leather seat. His posture conveyed a sense of defeat, a silent acknowledgment of his responsibility.

"Well, we're screwed."

One officer emerged from behind the bus, his imposing figure clad in a sleek black uniform, a riot helmet firmly secured atop his head. He raised a bullhorn to his mouth, pausing momentarily before reaching for the radio mic clipped to his right shoulder. After a moment, he turned to his left, where another man approached, phone in hand, ready to relay the unfolding situation.

Blake reached for his device. "Something's going on. That guy is talking to someone." He searched for any new texts he received. His inbox was empty.

Evelyn tapped his knee. "Blake?"

He refocused on the scene unfolding before them. The man with the bullhorn was approaching with his hands in the air. When he was half the distance, he stopped and spoke. "Can you lower your window? I need to come and talk to you. I'm unarmed."

She did as he requested while he stepped forward.

"Are you Blake MacKay and Evelyn Cathey?"

They both nodded.

"You have some important friends. I received a phone call from your president, Mr. MacKay. She explained the situation. You're not in any trouble. It was our mistake. You and Miss Cathey are free to go on your way."

Both turned to each other. A smile creased his face.

———◉———

BLAKE SAT AT THE TABLE of a restaurant a stone's throw away from Evelyn's hotel. It was outside and adjacent to the same road on which the police chased them only an hour ago. He typed notes into his device of things he wanted to ask her.

A floral scent, reminiscent of Japanese cherry blossoms, enveloped his senses, drawing him in. He raised his head and caught sight of the young agent from Canada approaching. Her hair flowed like rich milk chocolate, cascading over her shoulders in soft waves. She exuded an effortless beauty, her striking features framed by delicate curls. The way she carried herself radiated confidence, accentuating her graceful figure that turned heads. She pulled back the chair, placed her purse under the table, and sat.

"Thanks for letting me take a shower. I wasn't exactly expecting such an action-packed afternoon."

"No worries. I took the liberty of ordering a drink for you."

A playful smile tugged at one corner of her mouth as she chuckled. She examined the potent drink before her, touching the glass with her fingertips and rotating it. The light from above danced across her nails, creating a shimmering reflection.

"Well, this is interesting. What is it?"

"Cherry lime Ricky. It's gin. You'll like it."

Cracking a smile, she chuckled. "Oh, you think so, huh?" Raising her cocktail and giving it a tiny stir with the straw, she sipped. "Mmm, yes. I do like it. Thank you."

"So, what are you doing here? If you're not officially working for CSIS, what's your connection?"

Her smile dissipated as she returned her drink to the table. "Well, you don't beat around the bush, do you?"

"I'm trying to get to the bottom of it all. I'm more than positive you have some personal interest in all of this, so doesn't it make sense to compare notes?"

She sneered and pursed her lips. "All right." Folding her arms on the surface, she leaned in. "My brother was on an oil exploration ship called the Arctic Drill. He was looking for oil below the ocean floor in the North Atlantic and a couple of months ago, he and the entire ship disappeared. No sign, no signal, nothing."

"Okay. Go on."

"I saw on the news the Russians attacked the oil platform and there was a survivor. I then read about the attack the Americans did on the Russian oil research station."

He shifted in his chair. "Yeah, you know that's bullshit, right?"

"Yeah, same for my country attacking the oilfield in Alaska. I thought there was a connection to what happened to my brother's ship, so I came over here to find some clues."

He sipped his beer.

Her eyes went wide as she slapped the table with both hands. "Oh, my gosh! Holy shit!"

"What?"

"I just realized this. Oh my God. My brother. He sent a cryptic text to me months ago. It was the last thing he ever sent me. It was from a satellite phone. It said something about an oven and the Danes. Do you think the Danish army attacked the ship?"

He shook his head. "No," Waving off her revelation. "They've known about that for months. It wasn't them. It's whoever the hell is attacking all of us. The U.S., the Russians, the Danes, and you, the Canadians. Whoever it is, wants to make it look like all these nations are attacking each other. But why?"

She tapped her finger on the red and white checkered tablecloth. "A diversion of some kind?"

"Yes, it's possible." He polished off his beer and signaled the waiter. "But from what? Is your brother's ship still missing?"

Sipping her cocktail, she gazed out at the harbor as a cruise liner set sail, its horn echoing a warm farewell across the water. Blake leaned forward and acted as if his legged itched and slipped a small tracking device into her purse.

She turned her attention back to Blake as he straightened. "Yes. It's still missing. Canada Oil has no known location."

25

Prince Awadi Salib Property South of Trongisvágur
Faroe Islands

June 28th 08:30 (07:30 UTC)

A flurry of sparks burst forth, dancing in the air chaotically like fiery sprites. They sizzled and crackled before gracefully descending, a few playfully rebounding off the surface before fizzling into darkness.

Madison raised the welding mask to inspect her work.

Sweating profusely after hours of labor on the new bracket, extending the laser drill by three feet from the submersible's hull, she fervently hoped the man with the mangled ear would secure it successfully. She forcefully expelled any traces of violence from her thoughts.

Inspecting her latest weld, she blew on it, taking pride in her meticulous work.

Damn, that's pretty good.

Zaanjar approached her and reached out to examine the fabrication when Madison grabbed her forearm. "Careful, it's still hot. I finished with the last weld about thirty seconds ago."

"Oh. Thank you." She withdrew her hand and walked around the table, scrutinizing her colleague's recent work. "This is excellent. And professional. Much better than the first one."

Madison stood from her rolling stool and nodded. "Let's hope so." She attempted to wipe some of the black soot off her blue coveralls and then laughed at herself. "Ah, I'm an idiot. These are burn holes."

They shared the humorous moment when Madison's smile faded to a straight line. Her eyes were drawn to the approaching man clad in a flowing white *thawb*, its tails dancing and bobbing with each step he took.

She sighed and focused on her friend. "You'd better get back to whatever you were doing. I know he's coming to talk to me."

"All right. Let me know how it goes."

"I will." She removed her mask and placed it on the stainless-steel worktable.

Zaanjar stepped to the side and dipped her chin as he approached. "Your Majesty."

He waved her off as he continued to Madison. Stepping to the workbench, his eyes scanned over her newest concoction. "I assume this is the new mount for the drill?"

"Good morning, Your Highness. Yes. I recently finished the final welds."

"And it's long enough so we don't have a repeat and another implosion?"

"Yes, sir. I calculated the safe distance it has to be and then added twenty percent. To be safe."

He nodded and motioned with his head to follow her. His expression was blank.

Oh-oh. Something's wrong.

They walked near the water of the inside dock. When they were near the far wall and away from any prying ears, he stopped. "I've put your plan into action. My man and his team have located the Deep Wave research vessel, it is where you said. It's three hundred and fifty miles east of here. Three degrees east and sixty-one north."

"Okay. Where about is that?"

"Northwest of Bergen, Norway by forty kilometers."

A hopeful smile creased her lips. "Well, that's good—isn't it? It's close."

"Close is a relative term, Doctor. It's close when you have a Gulfstream and you're jetting off to Paris for dinner. It might as well be on the moon when you're stealing a submarine."

A small splash in the water caught her attention. She turned to witness the ripples forming where a fish broke the surface to feed, its movements creating circles spreading outward like visible sound waves fading into oblivion.

"I understand. When is this going to happen?"

She remained fixated on the water. With the prince's silence lingering, she shifted her attention back to him.

"Tonight, so be prepared. We should have your new sub tomorrow."

THE NORWEGIAN SEA
23:52 (21:52 UTC)

Thirty miles off the coast of Norway, the Sea-Ray L650's twin engines came to a halt, and the boat drifted to a still, gentle bob. The crescent moon's sliver of light was bright enough to shimmer off the waves, but too dark to see on the deck. Nazir illuminated the rear of the boat with the built-in lights.

They'd stolen the cruiser from a retired couple in Bergen. His team required a boat large enough to hold their Zodiac and a fuel capacity to reach their destination, yet one with reasonable speed. The docks at Hjellestadt Harbour South had the most options for private pleasure boats. Upon stepping into the facility, their eyes landed on the couple aboard the vessel, and in that moment of comparison with their alternative options, the choice became unmistakable.

The elderly couple begged for their lives in the cramped cabin, but bullets pierced the air, tearing through flesh with a sickening thud. Blood sprayed like crimson fountains as life drained from their bodies.

Silent except for the haunting whispers of death, they dragged the limp forms, along with their dead beloved Shih Tzu, to the rear crew quarters. They shoved the corpses into the confined space, limbs awkwardly contorted into unnatural angles.

As the boat cut through the waves, the stench of gunpowder mixed with coppery blood saturated the air.

Once they reached the desolate expanse of the sea, devoid of witnesses, they fastened the lifeless bodies to a spare anchor. The harsh cawing of seagulls overhead seemed to mock their heinous act as they watched gravity claim their victims into the depths below.

They filled the vessel's fuel tanks with diesel, using the old man's credit card. The mechanical hum of machinery, masked by the eerie silence surrounding them, was a grim reminder of their treacherous journey into darkness.

Nazir went below, turned, and headed aft to the master stateroom. He planted a small block of C4 with a remote detonator on the floor of the shower in the master head. Coming out of the cabin, he went to the bar, poured a shot of vodka, and slammed it back. "Make sure you have everything we need in the Zodiac. I've planted an explosive to detonate after we leave."

The men he brought with him were the same as he used when they attacked the petroleum refinery in Prudhoe Bay, Alaska. Wayne, known as 'Wiggle' on missions, finished stowing his silenced H & K MP5 in the inflatable. "How far are we from the target?"

Nazir raised his tablet and accessed the live satellite feed Prince Salib had provided for them. "Looks like three klicks to the east."

Once on the inflatable and at a safe distance, he removed the detonator from this pocket and pressed the button. There was no brilliant explosion. A bright flaming fireball could be seen for miles—attracting unwanted attention. Instead, he used a small amount of C4 to blow a sizable hole in the hull below the waterline to make the luxury boat sink.

The zodiac appeared to float above the water as it moved over the unusually calm sea. The surface was like skating across the ice. A rare temperature inversion kept them comfortable as the warm summer night trapped the cool air near the surface. The boat was outfitted with a special Raider Outboard, which was submersible and allowed for a near-silent operation, enhancing their stealth as they navigated toward their target. Tim "Tapeworm" was at the helm while Jackson "Jackyl" was at the bow with his binoculars pressed to his eyes.

"I've got a visual on our target." He raised his hand and pointed. "Head three degrees east. It's about a klick out."

Soon, the navigation lights on the 238-foot vessel came into view. Nazir sat next to Tim. "Half the distance and we'll creep in from there." Tim nodded. "I assume the stern, where the crane is?"

"Head forward first. We'll let Luca shimmy the anchor line. We'll meet in the middle."

He nodded. "Sounds good. Do we have a number?"

"Prince Salib said his contact reported an approximate number. Somewhere between twenty-five to thirty." He checked his watch. "This late, there will be only a few people awake. We'll take them out first, then to the accommodation decks for the others. There are two of them, just below the pilothouse."

Silently, the small inflatable glided to the bow, a silhouette against the darkening sky. The only sound was the gentle thrum of waves lapping at the zodiac's hull. Clad in black, Luca slung his silenced MP5 across his back and, in a voice almost inaudible, checked his mic. "Radio check. This is Moonbeam." Nazir responded with a subtle thumbs up. As did the others.

He climbed onto the anchor chain and started his way to the deck. The other four men continued to the ship's rear to the launch platform. The reason for their mission, the submersible; hung from the ship's overhead crane. Its outline was a black outline against a starry backdrop.

On the aft deck, Wayne "Wiggle" signaled a halt with a swift hand gesture.

"Someone is working on a winch ahead. Hold here." Nazir and the other two stood down and watched. The silent assassin crept toward the unsuspecting victim. Each step he took was deliberate, careful not to make any noise. His muscles tensed as he grew ever closer. Keeping his rifle slung, he reached for the large knife sheathed in the front of his tactical vest. His prey crouched, wearing a headlamp, one hand on a wrench, the other holding the top of the box housing the small engine.

He lurched forward, wrapping his left arm around the man's neck and pulling his head back, and pinched his nose with his thumb and forefinger. Grasping the ten-inch blade with his other hand, he pushed it into the side of his victim's neck, just inside his collarbone until it pierced his heart. Pressing the man's head over to the side until the heart stopped, he withdrew the knife and thrust the head hard over to prevent any arterial spray. He then gently placed the body on the deck.

Clean and silent.

Grabbing his shoulders, he pulled him behind some crates to hide the body, then waved them forward.

The bridge sat four decks above. Nazir activated his radio. "Moonbeam, what's your twenty? We're headed to the bridge from the stern."

"I took out one person. I can access the bridge from the front. There are stairs leading to it. I see the movement of at least two people."

"Sit tight. We'll take care of the bridge. I want to avoid any crossfire."

"Copy. Standing by."

Nazir turned and nodded to the three men behind them. They climbed the stairs, ascending to the rear of the bridge. Peering through the window, they observed three men and one woman inside. Two men studied a chart, pointing at it and nodding in agreement. Meanwhile, the other pair lounged in high swivel chairs at the helm. The woman rested her foot on the control panel, while the other sipped from a mug, engrossed in conversation.

Turning to his men, he displayed four fingers to indicate the number of people on the bridge. "Two are reviewing some charts. The other's at the helm." They readied their weapons, and Nazir counted. "Three, two, one."

Not wanting to create unnecessary noise, Nazir stood from his crouched position, opened the door, and entered.

All occupants turned to them, their brows furrowed and expressions a mix of confusion and curiosity. One of the two who'd been leaning over the chart table straightened. "Who the hell are you?"

All four men chose a body and squeezed their triggers. The weapons were semi-automatic—single shot—double tap. Heart, then head. The bullets flew with deadly precision, each finding its target as if guided by an unseen hand. Silent and fatal, they obeyed their sole command: to kill. Mission accomplished.

Nazir stepped over to where the men had been reviewing the maps. One of the crew lying on their back turned his head. A red line on his temple marked where the bullet grazed him. Coughing, his lips struggled to form the word, "Why?" He fired once more, opening the man's skull like a busted melon. Afterward, noticing a satellite phone on the corner of the table, he picked it up and showed it to his men.

"Yank the fuses for the radio and transponder and we can use this if we need to communicate with the outside." Placing it back on the chart table, he pressed his throat mic. "All clear up here."

Moonbeam entered the bridge. Nazir nodded to his men. "Full sweep, every deck. No survivors."

The five-man team started with the deck below the bridge, one of two accommodation decks. Each room held a single berth. The first floor's body count, plus the seven they eliminated earlier, made the total eighteen. Moving silently, the five men descended the stairs to the next level, repeating the same killing sweep.

Tapeworm swung open the door to reveal two women entwined in each other's arms, their naked bodies glistening in the dim light. Without a moment's hesitation, he unleashed a torrent of 9mm rounds into the bed, transforming the sheets into a crimson banner. The brunette on top slid off the bunk and hit the deck with a heavy thud. Her eyes, wide and vacant, remained fixed on her blood-stained face, still frozen in shock.

The furthest door swung open. A twenty-something man wearing gray sweatpants and an orange long-sleeve T-shirt exited the room. His eyes were wide with fear as he stared down Wiggle and Jackyl. Turning to his right, he left the hall for the main deck. Jackyl raised his weapon and fired. A scream of pain exited the young man's lungs as the door slammed.

"Shit. We've got a runner." Jackyl followed him out to the main deck. Blood drops littered the white-painted surface. A sign that at least one projectile hit its mark. Movement toward the prow caught his attention. As he approached, his prey came into view. Clutching his right shoulder, he turned to face him.

"No. Please!"

With each step, his pleas became more desperate and louder.

His blond hair blew in the gentle night breeze. His knees quaked as he shook his head.

"For the love of God. Please, no! What do you want? Please don't kill me!"

"Will you shut the fuck up?"

Like a cornered animal, the frightened man stared past him and ran down the starboard side, screaming as he tried to escape.

"Noooo!"

His speed was no match for the searing fire erupting from the Jackyl's barrel. In a relentless burst of full-auto, he unleashed no less than ten rounds into the man's back. The impact of the subsonic lead sent him lurching forward, propelled by the force of the rounds. He collided with the railing, losing his balance, and tumbled over, plunging into his dark, watery grave.

ONE DECK BELOW, CLAIRE Davis, had her feet outstretched on the dark wood coffee table. Her favorite playlist filled the room from the Bluetooth speakers. She was waiting on the results of a Thermoluminescence Dating test on some of the pottery they'd recovered from the treasure trove of Viking ships discovered below them in fifty feet of water off the coast of Norway. The method is used to date the last time the clay was heated. By measuring the accumulated radiation dosage, they can estimate when it was fired, and it can help place it within a historical context. Her colleague, Satish Patel, sat at the table with the television remote in his hand, changing the channels when they heard the thud.

Claire laughed. "Kinsey and Sue must be going at it again."

Half paying attention, Satish mumbled, "Huh? Oh—yeah." He switched the channel once more.

"What are you looking for on the damn TV? Pick a channel and keep it there."

"I'm looking for a cricket game. I know they are on here but can't remember what channel."

Righting herself, stretching and capping it with a deep yawn, she released her black hair from the confines of a rubber band and let it flow over her shoulders before standing. "Oh, well, have fun. I'm going to grab a coffee. It'll be another hour before I get the results of my test. I want to try to stay awake. I can't wait until morning. Besides, I'm too excited to sleep."

The galley was adjacent to the lounge, separated by a sliding door with a small window. Pressing the activation button, the door slid open; she entered and headed for the Keurig.

As the machine boiled the water and spat the steamy black liquid into her cup, she thought she heard Satish yelling.

He must have found his stupid game.

It was a loud thud, followed by the chatter of other voices, making her eyes narrow and nose scrunch with curiosity.

Stepping over to the small window, there was a black-clad elbow. As she moved her head for a better view, she made out the assault rifle he was carrying. Another crew member must have heard the commotion and entered the break room.

"Hey, who the f—"

Metal on metal rapidly clapped against each other, followed by empty brass shells bouncing on the metal deck, assaulting her ears. She caught a glimpse of the red spray filling the air as bullets peppered her shipmate's chest, ripping the flesh and breaking bone.

Her eyes were wide with terror. She pressed her hand to her mouth to stifle a scream and ducked away from the window, scanning for the exit to the forward stairwell. With a careful, measured step, she began to move toward her only escape route.

Ascending to the next level, she went along the accommodation hall. In each room, the door was open. Inside most rooms were the bodies of her dead friends and co-workers. Her breathing increased. A wave of panic and anxiety washed over her. "Oh, my God!"

I've got to call for help. The pilot house. I don't know how to work the radio. I have to figure it out.

She moved as fast and silent as she could to the amidship stairwell. It would take her up the next two decks to the bridge. Once on top, she searched for the radio station. Knobs, dials, digital readouts, and all sorts of things she didn't know how to operate filled the radio station. She grabbed the mic and pressed the button. "Hello? Mayday, mayday."

Silence followed. *Oh, for Christ's sake. I don't even know if this damn thing is on.*

Distant voices came from the stairwell.

Oh, shit.

She hurried to the top of the stairs as movement came her way.

The hairs on the back of her neck stood, rising like blooming flowers stretching for the warmth of the summer sun. She searched for somewhere to hide. A storage closet, past the chart table, caught her attention. Sliding the door open, she pushed life jackets aside and contorted her five-foot-four-inch frame into the tiny space. As she was closing the door, something drew her eye. Sitting on the edge of the chart table, the one thing she knew how to use. Her voice to the outside world. Her lifeline.

A satellite phone.

26

7 hours earlier
Bergen, Norway

June 28th 16:54 (14:54 UTC)

Evelyn jogged along the winding pathways of the quaint park; a serene oasis tucked amid the majestic architecture of the surrounding buildings. Young mothers laughed and played with their toddlers on colorful blankets, spread across the manicured grass. Nearby, others strolled with their dogs, while an elderly couple delighted in the simple pleasure of feeding ducks by the small pond at the park's edge. The tantalizing aromas of sizzling meats, fragrant spices, and freshly chopped herbs wafted through the air, blending seamlessly from the apartment balconies and the charming restaurants lining the nearby harbor.

Her phone's ring interrupted the music streaming through her earbuds. Checking her smartwatch, she didn't recognize the number, but the '44' country code told her it was a UK number.

She stopped and let it ring once more while she caught her breath. Wiping her brow with her sleeve, she tapped the green 'answer' icon on her smartwatch.

"Hello?"

"Aye, Special Agent Cathey?"

"It is."

"Angus Bruce, ma'am. Ah'd be the pailot comin' to get ye to fly ye out to the ship. Ah shud be thar in about an our. Ah've found a place to land that's close to yer hotel. It's a wee park, it's call'd—Ny... Nygards—ach, forgive me, lass, ah can't pronounce foony lingo."

She chuckled. "Nygardsparken."

"Aye, lass. That'd be it."

She turned around and took in her surroundings. "Yes. I'm familiar with it. I'm here right now."

"Oh, perfect. Th' patch o' grass west of the fountain. So, if yer facin' th'—oh, what th' hell am Ah doin? Ye'll see ma chopper. Just be there. And check out' yer hotel. Ah don't know how lang ye'll be gone."

"Okay, so to confirm, be back here in an hour?"

"Aye."

Evelyn disconnected the call, thankful his accent wasn't as strong as the CEO's she spoke with the other day, then double-timed it back to her hotel. She had under an hour to shower, pack, and return to catch her ride.

Even after a cool shower and the sun setting, she was sweating. Dragging one suitcase, her laptop, and purse was difficult enough, but she had to buy another bag to hold all the new cold weather gear she bought for this trip, making the three-block trip problematic.

Why didn't I get a damn cab?

People were still feeding the ducks, although now, it was a young couple. They stood hand in hand while the pretty blonde tossed small pieces of bread into the water. It was possibly their first or second date, discovering blossoming love for each other. The first sign of the whirring blades, the ducks retreated to the far side of the pond. Strands of her hair escaped the confines of her ponytail and blew in her face. She attempted to keep them at bay, but it was pointless. The Bell 505 landed in a flat place on the lush lawn. Its blue and white paint scheme matched the DavCo website she had perused earlier.

The blades slowed but never quit. The man she had spoken with earlier exited the craft, crouching as he came and grabbed her bags. He spoke out above the din of the engine. "Ah assume ye're Agent Cathey?"

With her hand holding her hair back, she smiled and nodded.

Returning a similar gesture, he guided her to the chopper to fly them to the DavCo Deep Drill, waiting a hundred kilometers offshore.

⸻◆⸻

DAVCO DEEP DRILL

165 Kilometers WNW of Bergen, Norway 19:36 (17:36 UTC)

Shoveling in the last bit of her meal into her mouth in the ship's mess hall, Evelyn wiped her chin with her napkin.

"Ah trust th' food tasted like shite."

She glanced up at the surprise announcement directed toward her. An elderly gentleman, attractive for his age, with chiseled features, slicked-back hair, and a close-trimmed beard, approached her, extending his hand.

"Kenny MacIntosh. CEO o' DavCo. Pleasure tae mak' yer acquaintance."

She accepted his hand. "Oh, Mr. MacIntosh. Yes, it's a pleasure to meet you too. And—no. Uh...the food—it was quite good. Exceptional, really."

He let loose a gentle laugh. "Guid. Ah was just teasin' ye. Ah pay thae fuckers enough tae mak' a damn guid meal, and Ah'm glad tae see ye agree. Ah'd chew 'em a new ane if they didnae."

She chuckled and placed her palm over her mouth. "You're funny." *Oh, my God, I can hardly understand you.*

From behind him, a young woman dressed fashionably in what young thirty-somethings were sporting these days; khaki skinny jeans, a white blouse, and a black jacket approached and extended her hand.

"Hi, I'm Nicole and I'm Mr. MacIntosh's assistant. I'll be assisting you with anything you need. Has anyone shown you the way to your cabin yet?"

Standing to accept her greeting, she shook her head. "No, I'm afraid not. Honestly—I was so hungry; this was my first stop."

"Aye, weel lassies. Ah'll leave ye tae get acquaint'ed, then. Ye're in guid hands wi' Nikki, Special Agent Cathey. We'll be speakin' later, aye?" He made a slight bowing gesture and walked out of the dining hall.

Evelyn smiled and then turned to her. "Your accent—it's so beautiful. Where's it from?"

Her tastefully colored red lips parted to reveal a gleaming white smile. "Thank you. I was born and raised in Wales."

Evelyn leaned in and spoke under her breath. "Well, I gotta tell you, you're a whole lot easier to understand than your boss."

They both shared a laugh. "Right. It—does take some time to get used to, but now—" She waved it off. "It's second nature to me. But I get how a westerner would have difficulty." She sighed. "Well, let's get you to your quarters now, shall we?"

DAVCO DEEP DRILL

233 Kilometers WNW of Bergen, Norway 23:51 (21:51 UTC)

Evelyn awoke in her cabin with the lights still on. After she'd unpacked, she decided to lay on the bunk and close her eyes. Righting herself, she rubbed her eyes.

Well, I guess I was more tired than I thought.

Reaching for her phone, she glanced at the time. Feeling her stomach growl, she decided to check out the odd ship she was on after getting something to settle her stomach.

Selecting a prepackaged Honeybun and a cup of chamomile tea, she made her way to the bridge, using the set of stairs outside the ship. The cool air gave her chicken skin, and she brushed off a chill, but it was also refreshing at the same time.

Stepping through the exterior bridge door, the room shimmered with a soft, ethereal blue hue emanating from a myriad of screens displaying data on the ship's functions and environmental conditions.

Three men stood around a console having a rather heated conversation when they noticed her. A tall Asian man wearing clothes typical of a ship's crew approached and tipped his hat. "Welcome aboard, Ma'am, I'm Deung Si-woo. I'm the captain. You can call me Woo. I take it you're the investigator from Canadian Intelligence?"

After setting her tea on a counter, she rubbed her arms briskly to warm them. "Yes, and thank you, Woo." She motioned with her head. "What was going on over there? Anything to be concerned about?"

"What?" He snickered. "Oh—no. We had a blip on the radar that was pretty solid, then suddenly disappeared."

Her brow rose. "You mean like it sunk or something?"

"Or something." He adjusted his hat on his head. "I wouldn't worry about it. It wasn't very big, maybe sixty or seventy feet. That's too small for a pleasure boat to be this far out at night. It could have been the conning tower of a Russian sub submerging."

Her eyes widened and her mouth went agape. "Seriously?"

The rapidly rising anxiety dissipated when he smiled and let out a satisfying laugh. "No. In all likelihood, it was two or three lost shipping containers. Together, they're big enough for radar to sense them. They'll float around until they take in too much water and sink."

She rubbed her arms again. "Ah, makes sense. It's fairly common then?"

Nodding, he rubbed the side of his nose. "More than you know. Ships lose thousands each year. Last year, one ship lost almost three hundred in these frigid waters. Look, do you want a blanket? I've got a bunch in a locker over there."

"Uh..."

"Yeah, you do." He stepped over to the locker, grabbed a blue blanket with the DavCo logo, returned and handed it to her.

"Oh, yes." Unfolding it, she wrapped it around her shoulders. "Much better. Thanks." She reached for her tea and took a sip. "Have you worked for DavCo long?"

He shook his head. "I don't work for them. I work for the company that built her. We're the shipyard responsible for the construction of the Arctic Deep Drill. I know her inside and out. As does the small crew of engineers I've brought to figure out what the heck happened and get her running again. I've got an equally capable colleague to pilot her back to Edinburgh, where we can go over her from stem to stern and ensure everything is working properly."

She took another sip of her tea. Her nose scrunched at its cold temperature. "How long do you think it will take to fix it and get her running again?"

Squinting his left eye, he rubbed the stubble on his chin. "Could be a week, ten days. Two weeks max. We've brought enough supplies and parts to finish the job in that time."

She nodded. "All right, that makes sense. When do you believe we'll get to it?"

He removed his hat and scratched his scalp, with his graying black hair. "Uh, well, depending on how she drifts." He glanced at his watch. "It's a little past twelve-thirty." His eyes moved toward the pilot house ceiling as he made mental calculations. "About seventy-two hours."

Evelyn's brow furrowed and her eyes went wide. "What? Three days?"

"Yes, ma'am. She's nine hundred nautical miles from us, and this boat is maxed out at sixteen knots. And you're lucky all the holds are empty. If they're full, we can do eleven—twelve if we're lucky. One thing is for sure, she wasn't built for speed."

She inhaled a deep, long sigh. "Uh, I understand." Looking at her now cold tea, she swirled the cup. "Captain, thank you for your time and the conversation. I'll get a refill and go back to my cabin. Can I—keep the blanket?"

"Certainly. You know, you can get to your cabin without going outside. Would you like me to show you the way?"

Shifting her eyes toward the green glow of the exit sign in thought, she shook her head. "Uh... No. I think I like the blast of cool air. But I appreciate the offer."

"Of course."

She exited the bridge and descended the stairs. The 800-foot ship felt as if it was hardly inching along, its progress barely perceptible. Gazing over the tranquil sea, the waters calm and glassy. Only ninety minutes earlier, the sun had dipped below the horizon of the North Sea, bidding its farewell for the day. Yet its morning warmth would soon envelop the vessel again, as the first golden rays were set to return in three and a half hours. At least for now, she could still enjoy the darkness. Where they were heading, the sun shone almost twenty-four hours a day.

She stopped on the next level to gather her thoughts and enjoy the peaceful moment. Lights off the starboard bow caught her attention. The boat looked to be about a kilometer away. She closed one eye to judge if it was moving. She tilted her head, extended her arm, and raised her thumb.

Nope. I don't think they're moving. Oh well. Probably all asleep—speaking of which.

She took a tentative step, then paused, straining to listen. In the distance, a faint scream reached her ears, as if carried over the water. The cry seemed to be beckoning for help.

Nothing followed. "I'm hearing things." She shrugged. "And now I'm talking to myself."

Foregoing a second cup of tea, she tossed her cup in the nearest bin and returned to her cabin for the night.

OSOYRO, NORWAY

June 29th 17:40 (15:40 UTC)

Everything had been quiet, and Blake had no new leads, so he decided to take a few days to rest and recuperate from his aches and pains of the past few days. The location he chose was a thirty-minute drive Southeast of Bergen.

In front of the rugged hill, covered in sharp rocks and wild grass, stood the building overlooking the azure Bjornafiorden, known as "The Bear Fiord".

It was a windy day, with whitecaps lapping against the rugged shoreline. The Norwegian flag waved graciously in the gusting winds, its brass fittings clanging against the pole as if proudly announcing its presence.

Blake exited the spa at the Solstrand Hotel. The young woman behind the desk gave him a good once over with her eyes and smiled. He returned the gesture.

Walking through the lobby, fragrances from the hotel restaurant wafted in and filled the room with the scents of locally harvested fresh fish, grilled sausages, and other meats. Blake felt his stomach react and would have no qualms about answering its calls.

Upon entering his accommodation, he was fortunate to have booked a corner room. He was able to enjoy the sights of the fjord from multiple angles. Both French doors were open, letting in the cool summer evening air. A light breeze glided through the room, gently blowing the white curtains with a kiss of Odin's breath. The doors to the right of his king-sized bed provided a view of the resort's courtyard and beyond its grassy lawn, the fjord with silhouettes of the mountain islands beyond. To his left, the building sat only a few yards from the water's edge. Mountains were more prominent on the landmass across the inlet sea's span.

Noticing his phone blinking, it indicated he had had three missed calls. All from Veronica. He swiped away the notifications and undressed for a shower.

I'll call her after I'm done.

After getting dressed, he grabbed the phone and sat in one of the two wingback chairs in front of his balcony view.

"Hey, sorry. I was busy. What did you need?"

"Were you ever able to ascertain whether Miss Cathey had any leads?"

"Unfortunately, no. She mentioned having communicated with the CEO of DavCo the owner of the ship her brother was aboard, yet they remained clueless."

"Okay. Do you know what she will do now all our leads have either dissipated or been killed?"

"No. I assume she'll go home."

"Well, you know what happens when you assume?"

"Ha, ha. Yes. Makes an ass out of you and me."

"Right. So, where's she at? We got a hit. She checked out of her hotel."

"What? When?"

"Yesterday. There is no record of her being on any flights. And her rental car is still at the hotel."

Blake stood and started to pace the floor. "She must have a new lead. Wait. No. Why would her car still be there?" He snapped his fingers. "Veronica. Hold on. I put a tracker in her purse. I'm going to put you on speaker."

He opened the app to access the device he'd slid into her purse when they enjoyed a drink together after their chase through Bergen. The app opened and started displaying a map. Her location was as bland as could be. Only a flashing dot in a sea of blue. No streets, and no outlines of buildings, as expected. "What the hell?" He used his fingers to zoom out.

"Son of a bitch!"

"What is it?"

"She's in the middle of the ocean!"

27

The Norwegian Sea
June 30th 00:41 (22:41 UTC)

Claire emerged from her hiding place as voices filled the ship's bridge. Instinctively, she retreated, sliding the locker shut but leaving a narrow gap to catch a glimpse and listen in, hoping to identify the intruders and discover their intentions.

Fear washed over her like an unseen blanket, enshrouding her in a suffocating grip, making it hard to breathe. She could feel her heart pounding, each beat a reminder of her vulnerability.

The first man removed his balaclava and started barking orders. "Jackson, Tim, do a final sweep of the entire ship. Holds, lockers, anywhere to hide. I want to make sure nobody is left."

A tall, imposing brute stepped into her view. He towered over the other. "Don't use our real names. In case someone is still alive and lurking about."

The goon, who appeared to be their leader, waved him off. "Nonsense. Anyone we'd find, we'd kill. We've disabled the radio, so there is no way they can get a message out."

Panic and anxiety gripped her. Each heartbeat in her neck pulsed at breakneck speed. Now she *had* to get the satellite phone. The man in charge turned toward her.

Her nose wrinkled as she cringed. He was missing his right ear. It was as if it had been cut off. As he began to reach for the device, the man at the helm called to him.

"Nazir, come here a moment. I'm detecting something on the radar. It's close." He spun around and disappeared out of sight. They were speaking but she couldn't make out what they were saying.

He returned, grabbed a pack of cigarettes off the table, retrieved one, and placed it between his lips. "Give me those binoculars. Let's go outside and take a look. Luca, wind in the anchor and start the engines. We need to go. And somebody, remove these dead bodies from the bridge!"

The door closed, and she didn't hesitate. Leaving the safety of her locker, she reached out and snagged the phone. Exiting the starboard side, she hurried to the main deck. Every step was conscious and calculated. Her senses were at peak awareness. With each foot closer to her destination, she scanned her surroundings and designated the best hiding place if someone approached.

The anchor winch motor started, and her stomach leaped to her throat. Her muscles flinched, arousing her fight-or-flight modes. She took a deep breath when she realized what the mechanical sound was. Crouching, she reached the amidship main deck doors.

Rising enough to peek in the window, the rail to the stairs was a few feet past the entrance. On this deck was the lab. One level below was the science storeroom. Under that, the workshop. A single bulkhead beyond was the stern thruster machine room. In there, she would hide until she felt she could escape.

Stepping inside, she moved to the top of the stairwell and descended to the storeroom. Fearing discovery, she descended another deck deeper into the vessel's belly. Entering the workshop, she scanned the room full of tools where various wrenches and screwdrivers hung on the wall. A large vice was bolted to a steel table. Behind it, a shelf full of paints and lubricants. A loud clanking once again set her nerves on end. It was the propeller shaft starting to revolve.

We're underway wherever the hell we're going.

She cranked the steel wheel on the bulkhead door. Each turn, the creaking was louder than the previous. She stopped and inhaled a deep breath. Scanning the area, she spotted a bottle of WD-40 multipurpose lubricant. Applying a generous amount, she let it soak in before resuming.

After a minute, she applied pressure. It moved without resistance or noise. She entered the small room, found a crate to sit on, and examined her lifeline to the outside world. The screen illuminated as it powered on. Her stomach sank as the wave of dread pressed hard on her shoulders.

No signal.

Feeling deflated, she leaned back and rested her head against the bulkhead.

I'm going to have to wait.

Sitting at the stern, deep inside, the relentless churning of the propeller pushed them through icy waters, and she drifted into a gentle doze.

THE NORWEGIAN SEA

200 Nautical Miles E of the Faroe Islands 04:00 (03:00 UTC)

Nazir had finished a short nap in one of the few crew quarters that weren't splattered with blood or littered with dead bodies. Checking his watch, they should be close to rendezvousing with the Atlas to transfer the sub from the Deep Wave vessel. Luca was on the bridge when he entered with a cup of tea. "Any sign of them yet?"

He indicated with his left arm. "There—off the port side bow. Perhaps a klick, or less. We'll be alongside in two minutes."

Sipping his hot drink, he nodded his agreement. "Excellent." Turning toward the chart table, something obvious was missing. Setting his mug aside, he stepped over to see if it had fallen off. He peered at the floor and in all the surrounding cubby holes. "Hey, did you take the sat phone? It was here the last time I checked"

His partner shook his head. "No. Ask the others."

Grabbing the nearest handheld radio, he addressed his team. "Has anyone taken the bright yellow phone from the bridge? Answer immediately."

He felt a heavy weight in his gut when all answers were identical: "No."

Pressing the mic button once more, his voice was gruff and urgent. "We have a survivor! Find them! Search everywhere."

Luca remained at the helm while the other four searched the ship from top to bottom. The Atlas rendezvoused with them and moored at the rear to make the sub's transfer as simple as possible.

CLAIRE'S EYES SHOT open with the loud metallic clanging that appeared to come from all directions. The clomp of thumping feet descending the stairs into the mechanical area was obvious. The prop shaft had stopped spinning and other voices penetrated the hull at the ship's stern.

Footsteps got louder and her neck hair stood on end.

She focused on the wheel sealing the door between her and the killer outside her sanctuary.

It started to move, and she held her breath. Frantically she peered around for anything she could use as a weapon.

It cranked again. A meter-long wrench rested in the corner against a wooden crate full of cans of gear oil.

Grasping it with both hands, with silent and deliberate steps, she moved toward the hatch.

The handle turned—its groan no longer silenced from the spray lubricant she used earlier.

The mercenary's radio squawked.

She strained her ears, attempting to understand what was being said. All she could make out was a simple, "Okay." His fading footsteps took with them the anxiety she'd accumulated.

It feels like we've reached our destination. Wherever the hell that is. I'll wait until I know they're gone and make a call from up on the deck.

Voices and thunderous noises came from the work deck above her for over an hour. The winch for the submarine davit was right over her head. The racket was deafening, each noise amplified by the cramped, cold confines of the space. She put her hands over her ears in a feeble attempt to shut out the constant din.

Another hour went by, and the commotion continued. Silence followed. She waited for twenty minutes. There still wasn't a sound from overhead. Placing the phone in her jacket pocket, she stepped over to the steel barrier, grasped the wheel, and began to turn it when a loud explosion echoed through the ship. The shock knocked her onto her back.

"Holy shit! What the hell?"

The groaning metal under duress filled her ears. The floor beneath her was at a different angle. Then she heard it. Rushing water.

Oh my God, I've got to get out of here.

Her worst fear became a reality when she glanced at the hatch. Seawater seeped in over the bulkhead. Springing to her feet, she darted over and cranked as fast as her strength would allow. The pressure of the incoming sea from the next room forced it open. The deluge rushed in, slamming her into the back of the tiny space. Fighting against the current, she gasped for life-sustaining air.

Coughing and gasping, she realized what she needed to do.

I need to let the room flood so I can swim out.

As the ship started to list, she went to the far corner and found an air pocket. The lights flickered. The water was calm enough that she could swim. Its icy bite sent shocks through her muscles. She took a deep breath and swam to the door. Flickering one last time, they illuminated her path, and then—total darkness surrounded her.

She felt for the door's frame and used it to push herself toward the staircase. She was never good at holding her breath and could feel her lungs starting to burn. The aching of the metal bending under tremendous stress roared like a demon's growl through the water, a haunting symphony of the ship's impending doom.

She grabbed a step and pushed her body through the remorseless sea and to the next deck, into the science laboratory. Light from the main lab caught her attention.

Her chest burned.

Thrusting herself upward, she broke the water's surface near her workstation on the main deck. Instinctively gulping for air, she turned toward the rear of the doomed ship. It was sinking by the stern. As she stood in the water reaching her calves, she needed to get higher to make a call with the satellite phone.

The phone!

Her pocket was empty.

"Oh God, no." Looking down into the dark, churning water, she knew what she had to do. Pulling a waterproof emergency light from the wall, she switched it on and dove into the room she had narrowly escaped. Scanning the small area, the bright yellow phone wasn't anywhere to be seen. Fear washed over her. She pushed herself to the surface for a deep breath.

Dear God, please be with me.

Kicking hard, she grasped the steel railings, propelling her deeper into the boat's sinking belly through the science room and further to the workshop. The tortured wail of the dying vessel sent shivers through her. Into the lower room, she panned the light, hoping to catch a glimpse of her yellow savior.

Over in the corner. Shining like a beacon, there it was.

Kicking with all she had, she reached out. Her body quaked and convulsed. It needed oxygen. Her lungs were on fire. There was another convulsion. The air propelled forcefully from her. Bubbles surrounded her, rising to the top. The demonic growl of her tortured keeper gave her the will to keep going.

No! Kick harder!

Up to the storeroom and holding on with all her strength. More air escaped. Darkness started to fill her vision, and every muscle burned.

I don't wanna die! Not this way.

One more heave! She reached the surface. Precious oxygen.

She took a deep, life-sustaining gulp of air, the vital gas flowing through her body. Heading for the rear stairwell, water past her knees, the ship started listing to starboard. She climbed the steps, inhaling deep as she went. Desperate to fill her lungs, she would stop and breathe before continuing to another level.

Where are the inflatable rafts? Oh! I remember. They're in the front in a storage area.

Rushing to the front of the ship, she found the locker and pulled out a raft. She stumbled as the deck's angle increased from the bow rising out of the sea. Moving to the port side, she flung it over the edge, pulling the instant inflation cord as she released it. After landing, it filled itself with air.

Pressing the emergency button on the phone, she was connected to the Norwegian Coast Guard. After telling them she was sinking, they locked onto her coordinates and dispatched a chopper. Ending the call, she tossed it into the life raft and jumped.

She used the paddle to get herself away from the sinking vessel, fearful it could suck her into the dark abyss with it. She watched as the bridge bid farewell to the sun forever and slipped under on its descent to its watery grave three thousand feet below.

To her right was the Atlas, its twin screws propelling it and everyone onboard, along with the familiar ROV dangling from the davit, away to an unknown destination.

Unaware and unfeeling, the bullet tore through her skull, her head erupting in a cloud of crimson. Fragments of brain and bone splattered into the sea. The subsequent rounds punctured the raft. The weight of Claire's dead body pushed it beneath the water's surface, enveloping her in a cocoon of rubber, like the petals of a Venus flytrap, forever trapping its victim inside.

28

Near the North Pole
July 1st 08:00 (08:00 UTC)

Butterflies danced in Evelyn's stomach, tightening her chest with each passing moment. She stole one last glance through her portal at the ghostly ship, once brimming with the lives of countless souls, including her beloved brother, Richard. Now, it drifted aimlessly among the icebergs, an empty vessel echoing the memories of its former passengers.

What would she find over there? A ghastly display, like out of a slasher film with blood spatter and dead bodies lying about? A spectacle frozen in time of the horrific events and the torture those onboard endured. Or, did the attackers throw all the corpses overboard? Whatever it was, she was prepared the best she could be. Not having an evidence kit with her, she improvised. She'd purchased a box of rubber gloves and several spools of yellow caution ribbon to act as her crime scene tape she could use to cordon off areas of investigation.

A gentle rap on the door drew her attention from her thoughts. She wiped away a tear.

"Come in."

Nicole cracked the door and stuck her head in the room. "They're ready for you."

Nodding her understanding, she forced a smile. "Okay. Tell them I'll be there in three minutes."

"I will. Take your time."

Evelyn informed Mr. MacIntosh she needed to be the first to board the Arctic Deep Drill—and she had to do so alone. The vessel was now a crime scene. Under the control of a Canadian corporation, the ship enforced its authority by stressing the importance of safeguarding the area and blocking any outside interference. Whether her claim was entirely accurate was uncertain but framing it this way would help mitigate his company's liability in any potential wrongful death lawsuits. In the heated debate, her argument settled the matter for him.

Along with her initial items, she had her camera, fingerprint dust and brushes, a load of evidence bags, measuring tape, audio, and video recorders, as well as a notebook. The last item she secured was her pistol. Raising it and opening the slide enough to verify a round had been chambered, she double-checked the safety and holstered her weapon.

The chopper lifted from the Deep Drill's forward helipad and within seconds it landed on the Arctic's identical pad.

"Aye, lass." He handed her a walkie. "Use this if ye want anything. We've got a team ready tae come o'er and help ye if ye need it. Best of luck!"

Stepping out of the bird, she ducked and made her way to the exit. The sound of the helicopter's engines and blades increasing their revolutions drowned out everything, including the thoughts in her head. The gust of wind chilled the already freezing temperature to extreme conditions. In minutes, the chopper was back on the ship adjacent to her.

The sun shone, and the thermometer stood at an average of minus one degree Celsius. After a deep breath, she descended the stairs leading to the bridge. Black static lines, still connected to the rails with carabiners, blew in the wind, like tendrils of jellyfish floating in the sea. Broken windows were visible in the front windscreen, and the back wall showed numerous blood splatters.

Removing the video camera from her bag, she commenced the recording. "This is where they must have rappelled and entered initially. The crew were caught off guard and taken by surprise."

She took multiple pictures from different angles. Continuing to the pilothouse, she came to the door, closed her eyes, and prepared herself for whatever horrors lay beyond its icy-cold entrance.

Inside, the floor was strewn with shards of glass. Blood spatters adorned the interior, splattered across the walls and control panels, a grim testament to the violence that had transpired. The floor bore smears, revealing the path where bodies had been moved, leaving an unmistakable mark of chaos and horror.

Stepping further into the grizzly scene, she glanced to her right. The gray matter lay putrefying in the aisle, smeared as if someone had dragged a body over it. The stench of decomposing flesh assailed her nostrils, and she placed her hand over her nose and mouth while she gagged. Dashing for the exit, she burst through the door and projectile puked as she reached the outside railing. Swallowing the chunks left behind, she repeated the process and hurled the rest of her stomach's contents into the sea below.

"Ughhhh!"

She spat.

"God!"

"Oh, no!"

She heaved again as bile and what little content remained spewed out of her.

Taking a moment, she breathed in the crisp air. Putting her bag on a storage bin containing an inflatable raft, she rummaged through it until she found her menthol and a surgical mask.

Opening the jar, she applied an excessive amount to her upper lip. The refreshing, minty cool aroma was a pleasant scent, reminiscent of mint candies or a crisp winter breeze. After she gathered her composure, she descended to the next level. She planned to take a general walk around the ship and identify all areas where a criminal act had happened. She would also search for evidence and mark it with a marker. Afterward, she would return and forensically investigate them.

On each floor she combed, the scene was similar. There was confirmation of violence having taken place such as bullet holes, or blood on the walls and decking. Nothing screamed at her as anything of particular importance. The most intriguing piece of evidence was the lack of it. There were no brass casings and, more importantly—no bodies—anywhere.

She walked to the starboard side of the main deck and headed for the door. It was jammed when she pulled it. Checking the handle, it was disfigured and bent, with red paint scuffed on it as if smashed by some heavy object. The door's window was shattered and white residue was still on the frame and stuck to the broken glass.

Glancing at her watch, her stomach growled, so she ate her lunch. It had been hours since she vomited and after all the other blood she'd seen, she'd numbed her senses to it. She grabbed her radio and called the Deep Drill. "Captain Woo? Over."

"Yes, Special Agent Cathey, go ahead, over."

"I am going to be here a while. How long did you say I had daylight? Over."

"I didn't, but you have twenty-four hours. The sun doesn't set. It only dips toward the horizon before rising again. Over."

"Okay, that's what I figured. I'll check in at eighteen hundred and let you know when you can come retrieve me. Over."

"Copy and understand. Out."

---

30 NAUTICAL MILES SOUTH of the Arctic Deep Drill 11:48 (11:48 UTC)

Blake sat in the rear of the KC-130 preparing for the most dangerous jump he'd ever done. Most of his nervousness was not having affirmation of another vessel being there.

The last action he wanted to do was jump to an abandoned ship in the middle of the Arctic Ocean with no means to get back. Some worry subsided when he received confirmation from the navigator there were, two vessels present.

The next thing eating at him was he had a tiny target he had to hit. There was no room for mistakes. The forward helipad was his only option. Rigging, davits, and cranes covered the rest of the boat, providing no flat surface to land on.

He thought about all the hoops the U.S. Government had to jump through to get the Danish Airforce to fly him out to his destination. Money? Concessions? Relief on some import tariffs? Reminiscing, he remembered how President Pennington was a formidable adversary when bargaining. Perhaps she threatened to pull funding for some of their pet projects and they immediately agreed to help. It was in their best interest too for him to get to the bottom of this mystery. After all, they too were victims of an attack with losses.

The co-pilot's voice over the headset jerked him from his thoughts.

"Three minutes until we slow to jump speed, Mister MacKay. Five minutes to *fallskærmsudspring*."

He smiled. "Is that airborne in Danish?"

"No. Parachuting."

Blake's stomach rose as they descended to his jump altitude. The red light illuminated and the rear hatch opened. The cool air enveloped his body and shocked him, even through his thick, black cold weather gear.

He lowered his goggles and waited for the light to change.

A buzzer sounded, and the cabin filled with a green glow. Accelerating to a sprint he dove out of the rear of the plane.

He loved the rush of adrenaline and the feeling of acceleration as he was propelled towards the ground at terminal velocity. The wind rushed past him, filling his auditory senses.

A thin layer of clouds blocked his view of the ocean below as he tried to scan for two tiny dots floating in the vast Arctic. Being filled with thousands of ice chunks didn't help the matter.

Glancing at the phone he'd strapped to his wrist, he had locked onto Evelyn's tracker. He adjusted his flight path and broke through the misty veil.

Sitting in the sea were two identical boats. From studying photographs, they each had their name written along the side in huge letters, but he was approaching them from their bows so he could land on the raised helipad. As he kept falling and getting closer, the situation made his decision. On one sat a helicopter with some intimidating rotor blades. The empty one would have to be it. He pulled his cord, and his guts dropped to his feet as he slowed from 120 mph to an easy 10 to 15 mph.

Navigating the chute, he approached the empty landing pad. As he glanced to his left, the other ship had Deep Drill written in white along its blue hull.

The touchdown was soft and perfect, but as his chute started deflating a gust of arctic wind latched on and knocked him off his feet.

It dragged him toward the brink.

Clawing at the smooth, steel surface proved worthless, he reached for his sheathed, ten-inch blade attached to his chest and flipped himself on his back.

The edge was fifteen feet away. Grabbing at a heap of cords, he sliced them in half.

Now ten feet to a sixty-foot drop. Another set of cords filled his grasp, and he cut them.

Two feet away from plummeting into the icy waters below the chute released and drifted off like a wayward balloon.

He let out a deep sigh. "Fuck me!"

Rising to his feet, he surveyed the top of the ship. Facing aft, the only thing in his view was the Doppler radar housings, and beyond the central radar tower, stood the massive drill rigging. Making his way to the bridge, he peeked into the door's window, there was a site he recognized, the ending result of violent carnage. Blood, dried to a deep crimson, stained the walls and floors. Upon entering the bridge, the all too familiar stench of death permeated his nostrils. The wind howled as it entered the shattered front windscreens.

As he walked through the room, the ghosts of his hidden demons, brimming with furious rage, haunted his memories. He envisioned the attack, the sharp, rhythmic sound of silenced assault rifles echoing in his mind, delivering their deadly payload to unsuspecting victims caught off guard.

Stepping through to the rear of the pilothouse, he descended to the next level. Trails of blood from where bodies had been dragged marred the floor. Entering the captain's cabin, he went straight for the desk. He sat in the chair and started to rummage through the drawers, looking for anything to give him a clue to pursue.

A familiar voice filled his ears from behind him.

"Raise your hands in the air and stand up. Don't make any sudden moves or I'll put a bullet in the back of your head."

He did as he was commanded. After standing, he turned. "Hello, Evelyn."

Her brow furrowed, and she cocked her head. "Blake?"

Casting a warm smile, he gestured to the pistol in her hand. "You gonna keep pointing that thing at me?"

"What? Oh—sorry." Lowering her weapon, she stowed it in the holster on her belt.

"So, why are you here? How did you find me? Wait!" She pursed her lips and frowned. "Did you put a tracker on me?"

He stood, staring at her, before looking away.

Her hands went to her hips, and she shifted her weight to the other foot. "You son of a bitch. You did, didn't you? You don't trust me."

His eyes widened while his arms were outstretched. "Uh...Hello? What was it you said? Canada Oil had no idea where the ship was. I don't hear from you to discuss any new clues you or I might have found and the next thing I know, you're in the middle of the North Atlantic heading to only God knows where. I presumed it was the missing boat, and I was right."

He moved closer to her, inhaling the delicate scent of Japanese cherry blossoms stirring a long-dormant sensation within him. The ceiling lights danced in her vibrant green eyes, and to his surprise, she didn't recoil as he invaded her personal space.

"I thought you and I had an agreement to work together." He turned and stepped toward the desk before returning his gaze to her. "Might I remind you, you're not working on an official capacity, but you've probably fooled those people on the other ship, haven't you? I can surmise what they'd say if I told them. How did you know I was here anyhow? They called you?"

She turned her focus to the floor and waved the walkie, she held in her hand. "Yeah. They asked if I was expecting a visitor."

The radio squawked. "Agent Cathey, are ye all right? We saw the lad make his way onto the bridge. Over."

Lifting it to her mouth, she pressed the button. "Affirmative. I've made contact. He's a—" She released it. "You and I gonna play nicely?"

Blake cracked a smile and nodded.

Pressing back on the side of the transmitter, she added. "Uh, he's a colleague. Part of a joint investigation between us and the Americans. All is well. Over."

"Roger. Out."

She clipped the radio to her belt and nodded to him. "Are you gonna stand there or are you going to help?"

"Yes, ma'am."

They left the captain's quarters and set off toward the staircase. He unzipped his coat. "So, what have you discovered so far?" They descended the stairs.

"It's not what I *have* found, it's what I haven't. Do you notice any bodies or ammo brass lying around?"

"Can't say I do."

They reached the first landing and continued their downward climb. "Don't you find it a little weird? I mean, who the hell comes in, slaughters everyone, and cleans up afterward?"

The next landing approached, and she waved him on. "Come on, one more deck."

He cleared his throat. "It would make sense if they needed the ship for a few days and didn't want to be stepping over rotting corpses. But the brass? I'm not so sure. They'd be smart enough to load their weapons wearing gloves to avoid leaving fingerprints, but on the other hand, if they stayed on board for several days, they must have left evidence everywhere. So, in answer to your question—yes. It is odd. Where are we going, by the way?"

"Remember when I told you about the text message from my brother?"

"Vaguely."

"It's in the oven, the Danes." They arrived at the bottom, and she opened a door for him. "Through there." After the door slammed, she moved in front and continued to walk. The hallway was bland and sterile, with light beige tile and walls. "Up here is the galley. I was on my way to check the oven when I got the call of some idiot parachuting onto the ship." She glanced back with a playful smile on her face. Blake returned the gesture.

"Guilty as charged."

They entered the galley and stopped. She placed her hands on her hips and let out a long sigh. Before them was a room of tables with pots, pans, and utensils hanging overhead. Below them were dozens of drawers and cabinets, and a wall with six ovens. All stainless-steel. "Well, you take the three on the right and I'll take the others on the left."

They'd searched two of their three ovens without success when she froze in place. "*Shhh*! Quiet."

Blake halted. They listened. "Wha—"

"*Shhh!*"

After a few moments, she shook her head. "I dunno. I might be hearing things. I swear I heard a door open and close." She concentrated for a moment longer. "I guess not. Any luck?"

"No, nothing so far."

After tearing apart the interior of the last oven, she slammed the door shut. "Well, shit! Not a damn thing! Richard! Goddammit! Where did you put whatever the hell you were talking about?"

He was still searching through his final one when she turned around and froze.

Standing before her was a man with untidy hair in dirty khaki pants and a blood-stained sweater. He was holding a flash drive pinched between his forefinger and thumb.

Her eyes went wide.

"Richard?"

29

On the DavCo Arctic Drill, The North Sea

July 1st 14:00 (14:00 UTC)

"Richard!"

Evelyn ran to her brother and embraced him. He returned the gesture with a warm hug. "Sis!" Pulling back, their eyes met, and she began patting him while tears formed in the corners of her eyes. "Are—are you real? I—I can't believe it. How can this be? What happened? Oh, my God." Embracing him again, his eyes widened as he grunted, caused by the air escaping from his lungs.

"Woah. Not so tight, Ev. I can't breathe."

She released him. "I'm sorry. I'm—thrilled you're okay. For the past six weeks, I've been mourning you. I thought you were dead. Please, tell us what you went through." His focus shifted to the man behind her. "All in good time, sis. I'll tell you everything." He stepped toward Blake and offered his hand. "Hi, Richard Cathey. I assume you know who I am by now."

He returned the greeting. "Blake MacKay. Yes. It's a pleasure to meet you. She speaks highly of you."

He put his hands on his hips. "Well, I'm sure you have plenty of questions for me. Where is Josh? Is he no longer your partner?"

Evelyn's brow furrowed. "Huh? Oh, yeah." She gestured at Blake with her thumb. "He's with the Central Intelligence Agency and we've been working together on this."

He jerked his head back. "CIA?" Turning to his sister's companion, he squinted at him. "Why are you guys involved?"

"I'm afraid this is much bigger than you know. If you've got somewhere comfortable, we can talk, you can tell us what happened, and we'll fill you in on the expanded picture."

Blake and Evelyn sat on a brown, fake leather sofa with cracks in the upholstery. Richard handed her a cup of hot tea and Blake a bottle of water. As he opened a Dr. Pepper for his enjoyment, he reclined in a blue wing-back chair across from them both. A scuffed, dark wooden coffee table separated them.

He sipped his soft drink and rubbed his palms together after setting it on the table before him. "So, where do you want to start, eh?"

She jumped in. "My first question is what did you do with all the bodies?"

His eyes squinted while his nose scrunched. "Ew. You had to go there first?" He sighed. "They're all stacked in a pile on the back of the ship and covered with a tarp. It stays, for the most part, below freezing, so I figured it would be the best location. I—didn't want to dump them in the sea. They were my friends and colleagues."

The two intelligence agents eyed each other and nodded in agreement.

Blake opened his bottle. "So, who attacked you? We know it wasn't the Danes."

Richard's eyes stared past them and focused on the wall. "I don't know. And yes, I can tell you it was not the Danes."

Sipping his water, Blake wiped his mouth. "Why did you think it was them in the first place and why are you so positive now it wasn't them?"

"I was on the bridge when one of the bridge crew said a chopper was coming from Copenhagen."

He leaned forward. "So, you were there when they attacked?"

Turning his head, he paused, as if resurrecting painful memories he tried to bury. "Yeah—I was."

Both agents gave him his time.

"Men in Danish military fatigues burst through the front windows and immediately began firing. They killed everyone in sight. My buddy got his brains blown out in front of me."

He started rubbing his beard in thought.

Evelyn stood and stepped to her brother. She rubbed his back. "I know this is distressing, but it's important."

He turned to her. "They went through the entire ship and anyone they saw, they gunned down."

She continued comforting him. "How did you survive?"

"I got the heck outta there. I ran like hell, and I hid. Unfortunately, they found me."

She stopped and went to face him. "Oh, my God. What did you do?"

"Well, I was hiding in one of the lifeboats. That's where I called you from. I took a satellite phone out of the emergency kit onboard. You didn't answer, so I thought I should text you."

"Yeah, I want to ask you about that in a minute, but go ahead and finish your story."

"Well, I heard voices, and they weren't speaking Danish. It sounded more Arabic or some Middle Eastern language." He took a sip of his drink. "Anyway, some guy came into the life raft and aimed his pistol at my face and pulled the trigger."

She pressed her hand to her mouth, her eyes brimming with tears. As a few slipped past her lashes, he continued talking. "The bullet." He shook his head. "I'm not sure how, but it must have grazed me. Or my reflexes reacted too fast. I was in a confined space, so it could be a combination of the two. I think when I flinched to avoid getting hit, I slammed my head on the side of the boat. It knocked me out. When I woke, there was blood in my hair. On the left where I bashed it and, on the right, where the bullet grazed me."

Blake shifted his weight on the couch. "How long were you out? Did you happen to get a good look at any of them?"

"I honestly don't know. They were gone by the time I came to. As far as getting a look—I only saw one. And I'll never forget that son of a bitch. He was an evil-looking asshole. His right ear was chewed to hell."

Blake jerked forward. Evelyn glanced back at him. "What? Are you sure?"

Richard double-downed. "Oh, one hundred percent. That wicked prick's face is imprinted in my brain."

Blake's eyes shifted toward the floor in thought. "After they left, and you came to, why didn't you call your sister again?"

"They removed every sat phone from the ship, destroyed the radio and internet satellite dish. I had no way of communicating. I got partial power restored and hell, I have more than enough food. I was hoping I'd drift, and someone would find me."

Evelyn leaned in. "But the transponder. How did you turn that on and why did it take you so long to do it?"

He shook his head. "Sis. Until a few days ago, I didn't even know what a transponder was. I was reading a repair manual on the ship and came across it by accident. When I went to where it was, I honestly expected to see it destroyed, but it was just turned off. So, after I directed some power to the bridge, I—flipped it on." With a departing smile, he shrugged.

Both agents gave each other a confirming nod, as if communicating what to do next without saying a word. Evelyn placed her hand on his shoulder. "Bubby, do you know *why* or *what* they came here for?"

He turned to his sister. "I do. Yes."

The pair of them responded together. "Why?"

He stood and sighed. "It would be better if I showed you. Follow me."

After they went four decks into the belly of the ship, they arrived at some double doors. Richard opened them. "After you."

She entered, and Blake followed. "Hey, tell me how you repaired the power."

"Oh, I wouldn't say I—" He made air quotes. "'*Restored power*'. I got one of the backup generators running and diverted the main fuel line to it so I would have a constant supply. I have it operate everything in the galley, temperature control, water pumps, desalination system, and only a few rooms I use regularly, like my cabin, lab, galley, and the break room we were in."

"I see."

"This ship is quite remarkable. It has triple redundancy on everything necessary to function. Unfortunately, I don't have a clue how to undo what they did to bust it."

They came to another set of doors. "Ah. Here we are. When you enter, you'll see a small glass enclosure. When you go in, you'll see some glasses on a shelf. Grab a pair and put them on. They are essential for unveiling what I am about to reveal to you."

Blake and Evelyn entered the enclosure. Each selected a pair of spectacles. Once they were snug on their face, Richard gave a thumbs up and sat at his computer.

"Okay, are you ready?"

They both nodded and answered, "Yeah."

"Sis, what I meant in the text was the information on this flash drive." He held it before him. "I hid it in the oven, and when I did, I thought the Danes were the ones attacking us."

She grinned. "Yes. I understand now."

"Are you all set? Here we go." The space darkened and a full three-dimensional image appeared. Evelyn smiled as Blake tried to study what he was looking at. She strode around it and reached out as if expecting to feel something. "What is it?"

Blake took off his glasses. "It's oil. And a shit ton of it, if I were to guess. Correct?"

She removed hers and turned to her brother.

"Correct. As far as size goes, it's the largest oil reserve known to man. Hundreds of trillions of dollars. All sitting here, waiting to be plundered."

Blake gestured to her, and they walked out of the room. "Worth starting a war for." Richard's forehead wrinkled. "War? What do you mean?"

She stepped over to him. "Remember when we said this thing was bigger than you know?"

"Yes."

She glanced over at her new partner. "You want to tell him?"

"Sure." He took a sip of his water. "The attack on this ship was only the beginning. The men donned Danish military uniforms, aiming to deceive the Canadians into believing they were under attack by Denmark."

He paused. "In similar attacks, one took place making it as if the U.S. assaulted a Russian base, you guys, our friends to the north, stormed an American refinery in Alaska and the Russians wiped out everyone at a deep-sea platform operated by the Danes in the North Sea."

Richard's jaw dropped as he placed his hand over his mouth. "Oh, my God."

"There's more. In each case, the assailants waited until a message was dispatched blaming the offending country for the attack. After they confirmed a communication had been sent, they'd kill the person who sent it. They were only a tool for part of their plan."

Evelyn shifted her weight. "All except the oil rig."

He nodded. "Right. They left a single guy alive, but they were careless. One of them revealed himself and the lone survivor mentioned a unique characteristic of one of the attackers."

Richard chuckled. "Let me guess. A jacked-up ear."

Blake made the pistol gesture with his forefinger and thumb and winked. "Bingo."

"So, this person was able to identify him?"

She sat on the edge of a desk. "No. He was supposed to describe him to a world-renowned sketch artist so we could get an idea of what he looked like, but someone murdered both of them."

He rolled his eyes. "Oh, holy shit."

Blake folded his arms. "Right. They were professional hits."

Richard leaned back against a table opposite his sister. "So, what are we going to do?"

"We need to find out who this guy is. He is the key to discovering who is behind all of this. Are there any cameras on the ship?"

"No, well—yes, but no working ones. They destroyed them and deleted all the recording files. They also eliminated the satellite dishes, killing my internet. So—I have a question."

"Fire away."

"Is all this so they can drill and claim this oil?"

"One hundred percent."

"Well—we have a much bigger problem then."

Evelyn shifted her gaze from her new partner to her brother. "What do you mean?"

Richard strode to his desk, yanked open the central drawer, and extracted papers adorned with intricate designs.

He scanned the room and stepped to a table large enough to piece them together. "Come over here and I'll try to explain. It might be difficult, but you'll get the idea when I tell you the issue."

They joined him and perused the graphics strewn out before them. It appeared to be a bunch of colored traces from some type of instrument. Blake cleared his throat. "I give up. What am I looking at?"

Richard put his finger on the lines. "This is the raw data from the ground-penetrating radar. These represent solid rock, here. And this is the void for the crude deposit. Follow me, so far?"

Both nodded.

"What I'm concerned with is this under here."

Blake pointed. "This?"

"Yes."

She leaned closer. "It appears to be another void."

"Right. It is."

"Is it more oil?"

"No, Sis, it's not."

Blake sighed. "Can you get to the point? It's obvious it's concerning to you, so quit being so melodramatic and tell us what it is."

He closed his eyes and raised his hands. "Okay. Sorry. It is a giant magma bubble."

"And? It's been there, what, twenty million years, along with the crude? So, what's the problem?"

"More like a couple hundred million. The region of concern is this key zone here." He pointed to a small thin area separating the oil and the magma. "All of this is under extremely high pressure. The Earth has its tension-release valves."

He gestured with his hands. "Thousands of volcanoes. A majority of them are deep in the ocean and they're opening and closing all the time. So, not a huge deal. Right? What concerns me is this narrow layer dividing the two. The immense deposit exerts tremendous pressure, anchoring the divider firmly against the searing molten rock."

Blake shifted his weight from his left to his right. "I don't like where this is going."

Richard chuckled. "And you shouldn't. If we drill and remove this oil, the pressure holding this rock in place will loosen, and eventually, the force of the magma pressing on this thin wall will burst through. The result would be a cataclysmic event, altering life as we know it. The oil would catch fire and would boil the ocean. All the arctic ice within a thousand miles in every direction would melt. We're talking over three million square miles. Most coastal cities would be underwater. I don't even want to think about the sea life affected."

Blake pinched the bridge of his nose with his thumb and forefinger while his eyes were shut tight.

Evelyn studied their faces. "How long would it burn?"

He laughed. "Don't get me started. Have either of you heard of Centralia, Pennsylvania?"

They shook their heads.

"In nineteen sixty-two, a landfill burst into flames and it spread to the labyrinthine coal tunnels the miners dug a thousand feet below the surface. Despite all their efforts to extinguish the flames, the fire took hold in a coal seam. It's still burning today! Sixty-plus years later. Sixty! The place is a ghost town. And this? This is ten thousand times bigger."

Blake walked over to the portal and stared out over the vast ice expanse on the horizon. He imagined all of it gone. The destruction and harm it would cause. Anxiety flowed through him like electricity, jolting his nerves with every heartbeat. He spun around.

"Evelyn, call the other ship. Have them come to get us. Let them dump off their crew to start their work here. We must head south, ASAP. I'll get on the horn with my handler and tell her what's going on and we'll figure out our next move. We need to find out who is behind this now. The fate of the world as we know it is in our hands."

30

Prince Awadi Salib Property South of Trongisvágur
Faroe Islands
July 1st 16:30 (15:30 UTC)

The reverberating echoes of clinking chains resonated through the underground dock, mingling with the faint scent of saltwater and engine oil lingering in the air. Amidst the bustling activity of workers securing the ship's docking lines and unloading the stolen submarine from the Atlas, Madison's focus was elsewhere. Her narrowed eyes betrayed a simmering rage, threatening to boil over at any moment.

With a steely determination, she observed Prince Awadi Salib's entrance into his secluded office, her jaw clenched tightly against the mounting fury within her. Approaching the imposing guards with a calculated composure to avoid arousing suspicion, Madison couldn't shake off the prickling sensation crawling beneath her skin. It was as if a swarm of invisible needles relentlessly prodded at her nerves, setting her on edge amidst the clandestine operation unfolding around her.

"I have something to discuss with the prince. It's about the new sub."

Both men nodded and allowed her to proceed inside.

Salib had his back to her and was organizing some files on his desk. He turned and started to welcome her. "Ah, Doctor Wy—"

She lunged at him. "You son of a bitch!" Swinging with all her might, she hit him in the jaw with her closed fist.

Taken aback, his eyes were wide. She struck again. This time, his hands grasped firmly around her wrists. The guards burst into the room. She wiggled to get free of his viselike grip. "Let me go!"

"No! What is the meaning of this?"

The two behemoths latched onto her arms and pulled her off while she continued to protest. The prince backhanded her across the face, his rage was building. With a flushed face, he barred his teeth and lashed out at her. "How *dare* you!"

Clenching his fist, he punched her in the mouth. "I should kill you for your insolence!" Driving a hard punch into her gut, she bent over in pain. He nodded to his guards to drop her. Lying in a fetal position, her eyes were shut tight.

Pacing hurriedly, he was wringing his hands while he muttered to himself. "What do I do with you? The audacity. You little bitch." His breathing was fast and erratic. His anger reached another pinnacle.

Stepping toward her, he reared back and kicked her. "Why?" She coughed as his foot slammed into her again and again. "Why?" Spittle shot out of his mouth. Another. "Why?" Veins throbbed near the surface of his neck. Another kick, this time connecting with her face.

Leaning over, he grabbed her by the hair and forced her to rise. "Stand up! Get to your feet, you fucking whore!" Blood trickled from her busted lip. She gasped for air. He pulled down on her ponytail, forcing her chin to rise and look at him. "If I didn't need you to fix and operate the sub, I'd chop you into little bits and throw you into the sea."

He caught the eye of one of the guards. "Help the doctor to find a place to sit."

The two men grabbed an arm, lifted her, and plopped her into the leather and chrome seat before Salib's desk. He moved to his wet bar, poured a shot of single malt, and tossed it back in one gulp.

She sat, glassy-eyed, staring at the wall behind him, her gaze drifting past the dozens of framed photographs of him with celebrities and dignitaries. He sat across from her, calmed himself with some deep breaths, and drummed his fingers on the surface, the tension between them thick and palpable.

After several moments of stressed silence, he rose, grabbed a towel, and filled it with ice from the minibar. He crossed the room and held it in front of Madison. "Here. It'll reduce the swelling."

She remained stoic. While shaking the towel, he barely contained his fury. "Take it, Goddammit!"

Reluctantly, she accepted his offering and pressed it to the corner of her mouth.

Leaning against the desk, he crossed his arms over his chest. "Now. You're angry with me. You've dodged my questions every time I've asked for clarification. I'm no longer asking."

Her head didn't move as her eyes shifted to meet his. "You know damn well what you did."

His hand slammed on top of his desk. She flinched and closed her eyes, expecting another strike from his hand.

"No! I wouldn't be asking if I knew the answer already, would I?"

She took a deep breath. "When I told you about the submersible we could steal, I didn't think you were going to kill everyone!" She leaned forward. "I had a friend there!"

His gaze flicked to the two intimidating guards flanking Madison before snapping back to her. "How did you stumble upon this information?" His tone was as cold as a winter's night.

She attempted to keep her voice steady. "From my phone's newsfeed. The report said the ship vanished, feared lost."

His fingers snapped, the sound reverberating in the room as he extended his palm toward her.

She unlocked her phone and handed it over, displaying the news story that had caught her attention.

Watching him as his eyes darted across the screen, he absorbed every word of the article with a predatory intensity. He returned the device to her and rose from the desk—a tall figure casting an imposing shadow. "This doesn't bode well for our timeline." His tone was grim and carried a hint of anxiety.

"We need to move right away, Doctor. If needed, you can make any final adjustments to the sub on board the Atlas, while en route to our destination." He began pacing like a caged tiger preparing for its next hunt. "I'll handle logistics—fueling up, gathering provisions, and assembling a crew. I will need Nazir and his men." He pointed at her—a silent order hanging in the air. "Ensure the damn submersible is ready for deployment without further delay!"

He reached behind him and retrieved a manila folder, which he tossed onto the table between them.

She glanced at it and lifted her eyes to his face. "And what might this be?"

His smile was icy. "Take a peek."

As she opened it up, photographs spilled out—images of her family captured outside their home. Fear ran through her body as she sifted through them before placing them back into the folder with trembling hands.

"Is this some kind of warning?" She tilted her head and narrowed her eyes at him with suspicion. "Your Highness?"

His response was a chilling grin, his eyes glinting with cruel intent. "Mind your tone, Doctor." His intentions were sinister and clear. "I believe you're well aware of the extent of my influence. The mere idea of any misfortune befalling your loved ones would be a major tragedy."

His threat hung in the air, causing her heart to pound.

"Understood?" His voice was as cold as ice.

Her fear was unmistakable as she bowed her head. "Yes, Your Majesty."

THE DAVCO DEEP DRILL
700 NM NNW of Bergen, Norway

July 2nd 09:15 (08:15 UTC)

Blake savored the last bites of his fluffy scrambled eggs, bacon, and toast with raspberry jam. The clinking of cutlery against plates filled the room as Evelyn entered the cafeteria. She twisted her dark brown ponytail into a bun atop her head, though a few rebellious strands danced around her face like whispers in the wind.

The cable-knit turtleneck molded to her form, tracing every contour to perfection.

A delicate fragrance of Japanese cherry blossoms trailed behind her, weaving through the mingling scents of coffee and toast. Blake admired how effortlessly she carried herself as she approached his table, with subtle grace in each step.

"Good morning." He greeted her with a soft smile, his eyes lingering on her momentarily before meeting hers.

"Hello." Evelyn's hands instinctively reached out to pull back the chair opposite him and then hesitated mid-motion. "I'm sorry. Do you mind if I join you?" Her voice held a hint of eagerness as she awaited his response.

Blake's gesture was inviting as he extended his arm toward the empty seat, silently granting her permission to sit.

Seating herself, she removed her phone and was fidgeting with the screen.

"So, I like to hurkle-durkle after I wake, and I was—"

Blake almost spit out his coffee. He swallowed. "Wait! You what?"

She scrunched her nose. "Huh? Oh. Hurkle-durkle. You know it?"

He smiled and shook his head. "Lady, I have no freaking idea what you're talking about. Is it some weird Canadian thing?"

"Uh, no. It's Scottish. Thank you."

"It is? Well, what the hell is it?"

"It's lounging in bed long after you should be getting up. I do it in the morning to read the news on my phone." She reached out and touched his arm. Her hand stayed in place and gave him a chill. One he hadn't felt in a long time. "So, anyway, there was one article I read. A couple who moor their boat at a marina in Bergen have disappeared."

Blake's gaze momentarily drifted toward a person waiting in line to order food, his mind racing to decipher the implications of the unfolding story.

"And there's this." She placed her phone flat on the table for him to see. The headline glared back at him, adding another layer of intrigue to an already puzzling situation.

Deep Wave Research Vessel Disappears Off Coast of Bergen

He propped his chin on his hand, his brow furrowed in concentration. "Hmm. Two boats vanish off the coast simultaneously. Coincidence doesn't sit right with me. What's your plan?"

"The article about the elderly couple mentions their daughter. She's en route to Bergen to join the search efforts and I reached out to her. She should arrive tomorrow."

Calculating the time frame, he glanced at his watch and tilted his head back, eyes shut, as if mentally mapping out the remaining time ahead. "It'll be... At least thirty hours before we reach a distance close enough for the helicopter transfer. I'll have words with the captain and persuade him to push this slow-ass boat harder to gain us some precious time over the next day. The company will cover the extra fuel costs. With some luck, we might have a chance to speak with her by tomorrow night."

She nodded in understanding, determination flickering in her gaze. "I'll make the necessary arrangements."

HOME OF OSKAR AND LINNEA Gunderson
Bergen, Norway
July 3rd 18:38 (16:38 UTC)

A parking space beckoned him from the roadside, nestled conveniently in front of the elderly couple's abode. The house stood proudly, evidence of meticulous care, boasting two floors of elegance. Its exterior, akin to its neighbors on the charming lane, gleamed in white stucco with windows framed in bold chocolate brown and a roof adorned with sleek black tiles. The entrance door, fashioned from rich dark wood, featured a leaded glass window that hinted at the warmth within. Surrounding the property were verdant hedges bursting with life, their leaves lush and vibrant, but in need of an overdue grooming.

Blake guided her across the street, his senses alive to her presence as her alluring fragrance enveloped him once more. Battling back primitive instincts, he trailed behind her as she led the way to the entrance. Just before she could announce their arrival with a knock, the door swung open to reveal a woman in her middle years. Her shoulder-length blond hair caught the sunlight as she greeted them with a warm smile.

"Hello, I'm Ingrid Jorgensen—Jim and Margaret's daughter. We spoke on the phone."

"Yes, I'm Evelyn Cathey and this is Blake MacKay. Can we come in and ask you a few questions?"

"Absolutely." She stepped aside and welcomed them inside. After retrieving both glasses of water, they convened in the living room. The two made themselves comfortable on a long, dark blue cloth couch. It was simple. No patterned material, it had straight contemporary lines. Perched on a Scandinavian chair, she settled into the smooth wooden frame topped with pristine white cushions.

All the furnishings rested on a pale cream-woven rug. In the center of the room sat a sleek mid-century modern coffee table crafted from rich mahogany, its surface adorned with an intricate chessboard ready for a strategic game. Next to it, a gleaming gold-colored bowl added a touch of indulgence to the elegant setting. A picture book of luxury watches nestled in the nook under the table.

Evelyn admired the room. "Your parents' place is beautiful. Is this where you grew up?"

She smiled, her eyes glinting with nostalgia as she recalled events etched into every corner of the room. "Thank you. Yes, it is. It holds a great number of memories for me."

"I'm sure it does." Evelyn nodded empathetically, taking in the scent of freshly cut flowers permeating the air, mingling with hints of sandalwood from burning incense nearby.

"What got you concerned something was wrong?" Blake leaned forward, his gaze scanning the room discreetly.

She crossed her legs gracefully, her silver anklet softly chiming with each movement. "They're older and are never out late." The ticking of an antique clock on the mantelpiece filled the silence between words, like an ominous reminder of time slipping by unnoticed.

"I kept trying to call and they wouldn't answer." As she spoke, a faint breeze wafted through an open window carrying distant sounds of seagulls squawking by the harbor.

"I know they go to the boat some nights and have dinner." Her fingers traced patterns on the armrest of her chair, "but they never take it out after dark." The soft creaking of floorboards underlined her concern, like an unsettling melody playing in the background.

Blake raised his finger as he studied a family portrait hanging crookedly on the wall behind her. "You live in Copenhagen."

He paused as a hint of cinnamon wafted towards him, a tempting trail from the nearby bakery's oven-fresh pastries. "How did you know they took the boat out?"

"I didn't." Her voice was barely above a whisper amidst the gentle rustling of leaves outside carried by an evening breeze dancing through lace curtains framing the window behind her. "I was getting desperate to find out what happened and was about to call one of our neighbors and wake them to come over here..." Her words trailed off momentarily as distant church bells tolled in the twilight, "...and then I remembered my mom always takes her little Yorkshire Terrier with her."

Blake's brow furrowed. "I'm sorry. I don't understand. What does her taking the pet have to do with anything?"

"Well, my mother just loves her dog and was always afraid something would happen to her—she'd run off or—" She chuckled. "Get kidnapped. Anyway, I bought her one of those GPS tracker collars. So, I logged onto the company's website to check where Oscar was and low and behold, they're thirty miles off the coast?"

They both turned to each other. Evelyn stood. "Do you think you could log on and show us now?"

"Of course. I can do it on my phone."

While she opened the app, Evelyn called the Deep Drill's Captain.

"Woo, if I send you a bunch of coordinates, can you review your radar's historical data and tell me what, if anything, occurred there?"

"Yes."

"Okay. Standby."

She took Ingrid's mobile, glanced at the screen, and back to her. "Is this the last known location of the dog?"

She nodded, her long, slender fingers navigating the phone screen. "Okay. Thank you." The device's soft glow illuminated her face as she pressed on it to set a pin and retrieve the coordinates.

"Captain Woo. Try this on for size. Picture sixty degrees, thirty-six minutes, thirty seconds north; three degrees, thirty-five minutes, fifty-five seconds east."

After a few moments of silence apart from the rustle of papers. Woo coughed. "Hold on a moment. Let me check my—oh, never mind. I don't need to consult any reports. I know this location. Remember when I talked about some containers sinking? That's the exact spot."

Evelyn pursed her lips, deep in thought, and glanced over at Blake for confirmation. "And how did it appear on the radar? Not just your assumptions. As you mentioned, multiple boxes could be clustered together and partially submerged."

Blake's eyes narrowed as he listened to the conversation. "It appeared to be between sixty and seventy feet. Around that range."

"Okay," she acknowledged with a nod of gratitude before ending the call. "Thank you, sir." She lowered the phone.

Ingrid's face had an expression of curiosity as she turned to her. "What was the size of your parents' boat?"

Ingrid stared at her. "Sixty-five feet."

Taking a step forward towards her, their eyes made contact. "Do you know where your folks usually docked it?"

Ingrid nodded. "Yes, of course. Hjellestadt Harbour South."

HALF AN HOUR LATER, they pulled into the marina. She got hold of her door handle when Blake touched her other arm. "Hold on."

He reached around to the back seat and grabbed his laptop.

"What are you doing?"

"Well, we just can't go in there and ask to see their videos."

"Why not?"

He smirked. "Seriously? You are law enforcement operating outside your jurisdiction and not even here on official business. While I have the authority to operate in this area, they won't take my word for it. I'm familiar enough with Norwegian law to know they won't give us shit without a warrant."

"Besides—" He pointed to the clock on the dash. "They closed over an hour and a half ago. We'd have to break in."

"So, what are you going to do?"

"I'm gonna steal it."

He stepped out of the car and set the computer on the roof. As it was booting, he gazed out over the harbor. "This place offers internet to the slip owners. It's most likely they didn't change the default admin username and password to access their router. I've memorized all the major manufacturers' passwords. I'll hack into their system, and we'll review any security video from the night they stole the boat and cross our fingers."

Raising her hand to shield her eyes from the light illuminating the parking lot, she looked back at Blake. "While you're hacking away, I'm going to ask around. See if anybody saw anything."

After the third guess, he gained entry to the harbor's network. It took several minutes before he found the file folders for the recordings.

The system maintained compact folder sizes by automatically removing files older than 132 hours. The old couple and their small yacht disappeared five days ago.

Whew, barely made it. I'm glad they haven't deleted them yet.

The soft glow of the computer screen illuminated Blake's expression of concentration as he navigated through the digital labyrinth. His fingers danced across the keyboard, clicking on the folder labeled "June 28th." A mosaic of video thumbnails populated the monitor, each representing a different vantage point of the docks.

As he meticulously examined over a dozen recordings, the monotony was suddenly broken by a flicker of movement. On the monitor, five shadowy figures materialized on the main dock, their dark clothing melding with the night. Blake leaned in, his nose almost touching the screen, but frustration creased his brow as he realized their backs were turned to the camera.

Turning his attention to a different feed, he observed the indistinct cluster of individuals gliding past the Gunderson's yacht. The imposing silhouette of a nearby cruiser cast an inky blanket over the area, obscuring any hope of identifying the intruders.

His fist connected with the roof of the car. "Dammit!"

A familiar scent wafted through the air, a delicate blend of cherry blossoms and powder that could only belong to one person. Soft footsteps approached from behind, and a warm breath tickled his ear. "Boo."

A shiver ran along his spine as he turned, a smile playing on his lips. "Hey."

Her eyes sparkled with curiosity. "Did you get in?"

His shoulders sagged. "Yeah. And I have some film, but every shot hides their faces." He raised an eyebrow. "Did you have any luck?"

Her lips formed a tight line as she shook her head. "No. None. It's getting late and there is hardly anyone here. Of the people I met, only two spoke English, and they weren't here when the boat was stolen."

His fingers flitted across the keyboard, pulling up footage of the car park. A dark SUV rolled into view, disgorging five men into the night. Both agents leaned in, eyes scanning every pixel. Her finger shot out, pointing to a Land Rover in the distance. "It's still here. I'll get my kit and dust it for fingerprints."

"Hold on." His hand reached out, freezing the frame. He zoomed in on a figure tugging at his memory. "I may have something."

Evelyn stepped closer, her warmth radiating against his side as he advanced the recording. His face fell. "No. Dammit! They keep away from lighting. Not on purpose, though. It was damn luck."

She inched nearer, her perfume enveloping him in a cocoon of memories. "Perhaps another one will give you a better angle."

His eyes widened as an idea struck him. Without a word, he bolted from the side of the car and sprinted to the harbor's entrance. His finger jabbed at the stoplight before he raced back, chest heaving.

Breathless but exhilarated, he exclaimed, "Cameras at the intersections. I have the timeframe. I can easily hack into the city's closed-circuit system and view this guy's face."

Once again, going to work hacking into the surveillance cameras, he found the camera at the intersection.

Looking at the parking lot's video timestamp, he chose a file date stamped near the time he thought they'd be turning in.

A full face-on shot of two of the five men in the SUV appeared on his screen. The driver turned to his left, and he paused the frame.

He didn't say a word. Frozen, his eyes locked on to the man they'd been searching for.

She stepped to the computer and pointed. "He has no right ear! Is this the man we're seeking? It's not disfigured like Richard said."

He nodded. "Oh, it's him."

She smiled. "Well, that's good. We can run him through the facial recognition database and figure out who he is."

He frowned. "It won't be necessary."

"But why not?"

"Because I know who he is." He took a deep breath and turned to her. "His name is Nazir Farhi. He got his training with the Jordanian Special Forces and is known to have terrorist ties to Al Qaeda and Hezbollah. I believe he does private contract work most of the time now. The question is, who is he working for, and what the fuck is he doing for them?"

She stood silent. Her green eyes sparkled under the overhead lights, reflecting a deep concern for him, and making his heart race. Visions of Adriana, the love he lost, ran through his mind's eye. Evelyn reminded him of her. Her gaze was steady, and her expression of apprehension ignited something within him—a determination to open up. "I can't keep pretending." His voice was almost inaudible.

Her brow furrowed. "About what?"

Blake's phone rang and shattered the awkward moment.

Retrieving his mobile, he answered it. "MacKay."

"Right. Okay. On our way."

He folded the laptop shut. "We have to go. That was Alice. He knows what happened to the other ship."

He flung the computer into the car's back seat as she strolled to the opposite side.

"But you didn't finish telling me about Nazir. How do you know he and the guy Richard mentioned are the same person?"

"Because I'm the one who destroyed his ear."

31

CIA Safe House
Bergen, Norway
July 3rd 20:45 (18:45 UTC)

The night air sent a chill coursing through Evelyn, and Blake couldn't help but notice the goosebumps on her skin as he pushed open the gate to the courtyard. It groaned in protest, a sound echoing years of wear and neglect. The black wrought iron, burdened by countless layers of paint, stood as a testament to time. With a few drops of oil on the hinges, it would reclaim its former grace.

A few feet from the gate, stone pavers lined their path. They ascended the three steps to the front door, her perfume continuing to drive primal thoughts within him. He shook them away and pressed the button. A camera kept a watchful eye on them and an electronic lock buzzed, indicating they could enter. He opened the door and motioned her inside.

Upon entering, the narrow foyer welcomed them with a crackling fireplace that chased away the evening's lingering chill. Evelyn's heels clicked softly against the polished, light hardwood floor, partially muffled by a small, plush rug that invited touch. The subtle scent of lemon polish mingled with a hint of lavender, emanating from the coat rack where a forgotten scarf hung limply.

To their left, a cozy living area beckoned. The leather couch and two easy chairs, their clean lines hinting at Scandinavian design, faced a brick fireplace where flames danced merrily, casting flickering shadows and flooding the room with a gentle, golden glow.

Blake's gaze wandered to the opposite side, where the dining room stood in silent elegance. As they moved further in, the home revealed itself as an Ikea showroom come to life, each element precisely placed, yet somehow inviting. Framed black-and-white photographs adorned the walls, softened by the warm lighting.

On the coffee and end tables, succulents added spots of green life, their fleshy leaves cool to the touch. Beside them, drink coasters waited patiently, their smooth surfaces reflecting the firelight.

She nodded her approval and gave a coy smile. "Clean. Since when did the CIA have a safe house in Bergen?"

He smiled and waved her to walk toward the rear of the home. "About four days ago."

As they approached the entrance with steps leading to the basement, another buzz and click motioned them to where the action happened. Reaching the landing at the bottom of the stairs, the space opened with a row of cream-colored plastic folding tables. It smelled of fresh pine, glue, and vinyl. Everything was new. Sitting before them were no less than eight analysts typing furiously at their keyboards, searching for information, sending emails, or God knows what else.

Fluorescent lights dangled from the unfinished ceiling, held in place with flimsy chains and twine. Out of a single office in the back corner came Jackson King, the Chief of Station assigned to the temporary command center, while it was an active site. He was of average height but built like a tank. He formerly used his tree trunk legs as the running back with the second-most career rushing yards for the University of Louisiana. His thick New Orleans drawl was evident when he spoke.

"Blake MacKay, huh? How ya doin'? I reckon you're behind this whole mess that's been stirred up, ain't ya?"

Blake chuckled and shook his head.

The COS turned to Evelyn with a charming grin. "And I reckon you must be Miss Cathey?" He extended his hand. As she accepted his offer, her radiant smile brightened the room. "Yes, it's a pleasure to meet you." His eyes widened, lingering on her curves with evident appreciation. "Oh, the pleasure is all mine, ma'am. Truly, all mine."

Blake's eyes narrowed as he contemplated ramming his fist into the man's face after he thought about what might be running through the chief's mind. A pang of jealousy stirred within him, reviving old emotions he felt was a distant memory. He shook them away and diverted his attention to other business. "Is our super techie around? He mentioned finding the missing research ship and needed some help to confirm it."

"Oh, yes." Raising his arm to point toward the opposite corner. "Back there. Kinda keeps to himself."

Blake shrugged. "Meh. Typical. He's probably inventing some new crazy device. We'll go say hello and try to help." He placed his palm on the small of Evelyn's back to guide her toward his colleague. "Thanks, Jackson."

Mumbling under his breath, he started walking. "Stay away from him."

She turned her head back as they walked. "Why?"

"I heard he's a womanizer."

He saw the side of her mouth curl and was happy to see her smile. As they approached Alice's corner of the basement, he stood to greet them.

"Hey, Mister MacKay."

"Alice. My man." They high-fived. When Blake turned to her, she was frozen in place, with her jaw open.

He chuckled. "Yes, he's tall. You can close your mouth now."

Shaking her head to clear away the shock, she shook his hand. "I'm sorry. You're so tall."

"Really? I hadn't noticed."

They all laughed. Evelyn grabbed an empty chair and rolled it over. "I'm sorry. That was rude of me."

He waved it off. "Ah, don't worry about it. I get it often. I'm used to it."

"How tall are you—if you don't mind me asking?"

"A little over six-nine. Six-ten in shoes."

"Did you play basketball?"

Blake clapped his hands. "Hey! That's a conversation for a different time. He said he has a lead on the elusive research vessel." He wheeled over a stool and sat. "So, show us what'cha got."

Alice sat, spun his long legs around, and attacked the keyboard. His desk was somewhat untidy, with assorted papers scattered haphazardly. A solitary white mug adorned with the Norwegian flag rested on a warmer plugged into a USB port. Four large monitors stacked two high and positioned side by side formed a virtual digital wall displaying documents, satellite images, and various data.

Shortly, he opened several snapshots from satellites of the Deep Wave vessel at its mooring place off the coast of Norway, where they were exploring the sunken Viking ships.

He pointed to a timestamp on the screen. "See here? This is two-thirty in the afternoon on the 28th." Switching to the adjacent monitor, his finger tapped on an icon representing a ship on a marine traffic website. "And here is the corresponding transponder report, showing they were at these exact coordinates."

Blake leaned in. "Okay. The Discovery. Well, now we know its name. When was the last time the transponder reported?"

"Ah. Yes." Alice shuffled some papers on his desk. "Found it." Taking a moment to think after glancing at the paper and then at the clock on the monitor, he sighed. "Approximately one hundred and fourteen hours and forty-five minutes."

Blake cracked a smile and shook his head. "Couldn't you have said four and a half days?"

His colleague's face was blank and emotionless. "No. That would be inaccurate."

He raised one long boney finger. "There's more. As each satellite passed over, I took thousands of photos and incorporated artificial intelligence to find objects on the water and I found this." He pressed a button, and an image of the ship appeared. "You can thank the long hours of daylight in the summer. It wouldn't have been visible in the dark if it wasn't so far in the north."

Evelyn stood and leaned in to focus on the screen. "It's stamped seven in the morning. Where is this?"

Alice reached for his mouse. "Well, another interesting oddity. It's about two hundred miles east of the Faroe Islands. But look at this." He zoomed out.

Blake squinted as he concentrated on the screen. "There's another ship."

"Right."

Silence filled the air as all three stared at the monitor when Alice broke the lull. "Now check this out." He zoomed in tight to the stern of the Deep Wave ship. "Does anything catch your eye here?"

"You mean something other than the glaringly bright yellow submarine?"

"Nope. You got it." He clicked a few buttons, opened another image, and zoomed into the rear of the mystery ship. "And now?"

Evelyn grabbed Blake's knee. "The sub! It's on the back of the other ship."

He enjoyed the tingle running along his leg at her touch.

"And..." Alice drew out the word as he expanded the image. "Now the research ship is not there—anywhere."

Blake stood and stretched. "They sunk it. They stole the sub and sunk the Discovery. My instincts tell me they killed everyone on board, too." He stepped away, then back. "Please say they have a transponder."

He puckered his lips while shaking his head. "According to maritime law, a ship this size is required to have one, but unfortunately, it hasn't been on in months."

"Dammit!"

Alice raised his index finger. "Hold on Buddy ol' Buddy. Have I ever left you feeling disappointed?"

Blake started to reply when his tech-savvy friend interrupted.

"Don't answer that. I've got something you're going to like." Opening additional images, he continued. "I was able to follow them, based on their trajectory. It kept heading west until it got to the Faroe Islands where it disappeared in—"

"Disappeared?"

"Standby." He clicked and displayed a final image. "This is the entrance to an indoor or underground dock. The ship went in there."

"What is that place? Who owns it?"

"Well, it's owned by a corporation, which, of course, was a shell company, owned by another shell company, and so on, and I didn't feel like going down that rabbit hole. So, I searched through all kinds of permits in the Danish government system. Plumbing permits, electrical, etcetera."

Evelyn shook her head. "Good God, you're thorough. Did you find anything?"

"No. But then I remembered even though they're under the control of the Danish parliament, they're still an autonomous territory. It's a unique political arrangement."

Blake made a circular motion with his hand. "Right, right. Get on with it."

"Yeah, so I got into their local system and found an application for a dredging permit. Signed by Abdulaziz Farouk." He closed his eyes and raised his palm. "I know, I know. Who the hell is he, right?"

Blake responded in a low, monotone voice. "Amazing. You read my mind."

Evelyn chuckled. He caught her warm smile out of the corner of his eye.

"Yeah, well, read this. This guy handles a lot of business affairs for none other than…" He worked his magic again, clicking and moving windows. "This guy." He tapped his keyboard. "His Royal Highness, Prince Awadi Salib, of Saudi Arabia. Removed."

Blake's brow furrowed. "Removed? What do you mean?"

"Not sure, but he's not a nice guy. The Royal Family has disowned him. But they provided him with enough money to live *very* comfortably for the rest of his life." He zoomed into a large boat. "This is his yacht. The Midnight Oil. Well—it's in Arabic, but I think I translated it correctly. But anyway. He's got a big boat."

Blake stood. He took a few steps back and then started pacing. "What does this guy have to do with this?" He snapped his fingers. "Follow the money. Alice! Can you look and find any kind of relationship or connection to a man named Nazir Farhi."

"I can try, but doubtful. Anything nefarious he's done for him; he probably paid him in crypto or diamonds—something untraceable."

"Right. Run our buddy Nazir through facial recognition. See if you can get a hit on him at airports, bus terminals, and train stations. Anyplace that puts him at the same location as Salib or near where some of the attacks have happened. Let me know if you discover something."

"You'll be the first to know. What are you two doing?"

Blake and Evelyn's eyes met, and he smiled. "We're going to the Faroe Islands."

32

1260 Nautical Miles NNE of the Faroe Islands
Greenland Sea

July 5th 17:15 (15:15 UTC)

Madison finished the last weld and raised her mask. The sweat left trails on her cheeks like sled trails through snow. She sighed deeply, stood, and removed the dark shield from her head. Placing it on the workstation, she closed her eyes and pinched the bridge of her nose with her thumb and forefinger. The release of pressure felt calming.

"All done?"

The words startled her. She turned to her friend and colleague, Zaanjar. She smiled while reaching for a towel. "As done as it's going to be." The words sounded muffled through the cloth as she wiped the sweat from her face.

The frigid air did a swift job of cooling her off. Looking aft, the trail left behind by the churning propellers, left her filled with anxiety, as she realized what lay ahead was as unpredictable as the shifting tides beneath the ship.

She tossed the cloth on the counter. "Do you have any idea where we are?"

Her colleague focused on the final welds she'd completed. She shook her head as she continued her inspection. "No. But I think I heard someone say Greenland is about sixty kilometers off the port side."

"All right. I suppose I'll ask his royal pain. I need to let him know I'm finished anyhow."

Zaanjar's brow furrowed. "He's here? I didn't notice him when we were boarding or loading."

"He took his yacht and flew here on that fancy chopper. I don't know how you could have missed it landing. Thing's got a range of over a thousand miles."

Her friend strolled over to the railing and leaned forward, gazing out toward the helicopter perched on the landing pad at the bow of the Atlas.

She walked back. "I think I was napping. We're all freaking exhausted from the timeline he—what did you call him? His royal pain?"

"Yeah. Pain in the ass."

They both laughed.

She continued. "Right. The deadline he set on us. I was asleep. It would take the ship sinking to wake me."

Madison nodded and leaned back against the table while folding her arms. "Well, it's all done now."

"Finally. Great job. And you think this one is safe from imploding unlike the other?"

"Oh, for sure, a hundred percent."

"That's good. I'd still hate to be the pilot." Zaanjar's head tilted as her nose scrunched. "Speaking of which. Who *is* going to run it?"

A sinking feeling washed through Madison, and her stomach tied into a knot. She straightened herself and unfolded her arms. "Oh, fuck! He mentioned needing me to operate the sub while we screamed at each other. I hadn't thought about it until now." She tilted her head back and let out a grunt. "Ughhhh. I guess I'd better go and find out. Meet for a drink later?"

Her friend's pearly whites showed through her wide smile. The thought of some well-earned celebratory drinks got her excited. "Sounds great. Good luck, Madison. Drop by when you're done."

THE FAROE ISLANDS

July 5th 17:30 (16:30 UTC)

The coastline bobbed and moved in rhythm with the sea. Blake lowered his binoculars and set them on the table. Evelyn exited the cabin of the Cruisers Yachts 50 GLS. She played the part and dressed in a black bikini in case anyone from shore was watching them. She opened a bottle of water as she approached. "Do you see anything interesting?" He turned to her.

Oh, dear God. I do now.

Desire swelled within him. Something he hadn't felt since he met Adriana in Cuba. The tiny top didn't leave much to the imagination and the thin sarong wrap, tied around her waist, hugged her hips and accentuated her curves. Remembering his lost love and the pain of not knowing what happened to her helped to mitigate the lust building inside him. "Uh, well, I spotted the opening to the underground marina." He glanced at his Panerai GMT. "It's five-thirty. Let's go somewhere out of their line of sight and wait until dark. Then we'll return. I think I can gain entry through the marina. I'll poke around and see what I can find."

He moved around the aft station housing the twin gas grills and integrated sink and brushed against her as he went. Her scent invigorated the feelings he was desperately trying to suppress. As he passed, he turned back to her. "Hey, do you know how to drive this thing? Because I may need you to come and retrieve me in a hurry."

She shook her head and pointed her thumb at herself. "Me? No." Her grin grew wide. "But show me."

The bridge was an impressive array of three large digital touch screens, each one displaying everything a captain would need to know about the vessel. It exuded a sense of modern sophistication and control. With a burst of excitement, she jumped into the long bench seat, her energy infectious, radiating like a giddy schoolgirl. She slid effortlessly in front of the steering wheel, her movements confident and playful. Turning to him, she patted the seat cushion beside her with a teasing smile. "Come on, big boy. Don't be shy," she coaxed, her voice laced with an inviting charm sending a thrill down his spine.

Blake positioned himself next to her and pointed out the various controls. "This is the bilge blower. You want to run this for a couple of minutes before you start the motors, otherwise, you'll blow yourself to hell and back."

She playfully slapped his shoulder. "What? You're kidding."

He couldn't help but return the smile. "No. Seriously. You've got to eliminate all the accumulated explosive fumes. Not so much when we have outboards, but they still get in the bilge, and—better safe than sorry, right?"

"What's all this?" she asked, leaning across him, her finger gracefully tracing the edge of the far-left screen. The warmth of her body radiated against him, and he found himself momentarily distracted by her intoxicating scent—a delicate blend of cherry blossoms and something uniquely her. As her skin brushed against his, a rush of warmth spread through him, the softness of her touch igniting a spark that lingered in the air between them.

Oh, dear God, help me.

He swallowed. "It displays your depth, engine revs, hours, etcetera."

"Why are there three of them listed?"

He chuckled. "Look behind us."

She turned around. Her breast pressed against his arm. "Oh."

"Exactly. Three, six-hundred horsepower engines. Now let me show you how to turn me on. Them—them. Turn *them* on."

Oh, God.

She chuckled. Blake could feel the blood rushing to his cheeks. He cleared his throat. "After you've run the blowers for a couple of minutes, you can hit each of these buttons. They start each engine. Go ahead."

Each of the powerful V-12 outboards roared to life. Lights and information came to display on the screens before her. "Okay. What's next?" She touched a round knob on the starboard console. "What's this do?"

"Those are the thrusters. You don't need them."

"Maybe I do. I like to be thrusted."

Blake's gaze locked with hers, and for a moment, it felt as though the world around them faded away. If eyes could smile, hers were beaming with warmth and mischief. A flutter of uncertainty danced in his chest—was she flirting with him? The thought sent a thrill through him.

She has to be, isn't she?

The playful glimmer in her eyes suggested a connection getting increasingly difficult to ignore. He giggled. "Okay. Let's keep it professional."

She frowned.

"Those handles to your right. The left one shifts it into gear. Forward is that way." He pointed to the bow of the yacht. "And you can guess what backward does."

She saluted. "Aye, aye, captain."

"The one furthest right is the throttle. So, now you know what to do, show me. Take us around to the other side of the island. Get to where we're in about twelve to twenty feet of water and use this button to drop the anchor."

She brushed a wayward hair from her eyes. "What are you going to do?"

"I'm going to take a nap."

1268 NAUTICAL MILES NNE of the Faroe Islands
Greenland Sea

July 5th 17:52 (15:52 UTC)

Madison knocked on the private quarters of Prince Salib and waited for an answer.

"Who is there?"

"It's me, Madison."

The butterflies in her stomach started to flutter in anticipation of another topic of conflict. The last thing she wanted to do was dive over 8000 feet and use the untested drill, especially after what happened to the other jerk.

"Enter."

The prince stood poised, cradling a clear container filled with a viscous black liquid that seemed to absorb the light around it. Dressed in stylish western attire, he sported sleek black pleated slacks, while a crisp white button-down shirt, crafted from a soft fabric reminiscent of flannel, hinted at a blend of comfort and sophistication. His beard was meticulously trimmed, lending an air of refined masculinity to his appearance. His rolled sleeves revealed the exquisite glimmer of his rose gold Jaeger LeCoultre Duometre Heliotourbillon, its intricate mechanisms catching the light with every subtle movement, a testament to craftsmanship and elegance. The scene was one of striking contrast: the dark liquid in his grasp, against the pristine whiteness of his shirt, and the luxurious timepiece that whispered of a world where time was both an ally and a foe.

As she stepped into the room, his gaze tracked her every movement, gliding from her head to her toes in an unmistakable appraisal, as if he were undressing her with his eyes. The scrutiny felt invasive, reducing her to little more than a commodity on display for his amusement.

He extended the container to her. "Have I ever shown you this?"

Accepting the jar, her eyes narrowed. "I don't believe so." Taking a moment to inspect what it held; she returned to him. "Oil?"

"Yes. Raw crude." He placed it meticulously on a small pedestal centered on a shelf. "You are familiar with Lake Superior, I presume?"

"Of course."

He smiled. "It is the largest freshwater body by surface area in the world. As far as depth, it is much deeper than the other Great Lakes. It holds three quadrillion gallons of water. By comparison, Lake Huron holds a mere three and a half trillion gallons." He stepped over to her and ran the back of his finger along her arm as he circled behind her. Her nerves pricked at her as the uncertainty of his intentions rose. "Now, imagine if you will, a sea of crude the same size." Stepping in front of her, her disgust peaked as he invaded her space. She could smell the liquor on his breath. "*That* is what you'll be drilling for, Doctor."

It wasn't until he finally removed himself from her personal boundary that the realization of what he said hit her.

"Wait. Me?"

He sat on the edge of his desk. "Absolutely! It will be the—crowning event of your hard work."

She stood speechless. A competing battle between her ire and anxiety boiled within her as she thought of some excuse to get out of stepping into the yellow tomb hanging on the stern of the ship. His next words sealed her fate.

"To earn the twenty-five million I promised you, it is your final requirement."

Some of her anxiety released itself in the form of a sigh. "I understand. How long until we get there?"

"Thirty hours or so. We will launch first thing in the morning on the seventh."

He dismissed her as if she was an annoying child. "Move along. I have things I need to do." Standing from his perch, he went around his desk, retrieved a folder from a drawer, and sat. He turned to her. "Was there something else, Doctor?"

Her eyes shifted away from him as her head and shoulders dropped. "No, Your Highness. I'll be ready to dive."

She turned and left the room. After the door closed behind her, she stopped in her tracks and whispered, "Shit! Now I definitely need a drink."

33

The Faroe Islands
July 6th 01:30 (00:30 UTC)

They had spent the past eight hours resting, making dinner, and talking. They sat on the main outer deck in the plush confines of the small yacht, and they spoke a lot. He discovered a wealth of information about his temporary partner-in-crime and her relationship with her brother, Richard. They also had much in common concerning extracurricular activities. Snow skiing was a favorite pastime, as were riding snowmobiles, and ice skating. Although her passion was figure skating, his was geared more toward hockey.

Each had extensive fighting experience and worked for intelligence agencies in their respective countries.

The question he didn't want to answer but knew was coming, made him cringe when he heard it.

"So, I told you why I am single. What's a good-looking guy like you doing all alone?"

Sitting on the bench seat at the table he leaned forward and rested on his elbows. "I suppose it's some of the same reasons as you. This job doesn't allow it."

She tilted her head to the side. "You've been hurt, haven't you?"

He straightened and put his palms flat against the surface. "Ah. I don't want to talk about it."

Her hand delicately touched the top of his. "I'm sorry. She must have been special."

What was happening and who was this woman who was stirring old feelings and desires he lost? Part of him wanted to tell her about Adriana and how he killed her father on a mission and together they foiled a coup and terrorist attack. He wished he could discuss what happened to her and how it destroyed him inside. But now was not the time. He withdrew his hand. "Yes. She was."

Glancing at his watch, he slid out from behind the table. "It's time to go. Get this beast started and get us around to the other side of the island." Trying to change the mood, he smiled at her. "You remember how to drive this thing, don't you?"

She didn't smile back. "Of course."

He went below while she slid into the helm. Inside the cabin, Blake slipped into his wet suit. He left the top peeled open to keep cool, exposing his six-pack abs, muscular chest, and arms. Evelyn's shadow filled his peripheral vision. He could sense her eyes on him. She looked away as he turned to her.

He pointed to her. "Ah, caught you looking."

She chuckled. "Naw, MacKay. You're not my type."

"What. Strong and attractive?" He climbed the steps out of the cabin. She moved out of his way. "No. Damaged goods."

Those words cut through him in a way he didn't expect. Did he blow something before it even started? His face went emotionless as he headed to the rear of the boat. He dragged out his re-breather, flippers, diver propulsion vehicle (DPV), and all the other things he would need for his dive to the mystery base. They said nothing while he finished getting on his wetsuit and equipment. After attaching his whisper mic to his throat, he passed her a handheld radio. "Go below so I can test the reception. It's on the right channel, twelve. If coms become compromised, switch to twenty-three."

After testing communications, she stepped out of the cabin. He struggled to divert his gaze. Her long legs and flawless figure drew him in. How her silky brown hair framed her striking green eyes reminded him so much of Adriana. And her intoxicating scent. He shook his head, trying to clear his thoughts.

"Blake?"

Air blew out of his mouthpiece as he tested it. *Don't sound like a stupid little child who got his feelings hurt.* "Yeah. What's up?"

"I'm sorry. What I said was mean of me and uncalled for."

He continued to check his equipment. "Don't worry about it. I'm a big boy."

She extended her hand. "Friends?"

As he grasped her hand, she reached in and kissed his cheek. "Now go find out what this guy is planning."

A smile crept onto his face, impossible to suppress. With a gentle grip on the back of her arm, he drew her nearer and locked his lips with hers in a passionate kiss.

She stepped in, savoring the warmth of his full embrace. A current of electricity surged through him. Her lips were soft and inviting, and her touch was invigorating. They kissed and held each other for what felt like an eternity. Finally, he pulled away, breathless. "Make sure you keep your coms close."

She nodded. Speechless. "Uh... of course. I will."

Stepping onto the boat's lowered side, which functioned as a swimming platform, he jumped into the sea.

LIKE A SILENT PREDATOR stalking its prey, he surfaced inside the underground dock. It was quiet and empty. After securing his flippers and DPV to the swim ladder, he climbed out of the water, crouched behind a steel cabinet, operated his mic, and spoke in a whisper.

"Evelyn, I'm inside and on the dock. Can you get the infrared camera? It says FLIR on it. Tell me what you see?"

"Yes, give me a second to grab it."

He paused briefly to absorb the enormity of the faintly illuminated space. The scent of lubricant and machinery intertwined with the saline breeze evoked memories of his time aboard a submarine, scouring the depths of the Bering Sea for a nuclear weapon pilfered by North Koreans in an antiquated Russian Whiskey Class Submarine.

Chains hung from several cranes on tracks near the ceiling. One was grasping a giant steel beam. He speculated the chains were for transporting and hoisting heavy equipment or a compact deep-sea submersible. In the distance, he saw a space appearing to be an office."

"Blake, you there?"

"Indeed. Where else would I be?"

"Funny. You're all clear."

"Roger. Keep an eye on the infrared camera and let me know if anyone comes."

After she acknowledged, he moved swiftly and silently towards the double doors. Removing a lock pick, he easily broke into the office and flicked on his flashlight. It wasn't what he was expecting. It was a repository for more equipment. Many were still in their boxes, sealed, with years of dust collected on them. "Shit."

"What's the matter?"

Forgetting he had the whisper mic on constant broadcast he shook his head. "I'm okay. It's a dead end. Stand by."

He glanced to the right as he stepped from the storage closet, revealing a gloomy corridor stretching before him. With extreme caution, he ventured forward. The hallway eventually opened up to a grand chamber, its high ceilings echoing with a sense of history. On the far side, two colossal wooden doors stood sentinel, their surfaces intricately carved and adorned with ancient bronze knockers, each bearing the likeness of Thor's Hammer. *"That's it."*

He approached them with discretion. Withdrawing his phone, he chose an application, one of Alice's concoctions, and started scanning all around the door's perimeter. *Nothing.*

He grabbed the right door's handle, closed his eyes, and held his breath. It opened.

"It can't be this easy."

"What are you talking about?"

He sighed. "You don't need to answer me every time I say something. I tend to talk to myself in mission."

"Oh! I do it too! Another thing we have in common. The question I have for you though, is do you answer yourself?"

He let out a chuckle. "Just keep an eye out. It's possible I triggered a silent alarm."

Inside, it was vast. It looked more like the grand hall in a Viking village than an office. A long wooden table was to his left and an ancient-looking desk with Nordic symbols carved into it was in front of him.

With his penlight clutched between his teeth, he rummaged through the drawers. Ten minutes later, after no clues, he inspected the room. His hands searched under the desk for a button or lever. Over to the bookcase, he removed books, searching for a switch, but none were found. He sighed once again. Above the bar was a flat mirror. Shining the light, its reflection was more reminiscent of a two-way mirror, than a regular one. He searched every drawer. Nothing materialized until the last one, only a lone remote control for a Samsung television.

Taking in his environment, Blake found no television anywhere. His fingers grazed the power switch and a screen illuminated from behind the mirror, projecting a map. Blake narrowed his eyes, gradually comprehending what lay before him.

"Hey. I found something."

"Are you talking to me or yourself?"

"Hold on." He removed his waterproof camera and snapped several pictures. "I'm looking at a map of the oil field your brother told us about and there is a big fat red x on here. Grab something to write with. I want a backup in case something happens to my camera."

"Uh, okay. Gimme a second."

He kept his eye on the entrance to the room while he waited. The last thing he wanted was to be surprised by armed men bursting through the doors.

"Right, I'm ready."

He focused his attention back on the screen and looked at the coordinates for the large X. "Eighty-two degrees, thirty-three minutes, one point three four seconds north and thirty-seven degrees, twenty-eight minutes, forty-six point six five seconds east. And then put in a depth of eighty-one hundred feet."

A noise alerted him. "Dammit." He grabbed the remote and turned off the television. "Grab the FLIR. I heard something."

He ducked below the bar and waited for confirmation from Evelyn. "Blake. You're too deep inside for it to detect anything. Sorry."

"It's okay. I'm outta here. Be prepared." He remained crouched and peeked around the corner. A trio of light streams from flashlights lit the room and scanned it from side to side.

The men spoke Arabic. Fortunately for him, he understood. The first was going to his left, the other his opposite, and the third was to check his hiding space.

Raising his arm, he felt for one of the many liquor bottles, grasped the base, and brought it to him. The warm glow of the flashlight filled his vision to his right. He gripped the glass container's neck. His timing had to be perfect.

Footsteps closed in, and with each one, his heart pumped harder. He could feel the throbbing in his neck.

The guard further out, spoke, indicating it was clear. "*Al-amr wadih huna. Enta?*"

The man adjacent to him answered. "*Ana dhahib lil-tahqiq wara'a al-'aridah.*"

Great. He has to check behind the bar.

The man took another step, and Blake sprang to his feet, swung the bottle at the guard's head, and crushed it across his skull. Vodka splashed out, and the man fell to his knees and onto his face, out cold.

He grabbed two more bottles and flung them at the sentinel on his right. As he approached him, he poked him in both eyes.

When the man's hands went to his face, Blake cupped his hands and slapped them over each ear, rupturing his adversary's eardrums. He then swept his feet, and his opponent was on his back. Pouncing on him, he elbowed him in the forehead in three quick successions, then snapped his neck.

He heard through his radio, Evelyn's pleas. "What's happening?"

Bullets ricocheted off the concrete floor next to him. "Bring the boat! Now!" He bolted for the exit. Splinters from the ancient doors filled the air as rounds penetrated the surrounding wood. "*Waqif! La tataharrak. Amurak bil-tawaqquf!*"

Yeah, I'm not stopping.

He sprinted toward the water where he had entered. The pursuing guard kept yelling to stop. "*Waqif! Waqif!*"

A bullet whizzed by his head and buried itself in the wall as he changed direction to turn into the underground marina.

His partner was nowhere to be seen. Scanning the area, he desperately searched for somewhere to hide. He ran for cover as the last of the three men stopped and opened fire. Hot lead peppered the floor to his rear. The roaring of V-12 motors filled his ears. *Oh, thank God.*

"I'm almost there."

One of the two adversaries he had incapacitated stirred back to consciousness and reentered the room.

Bullets riddled the desk where he sought cover. To his right, hung crane controls suspended by cables. Scanning for their target, his eyes locked onto it—a sturdy girder stretching nearly ten feet in length gripped firmly within its mechanical grasp.

Opting to peer from behind his barricade, he spotted both foes positioned twenty feet ahead. Seizing the control panel, he maneuvered the crane towards them. The thunderous roar of the boat's engines reverberated through the expansive chamber.

The yacht approached at full speed. She masterfully turned around in the tight space. He stood as the two aimed at the boat, ready to fire.

He released the heavy beam. One man screamed right before it crushed him, spilling brain matter across the floor.

The other man dodged and started firing after he regained composure. Blake took off running for his life.

As he was judging the distance he was about to jump, he witnessed her emerge with an MP5. She unleashed a barrage of her own toward the remaining guard.

Blake dove onto the small yacht and immediately went to the helm. "Hang on!"

He pushed the throttle wide open. She remained suppressing fire in three and four-round bursts until her mag was empty. By then, they had exited the marina. He kept it at full speed until they were far away and verified no one was following them.

She slid in next to him and their eyes met. They both laughed but didn't exchange words. She grasped his upper arm, leaned her head onto his shoulder and stayed there while they drove off. His thoughts drifted to Adriana and what was happening now with this woman. Did he dare go down this path, again?

An hour later, they found a safe natural harbor and anchored. They went below and he lay flat on his back, exhausted. He wasn't going to make any moves on her. His mind was a blend of emotions. The last thing he desired or needed was a relationship. If she wanted to seduce him, then so be it. He chuckled to himself. *Wishful thinking.*

She gently closed the door to the cabin, sealing off the outside world. With a playful determination, she got on all fours and crawled onto the bed, positioning herself atop him. Her thighs pressed tightly against his—an embrace radiating warmth and stirring questions of what might be next. Her emerald eyes danced across his body, exploring every contour and detail, filled with a mix of desire and mischief. She bit her lip with a hint of teasing.

A sigh escaped her lips as she slowly removed her top, revealing her breasts to the soft glow of the cabin light, inviting him into an intimate moment that felt both electric and timeless.

Blake tilted his head to take in the entire scene before him. *Well, I guess I know the answer.* He opened his arms and welcomed her into his embrace. For the next few hours, they lost themselves in each other, their bodies entwined in a passionate dance of love and discovery. They explored every curve and contour, savoring the intimacy blossoming between them. As the night deepened, they succumbed to the sweet grasp of sleep, cocooned in each other's arms, their hearts beating in perfect harmony.

As daylight broke, he awoke and made coffee while she stepped out into the sunlight. He'd finished filling two mugs when she called out. "Uh, hey. Better get out here."

He emerged and handed her a warm mug. The aroma filled her senses, and she took a sip.

He sat his coffee on the helm. "What's the matter?"

Taking a few steps to the starboard side, she pointed. "Bullet holes. How will you explain these to the place you rented this from?"

He shrugged. "Pirates? I dunno. That's what the deposit's for. I'll call my handler and figure out a way to those coordinates I gave you. What did those people on the dock say when we asked them about the last time they saw the ship with the sub on it? Three days? Four?"

She swallowed. "They said three, but now it's been four."

"Right, so they have a four-day head start and it's about seventeen hundred miles." He placed his hands on his hips and let out a deep sigh. "Aughhh, this keeps getting better."

He went below, fished out his satellite phone from his bag, and dialed Veronica.

A groggy voice answered. "I am assuming this is of great importance, Mister MacKay, otherwise you wouldn't be calling me in the middle of the night?"

Blake gritted his teeth when he remembered the time difference but got pleasure knowing he disturbed her. "Right. We've confirmed the prince is behind this, and I've located the drilling site."

She cleared her throat and sounded more awake since he told her the confirmation of their suspicion. "This is concerning news. Where are you now?"

"The Faroe Islands. We have to get to the North Pole. It's over sixteen hundred miles and they have a big head start. We need a fast ship with a good range."

"When I spoke to the Norwegian Ambassador to secure your plane ride to the Arctic Drilling vessel, he mentioned a Skjold class corvette which is fast and could be at our disposal."

He walked out to the deck and grabbed his coffee. "No. They don't have the range. Do we have any Independence-class ships nearby?"

"I don't have a clue. Let me make some calls and I'll get back to you."

"Sounds good."

Blake descended below deck to change his clothes. As he stepped out of the cabin, he was enveloped in Evelyn's embrace, punctuated by a soft, warm kiss that made him feel like he did with Adriana. Feelings of doubt and fear crept in. He was determined not to make a mistake. He started the engines and headed back to the marina in Torshavn.

Once docked and after having a lengthy discussion with the boat owner about the four bullet holes, they exited the dock when his phone rang.

"Hello Veronica"

"Can you get to Reykjavik? If so, the USS Jackson can take you to your destination. The President has contacted the captain personally and ordered him to give you his full cooperation."

"Yes Ma'am. On the way."

He disconnected the call and placed his bag in the trunk of their rental car. He took Evelyn's and did the same. She tilted her head and shrugged. "So, where are we going?"

He opened the door and met her gaze. "Reykjavik. We're catching a fast boat to the North Pole."

34

USS Jackson
1169 Nautical Miles from Reykjavek, Iceland
68 NM off the NNE coast of Greenland

July 8th 11:17 (10:17 UTC)

Barreling along near maximum speed, the Independence-class ship looked like a gray flint arrowhead piercing the sea. It sped along the Greenland coast toward its final destination, a rendezvous with the Atlas. The mission: Prevent drilling at all costs.

Blake, Evelyn, Captain Jerrod Tyson (Captain of the Independence), Captain Isaac Pendelton (SEAL team six leader), and Lieutenant Commander Jimmy Torres huddled around the conference table in the captain's ready room. Captain Tyson waited for everyone to get seated, then drummed his fingers on the hard surface. "All right, gentlemen." He turned his head to Evelyn and smiled. "And lady."

She returned the gesture. "Thank you."

He grabbed a stack of folders with the typical classified red dashes along the edges and started passing them out like a deck of cards. "This one we're calling operation 'misfit toys'. You will notice it is classified and will remain so. Everyone understands?"

A collective "Yes sir." filled the confined space.

"Special Agent Cathey, I'm extending this courtesy to your nation under President Pennington's orders. Mister MacKay, I understand you know these two delinquents and have worked with them in the past?"

He chuckled. "Yes sir, I have."

"Great. Then, in a nutshell, inform all of us what the hell is going on."

Blake nodded. "Right. So, Prince Awadi Salib."

Evelyn placed her hand on his sleeve. "Remember, he's been exiled."

"Oh, yes. Exiled Prince. Nonetheless, he's discovered an oil reserve under the seabed, the largest in the known world. The ideal drilling point is at the coordinates we're presently headed to. Several problems, though. One. It's in an EEZ and technically it can't be drilled in unless all nations claiming ownership agree and share in the profits. Those nations are Russia, Denmark, Canada, and us. Now, if hearing those four countries together rings a bell, and it should, those are the ones who all got attacked at several of their oil-related sites."

Captain Tyson cleared his throat. "Sorry. Can you go back a little and give us some background info? I don't know about the rest of you, but I'm kind of lost."

"Sure thing." He stood and started to walk to a chart on the wall. "What we believe is sometime in March, Salib discovered there was oil here." He pointed to a location on the map. "Earlier this year, underwater sonobuoys detected an anomaly. Some scientists claimed it was volcanic activity, others said it was an old mine, maybe getting hit by a chunk of ice and detonating, blah, blah, blah. But after some intercepted chatter from the Russians, we think it was the implosion of a Russian sub modified with sonar equipment."

Captain Pendelton shifted in his chair. "What makes you say that?"

"Ah." Blake pointed to him. "Good question. Follow the money. Now stick with me. It gets a little confusing here." Moving to the table, he pressed a button on his laptop and the information on his screen displayed on a large monitor behind him. "On March eighth, a mere minutes before the buoys sensed, what we believe was an implosion, there was a large bitcoin transaction divided into a hundred and twenty-one different accounts and then after the destruction of the sub, all of it came out of every account except one."

Lieutenant Commander Jimmy Torres crossed his arms. "I thought crypto was untraceable."

Blake got somewhat animated and pointed to the young SEAL. "Not true. The entire transaction history is visible. The identities behind the wallets are problematic and can't be seen. But again."

His palms faced his audience. "Stick with me. I said all the accounts were drained but one. The owner of that account sold the bitcoin and transferred the cash to a different bank in the form of U.S. currency belonging to this man."

He clicked his remote, and an image filled the screen of a Middle Eastern man. "This is Akram Saman, and he has known ties to our buddy, the prince. Now, we have a database of known POIs and when any—" He made air quotes with his fingers. "Person of interest does a bunch of traveling; it will notify our system to investigate."

Torres laughed. "God, I love our intelligence. You can't hide from us."

The room filled with laughter.

"Right. Wait till you hear this. On February twenty-seventh, Mr. Saman left Bahrain and flew to Amsterdam. From there, he boarded a short flight to Oslo and spent the night. The next morning, he flew to Andenes. in the extreme north. Now why is this important? I'm getting there." He walked over, grabbed a bottle of water, and took a drink.

"Okay, we believe he chartered a boat and loaded some equipment. We don't have it on video, but we believe it from the witness statements they gathered. They never returned, and the boat was discovered two weeks later adrift in the Norwegian Sea, abandoned. The owners haven't been seen since. He more than likely killed the men on board, dumped them overboard, navigated to a designated area, and rendezvoused with the Russians."

Captain Tyson leaned back in his chair. "And what is it you believe he did?"

"Another good question. Our theory is that he modified the submarine, equipping it with sonar technology, which led him to the discovery of oil. Subsequently, he set off an explosive device, obliterating everyone on board. Following his tragic demise, his family received compensation for his ultimate sacrifice."

Captain Tyson straightened. "Is there any confirmation from the Soviets they have a sub missing?"

Blake's nose scrunched, and he blubbered his lips. "What? Do you think those commies will tell us about anything they are missing? Heck no. But I can tell you this. There were an awful lot of funerals, all within a few days of each other, and several were for high-ranking naval officers, all confirmed to be on the sub. We can all assume what that means."

They collectively nodded.

"So, back to what I was saying. Salib found out, we think he had a mole working for Canada Oil, but he found out the folks on the DavCo

Artic Drill ship stumbled onto this discovery. Through a loophole in the EEZ regulations, if he drilled and capped a well, he could claim ownership, regardless of any other claims. It's a first come, first serve thing. Anyway, to keep the four nations busy, rather than claiming it, he had teams of mercenaries attack various outposts, all dressed in another country's uniforms, setting off false flags."

"And those were the strikes that were happening all around the world?"

"Yeah, Isaac. That's right. The Danes attacked the Canadian ship. We supposedly invaded the Russian outpost on Kotelney Island. The Canadians struck the refinery at Prudhoe Bay and the Russians went on a killing spree against the Danes on the Thistle Oil Platform."

Evelyn chimed in. "He did all of this to keep us occupied on each other while he developed a way to drill the well, all while being completely invisible."

Shuffling through the various photos in the file, the Lieutenant Commander's eyes met hers. "Can you explain a little further?"

Blake nodded to her to continue. "He needed stealth. If he deployed a drill ship or a platform, then we'd know about it. A submarine with a drill attachment would be the only way he could accomplish his goal."

An image of a large vessel appeared on the screen, and he took over from Evelyn. "This is the Atlas. It is the ship we're looking for. This picture was taken after some of the prince's henchmen stole the submarine from the Deep Wave Institute. They attacked their research vessel, the Discovery, off the coast of Bergen, Norway. They killed everyone on board and sunk the ship. From the information I gathered at a facility on the Faroe Islands, believed to be owned by Salib through various shell companies, they've retrofitted this sub with a laser drill, and that is how they will get to the crude while remaining undetectable."

Everyone remained silent as they absorbed the information. Blake took a sip of his water and swallowed.

"Now for the *bad* news."

Captain Tyson removed his glasses and rubbed his eyes. "What do you mean?"

"Gentlemen, this next thing I'm about to tell you is frightening. It is why President Pennington called you personally, Captain, and why this mission has such a *must-succeed* mandate." He displayed an illustration of the reservoir field and a magma bubble underneath it. "This is the oil, and this—is a lake of molten rock." He pointed to a thin line. "This area here represents an extremely thin layer of rock separating the two. It is held in place by the weight and pressure of the crude bearing down on it."

The lieutenant started to shake his head. "Oh, no, no. I already know what you're gonna say. If they start pumping out the oil, the rock layer will be weakened. It will collapse and the two will mix, and—"

Blake nodded. "Yes, and boom. Catastrophic event. Everyone—let me be abundantly clear. This *is* a life-altering event on Earth as we know it. It is, for all intents and purposes, Armageddon, and we must stop it. Beyond all measure."

The SEAL leader stood, walked over to his gear bag, and removed his laptop. He turned to Blake. "So, what are your plans?"

"Well, there is no darkness here so you can forget the advantage of surprise." Blake addressed the ship's captain. "Sir, what is our ETA?"

"Last I checked, we were three hundred and fifty nautical miles—a little over six hours. But we're loaded with TLAMs and we're well within range. We could blow 'em to hell from here and they'd never know what hit 'em."

"Thanks, Captain. Sending a barrage of TLAMs—" He turned to Evelyn. "Otherwise known as Tomahawk missiles, is, at this point, not the optimal solution. I've been told to take the prince alive and there is a possibility of an American citizen on board."

The officer's eyes narrowed. "Pardon me, Mister MacKay, but did I miss something when you said *beyond all measure?* To me, if *whatever it costs* causes the death of some asshole rogue royal or some U.S. citizen who lost their way, so be it. I mean—if this is as bad as you claim."

"I have my orders, Captain, but I'll keep your idea as a last option backup." He turned to the SEAL Commander. "We send them a message upon arrival we're boarding. Evelyn, I, and five of your men will take a tender over. You and the rest can take the chopper. There is a pad on it, but it will probably be occupied so prepare to fast rope to the deck."

"I'd prefer that, to be honest."

Blake nodded. "All right. There ya go. You secure the prince and I'll—oh, dammit! I forgot. Hold on."

He went to his laptop and flipped through various slides until a Middle Eastern man's photo appeared. He backed away. "Everyone, listen up. This is Nazir Farhi. He has been the mastermind behind three of the four attacks. There will be a good chance he will be on the Atlas. He should be considered extremely dangerous and hostile, and you are authorized to use extreme prejudice if you encounter him."

The Lieutenant Commander made a fist and rammed it into his opposite palm. "Fuck yeah!"

Blake chuckled and glanced over at Evelyn. She was smiling and laughing at the SEAL's zest for violence. Their eyes met and her smile widened. A tingle traveled from his feet to the top of his head.

"What else MacKay?"

"I've had the displeasure of dealing with this guy personally. I'm the reason his ear is all messed up. Although a recent photo suggests he no longer has it. So, if he sees me—let's just say it won't be a warm welcome. Uh—what else? Oh, right. While the SEAL team from the chopper gets the prince, we'll work on disabling the sub so it can't dive or drill."

Evelyn chimed in. "What if it's already deployed?"

He sighed. "According to my calculations, since their vessel is considerably slower than ours, they will arrive only two or three hours before we do. I don't think they will have time to launch immediately."

"We've got depth charges. They can take care of the sub."

"Thank you, Captain, but we're talking a depth of over five thousand feet. What is the maximum you can set the charges for?"

He dipped his chin. "Oh. Never mind. Nine Hundred feet, max."

"Right. I have a small mine I will attach to the sub. It's not enough to destroy it, but it will damage it so it can't dive. Once I do that, I'll find the American, you'll have the prince, we'll take them into custody and bring them over and put them in the brig."

Evelyn raised her eyebrows. "What about the others?"

Captain Tyson grabbed a pen and made circular motions on a sheet of paper. "We'll tow the ship. Interpol can decide what to do with them."

Blake clapped his hands. "All right. So, we have a plan. I suggest everyone get something to eat and then rest. We have some heavy work ahead of us."

35

The North Pole
July 8th 19:30 (19:30 UTC)

Madison's stomach was already in knots. Her anxiety was through the roof in anticipation of the dive she was going to make the next day. The cold arctic air did little to dissipate the heavy sweat under her jacket. Seeing an American warship off the port side of the Atlas exacerbated everything. She rushed to the rail and vomited her dinner into the icy water below. After wiping her mouth on her sleeve, she hurried to talk with Prince Salib.

Upon entering his plush suite on the vessel, he was on the radio with someone. He slammed his fist on his desk and shouted. *"Ibn al-ʿāhira!"*

He stepped toward the wide window, pulled back the curtain, and stared into the void. His scowl conveyed all she needed to understand.

Choose your words carefully.

Frustrated, he rubbed his temple. "Okay. How long?" His gaze locked onto Madison's, and a knot of anxiety tightened in her throat, making her neck ache.

The tension in the air was palpable. "Very well. Thank you, Captain."

He sighed as he tossed the radio aside. "I assume you're aware of our visitor's, Doctor?"

"I am." Stepping closer, she kept a keen eye out for any signs of an outburst of violence, the likes of which he was known for. "Do we know what they want or why they are here?"

He clenched his jaw. "We do not. But we're about to find out."

Her brow furrowed. "How so?"

Grasping a pen and taping it on the desk like a drumstick, he looked away, then back. "They're boarding us. Something about the transponder."

She outstretched her arms. "What do we do?"

"Get ready to launch. If they ask, you're on a sample-gathering mission. I don't want them to see a laser drill attached to the front. They'll know how powerful it is and what it is for."

Madison froze in place. She wasn't mentally prepared for this dive now.

"Go earn your twenty-five million, Doctor."

BLAKE, EVELYN, AND half of the SEAL team rode to the Atlas on the USS Jackson's tender. The rest of the squad flew over on the MH-60S Sea Hawk.

Captain Tyson contacted Atlas and notified them they were doing a basic safety check because the ship's Automatic Identification System (AIS) transponder was not sending a signal, which is considered a breach of maritime law.

Turning off the AIS allows a ship to operate undetected, which can be associated with illegal activities.

They were met at the vessel's stern. Blake hopped off and offered his hand to Evelyn.

Once everyone was on board, he panned the area and observed the yellow sub. The rhythmic chuff chuff sound the Seahawk created as it hovered above the bow made it difficult to speak without yelling. Tapping her on the arm, he pointed to the submersible hanging from chains on the stern. "Go over there and try to disable it—enough to prevent it from diving! I don't want to use this mine if I don't have to!"

She nodded her understanding. As he turned back to the SEALS on the deck, near the rear entrance, he made eye contact with an old adversary. Nazir's stare cut right through him. The one-eared mercenary lifted his chin and sneered at him before a wry smile creased his face and he ducked inside at a hurried pace.

Blake placed his hand on the shoulder of the nearest man. "Keep an eye on—"

Bullets ricocheted off the davit's steel beam. Isaac, the SEAL closest to him, winced and hit the deck, blood seeping out of his leg. Doc, the medic, rushed to him and started treatment as the other two bore down with their

MK18 CQBR assault rifles and returned fire. Blake's head was on a swivel, searching for Evelyn. She took cover and was crouched behind the sub, her pistol in her hand.

"Stay there! I'm going after Nazir."

The SEALS maintained a covering fire while Blake darted inside the vessel. One of Nazir's men, Drew, stepped out of his hiding place, adrenaline surging as he returned fire.

In an instant, Blake raised his HK416, the weapon's familiar weight steady in his hands. He squeezed the trigger, unleashing a trio of rounds tearing through the air, silent with deadly accuracy.

Each bullet found its mark, driving into Drew's skull with brutal precision. The impact was catastrophic; the back of his head exploded.

The ship's pristine white sides transformed into a grotesque canvas, splattered with a horrific collage of blood, brains, and bone fragments.

He stepped over the lifeless form, a grim reminder of the violence that had unfolded, and entered the ship. Heavy silence enveloped him, broken only by the echo of his footsteps reverberating through the dim corridor. As he ventured deeper into the vessel, the air thickened with the pungent stench of fresh death, transforming the long passageway into a chilling mausoleum. The plinking of bullets on the main deck confirmed the remainder of the men were fully engaged with Nazir's crew.

A door slammed and echoed from the steep stairwell. He pointed his rifle over the edge, searching for movement. He activated his microphone. "Evelyn, when you get a chance, try and sabotage the sub. I'm going to the engine room."

"No! Don't. It'll be a trap. Wait for the rest of the team."

"No time. I know where he's at. If I stick around, no telling where he—"

The shadow betrayed the intentions of the man lurking behind him. Blake instinctively raised his arms defensively as the fire extinguisher crashed into them. His adversary pressed all his weight against Blake, his rifle bearing onto his chest, forcing him to bend backward over the railing, the mercenary's strength overwhelming. With a surge of adrenaline, Blake delivered a heel kick to the man's left knee, the sickening sound of snapping bone and tearing ligaments echoing in the air. The soldier's leg bent at an unnatural angle, was painful to witness.

Letting out a primal scream of agony, his opponent crumpled to the deck. Seizing the moment, Blake wrenched the metal canister from the other's grasp and swung it as hard as he could, the impact connecting with his opponent's temple and sending him sprawling. In a swift motion, he grabbed both sides of the man's head and twisted, ensuring he would fall into a permanent slumber.

He hadn't noticed Evelyn's pleas in his ears. "Blake! Blake!"

Out of breath and breathing hard, he answered. "I'm okay. I had a slight detour. Heading below now."

Two decks later, he was in front of the engine room's doors. He slung his rifle for his Glock 23 and proceeded with caution.

The engines were still, but the room was still filled with the constant hum of the generators, water desalination system, pumps, water heaters, and various mechanisms required for a ship this size. He peered in every corner. *Come on, you son of a bitch. Where are you?*

A sign on the port side caught his attention. *"Davit Winch Motor"* He nodded to himself as if he needed affirmation. He stepped to the other side and scanned the room. There was no sign of his old nemesis. With his free hand, he removed the explosive.

If I disabled the davit, they can't launch the sub.

He powered on the mine to set the timer for 5:00 minutes.

The weight of Nazir crashing into him from behind expelled all the air in his lungs. He lost hold of the mine, and it landed somewhere. There was the clank of it hitting steel and the grunt and anger from his old adversary.

"Mister MacKay. Not a pleasure seeing you again." Nazir's boot bit into Blake's side, already bruised from previous battles. Nazir turned and walked away to retrieve something. "I'm going to take my time and enjoy this."

Blake closed his eyes and used an old technique of body scan meditation to push his anxiety away and focus on his lungs to regain his breath.

The thump of each step echoing through the steel plates grew in intensity on his back as his enemy got closer.

Opening his eyes, Blake's field of view was filled with a crowbar bearing down on him. He rolled to his left as it hit the metal floor.

He rolled right as it missed again. Rolling back, Blake leaped to his feet. *Where's the damn mine?*

Panning to his right, the red glow of the digital numbers caught his eye. It was wedged behind a grating, head height, pressed against the hull.

He didn't set it for 05:00 minutes. It displayed 50 seconds. And it was activated.

00:22, 00:21.

He ducked as the iron bar crashed against the Caterpillar diesel engine. Blake let loose with two uppercut punches to Nazir's gut.

The clang of the bar hitting the floor reverberated in the tiny confines of the engine room. A clenched fist landed a blow on the top of Blake's head as he was bent over trying to deliver another hit.

A sharp kick to his side made him grit his teeth in pain. Blake retreated, successfully blocking the incoming front kick. As he regained his stance, he shot a glance past the man, his eyes blazing with hatred.

00:13, 00:12.

Nazir charged in, attempting to tackle him. Blake braced himself, stretching his right leg behind him for stability. With Nazir leaning in to try to wrestle him to the ground, he seized the opportunity and delivered three swift punches to his kidneys.

00:09, 00:08.

Reaching around, he unsheathed his eight-inch blade from his vest and drove it into his attacker's kidney. Nazir released his grip and arched his back while screaming in agony.

00:03, 00:02.

Blake leaped up and grasped an overhead pipe. With a powerful thrust of his legs, he swung forward and drove both feet into his old enemy's chest. The impact sent him crashing back against the side of the hull.

00:01, 00:00.

Blake turned and hit the deck as the mine detonated, obliterating Nazir's head and most of his shoulders in an instant. In the aftermath, a three-foot gash marred the ship's hull right at the waterline, an unwelcome consequence of the detonation.

He gagged and turned away from the grotesque scene.

"Well, now your face matches your ear. Fucker!"

As the water spilled in, he searched for his rifle and Glock. Grabbing both, he exited to head to the deck. He was met with rifle fire from above and ducked back in for cover. "Dammit!"

He opened his mic and called out to the team leader. "Isaac! I've got a hostile shooting at me from the main deck level. Aft stairwell to the engine room. It's starting to flood. Come and help ASAP. Over."

"On our way after I take care of this problem. Over."

"Understood."

MADISON BRACED HERSELF against the wall. "What the hell was that?" Black smoke rose in tendrils, like demonic fingers grasping for souls as it guided her to the railing. Leaning over to inspect what caused the explosion, she gasped at the gaping hole in the hull. Water was being sucked in at an alarming pace.

"Holy shit!"

Running back to Salib's quarters, she entered as he was pacing back and forth while on his phone.

"Do it! I'll be there as soon as possible!"

He ended the call and started assembling his things. Madison's eyes were wide, her hands open, with her arms raised. "What are you doing? Did you hear the explosion? The ship's going down!"

His eyes met hers as he continued to scramble, gathering stuff. "Of course I did, you idiot. Shouldn't you be in the sub?"

Her brow furrowed. "What? You've got to be kidding. Didn't you hear me? The ship—is—sinking!"

"And you have a job to do, doctor! I expect you to finish it!"

A crease fell across her brow as she shook her head. "Hell no. Forget—"

"Doctor! For fuck's sake!" He stopped and turned to her. He stood in contemplation. "To hell with it. One hundred million!"

Her mouth went agape. "What?"

He stepped toward her while pointing. "You heard me. One hundred million dollars. You cap the well, and I'll quadruple your payment."

She stood silent and in disbelief.

"But you'd better hurry, because like you said. We're going down."

He brushed her shoulder as he rushed past her. She turned to him as he was exiting the room. "Where are you going?"

"I'm flying the hell outta here. The well, doctor! Time is ticking."

She burst out of the room and raced to the main deck, where chaos reigned. People were scrambling for lifeboats, and the dead bodies of Nazir's men were sprawled across the decks and corridors. The air was thick with the sound of gunfire, punctuated by the shouts and commands of military personnel. Amidst the turmoil, she could hear her name echoing through the mayhem. "Madison!"

Zaanjar ran to her and grasped her shoulders. "What are you doing? We need to get out of here. Come on!"

"No! I can't. I have to launch the sub. I can't do it by myself. Please come help me."

Her nose scrunched as her chin dipped. "What are you, crazy? Forget about the damn thing. Come on." She started to pull her in the opposite direction. Madison yanked her arm loose.

"No!"

"Madison? What's wrong with you?"

She placed a gentle touch on her friend's arm. "I'm sorry. He's paying me a ton of money to drill this well. I will give you a hundred thousand dollars to assist me in launching the sub."

Her right brow raised. "You're kidding me."

"No. I need your help. A hundred grand."

She sighed. "Ok, but let's hurry."

36

The North Pole
July 8th 19:51 (19:51 UTC)

Evelyn kept out of sight of the mayhem continuing on deck between the SEALs and what was left of Nazir's team of mercenaries. The resonating sound of gunfire piercing the otherwise serene arctic air had relinquished itself toward the ship's bow, so she made a closer inspection of the apparatus attached to the front of the submarine.

What the hell? I think this is a drill. This is what they're going to use to create the well.

She traced her fingers along the line of welded steel extending from the submersible. Its touch was cold. The coldness was a warning. A chilling reminder of what lay beneath them. At the end, eight bolts secured the laser in place. To her left, she spotted a toolbox. She holstered her pistol and searched through the drawers. As she rummaged, she found a socket wrench with several sockets.

Not knowing what size she needed, she placed each socket on a bolt head to test. Finding the correct fit, she wrangled with the first of the fasteners. Screaming from behind her, followed by a flash of severe pain in her right hand as a pipe knocked the tool out of her grasp, crashing into it.

"What are you doing? Stay away from this!"

Evelyn grasped her hand and worked through the torment as she tried to make a fist. Nothing was broken but she could sense it starting to swell. There was no way she could grip her pistol. Standing before her was a tall blonde wearing a University of Tennessee sweatshirt. With a clenched jaw, she looked as if she wanted to kill her with her eyes.

"I asked you a question! Now go away. We need to launch it." She turned her head for a moment. "Zaanjar, get to the hoist controls. We're getting this in the water."

The crane was activated. The motor's growl harmonized with the metallic symphony of tensioned steel cables, creating a cacophony rivaling the chaos unfolding at the forefront.

The yellow deep-sea explorer started to rise. The blonde shifted her focus and Evelyn her move. She lunged at the blonde. Attacking low, Evelyn rammed her shoulders into Madison's midsection and wrapped her arms around her opponent. They both fell to the metal decking with a thud. Straddling her, Madison punched Miss Tennessee in the face with a left hook. The weaker of her two hands had little effect, only to enrage her.

Evelyn's adversary's eyes squinted, and she clenched her teeth. The pipe she held came unbounded toward the side of Evelyn's head. Evelyn rolled to her right and raised her left arm in defense. The makeshift weapon crashed into her elbow with punishing force. "Get off of me! You don't understand. I have to launch this sub. It's for my brother!"

Pain pulsed from her elbow, a relentless ache that shot through Evelyn's arm like a storm, reaching to her fingertips, turning even the simplest action into a struggle. Getting up proved challenging. Her hand throbbed insistently while her other elbow protested fiercely. As she knelt on one arm, she inadvertently exposed her vulnerable midsection.

Madison took advantage of the opening, drawing back her leg before delivering two powerful kicks to Evelyn's ribs.

The sub cleared the stern and entered the water while the ship listed to the port side as the sea rushed in. The gunfire came closer, as did the voices of Nazir's team and the SEALs. Chaos surrounded her.

Madison yelled out to her friend. "Zaanjar, keep lowering it until there is slack in the line."

Evelyn faked defeat and waited until her adversary wasn't paying attention to her.

A thud diverted her attention as a bloodied body plummeted from the level above, riddled with bleeding holes, half of his jaw missing.

Bullets whizzed overhead. Some ricocheted off the davit, adding to the turmoil. Madison strode along the rail on the port side. Evelyn winced in pain as she struggled to her feet and rushed her foe.

The two collided at the edge of the sinking vessel. Ignoring the agony in her arms and hands, Evelyn grasped Madison, attempting to throw her overboard. But her injuries were too severe, and her opponent's strength was overwhelming.

"You bitch!" Madison screamed, rage consuming her like an insatiable fire. "Nobody will stop me! Fucking die!" She crouched, reached around Evelyn, and with a heave, lifted her and tossed her over the railing.

"ZAANJAR. MORE SLACK." When she didn't hear a response from her friend, she turned. Zaanjar was lying on her back, bleeding from multiple gunshot wounds. "Shit!"

Bounding to the controls, her anxiety was through the roof. "Come on, come on!"

She released enough slack to remove the cables, her heart racing.

"Good enough!"

Sprinting toward the stern, she launched into the air and landed on the submersible. After freeing it from its steel restraints, she opened the watertight hatch and entered.

BLAKE RUSHED OUT ONTO the rear of the boat, where he'd heard Evelyn's voice moments earlier. Before him was a dead woman near the davit controls, a mercenary bloodied with holes and the DSV bobbing in the sea. "Evelyn!" He glanced at the upper deck and called out again. "Evelyn!" One of the SEALs appeared, his breath dissipating against the frigid air. "Frank, have you seen her?"

He shook his head. "No, bud, I've been a little busy. We need to go. The threat's been neutralized, and this vessel is sinking."

There was a faint cry. "I'm down here. Help."

Blake raced to the edge as her body was sucked into the engine room with the rushing water. "Oh, my God!"

Blake sprinted inside and into the belly of the ship. When he reached the lower level, the water was at chest height. It was bitterly cold. The door was ajar, and the icy sea rushed out. "Evelyn!"

"I'm—here! I'm stuck!"

He grasped the door with both hands and pulled. Placing his left foot on the wall for leverage, he strained as the ocean consumed the doomed vessel. As he slipped in, she was pinned near the opening in the hull. Her clothes were snagged on the torn steel. He waded over and inspected the situation. A stream of crimson mixed with the swirling around her revealed more than he could see.

He unsheathed his knife and started to cut her loose. A sharp corner of metal had pierced her side. She was bleeding profusely. Water was now past his shoulders. She was shaking, her lips were turning blue, and her eyebrows were raised and pulled together. "Hey! What's wrong?"

"Hold on. I have you." He took a deep breath and submerged. He continued to chop at the cloth binding her to the ship's mercy. After removing strips of Evelyn's clothing, he clamped them between his teeth. Her body was free, and he popped his head out of the water. Grabbing the remnants of her clothes, he handed them to her. "Press this on your wound. You're bleeding pretty bad, but Doc's on deck and he'll take care of you as soon as we get you outta here, okay?"

Groans and creaks filled the room as the weight of the sea pressed hard against the steel. "We gotta swim. Fast."

Nodding, Evelyn was already shivering from the severe cold. His eyes fixed on hers. "I've got you. I won't let anything happen to you. Look at it this way. Now you know what people on the Titanic felt like."

Her teeth started to chatter. "That's—not—funny."

He smiled. "Come on, let's go. Deep breath."

Taking in a gasp of air, they submerged and swam to the exit. The first flight of stairs was underwater. An evil growl like a chorus of damned souls echoed within the ship. Blake grabbed hold of the stair rail and used it to propel them upward. Only a few more feet and they climbed the dry steps. "Okay, Move it." He opened his mic, reached under her legs and scooped her into his arms. "Doc! You there? Over."

"We're here, Blake. I'm on deck and the rest are in the tender. Over."

"What about the chopper? Evelyn is wounded. Over."

"Copy. I'll order its return, and ride back with her. Where is the wound? Is it a gunshot? Over."

"Negative. A gash in her side from a sharp piece of metal. Over."

"Affirmative. Tell her we call that a million-dollar wound. Over."

"I'll let you tell her yourself. We're approaching the deck. Over."

Moments later, the Seahawk descended, its rotors roaring as it hovered over the ship's bow. With urgency, the two men loaded Evelyn onto a stretcher before hoisting her into the chopper. As the aircraft lifted off, they took their places beside her, the thrum of the engines a stark contrast to the chaos they had escaped.

Blake and Doc gazed out from the open door as the Atlas disappeared beneath the waves, vanishing into the depths of the ocean's embrace, destined for its permanent resting place five thousand feet below. The weight of the moment settled heavily on them, a silent farewell to those who lost their lives.

The pilot came over their headsets. "We'll have them retrieve the survivors from their lifeboats. I'm sure you'll have lots of questions for them."

Blake nodded. "Right. Hey. Wait a second. The sub. Did it dive?"

A collective pool of replies indicating nobody had any clue shot a wave of apprehension through him.

"We've got another problem."

MADISON GRIPPED THE controls. Her view into the abyss invoked fear and anxiety. She wiped her brow and was surprised by the amount of her sweat, considering the cool temperature of her surroundings. She tried to focus on the job ahead to control her uneasiness after what she'd been through moments ago.

A deep moan echoed throughout the inside of her confines. "What the hell was that? A whale?"

The sound intensified, overwhelming the submersible. She flicked on the outside lights, only to be met with a void of illuminated black, punctuated by occasional bubbles and the eerie silhouette of floating organic matter. Suddenly, the DSV jolted violently, and her descent accelerated. Alarms blared around her. "Oh, my God!"

Her rate of descent was initially set at 60 feet per minute, but the dial surged upward: 100, 125, 140. A hull pressure alarm shrieked, sending a chill along her spine. Her hair stood on end, and panic clawed at her throat as she was dragged deeper. 170, 190. At this rate, she would implode in less than two minutes.

"Fuck it!" She slammed the controls to full power and veered to her left. The reflection of a white panel illuminated the cramped interior. It was the Atlas. With a sudden shift, her descent slowed as she escaped the pull of the doomed vessel. She sat in stunned silence, her mouth agape, watching as the bow slipped past her and faded into the darkness below.

BLAKE HAD CHANGED OUT of his soaking-wet combat gear. His hair was still damp from their unexpected swim. He entered the infirmary to witness Evelyn lying on her side with Doc focused on her body above her right hip. He pulled on the suture, cut it, and removed his gloves. "That's it, young lady. Eighteen stitches. No charge."

"Thanks." She winced as he helped her sit upright. She held a bag of ice against her hand while another was taped to her elbow.

Their eyes met. They seemed to speak volumes to each other without saying a word. He put his arm around her, and she leaned in and rested her head on his chest. "Thank you."

He chuckled. "For what?" She initiated a playful tap of her head against him. "You know. I hope you killed the bitch."

Blake's and Doc's eyes shifted uncomfortably and met. Doc's eyes widened, and he frowned. "That's my cue to leave." He handed her a pill bottle. "These are for the pain. One every six hours. I'll check on you tomorrow, but let me know if you have any problems or further discomfort."

She nodded. "Thanks, Doc."

After he left, she sighed. "I gather there is a situation?"

"Uh, yeah. We think she got in the sub and is on her way to start drilling."

Her brow furrowed. "Seriously? What happened to Salib?"

"He took off on his helicopter, but one of the guys attached a tracker to it, so we're not too worried about him right now. The critical problem is that crazy bitch with the drill. This ship doesn't have the technology to scan at those depths, and it's—well, you heard the captain. The depth charges are only good for nine hundred feet at the most, and she's well past that by now."

Evelyn reached for Blake's hand and started rubbing the top of it with her thumb. Her chin rose. "Hey! I have an idea. The uh...the Arctic. The captain said they'd be here for ten days to two weeks making repairs. It has the equipment to find it."

He shook his head. "It could be a thousand miles from here."

"But what if it's not? Let me at least make the call. Help me to stand and bring me a satellite phone. I'll get an answer."

He glanced at the clock on the wall. "It's after midnight here. What time is it in the UK?"

"They're three hours behind us."

Evelyn retrieved the CEO's business card and called his mobile. He confirmed the location of the Arctic Drill. She contacted the captain and discovered the vessel was operational and only fifty nautical miles away. The drill ship started and would be there in three hours. Blake calculated the descent would take an additional sixty minutes with another thirty to find the target. He had no idea how long it would take to reach 1000 feet into the oil field. He decided to grab something to eat and get some rest until the drill ship arrived.

THE ARCTIC DRILL SHIP

July 9th 00:13 (00:13 UTC)

The soft glow of the midnight sun filled the bridge of the Artic Drill. They'd mapped out a two square mile grid pattern from the center of the area where the Atlas sank and searched for the submersible working their way out. Blake approached the man in charge. "Captain Keng, what do you know about laser drills?"

He sighed and stroked his beard. "That's a question for the engineers. I pilot the ship. However, since they aren't aboard, I'll try to explain. I've been in this business long enough to have picked up some knowledge."

Blake nodded. "I'm fine with testing your skills. How fast would it take to use a laser drill to cut through a thousand feet of rock?"

He shifted the weight on his feet. "Oh, you gave me an easy one. Just over two hours running at maximum output. Maybe two and a half if they encounter something dense."

"But what kind of power source would they have? What if it came from a small submersible?"

"Hmm, well. With an inadequate energy supply, anticipate at least eight hours." His eyes widened and he raised a finger. "Uh, you also have to accommodate for the hydro drill."

"Hydro drill? What do you mean?"

"You can't drill into an oil reserve with a flaming hot laser. What do you think will happen?"

"Fair enough. How much time would that add?"

"A couple of hours at best."

Blake glanced at his watch. "Dammit. We're still way too close. Where are we on finding the damn sub?"

The phone on the wall rang and Captain Keng answered. "Yes." He covered the mouthpiece with the palm of his hand. "All stop. Mark coordinates and heave to." He uncovered the mouthpiece. "Thank you."

He replaced the receiver and turned to Blake. "Your timing is impeccable, Mister MacKay. We've identified a target. We're right above it."

Blake put his hand on his chin, gazed out of the bridge's rear window, and stared at the rigging in the middle of the ship. His eyes darted from the top and then to the bottom. He focused on the cables and the shafts stacked on storage racks on the side and turned back to Keng.

"How deep can this thing drill?"

"Ten thousand feet."

"How accurate can you get?"

He smirked. "I could punch a hole in a dime if I had a bit small enough. What are you thinking?"

Blake turned toward the davit and then back. "I need you to poke one in the sub."

He nodded and rubbed his cheek. "It's going to take a lot of time. We have to assemble the shafts, and then there are security measures."

"What of those, if any, can you skip if you're not drilling a well?"

Blake stood and waited while the captain thought for a moment. He then looked at the clock on the wall.

"Captain, I haven't mentioned this, but if she succeeds in her mission, the entire world's fate will hang in the balance. This is a global catastrophic event. We are running out of time."

"Well, when you paint such a dark picture, we can pass on *all* of them. We'll need all hands on deck for this."

The ship maintained its location above the target, and the crew started connecting the segments of the shafts. Each was 46 feet long and had to be lifted into place by a crane and connected by a team on the deck floor. The normal process would take fourteen hours, but without all the safety measures, they could cut it to six.

5,017 FT DEEP BOTTOM of the Arctic Ocean

July 9th 07:11 (07:11 UTC)

Madison woke from a two-hour nap. She had reached a depth of 875 feet and needed another 162 feet to reach well depth. She would cap it, surface and reap the reward of 100 million dollars from Prince Salib. All had gone smoothly so far. She had fifteen more hours of oxygen left. But it was more than enough to complete her assignment and surface safely. She had a satellite phone to call for help and told herself she'd think of a story on how the Atlas sank on her ascent.

She adjusted the hydro drill in place for the final drilling session, making sure the anchors were holding tight and turned it on. The debris which settled into the hole blew out and clouded her view. The depth reader went to 895 in a few minutes.

The submarine vibrated steadily as the drill pierced through the rock, making the initial jolt feel like another routine occurrence. Within the narrow confines of the compartment, the ceaseless barrage of rock and sand hitting the metal shell reverberated, serving as a persistent indication of the fragments ejected by the freshly bored cavity.

Not until the full weight of the ship's drill pressing on the tiny sub did she realize something was amiss. It lurched hard. The lights flickered, and the DAV was pressed firmly into the soft silt ocean floor.

"What the hell?"

And then she heard it. The initial grinding of teeth scratching against the top of the sub, their sharp edges searching for something to bite and start its relentless assault on the hull. The noise sent a chill through Madison's spine, a prelude to the nightmare unfolding.

Her eyes were wide, and her hair stood at attention. The pounding in her chest intensified. She peeked at the depth. 970ft.

The grinding got louder. 982ft. She was so close to reaching the mass of black gold.

"Oh, God. No!"

Madison closed her eyes and a fraction of a second later, she and the sub imploded into a mass of steel, glass, and organic matter.

---

187 NAUTICAL MILES NNE of Greenland

July 9th 13:30 (13:30 UTC)

Blake pushed his empty plate away and watched Evelyn eat her salad. "What are your plans when we get back to Reykjavik?"

She finished chewing and washed it down with a sip of water. "I have some things to get caught up with at work and then I thought I'd return home. To my mom's."

His eyes shifted up in thought. "That's—British Columbia, right? Vancouver?"

"Close. Chilliwack. But it's essentially a suburb of Vancouver. About eighty klicks east. Richard is flying there on the 19th so I'm going out there to meet them. It's been a while since we were all together, especially after my dad passed away—I thought I'd take a few days to spend at home. How about you?"

He leaned forward on his elbows. "Waiting on orders. They're trying to determine if I follow Salib or let it go."

She placed her fork in her bowl and scrunched her eyebrows. "Let it go? How could your government—hell, how could my government or the other nations affected by him pass on bringing him to justice?"

He drummed his fingers on the surface. "I dunno. Something to do with the Saudis? Relations with them are always sketchy. I don't trust them as far as I could throw 'em, but we have to keep the illusion of diplomatic bullshit."

She nodded, reached out and started lightly rubbing the top of his hand. Then she smiled wide. "You know...I haven't properly thanked you for saving my life."

He smirked as a tiny knot formed in his stomach, and a thrill went down his leg. He also felt a slight flutter in his heart. "You don't say? How's your side?"

She stood. "Good enough." She motioned with her chin. "Come on MacKay. You're going to enjoy this."

37

The Burj Khalifa
Dubai

July 13th 01:13 (21:13 UTC July 12th)

The ascent to the top of the world's tallest building gave Blake time to reflect on the past few weeks. Most notably, he spent the final two days with Evelyn. One day onboard the USS Jackson, returning from the North Pole, and the last day—and spectacular night—in a luxury hotel in Reykjavik.

His mind flipped between joy and sorrow, caught in the bittersweet dance of emotions. The happiness she brought to his life, something he'd been missing for a long time, was overshadowed by the pain of her striking resemblance to Adriana. It stirred memories of a past he could not fully grasp. With every fleeting moment, his heart became a kaleidoscope of feelings, a vibrant yet tumultuous mix of longing, love, hope, and heartache.

The first elevator took him to the 138th floor. The second, to level 160, the third—the maintenance workers call the 'Washing Machine'—raised him to 166. After several more flights of stairs, he approached the final climb in the 243-meter spire.

Stepping into the confined area within the base, he discovered it was a mere ten feet wide. Facing him were a pair of slim pillars designed for climbing, each fitted with an extended steel rope. Fastening his ascender to the cable and double-checking his safety harness, he started his ascent. Exiting through the hatch reminiscent of a ship's porthole at the summit, he stood at an elevation of 829 meters above the city of Dubai spread out below him.

The wind whistled in his ears, and the relentless heat of the desert air enveloped him, even in the dead of night. He raised his binoculars and focused on the Persian Gulf. Moored 1,000 meters off the coast, *The Midnight Oil* floated still, while anchored near Jumeirah Bay.

The wind was at his face, promising to provide the immediate lift his glider required to reach the sea, which lay 3,000 meters from where he stood—a distance typically exceeding his gliding capabilities with normal equipment.

But Blake's setup was anything but standard. Modified by Alice, his gear promised an additional 1,000 to 1,500 meters of flight from his takeoff altitude, giving him the edge he needed for this daring leap.

The decision was made, and the mission approved. President Pennington had spoken directly to the Saudi royal family. The disavowed prince had broken the last straw, and the king had allowed the elimination of their lingering problem and embarrassment, once and for all. They had but one request. Make it look like an accident.

Having the royal family sanction the assassination provided an unexpected advantage: it granted the agency access to intelligence typically elusive. Salib had a notorious reputation in Dubai, infamous for his indulgent lifestyle marked by debauchery and illicit substances.

When anchored, he would often dismiss his entire crew, seizing the yacht for himself, allowing him to indulge his predilections without scrutiny. His encounters were not only scandalous; many of the young women involved were underage, ensnared in a grim underground sex trafficking ring.

This knowledge alone ignited Blake's fervent eagerness to terminate Salib's reign of depravity and put him out of his misery.

Dressed in all black, he perched at the edge of the spire and steadied his body by gripping one of the lightning rods. Despite having executed stunts like this countless times before, his heart raced.

The thrill of the impending fall sent a surge of adrenaline coursing through him, and every hair stood on end. He knew his faith in his equipment had to be absolute. He trusted both his gear and Alice.

With a determined resolve, he closed his eyes and sucked in a deep breath of warm, dry acrid air. With his arms raised, he leaped into the void.

The wind rushed by him, and physics took over. He slowed to a smooth glide and navigated toward his target. Skyscrapers rose from the desert, resembling a collection of gleaming pearls strewn across the sandy landscape, windows aglow, casting a pleasing light on the surrounding sands. The lights whizzed by his peripheral vision, resembling shooting stars as he raced through a tunnel.

The highway beneath him disappeared and left only the dark waters of the Persian Gulf. The yacht was swiftly approaching, and Blake readied himself to drop into the sea and close the remaining stretch by swimming.

Releasing his harness, he dropped a few meters into the ocean below. He swam the distance quickly. The side of the craft was open for the tender dock. He slid out of the sea in silence. Removing his sidearm, he prepared it for the upcoming battle and positioned his night vision over his eyes.

His world was now immersed in a soft, green glow. Entering the watercraft garage, a wake boat hung from its davit. On the opposite wall, he made a mental note of the two WaveRunners, then crept through the engine room.

Its bright lights and pristine white walls forced him to remove his night gear. Chrome covers were so clean you could eat off them concealing unsightly hoses and fans. The hum of the generators masked any sound.

He was grateful for the enthusiastic YouTuber who toured the vessel in the previous year's Monaco Yacht Show. Blake watched the video multiple times and knew exactly where the prince would be.

Ascending three levels, he entered a realm of luxury amidship on the main deck. The polished wooden floors gleamed underfoot, while walls of lustrous wood and marble tiles added to the elegance.

The curved central stairwell radiated opulence, and from the ceiling hung a breathtaking chandelier crafted of shimmering chrome and crystal, extending five decks in length. He moved with precision to the forward owner's suite.

Separated by a single door, his target lay on the other side. He switched to infrared and confirmed two bodies were lying in the bed. He needed to be swift and quiet. The green glow once again filled his vision. With a gloved hand, he grasped the door handle and turned it.

On entering, he found two young girls. They looked to be between fifteen and nineteen. Blake shook his head. *What a piece of shit!* The blonde girl's eyes fluttered open and fixed them on him. She gasped. He brought his finger to his lips. She nodded understanding, closed her eyes, and sank her head back into the pillow.

Exiting the room, the dim light in the hallway gave him multiple options; up, down, or stay on this deck. He decided to sweep where he was and move on from there. When he entered the main saloon, the hardwoods ended and were replaced by lush carpeting. To his right was a bar with four stools tucked neatly under its highly polished top. As he began to turn, the voice from behind startled him.

"That's far enough, Mr. MacKay."

He froze.

"I'll be kind and let you know I'm about to switch on the lighting. Please take off your night vision, but not before you hand me your sidearm."

Blake started to move his hand to his pistol when Salib intervened.

"Ah-ah. Your left hand."

Blake sighed and used his opposite hand to remove the 9mm from its holster on his right hip. He handed it to Salib's waiting grasp.

"Thank you. Take off your night goggles now."

As he removed them, the lights illuminated the interior.

"My father, the king, wants me dead. But a mother's love for her son would never betray me. I've known for days you'd be coming. I didn't know when."

Blake met Salib's cold stare. The prince was sitting on the leather couch facing the bar. He wore a silk, leopard-print robe, and a black sash with matching pajama bottoms.

"I guess it got tiring occupying yourself with fucking little girls—Your Highness?"

The smug man ignored his comment, inspected the weapon, and smirked. "A Hi-Point? Hardly the quality of firearm someone such as yourself would be using. I figured you for a Glock or Sig." He glanced at his palm and inspected his fingers. "And this oil. Did a child look after this piece for you?" He stood and wiped some of the residue on his garment. "I guess it doesn't matter at this moment. A shame you'll die at the hands of your own—" Glancing at the pistol, he shook his head as he smiled. "Weapon."

Blake chuckled. "You have a vivid imagination. I've got something to tell you about your greasy fingers."

The prince winced ever so slightly. He bent his right leg and leaned over to rub his calf. Straightening, he walked toward the bar. "I suppose I'll indulge you for one more moment before I shoot you."

"Gee, thanks." He waited while the prince reached for a bottle of vodka and poured a shot.

"Can I get you something, Mr. MacKay?"

Perusing the back of the bar, he spotted the 23-year-old Pappy Van Winkle Family Reserve.

"Well, since you're asking. The Pappy."

"At least you have excellent taste in one thing." Salib waved the gun, indicating Blake should help himself. While he poured the exceptional brown liquor, the prince swigged his vodka.

Blake noticed significant discomfort on the man's face. His nose scrunched and his forehead displayed deep wrinkles as his brow furrowed.

"I appreciate your concern for my—what did you say—greasy fingers?" He dispensed another drink and tipped it back. "Now, tell me about it."

"The oil you feel is a DMSO."

Salib's eyes narrowed. "Stop quizzing me on my knowledge of acronyms. Get on with it."

He raised his palms. "Fair enough. It's dimethyl sulfoxide. It's a colorless, oily fluid derived from trees as a by-product of paper production."

"So, it's not gun oil?"

He shook his head. "No. It's a delivery system."

Salib squinted. "Delivery system? For what?" He reached for a towel, wiping the sweat from his brow, his discomfort evident. His jaw was clenched tight, and Blake could sense he was struggling against the unmistakable signs of distress.

"Are you familiar with the South American poison arrow frog or the blue-ringed octopus?"

His lips began to quake, and his eyes narrowed. "Vaguely. What did you do to me?"

"Singularly, they are equally toxic. The frog produces a type of batrachotoxin so powerful that only 1/100,000 of an ounce can kill a human. However, the symbiotic bacteria in blue-ringed octopus salivary glands produce tetrodotoxin. This substance is potently neurotoxic, blocking the transmission of nerve impulses. This stops muscles from being able to contract and has deadly consequences. It explains the difficulty and discomfort you're having now."

Salib's body shook. "Argh!" His right hand holding the firearm was quaking.

Blake smiled. "You don't think I'd give you a loaded weapon, do you? I mean—in case the poison took too long to take effect."

Still wearing his special butyl gloves, he reached for the pistol and took it from Salib's weakened grasp.

He walked to the sliding door on the port side, adjacent to the bar. "By now, you're experiencing some paralysis." Opening the door, he tossed the gun overboard and listened for the splash. As he returned, the prince winced. Salib opened his eyes wide and blinked several times.

Blake nodded. "Your vision is starting to blur. It's about to get much worse." He retrieved some solution from his tactical vest and went to the sink. He poured the liquid over his gloved hands and washed them under the water. After removing a black mesh bag from his front pocket, he filled it with silverware from a drawer to weigh it down. Using a towel, he removed his gloves. Still wearing protective liners, he stuffed them and the cloth he used into the bag.

The doomed man's legs gave out, and he collapsed to the floor. He spoke in a broken and muffled voice. "You—won't—get—"

"Shut up. I'll save you the effort. This poison will run its course. There will be no trace. Any autopsy will not find anything and it will look as if you died from natural causes."

Curled in a fetal position, the prince tried to scream in agony, but he had trouble getting air into his lungs. Sweat poured from his brow, soaking his skin, and foam seeped from the corners of his mouth, highlighting his torment.

Blake made the short trip back outside and tossed the mesh bag into the sea. "Are you having breathing problems? It's because your intercostal muscles and diaphragm are being paralyzed. Your heart will be the last muscle to stop working and you know what happens then."

"Hey, if you don't mind, I'm going to get another bourbon." He retrieved a new glass, placed it on the shiny wood surface, and poured another drink.

He used a towel to grasp the bottle in case of any oily residue. "Hmm. No. Make that two." He laughed. "After all, you're not going to drink it."

Salib's body convulsed. Foam and spittle erupted from his mouth, marring the otherwise pristine white carpet with a disturbing contrast.

Blake savored esters of oak and vanilla as it filled his throat with a slight burn. After three more sips, the noise from the yacht's main saloon subsided. The stench of human feces assaulted his nostrils. He stepped to the side and saw the prince's corpse lying in a pool of his own waste. Removing his phone, he snapped a picture and sent it to Veronica.

He left the body where it lay, a grim proof of the night's events. After tossing his glass overboard, he wiped down the bar and the bottle of Pappy, ensuring no trace remained.

Descending below deck, he prepared the wake boat, expertly maneuvering the vessel out of the garage and into the water. Once it was securely tied to the cleats, he climbed the stairs back to the main stateroom to gather the young girls Salib had brought aboard.

He escorted them ashore, assisting them to contact their parents. Hidden in the shadows, he watched as they were reunited in the lobby of the Burj Al Arab.

CIA HEADQUARTERS
Langley, Virginia
July 15th
09:00 (14:00 UTC)

She wore a vintage ivory Chanel Boucle skirt suit with black double buttons and stitching. After being promoted to Director of Intelligence, she could negotiate a much nicer office than the former occupant, Mike Brennan. Sitting on the top floor, it occupied a highly sought corner with views of the surrounding trees at the rear of the building. She had also insisted on removing the old wood paneling on the walls to brighten the room. She walked over from her coffee bar and handed him a steaming cup of black Kona.

"Your favorite, if I recall?"

He lifted it to his nose. A symphony of aromas enveloped him. The rich, inviting scent was a delightful blend of fruity notes, reminiscent of ripe berries and tropical citrus, mingling with subtle hints of spice and chocolate.

He smiled. "You remembered."

Moving behind her glass and chrome desk, she placed her mug on the clean surface, sat in the black leather chair, and opened a file folder. "Well, it's official. Our friend, the prince, died of a brain aneurysm. Nice job."

Blake sat in one of the two matching easy chairs in front of her desk. He tipped his mug toward her. "Thanks."

"How'd you do it?"

He smirked. "It's complicated."

She raised her palm. "Never mind. I don't wanna know." Closing the folder, she tossed it on her desk. "What's next? Are you going to take some time to decompress?"

He nodded and turned his attention out the window. "Yeah." His voice seemed to fade along with his thoughts. Veronica stood and broke the silence by extending her hand. "Okay, enjoy yourself. I'll talk to you in a couple of weeks?"

He shook her hand. "Sounds about right."

She kept a grip on his hand. "I know we don't see eye-to-eye on a lot of things and... Well, I just wanted to tell you, good job."

His eyes widened, and some of the tension between them drifted away. "Thanks." He smiled and their hands separated.

HALIFAX, NOVA SCOTIA
July, 17th
10:40 (14:40 UTC)

He parked the rented Ford F-150 on the tree-lined street. The small 2-story home was quaint and well-maintained. Reddish maroon window and door trim contrasted with the taupe-painted siding. The BMW in the driveway indicated the occupant was at home. He grabbed the bouquet of lilies and daisies and headed for the house. He ascended the five steps to the covered porch. The butterflies in his stomach he'd felt for the last fifteen minutes wouldn't subside. Opening the storm door, he wrapped four times.

The door opened and Evelyn greeted him with a warm smile and a cheer of excitement. She flung her arms around his neck and squeezed tight. After a long embrace, she invited him in and closed the door.

END.

More titles by Thom Tate

Intercept
The Auroral Contingency
Spear Garden

Coming Early 2026
Who is Blake MacKay

For more information and to get inside information into Thom Tate's Covert World, visit www.tatescovertworld.com[1]

Exciting titles by Mr. Henry Martin
Sanctuary in Shadows
Element 115

Coming Summer 2025
Nexus of Deception
www.thriller-books.com[2]

---

1. http://www.tatescovertworld.com
2. http://www.thriller-books.com

Don't miss out!

Visit the website below and you can sign up to receive emails whenever Thom Tate publishes a new book. There's no charge and no obligation.

https://books2read.com/r/B-A-TRWHB-JLDZF

BOOKS 2 READ

Connecting independent readers to independent writers.

Also by Thom Tate

Covert World
Beyond All Measure

Standalone
Intercept
Spear Garden
The Auroral Contingency

Watch for more at https://www.tatescovertworld.com.

www.ingramcontent.com/pod-product-compliance
Ingram Content Group UK Ltd.
Pitfield, Milton Keynes, MK11 3LW, UK
UKHW030925060425
457073UK00002B/168